Oath of a Warrior

by

Mary Morgan

Legends of the Fenian Warriors,
Book 2

Oath of a Warrior

Cover Art by *Debbie Taylor*

The Wild Rose Press, Inc.
PO Box 708
Adams Basin, NY 14410-0708
Visit us at www.thewildrosepress.com

Publishing History
First Fantasy Rose Edition, 2018
Print ISBN 978-1-5092-2119-6
Digital ISBN 978-1-5092-2120-2

Legends of the Fenian Warriors, Book 2
Published in the United States of America

"Erina, mo ghrá," he groaned,
taking her mouth with savage intensity. She tasted of honey and spices, filling him completely and easing the torment that continually plagued him.

Breaking free, he placed his hands on either side of the door. Giving her all of him required something more from Erina. Without the assurance of accepting him for what he was, Rory would be a lost man.

"Are ye certain ye want to ken all of me? I want ye as sure as the sun rises and sets over the land each day, but ken this, Erina—there is more to me than a simple bedding. There are things about me that might frighten ye. What I'm about to share with ye may cause ye to question my existence, or worse, my sanity."

Her laugh was seductive and soothing as she wrapped her arms around his neck. "From the moment ye stepped through those trees that first day, I realized ye were not like any man I had encountered. It was as if the trees parted and ye came forth from inside them." She brushed her fingers along his brow. "For one, ye have the most mesmerizing eyes and they shift colors."

"And the second?"

Her face turned a rosy glow, yet, she held his gaze. "I thought your body chiseled from the old Gods, especially with all the markings on your back and arms."

His gaze swept over hers. "I am nae God, Erina, though some would call me a demon."

Praise for Mary Morgan

"Mary Morgan has quickly become one of my favorite authors. I adore her lyrical, vivid writing, the Celtic mythology, and the enchanting otherworldly element that she interweaves into her stories."

~Linda Townsend

~*~

"The author pulls you in, and you can feel the world evolving around you, and see it in your mind as you read along. A new-to-me author and it feels like I found a new favorite."

~Uncaged Book Reviews

~*~

"I loved this book and highly recommend it to anyone who loves not just fantasy and paranormal but a beautiful love story."

~Linda Tonis for Paranormal Romance Guild

~*~

"I truly love Ms. Morgan's books, but this one is breathtaking. She describes the land, flowers and especially the Fae Realm to the degree that I can almost smell Ivy's roses."

~Pknv

Dedication

To all of you who
adhere to a different path
or beat your own drum.
May you walk your own journey
and not worry about what the norm dictates.
You are each unique and beautiful.

Note:

Glossary of terms after page 383.

Prologue

In the beginning…when the world was new, Fae and humans lived peacefully together, but as the centuries passed, fear and distrust evolved. The Fae continued to love the humans, but they believed it was time to safeguard the realms. Therefore, they appointed the Fenian Warriors to protect the domain between human and faery. But most importantly, these warriors were to assist the humans.

When evil threatened to destroy a clan, country, or civilization, the Fae council called upon these warriors. Their orders were to steer a new course and aid the mortals. This group of elite Fae had the power to travel through the Veil of Ages, supporting those in need. They were not to alter the timeline or what the Fae believed to be the life strings of a human. To do so would be catastrophic.

Ancient and powerful, the Brotherhood of the Fenian Warriors was second only to the Fae King and Queen's powers. They have lived amongst us for thousands of years—watching, aiding, guiding. They could live in the guise of a professor, lawyer, knight, tavern owner, or a simple farmer.

Whatever was required, the warriors did so without complaint.

Yet, even these great warriors had their weaknesses as with any race. Though they used their powers for good, there have been times when a select few deemed it wiser to interfere *without* the knowledge of the Fae council. They twisted the laws to suit their own purpose and changed the course of time.

When three Fenian warriors left the Brotherhood to aid a clan—the Dragon Knights of Urquhart, they brought the fury of the Fae down upon their heads. Their punishment should have been swift, but the Fae always believed in redemption—even for one of their own.

A trial was ordered for all three Fae—the first was Conn MacRoich. His judgment had already been handed down. Now the second Fenian Warrior, Rory MacGregor, must face the Fae council and give his account.

Tales of this warrior's legendary acts swept through the Highlands with sagas of honor and nobility. Serving alongside Scottish chieftains, his guidance was deemed necessary before any battle. The human people rumored he was sent from the Gods and Goddesses to show them victory, and they were honored to have him sit at their feasting table.

Many sought him out, offering him riches, land, and marriage pacts to their daughters. However, he gave his assistance without accepting any accolades.

For all his laurels, Rory MacGregor conceals a dark secret—one he has kept hidden even from the Brotherhood. He carries the scar on his body as a constant reminder of his one failure. A badge of how he wronged another. But with any dark secret, time will eventually peel back the veil of reality.

When the truth is finally exposed, Rory will be forced to return and witness the event. If he so chooses, the warrior must face and conquer his demons, or surrender to the bleak abyss of torment and death. The Brotherhood will accept no other course.

Yet, another path of illumination beckons, and it will test this hardened warrior beyond his endurance.

Chapter One

"In the twilight moments before one wakes, be wary of the fragmented dreams of truth."

~Chronicles of the Fae

Beneath the Hill of Tara, Ireland, Mid Autumn— the season of harvest and feasting in the Fae Realm

Smoke filled his lungs, strangling his pitiful cries for mercy. Dust coated his mouth, and his eyes burned, reminding him of the flames of dragon fire during raging battles. Repeatedly, they continued to pummel his face, while his hands and feet remained bound as he knelt on the ground. Some threw stones at his head and others spouted vile obscenities and spat on him. He choked back the copper taste of blood and attempted to reason with any one of his captors.

Did they not understand who he was? Did they not know he could boil the blood within their bodies and peel the skin from their bones? He, a great Fenian Warrior could obliterate their entire city!

But he would not. Death would come far more quickly if he harmed so much as a hair on their pathetic bodies. In truth, he was honored bound by an oath to these deplorable humans.

"Bind...me to...the stake," he pleaded in a choked voice. "Take me." Fighting the wave of panic and the

4

pain slashing his body, mind, and soul, Rory blinked in an attempt to focus and faced his tormentor.

His captor grabbed a fistful of hair, forcing Rory to view the scene in front of him. *"Your time will come, ye spawn of the devil. But ye will first watch how your witch shall die."*

"Nae a witch," he hissed.

"Liar!" the man shrieked, spittle flying. *"Did she not tell wee Alan the charms came from the faeries?"*

"A lad's tale to amuse his friends," he argued, *during fits of coughing spasms.*

"Nae!" A woman protested, pushing through the crowds of people. She charged forward and delivered a slap to Rory's face. *"Ye are bewitched by the lass and spout lies about my son."*

She wagged a finger. *"Ye should burn with her. Ye have the painted markings of the devil on your body."*

"Leave and go tend to your son," ordered the man.

Hastily making the sign of the cross, she quickly departed.

"Please, have mercy," begged Rory.

"Mercy," he echoed. *"So that she may return and cast her evil ways upon us? Nae. She has been found guilty of her crimes."* Releasing his hold on Rory, the man nodded to another.

Rory uttered a curse and looked at the woman bound to the burning stake. Eyes wide with fear gazed back at him as the flames took hold of her dress, licking a path up her body. Not once did she let out a scream of terror. Choking on the scent of burning flesh, he swallowed the bile threatening to heave and attempted to stand. He would not let her die like this. She had done nothing wrong.

Yet, the effort cost Rory when his captor shoved a blade into his side. Pain dulled his senses, and he fought to move forward.

He broke free from his bindings and heard the crowd gasp in horror. No longer caring if any witnessed his power, he lifted his arms, only to have another bash him over the head.

Rory's last glimpse of the woman he had forsaken were her screams of his name before he succumbed into the dark abyss, praying death would take them both swiftly.

Awakening on a guttural cry, Rory turned and emptied what little he had in his stomach onto the ground. Gasping for breath, he waited for the spasms to settle within his body and rolled on his side. Wiping his mouth with the back of his hand, he leaned against the cool crystal wall of his prison, and let his head drop back. Gazing upward, he watched as the stars glittered like diamonds against an inky velvet night sky.

The dream had once again come unbidden to him during his time spent in the Room of Reflection. Never once had he dreamt of her until he entered his imprisonment. Nae. He had banished the memories—tucked them away to a remote part of his being. Hardened himself against any emotions. Struck her name from any thought and vowed never to reveal to his fellow Fenian brothers his involvement in her capture, imprisonment, and death.

Only one visible sign of evidence remained. And only Rory understood its meaning. It was hidden among the layers of his tattoos from the Brotherhood—twisted and puckered along his right rib cage.

His hand shook as he brushed his trembling fingers

over the ancient scar, recalling how he refused the pleas of the Fae healer to bind the skin. It would always be a reminder of how he failed *her*.

Rory dug his hands into the soft earth. "Why?" he uttered into the silence of his cage.

He snarled at the stillness mocking him. There would be no answers. Despair and bitterness were his companions, but they refused to offer him any comfort.

When he first entered his prison, days blended into weeks, and those turned into months. Then the first dream entered, sending him spiraling to the place within his mind he had locked away. It brought forth all the reasons why he often times despised the humans. Always narrow-minded and prejudiced in their thoughts and actions. They were quick to make judgments and feared any who were different.

Once, Rory had sought out the elders of the Brotherhood, requesting to leave mortal Earth, so he could return and remain in the Fae realm. They denied his appeal, since he gave no cause as to why he deemed it necessary to relinquish his powers and rights as a Fenian Warrior.

Now he could not fathom why the dreams had started, or why they continued in earnest to torture his soul.

Lowering his head, Rory rubbed vigorously at his eyes. "Enough," he muttered.

Bells chimed the morning hour, and he glanced upward. His starry attendants were fading as the dawn's dance started anew.

Folding his arms over his bent knees, Rory waited for the first meal of the day to appear magically within his prison, along with several books. He almost laughed out loud at the selection presented. Some were volumes of folk heroes and knights in shining armor. Occasionally, there would be one pertaining to his homeland of Taralyn, and his humor vanished.

Home. Green meadows, lush with foliage. Their colors made one's head spin, and teemed with wildlife that dwelt in harmony. Instead of one, there were three moons. When they rose in a luminous arc during their fullness, the sight would steal the breath from a Fae's body. And how could he forget the cool, scented waters of the lakes and streams that soothed the skin and calmed the mind.

These images teased him within the pages of the tome, calling him forth. Was this to be his curse—his punishment for helping the Dragon Knights? Only reading on parchment about places he could no longer visit? He growled his resentment at those who could not comprehend what he, Liam, and Conn had done for their world and the human realm.

A soft mist of colored lights flashed on the other side of the room, and a table appeared. Silver bowls held an array of fruit, vegetables, cheeses, and an assortment of breads. At the end set a goblet, as well as a wooden jug with water. There were a few other silver bowls, but Rory cared naught for food or drink.

It would not matter if the most delectable food in the realm appeared, it could not tempt him. His appetite had waned. In truth, he believed it was due to his imprisonment, since he no longer had the will to eat, drink, or even greet the new dawn.

Life did not reach out to him, so he retreated within, preferring the cold hard floor of his cell. Even his Fae guards had backed away when they issued an order demanding he take in some nourishment, and he responded by bellowing a curse at them. Eventually, the guards gave up and never returned to his prison.

As the first shaft of light entered the room, Rory pushed himself farther away from its radiance and retreated deeper into his anguish.

****

Conn MacRoich paced within the outer gardens of the royal palace. His hands fisted as he waited with uncertainty. His meeting with the Fae council had ended with terse words on both sides. He had argued that Rory MacGregor not be forced to endure a trial. His time spent in the Room of Reflection was enough punishment. Furthermore, he heard the account of how the Fenian Warrior had slipped deeper into a dark abyss, and Conn judged it was wise to step in and offer a solution.

The Fae council was not pleased. They found it difficult to argue with their prince, especially when he used his royal status to influence the other members. He reminded the council that Rory was under his command, and it was their duty to adhere to his convictions. In the end, they relented. Nevertheless, there were conditions.

Conn let out a frustrated sigh, and rested against a rowan tree. Folding his arms across his chest, he mulled over the multiple decisions and actions. For one, he could remove Rory and secure him in a place of his choosing. Another, simply ignore the Fae council entirely.

The air shimmered and Taran MacLean—friend and Fenian Warrior appeared.

Conn pushed away from the tree. "Give me the

9

account."

Taran shook his head. "Not good. The Fae guards no longer greet him daily. They bring his food inside the room magically."

Confused, Conn's brow furrowed, and he folded his arms over his chest. "Why?"

"Rory threatened them. They now fear the warrior."

"I heard the account given of how his mood shifted, but cannot fathom as to why he would do violence against another here in his homeland. Have you seen him?"

"Nae, he has blocked the vision mirrors in the room."

"By the hounds! There must be another way," argued Conn.

Taran shifted slightly. "You could seek him out."

Conn glanced sharply at his friend. "Asked and denied by the Fae council. Although, I might have a way to see inside the room."

Arching a brow, Taran inquired, "Care to share your knowledge?"

Clamping a hand on the warrior's shoulder, Conn responded, "I shall seek out the seer."

Taran snorted. "Good luck with gaining entrance. The last time you attempted any information, she banned you from her land."

"Yes, but I was only a Fenian Warrior. Now, I am the Prince of the Fae seeking help for one of our own. In the meantime, you return to Rory's room and stand guard. The Fae council has granted a stay of his trial, but I do not trust them. My instincts warn me it's only a matter of days before they call him forth. If they should come for him, seal the doors and alert me. Use whatever means, including how the orders came from *Prince* Conn."

His fellow warrior let out a soft curse. "Will the king support you?"

"He will always defend his son's actions."

Giving Conn a mock salute, Taran vanished in a flash of light.

Waiting for a few moments, Conn reflected on his friend's words about the seer. Shoving aside the doubt, he waved his hand in an arc and magically transported to the edge of the seer's lands.

Breathing in deeply of the crisp, autumn air, he strode with purpose across the wide path lined with oak and rowan trees. Her home was perched beyond the valley of the Fae, secluded within a thick grove of pines. She favored the forests and deep glens and never came to the palace. On the contrary, all went to seek her for wisdom and guidance. Her counsel was regarded with respect, though Conn knew firsthand that the seer's wisdom was not always accurate.

Closing the door on his own past, he moved along quickly. An owl hooted from within the thick branches, and he nodded in greeting. Dark eyes regarded him for a few seconds before taking flight deeper into the trees. Most likely, the bird was alerting its mistress of his presence. If Conn were not welcome, he would feel her wrath soon.

Shielding his eyes from the glare of the sun, he caught a glimpse of a lone figure at the end of the path. Her ebony cloak swayed in the light breeze, and she leaned upon her crystal staff. Stunned to find the seer waiting for him, he quickly masked his surprise and walked toward the woman.

The seer inclined her head slightly. "Prince Conn."

"Lady Emer," he acknowledged, and clasped his hands behind his back. "Thank you for greeting me."

A smile twitched at the corners of her mouth. "Did I have a choice?"

"There are always choices to be presented."

She waved him off. "I am in no mood to banter philosophy and words with you, Conn. I know what you seek."

Surprised for a second time, he asked, "Then you will grant what I need to see?"

"State your reason to see within the Fenian Warrior's prison."

"The warrior is refusing food, drink, and all communication. I fear he is retreating, and I must unravel the reason. This is not the warrior I know."

"It is his choice."

Tempering his fury, Conn explained, "A Fenian Warrior does not give up. Our training—"

"*Our?*" she interrupted. "You are no longer a Fenian Warrior."

"I will *always* be a part of the Brotherhood, Lady Emer. Furthermore, as the warriors are now under *my* command, I consider it my right to protect all, especially Rory as he awaits his trial. I have already spoken with the Fae council, and they will be calling him forth soon."

Lady Emer lifted her staff and stepped back from Conn. "Walk with me."

He followed alongside as she made her way through the trees. As he pushed away heavy pine limbs, the path narrowed and she took the lead. Onward they went, and he pondered why she did not magically transport them. Her movements were slow, but steady, and he found himself losing patience.

"Temper the anger," she ordered.

He rolled his eyes, but smiled. Taking a deep breath, he released his anxiety on the exhale.

As they made their way through the dense trees, the landscape opened to reveal a cave within a moss-covered hill. Vines snaked around the top, and Conn spotted the owl perched off to the side. Making their way upward through the soft grasses, they soon came upon the entrance.

The seer turned toward him. "Once you are inside, do not utter a word. Seal your mind and tongue. Do you understand?"

Conn nodded.

Upon entering the cavern, warmth enveloped them. Lady Emer lifted her staff, and brilliant lights glittered in the darkness. She tapped it once to the ground, and the place exploded in an array of dazzling colors. Crystals of different shapes and sizes littered the area. The walls of the cave were smooth, and the radiance of the crystals surrounded them in its glow. In the center of the cave sat a huge rose quartz fountain. Water bubbled softly upward, filling the cave with the scent of roses.

Gesturing for Conn to sit on a polished boulder, Lady Emer moved silently to the fountain. Placing her staff on the ledge, she raised her hands outward and the water took on a crystal globe suspended over the well. Lights sparkled within the sphere, changing and illuminating.

Conn leaned forward and braced his arms on his

thighs.

Images of the realm passed through the globe in a kaleidoscope of multicolored pictures until they settled and formed outside of the Room of Reflection.

"Brush aside the darkness and set forth the light of truth," the seer uttered softly and closed her eyes.

Conn stood and watched as the doors vanished to reveal Rory's prison. Memories of his own confinement opened old wounds, but he quickly banished them. As he searched within the room for his friend, worry took hold, and he took a step forward. Food, drink, and books remained untouched on a table, and his bed showed no signs of being used.

Finally, he glimpsed a black shadow in the far corner of the room, and his fists clenched by his sides. He barely registered the outline of his friend. Worry turned to fear, but Conn kept silent as he waited for the seer to finish.

Lady Emer frowned, and her hands shook. "No." Her voice shook with emotion. "This cannot be." Opening her eyes, she dropped her hands, and the image vanished, sending the crystal sphere spiraling back into the water.

Conn's patience was unraveling.

Eyes that held sadness gazed at him. "He *dreams*."

Stunned, he could no longer keep silent. "Not possible. Once we enter the Brotherhood and take our vows as a Fenian Warrior, we are no longer able to dream. The ability is stripped from us. It helps to keep us sane with all that we must do, especially for those who travel the Veil of Ages."

She arched a brow and pointed a finger at the fountain. "Nevertheless, Rory MacGregor is having the same dream—*nightmare* each night within his prison. He is hiding something."

"Can you tell me anything else?" he demanded.

"The answer to your question lies with the Fenian Warrior. The warriors are the most powerful—the elite. In addition, I have witnessed a similar occurrence. It is only spoken of in hushed circles within the realm of certain warriors who have walked this path of despair and loneliness hundreds of years before my time."

The walls of the cave felt as if they were closing in around him. Conn uttered a curse and stepped quickly out of the cavern. Glancing up at the azure sky, he took in deep calming breaths. This could *not* be possible. Not to a Fenian Warrior. Not to his friend.

Lady Emer joined him outside. "Then you realize what is happening to him?"

"Yes," he snapped, unable to control his fury. "Rory is slipping into the Realm of Sorrows. His guilt is too much to bear."

She placed a gentle hand on Conn's arm. "If he is not saved, he will cross over into the realm and walk the land as a shadow. *Forever*."

Chapter Two

"When the darkness brings comfort, beware the loss of emotions."

~*Chronicles of the Fae*

Pacing the length of the room within the inner chambers of the Brotherhood, Conn waited for Fenian Warrior and friend, Ronan MacGuinness. After leaving the seer, he'd considered it best to seek out more aid in protecting Rory. He was not about to surrender his friend to the Fae council. In Rory's condition, he would surely destroy everyone and then flee. He had heard the accounts only once as a Fenian Warrior. The elders had spoken of the few Fenian Warriors who had passed over to another chasm between the human and Fae worlds in hushed tones, fearing they would somehow appear if they uttered their names out loud. These warriors became outcast or worst, died, battling the dark shadows that plagued them.

Conn pounded his fist on the massive oak table. "I will not let you succumb to the void!"

"What troubles ye?" Ronan appeared in a flash of light by his side. He took a hold of Conn's arm. "'Tis Ivy? Is she unwell? As her former guardian, I would do anything for her. Those days I spent escorting her around the kingdom during her healing shall remain fond memories."

Letting out a frustrated sigh, Conn shook his head. "My *wife* is well. It is another." Pushing away from the table, he asked, "Have you concluded your mission in Scotland?"

Ronan frowned. "Aye, eons ago. Why?"

Folding his arms over his chest, Conn retorted, "You are continuing to speak in the old tongue of the humans."

The warrior shrugged. "I *favor* the language."

Giving his friend a slight smile, he motioned for him to sit. Taking a seat across from him, Conn placed his hands on the table. "I am preparing to take over the trial of Rory MacGregor. I must have witnesses who will swear an oath of silence to what happens at his trial."

Ronan leaned forward in his chair. "Ye ken the Fae council will not permit this act of interference. Ye may now command us, but ye were warned—*nae ye were forbidden* to stay away from Rory and Liam."

He snorted in disgust. "I can no longer sit idle and watch another warrior—my *friend* slip deeper into an abyss."

His friend rubbed his chin. "Whispers are traveling the realm of how he threatened his guards with one look. Did the council give ye permission to speak with him?"

Leaning back in his chair, Conn shook his head. "Not directly."

Ronan raised a brow in question. "Should I ask how?"

"No. Nevertheless, our friend is in grave danger if he stays within his confinement."

"Nae," he uttered in a shocked tone. "I cannae

believe he is in danger within—"

Conn held up his hand to stay his friend's words. "Furthermore, if and when he is to appear before the council, I believe it will be too late. In truth, I am doing the members a favor by relieving them of this dangerous situation. They have no idea how to control a Fenian Warrior when one begins to descend into the void. I risk much, including any others I bring in to hear his account. Yet, I surmise this is the only solution. It will be dangerous. This is why I have asked you here. You are one of the strongest and most powerful warriors."

Silence descended in the room.

Fisting his hands on the table, Ronan asked, "What do ye require of me?"

Relief coursed through Conn, and he let out the breath he was holding in. "Taran is presently guarding him. I require another to stand with him as well."

The warrior waved his hand. "Why not bring him here?"

"I might be Prince of the Fae, but I have no wish to start bending the laws of our people *without* permission."

"And your plan?"

"To seek approval from my king."

Ronan let out a groan. "Ye tempt fate asking your father to override the council's orders."

Conn laughed bitterly. "Did he not do the same for me?"

"True," Ronan agreed. "Yet, I cannae fathom what could have sent Rory into the darkness."

Sighing, Conn pinched the bridge of his nose. "He is dreaming."

The warrior stood. "'Tis madness! How?"

"He is holding onto a secret within his mind, body, and heart. When he entered his prison, they somehow surfaced. It is festering within him."

Ronan placed his hand over his heart. "Regardless of your conversation with the king, I am here to serve you and the Brotherhood. I will do what it takes to protect the life of a fellow warrior."

Conn rose slowly. "Now you understand my urgency to bring him forth. Speak of this to no one. Once the king hears my plea, I am positive he will grant me full disclosure and aid. I have no wish to see our friend's name blackened throughout the realm. His trial shall be handled with secrecy within the walls of the Brotherhood."

"Ye have my allegiance and trust." Drawing a sign in the air, the Fenian Warrior vanished.

Straightening his tunic, Conn magically transported himself to the royal chambers of his parents. Walking along the marbled pathway, he nodded to the guard in passing. The gilded doors opened silently, and he stepped through. Entering the vast chamber, he proceeded down the corridor on the left, praying he would find his father in his private office. Knowing the time of day, he often found the man alone with his favorite scrolls in this place of solace.

Pausing outside the rowan doors, he lifted his hand and knocked softly. When all remained quiet, Conn frowned and wove a single thought outward to his father.

"I wish to discuss an urgent matter with you. Are you nearby?"

"Meet me in the Library of the Ancients,"

commanded his father.

In a flash of light, Conn did as his father ordered. The library was one revered by every one of the Fae, since it held all the tomes, knowledge, and wisdom of his people from their homeland of *Taralyn*. Conn had recently ventured inside the sacred place. He had wished to study the lore of his home, particularly the flora and fauna. He yearned to recreate a flower for his wife, Ivy. Sadly, he was unable to get any to bloom, so he described in vivid detail every petal, stem, and the scent.

Conn smiled at the memory, especially at what followed afterward in their garden by the waterfall.

"I grant you permission," acknowledged King Ansgar.

Startled from his pleasurable thought, he turned around to face his father. "For what?"

The king slipped a ribbon in place between the silver pages of the book opened on the desk. "You must see to the Fenian Warrior's trial, and immediately." Closing the massive tome, he folded his arms over his chest.

Stunned by his father's declaration, Conn ran a hand down the back of his neck. "Then you have heard?"

"The moment his guards were threatened. They say his eyes are shifting to a darker color as well."

"Shit," he clipped out.

His father arched a brow at his use of the human curse word. "It is far worse than anyone imagines."

Conn braced his hands on the massive desk. "Any words of wisdom?"

Tapping the ancient tome, his father replied,

"There have only been two who have witnessed a Fenian Warrior descend to the Realm of Sorrows—one has since departed this realm to the land of *Tir na Og*."

Conn surmised the other person was his father. "Were you the other?"

King Ansgar shifted away from the desk. "No. At the time, I was courting your mother. I gave no thought to any others. I had recently ascended to the throne and was not concerned with the warriors."

Detecting sadness in his father's words, Conn stepped near him. "You are not responsible for the path a warrior chooses."

His father glanced away. "Seek out the elder, Loran. He must be present when you question the warrior."

Ahh…so Loran was the other Fae involved. "Thank you, Father."

Turning to leave, Conn paused and glanced over his shoulder. "If I may ask, who was the Fenian Warrior? And did he survive?"

Deep sorrow filled King Ansgar's eyes as he met Conn's gaze. "My brother, Baine, was the warrior. In a desperate attempt to slay me and claim the throne, Loran was forced to kill him. Baine's name has been stricken from all accounts, save one." King Ansgar nodded to the book.

"Father," he uttered in a shocked tone.

The king held up his hand. "Do not pity me. Nor ask for reasons." Moving toward Conn, he placed both hands on his shoulders. "Find the source of the warrior's misery and have him confront it. It is essential he be cleansed."

"If he fails?" whispered Conn.

King Ansgar stood back. "Then act swiftly on his death. For his mind will consume all who he is, and he will no longer be the Fae you know."

In a brilliant arc of light, his father left.

Clenching his fists, Conn shook his head. "*Death* is not an option for my friend!"

****

Shards of pain throbbed behind his temples, and Rory rubbed his eyes in an attempt to rid the demons tormenting his mind. In an effort to elude his dreams, he fought the desire to seek rest within his prison. His body, thoughts, and spirit sought out the land under him. Though during the quiet times, he thought he could hear the soft whisper of Mother Danu in his ears. Yet, when he concentrated, she always left him in the coldness of his own beleaguered nightmares and ramblings.

Crouching far back against the wall, Rory cloaked himself with darkness and shadows, believing the voices would cease to speak to him. No longer did he concern himself with the dawn or night. However, the voices lured him within, and the images returned with a vengeance. *Her* agonizing screams filled his mind, and the taste of smoke coated his tongue as he gasped for air.

He found his mouth parched and for a brief moment, Rory considered moving toward the table where a jug of water tempted him to quench his thirst. Lifting his head, he reached out with one hand, praying the jug would come to him. But he was a fool. There was no magic inside these four crystal walls. Furthermore, he was too weak and proud to move away from his haven of safety.

By the Gods, the water should come to him! He was a great Fenian Warrior! Or was the power taken from him when he entered the Room of Reflection? He clenched his fist and brought it to his chest. Confusion muddled his thoughts. And the voices mocked him from afar.

Distorted lights danced in front of his vision, and Rory blinked. Someone had dared to enter his prison unannounced. His fury rose at the intrusion. Did he not give orders to the guards to never return?

"Leave me," he growled in a hoarse voice.

"You have been summoned to appear for your trial," Taran replied calmly.

Rory snarled, recognizing the voice of the warrior. *Now they send those from the Brotherhood?* "I have done nothing which requires judgment."

"Even if it would mean your freedom from this prison?" inquired Ronan, stepping forward.

So they send two warriors. They must deem me mad. Rory clenched his hands. "You tempt fate by drawing near, my friend."

Ronan crouched down in front of him. "I dinnae fear ye, my Brother. And I am happy to hear ye call me *friend.*"

Rory swallowed. He did not want to hurt Ronan. All he longed for was the darkness of solitude.

"If ye have nae wish to go, I will keep ye company." Ronan shifted to sit alongside Rory. "However long ye require, I shall wait."

Rory glanced sharply at the warrior, but remained silent.

"I would have preferred liquid ambrosia or mead over water," Taran professed, pouring water into a mug.

"You always did like your drink sweet," Rory responded gruffly.

Taran winked. "And my women, too."

Ronan barked out in laughter, the sound echoing within the room, and Rory winced.

Taran strode over and sat down in front of Rory. Holding the mug toward him, he said, "Drink a few sips, and I shall tell you about my latest conquest in the Pleasure Gardens."

Rory eyed him skeptically. He hesitated briefly and then took the offered liquid. When the brush of the sweet water touched his cracked, dry lips, he almost let out a groan. His thirst was so great, he drank deeply. Meeting the hard stare of Taran, he handed the mug back to him. "More."

Taran stood and retrieved the jug. Returning, he handed it to Rory.

Lifting the jug to his mouth, he filled his parched body with the healing water. Stopping half way, he poured the rest over his head, splashing some on Ronan.

"Ye will need more than water to clean the grime from your body."

Rory rubbed his eyes and dropped the jug. He looked from one warrior to the other. "Even now, I carry the stench from when *we* fought the Dark One and Lachlan. Yet, not one of them from the council cares that evil was defeated and *we* saved two worlds."

"We are not here to pass judgment," uttered Ronan softly.

"Then why are you here?"

"Because ye need friends at your side when you appear for your trial."

"I deem two at your side are always better than one," added Taran and held out his hand.

Nodding slowly, Rory stretched out his legs. Though he was weak, the water had refreshed him and cleared the ghosts from the past within his mind. After grabbing the warrior's outstretched hand, he stood on shaky limbs.

Instantly, the four crystal walls splintered into shards of various colors, and the glass dome disappeared. All traces of his prison had vanished, and he found himself surrounded by pine trees. Sunlight streamed down through the canopy of branches, and Rory shielded his eyes from its intensity. He drew in a long breath of the clean, fresh air—filling his weak body. But his steps faltered when he started forward.

"Would ye like me to transport ye to your chambers? All has been prepared. There, ye may use your magic."

Rory nodded. "I have no plans on entering the Fae council as a battered and bruised Fenian Warrior, so yes."

"You are not meeting with the Fae council," interjected Taran.

Keeping his steps slow and steady, he glanced sideways at the warrior. "Have I been duly sentenced?"

Taran kept pace with him. "No. The king considered it wiser you should appear before an elder, away from the council."

"Why would he interest himself in the affairs of the Fenian—" Rory paused and rubbed a hand through his hair. "Of course. His son, Conn, is involved."

"It is not what ye think," corrected Ronan.

Rory resumed his steps. "No. I believe it is far

worse and now the king has chosen an elite elder to dictate a more severe punishment. King Ansgar never did favor his son entering the Brotherhood."

"Conn is no longer a Fenian Warrior."

Halting, Rory's eyes blazed with anger. "By the hounds, what mad realm have I entered into?"

Chapter Three

"One cannot favor the light over the darkness or the darkness over the light. Each is the balance to maintain a strong center."

~Chronicles of the Fae

Upon entering his chambers, Rory leaned against the oak doors for strength. Colors of the forest greeted him, along with the comforts he had forsaken in his prison. Food and drink were set out on a marble table, though he had requested none. Chairs, cushioned in green velvet beckoned him. Part of him longed to return to the darkness of his prison and for a brief moment, he almost called forth Ronan. Taking in deep calming breaths, he let his sight adjust to the soft glow of light filtering in through the quartz ceiling.

Glancing around, he observed his chair by the hearth. Open on a side maple table was the book he had been pursuing before his brother, Liam had stormed into his chamber announcing the news about the evil druid, Lachlan. The monster had slipped through the Veil of Ages, endangering another Dragon Knight, and Liam required his assistance to thwart the druid. Together, they convinced Conn MacRoich to aid them in their plan.

"So many moons ago," he muttered and raked a hand through his hair. "And where are you now, my brother? Or Conn?"

Pushing slowly away from the door, Rory strode into the innermost chamber. Removing a fresh tunic and pants from a massive trunk at the foot of his bed, he strode along the open corridor. Halting at the entrance, he stripped free from his torn clothing. The scent of the pine trees assaulted him. It was a haven like no other— trees, flowers, and the earth beneath him. In the center set an enormous copper tub, big enough for two or three people.

His mind screamed not to enter this sanctuary, since he should not be granted this luxury. Yet, his body was battered, weary, and in need of healing. Gritting back a curse, he lifted a trembling hand, and warm, scented water filled the tub. Sinking into the liquid depths, he washed the stench of a battle that was fought almost a year ago from his skin and hair with a healing soap that soothed. Leaning his head back on the rim, he closed his eyes.

We might have won the battle, but what about the other one? You saved two worlds, but were unable to rescue one human female. The voices taunted him.

"Enough!" His bellow reverberated throughout the enclosure of trees. Rubbing his eyes vigorously, he stepped out of the tub and quickly dressed.

Making his way back into his main chamber, Rory ignored the tempting fare displayed. Lifting a jug, he sniffed the contents. "Water." How he longed for whiskey or ambrosia and snapped his fingers.

A rare bottle of whiskey appeared. It was one made near the flowing waterfall of life close to the eastern border of the Fae realm. Opening the bottle, he guzzled deeply. The heat seared a path down his throat and into his body. Relishing the fiery liquid, he continued to drink until he judged the ghosts of the past had receded to the far reaches of his mind. Wiping his mouth with the back of his hand, Rory now believed he was ready to face his trial and tossed the empty bottle into the hearth.

Striding to his chamber door, he yanked it open. Ronan and Taran stood off to the side, speaking quietly. Halting their conversation, both warriors stepped forward and joined him.

Rory met their gazes. "I am ready to meet my fate." He gestured outward with his hand. "Lead the way."

Ronan nodded. "We are taking ye magically to the elder's chambers."

Arching a brow, he sneered. "I am not good enough to walk among our people?"

"Listen to us," reasoned Taran. "We are doing this for you. The council has objections, and we do not wish to meet any of them along the path."

"I don't fear them," snapped Rory.

"By the hounds," groaned Ronan and placed an arm on Rory's shoulder. In a brilliant flash, he transported them inside a chamber, lit only by torches along the dark, richly decorated paneled walls.

Rory stumbled forward, slamming against a gnarled oak desk. "Bastard," he growled. Righting himself, he turned on Ronan.

"There will be no quarrels or fighting inside my chambers, or I shall restrain you," shouted a familiar voice behind Rory.

"Loran?" Stunned, he twisted around to meet the hard gaze of the elder. "You are to be my judge?"

The Fae stepped forth, his arms clasped behind his back. "Yes. Do you give your sacred word there will be no violence in these chambers?"

Rory battled his fury and swallowed. He'd rather stand before a council of nine puny members than before one of the most revered Fae elders in their realm. His respect for Loran was immense, but not for the council members. "You have my word."

The elder gave a curt nod. "You may take your place." He gestured for Rory to take a seat in the center of the chamber.

"I wish to remain standing." Rory glanced at Ronan and Taran standing guard near the door.

Loran waved his hand in the air, and the chair slammed against the back of Rory's legs, forcing him to sit. "I have no desire to strain my neck to look up at you while I am sitting."

Turmoil bubbled to the surface, and Rory fought for control. "Did you choose to be my…arbitrator?"

The Fae elder adjusted his robes, and he took his seat behind the desk. "I was sought out by another."

Rory clenched his hands on the sides of the chair. "Is my crime so severe that I'm to be treated thusly? Hidden away, because you are all ashamed of what I did?"

Loran folded his arms over his chest. "What *crime* do you believe you've committed?"

"Nothing!" He shoved a fist into the air. "We saved two worlds that night. Lachlan had opened the door for the Dark One to enter. If not for us and the Dragon Knights, we would not be having this conversation."

Loran angled his head. "Why did you not alert your other Brothers? There is strength in numbers."

"We three were the guardians over the wives of the Dragon Knights. To involve other warriors would doom them to this unjust treatment."

"Surely you were prepared for the consequences."

Rory lifted his chin. "Of course. It was a path agreed upon. And one I would proudly venture into again."

"Did you not believe the Dragon Knights had the power to prevent this on their own?"

"No."

"I believe you."

Loran's response astonished Rory. "Then why am I here? Why confine me to the Room of Reflection for so long?"

The elder sighed. "Unfortunately, the council does not share my viewpoint on what happened. If it were up to them, they would send you to the Hall of Remembrance to reflect on that deed and any others."

A sliver of unease snaked its way up Rory's spine. The Hall of Remembrance was one place he feared to enter. The ghosts of his past lived there in vivid detail. They would surround him and fill him with their cries and sorrow. Beads of sweat broke out along his brow. Her whispered screams echoed near him, and Rory fought the urge to look over his shoulder, fearing *she* would be there. He fought the memories of the past within his mind.

"Where are you, Fenian Warrior?" demanded Loran.

Rory snapped his gaze back to the elder. "Here in this dungeon," he growled.

Taran stepped away from the door, and it did not go unnoticed by Rory.

"Is there a reason you stalk me, Taran?"

The warrior held his hands up. "I am only here as your friend."

Chaos swirled inside Rory's mind. His friends were all gone. Fragments of another time blinded his thoughts. Pushing aside one battle, another surged forth—one where they held victory over the evil who attempted to enter their worlds. He rubbed a hand over his eyes. Releasing a shuddering breath, he asked, "Where are Conn and Liam?"

"We are not here to discuss them," replied Loran.

His hands clawed into the sides of the chair. "Then what do you *want* of me?"

"What are you hiding, my friend?" inquired Conn, stepping forth from the shadows.

Standing slowly, Rory took in the form of the Fenian warrior. Shock, elation, and fury swept through him as one emotion. This was *not* the Fae he remembered. No longer was Conn part of the Brotherhood as his gaze swept over the royal garments and silver bands on his upper arms—denoting his true heritage. One of the royal household. *Traitor!*

Rory's fists clenched, and he inclined his head. "*Prince* Conn."

Conn nodded.

He leaned near him. "Did you barter for your freedom by taking your place as heir to the Fae kingdom?"

Conn's eyes flashed silver. "It was not my freedom I negotiated for. Now answer *my* question."

Rory sneered. "I will not answer to you. Leave."

"Listen to me—"

Dark fury burst inside Rory. His friend had

betrayed them all. Just like the events of the past. Must he suffer along with traitors—be it human or Fae? Did they not once stand together as brothers in a cause? "Never again!" he roared and leveled a blow against Conn. The Fae prince staggered, but quickly regained his footing.

Intense pain radiated throughout Rory's body as Conn directed a blast of power outward, sending him flying to the other side of the chamber. He slammed against the wall, dazed. Doing his best to shove the pain aside, Rory stood. Glaring at Conn, he watched as the Fae strode forward.

Despair and darkness clouded his judgment. "Do not come any closer," warned Rory.

Conn waved his hand in the air, enclosing them both within a sphere of magic. "Answer. My. Question."

Rory's jaw clenched so tight, he feared it would snap. "Nae!"

Conn arched a brow. "What time period are you in?"

Confused by the question, Rory glanced around. "This...realm." Conn's binding energy swirled tighter around them.

"Talk to me, Rory," Conn pleaded. "You cannot hold back any longer."

"There is naught to speak of."

"Shit! You speak in the old tongue," argued Conn and took another step closer. "And you *dream*."

Icy tendrils of fear swept over Rory. How did he know? How was it possible? He tried to breathe, the chamber closing in all around him, and the stench of another past battle filled his nostrils. The images flashed in front of him, and he blinked, forcing them away. "I have nau...*nothing* to say," he replied in a clipped tone.

Conn leveled a finger at him. "You may lie to me, but you can no longer do so to yourself. It is evident in your demeanor and your *eyes*. If you continue on this path of destruction, you will fade into the shadows. I am here to assist you, *not* condemn you."

Rory frowned. Using all his strength, he willed the visions away and cleared his mind. His hands clenched and unclenched. Drawing in a shaky breath, he released it slowly. Meeting Conn's intense gaze, he still did not intend to reveal his dark secret. He, Fenian Warrior, Rory MacGregor, was not some untrained warrior to be schooled by another, regardless if he was the Prince of the Fae.

"My path is my own, if I'm allowed, along with my past," stated Rory, crossing his arms over his chest. "Serve my punishment, or set me free."

Conn sneered. "Do you honestly believe I would set you free in your condition?" Fury showed in his eyes. "If you have no wish to share your dreams, then I have no choice than to order you into the Hall of Remembrance where we can all witness what you are hiding."

Rage mixed with fear took hold and Rory lashed out once again at Conn. This time, the prince did nothing to stop him, as he continued to slam his fists into the Fae. "I will never, *ever* step into that place," he bellowed, the sound reverberating throughout the chamber. The walls shook and the torches' flames snapped eerily.

"Stop!" shouted Loran, raising his staff into the air.

His wrath so great, the order barely registered within Rory's mind. As other hands dared to touch him, he fought the intrusion, striking out with ferocity. Yet, he found himself weakening, and his voice going hoarse. The struggle to remain standing was too much, and he collapsed onto the ground.

Instantly, crystal shackles were placed around his wrists. Sweat poured down his body, seeping into the earth. Bitterness clawed inside him as the land reached out in healing. He banished its soothing touch with a single thought.

Voices from those around him, mocked him. He shook his head to rid their cries. Where was he? Was *she* here?

"Rory MacGregor, Fenian Warrior to the Fae, *my brother*, I order you to speak what you have kept hidden from us. I *order* you to give your account—here in this place of silence. We—Taran, Ronan, and High Elder, Loran will guard your secret. This is not a choice any longer."

Weary and frustrated, Rory could no longer contain the emotions.

Conn knelt in front of him. "I give you my word, I shall keep whatever you say between us. All record will be banished even from the Hall of Remembrance.

Rory shuddered. She came to him unbidden as the maiden he knew from the first day they met, and as the ashen charred shell of her death. Pain tore into his heart, ripping apart what he had thought healed. Lifting his head, his eyes blazed with anger and sorrow, and one word tore free in a guttural cry.

"*Erina!*"

Chapter Four

"Keep your sight upon the stars and not the path in front of you. Stars are constant, but the ground is ever changing."

~Chronicles of the Fae

Village of Lindane, Loch Etive, West Coast of Scotland, October 1605

"For the love of the Goddess!" protested Erina, watching as the droplets of blood splattered across the white sleeve of her chemise, leaving a blotched pattern. Studying the odd shape, she swallowed. Was this a portent of ill tidings? Was the Goddess warning her? Her recent troubles followed her as surely as the river behind her cottage flowed toward the sea. She grasped the amethyst pendant hanging from her neck. The stone was cool and calming within her palm. Tossing aside the tremor of unease, she shook her head. Today was not one to dwell on what had yet to come.

Lifting her hand away from the spinning wheel, she let out a frustrated sigh. "I should have used the small *dealgan* to spin the wool." Glaring at the monster spinning wheel in front of her, she added, "'Tis much quicker with the old ways."

Standing, Erina reached for a cloth and wrapped her finger. Making her way toward her worktable, she poured water into a bowl. Removing the wrapping from her hand, she plunged her hand into the cool liquid and gazed outward into her garden. Sunlight danced along the fringes. Violets, foxglove, and bluebells waved in greeting coached by the morning breeze. Birds chirped in a nearby rowan tree, content to feed on the berries that were plentiful during the autumn months. And her faithful companion, Thane, was sprawled out among the wildflowers, sunning himself. Even her dog knew enough to be outdoors in the warm sun.

She sighed heavily. The land beckoned her to come and play. Yet, there were other pressing issues than tending to her garden. Betty Timmons required the spun wool today in exchange for fresh bread, dried beef, and other food supplies. Glancing over at her meager pantry, her stomach protested. If she did not get the wool to the woman soon, Erina would have to be content with the wild mushrooms, onions, and nuts for her daily meals. Her garden might be filled with herbs, but not vegetables or grain.

Removing her hand, she quickly inspected the injury and deemed it minor. Reaching for some fresh comfrey, Erina placed the leaves over her wound. Time was precious, and she had no desire to waste a single minute, even to properly boil the comfrey leaves. Standing on her tiptoes, she pulled down a box with fresh linen bandages. Pulling one forth, she quickly bandaged her hand.

Stretching out the ache in her shoulders, she padded back to her spinning wheel. No sooner did she begin than a pitiful bleating echoed outside. Grumbling a curse, she marched outside.

Thane was the first to greet her in excitable barking

as he circled around her.

"Aye, ye can stop your barking," commanded Erina, moving past the animal.

Three of her precious sheep had managed to escape from their pen and were helping themselves to her garden of herbs, and another was wedged between the gates. "Sweet Brigid! How did ye get out?"

The sheep's mournful protests continued as Erina approached the trapped animal. Uttering soothing words, she rubbed its head. "Ye have no one to blame but yourself, Tam. This is the third time ye have escaped. Ye should not have strayed with the others. Did your allies find a way to lift the latch, or is someone playing a malicious prank?" Freeing the animal, she directed it back inside.

Turning around, she gave a sharp whistle. Thane instantly reacted and charged toward the three intruders in her precious garden. "Bring them onward," she instructed.

Watching as the dog went after the sheep, Erina kept a watchful eye on all concerned. It took several attempts, as the animals considered their fare was far more important. Yet, with stealthlike moves, Thane maneuvered the sheep back inside the enclosure. Securing the latch in place, Erina bent and ruffled the fur of her faithful friend. "Well done, Thane."

The dog gave a sharp bark and then turned a critical eye toward the sheep.

"Aye, I cannot fathom the reason, or who is setting them free." Erina leaned against the gate, observing the animals. Two out of her dozen of sheep were still missing, and she noted another one was gone. "'Tis the third time this month." She glanced at her companion.

"Did ye not hear anything, Thane? I swear the thieving is increasing with each passing month."

The animal plopped down at her feet with a heavy sigh.

"Och, dearest, I ken ye dinnae hear so well." She bent to give the dog another pat behind the ears. Her heart ached realizing her beloved friend was aging. At ten winters, the dog had surely lost most of his hearing. However, his stamina was strong, and he roamed the hills with Erina often when she let her sheep graze on the southern pastures.

"Come the morn, we shall search for the others. I have nae time today." Erina glanced at the dog. "Guard them well," she whispered.

****

Securing the leather satchel filled with the spun wool, Erina reached for her plaid shawl and wrapped it around her shoulders. Saying a silent prayer Betty would be happy with the quantity, she made her way out of the cottage. Thane was settled in the cool shade of a rowan tree next to the sheep, and Erina smiled.

Entering her small stable, she placed the satchel over the back of the horse. "'Tis a fine day, Oberon. Do ye fancy a ride?"

The horse let out a soft whinny.

"I am shocked by your reaction, my friend." Stroking his mane, she added, "I would have expected a louder response, considering we shall be returning with carrots, and mayhap a turnip or two."

Oberon stomped the ground with his hoof, and shook his silky mane.

She laughed and patted his nose. "Ahh…much better."

Upon leaving the stable, Erina let the horse set his own pace. Breathing deeply, she relaxed and took in the blazing autumn colors that greeted her. Too soon winter would show her face and all traces of this beauty would vanish. If she did not prepare for the hardship the *Cailleach* brought, Erina would have no food or peat for her hearth.

Spring and summer should have been a bountiful one for her. Yet, the villagers were arriving less each season on her doorstep. Rarely did anyone seek her out for a simple love charm, or an herbal remedy to help in healing or sickness. Nae. Ever since the new king ascended the throne a few years ago, rumors circulated throughout the land he would reform the two countries. People became fearful, recalling the past burning of witches. Though there had been two years of peace, many judged it wise to keep away from Erina.

Aye, they treated her with respect, and there were those who continued to practice the old ways, but times were changing—bringing about an order of yet another religious belief.

"If only ye were here to give me counsel, Grandmother," she uttered softly. Straightening her shoulders, she let out a nervous laugh. "Ye would have tilted my chin up and reminded me of my blessings."

Maneuvering Oberon over the hill, Erina banished the negative thoughts. The Goddess had always looked after her, so there was no reason for her to dwell on unsettling thoughts. She did manage to have a few loyal to her healing ways, and there was always a demand for her services when a bairn was making its way into the world. Furthermore, Betty Timmons still required her wool.

As Betty's cottage emerged through the heavy pines, Erina dismounted and led the animal to the river. Giving him a firm pat, she removed her satchel and walked up the incline to the cottage.

Betty greeted her at the entrance, a frown marring her features, and her hands clasped firmly together. *Oh, Goddess, please spare me from an entire afternoon listening to her bantering about men.*

Giving her best smile to the woman, Erina reached outward. "Greetings, Betty. 'Tis a fine day, aye?"

Glancing quickly around, Betty pulled Erina inside the cottage and swiftly closed the door. "Nae," she sobbed out and collapsed onto a chair by the hearth.

Erina let out a sigh and placed the satchel on the table. "Can ye share your troubles?"

Tears flowed freely down Betty's cheeks. "Fergus will not speak with me."

"Can ye tell me why?" Erina pulled a nearby chair closer to the woman.

Betty snorted in disgust. "Because I refuse to let him kiss me a third time!" She held up three fingers to stress her words.

"I thought ye were interested in Robert Innes?"

The woman looked aghast, and wiped the tears from her face with her smock. "Goodness, that was several weeks ago. He had the most unpleasant odor."

"My apologies. I had forgotten." *Of course I have not seen ye for some time.* "Continue."

Her lip trembled. "I ken I am in love with Fergus." She clutched a hand to her chest. "He is the man I wish to marry. But I will not behave in a wanton manner."

As if ye have not done so already? Erina cleared her throat. "Have ye told him how ye feel?"

41

Shock replaced sorrow, and Betty squared her shoulders. "Why would I do such a thing? The man must declare his position first."

Erina nodded slowly. "Ye are correct."

"Aye. Ye cannot understand, since no man has come calling at your door." Betty regarded her coolly. "Why look at your clothing. Blood and dirt are smeared everywhere, and your hair is as wild as the grasses that cover the nearby hills."

Please help me to curb my tongue, Goddess, and temper the growing fury toward this woman. "If ye must ken, I pricked my hand on the spinning wheel this morn and had to rescue sheep that escaped from their pen. Pray forgive my appearance."

Betty shrugged.

Determined to avoid any more questions about her looks, Erina asked, "Have ye spoken with your mother regarding this matter with Fergus?"

"*Erina MacIntyre*, I'm stunned ye would ask. Ye ken how my parents have nae wish to see me marry a Campbell. My father would be furious." Betty leaned forward as if departing a great secret. "Ye will not speak of this to them. And I have a request for ye."

Erina reached for the woman's hand. "I give ye my promise. I have never spoken of our conversations with anyone."

Betty smiled knowingly. "We keep our secrets tucked within, aye?"

Releasing her hand, Erina sensed a cold prickle of warning. "'Tis nae secrets, Betty, only visits between friends."

Betty gave her smug look. "Ye cannot fool me."

Folding her hands in her lap, Erina asked, "What is

your request?"

Tears shimmered once again in the woman's eyes. "I must have my Fergus and ye will help me."

"How?" demanded Erina.

Standing, Betty went and retrieved a basket from the table. Placing the item beside Erina, she pulled forth a tiny package. "This is a lock of Fergus' hair. I wish to have ye make a love charm. I will give ye food from our larder 'til the next moon."

Erina eyed the full basket of food. If she refused, Betty might take back everything. Or worse, never seek her out for anything again.

Standing, Erina held out her hand. "If I do this, ye must honor the Fae by not speaking where ye came upon this love charm. Furthermore, ye must not be troubled if the charm fails to work on Fergus. The man might believe in the new religion, therefore making it impossible for him to be swayed. Remember, only those with a true heart can fall under a Fae love charm." Knowing how the woman regarded the Good Folk in high esteem, Erina believed in a favorable response to her demands.

Betty grasped Erina's hands, crushing the package. "Ye have my solemn vow I will follow your instructions. I only want his love." Releasing her, she picked up the basket and handed it to Erina.

"Thank ye, Betty." Moving toward the door, Erina paused. "Love can be lacking in harmony, Betty. If ye do love Fergus, think on your plan. Do ye not deem it wiser to let him come to ye without a charm?"

"Nae. There is no other alternative."

Erina nodded. "Come to my cottage on the eve of the full moon."

"I shall," she promised.

Quickly departing the cottage, Erina couldn't get her feet to move fast enough. Even though she was grateful for the food and more to come, her nerves bristled with uneasiness. Never before had any of her love charms failed, but that did nothing to halt the flood of misgivings about fulfilling Betty's wish to have Fergus.

Halting before the river's edge, Erina looked outward. "Guide my heart, my hands, and my words, dear Good Folk." Setting down the basket, she pulled out a small bun. Tearing it into pieces, Erina scattered them across the land. "Blessings to ye, my friends." After brushing the crumbs from her hands, Erina secured everything to Oberon and grabbed the reins.

She wandered slowly, judging it best to follow the path along the river. The journey back to her cottage would take longer, but she was in no hurry. The land called out to her, and Erina responded by banishing all negative thoughts and focusing on the items she would require for Betty's love charm.

"'Tis a shame ye cannot wait for love's first blossom to unfurl, Betty," she whispered.

Love! The emotion was foreign to her. Betty was correct. She'd never had a man court her. *Nae.* There were those who had attempted to steal kisses, but feared she would curse them after she scorned them with a tongue-lashing. In addition, what man would want to hold hands with her? Most days they were covered with the scent of her herbs. Or yet, grime from digging in the garden. Aye, her hair was unmanageable, but did not her grandmother say the color was rare and cherished among the Fae. "Humph!"

Therefore, the seasons blurred into the next without a man seeking her out.

Erina touched her lips. What would it be like to taste a man?

Lost in her thoughts, she tripped over a tree root and fell into a gorse bush.

"Bloody hell," she muttered, attempting to pull herself out of the golden flowers. Her horse let out a snort. Wiping her nose, she glanced over her shoulder at Oberon. "Ye are fortunate I did not land in nettles, or ye would have to suffer my complaints."

Gruff noises halted any further discussion with her horse. Shaking out her gown, Erina made her way slowly to the men arguing beyond the bend in the trees. Crouching down against a large pine, she observed the group. Four of the men she did not recognize, but the young lad was Thomas Dunlop from her village. Obviously, they were attempting to take what little food the lad had in his possession. Taunts and barbs continued to be tossed at him. Either he surrendered his leather bag, or they would be forced to draw their blades.

"Overbearing brutes," she hissed out.

Pulling forth her *sgian dubh* from her boots, Erina tucked the blade inside her belt and stepped forth from the tree. "Greetings, Thomas. Are ye fetching some mushrooms for your mother? 'Tis a fine day to search for the best, though ye did remember my words about foraging for the right ones, aye?" She moved slowly toward him, while keeping the other men in her sight. Placing her hand on his shoulder, she smiled. "Ye would not want to pick the poisonous ones."

"I…um." He coughed and nodded.

Wrapping one arm around his shoulders, Erina faced the surly group. "Are these friends of yours, Thomas?"

One of the men stepped forward. A wicked scar marred half of his face, giving him a grotesque look as he attempted to smile. "Nae, but I can be *your* friend." He wasted no time in leering at Erina.

She fought the urge to lash out with words. Deciding it best to ignore him, Erina squeezed the lad's shoulder. "Ye best get these mushrooms to your mother, before she sends out your brothers." She gave him a wink and prayed he would go along with the ploy, since Thomas had no siblings.

The lad swallowed. "Aye."

"No one is leaving," ordered the man.

Erina stepped in front of Thomas. Doing her best to temper her fury along with the fear, she lifted her chin. "Ye have no right to keep him from his chores."

The smile he gave Erina never reached his eyes. "I dinnae let any woman tell me what to do." Grabbing her by the arm, he crushed her to his chest, and used his other hand to cup her bottom.

A knot of cold fear churned in the pit of her stomach, and his stench made her want to heave. "Release me," she demanded.

He gripped her chin, forcing her to lift her head. "Nae."

Blinding pain radiated down her jaw, and her fingers fumbled for her blade. Her captor was swifter and blocked the attempt. Tossing her *sgian dubh* to the ground, he spat out, "Ye will regret your foolishness."

"Let her go!" yelled Thomas and flung the satchel at the man.

The bastard roared with laughter, and Erina used his momentary distraction to her advantage, and kneed him in the groin. "Run Thomas!" she screamed.

The lad did not need to be told twice and sprinted down the path along the river.

Howling in pain, the man slumped to the ground.

Yet, as Erina made to leave, her exit was blocked by three of his followers. Each drew forth their blades and leveled them at her.

"Ye…bitch!" bellowed the injured man. "I will see ye in pain before I am done with ye." He now stood on shaky limbs, drawing in deep gulps of air.

Turning around slowly, Erina fought the bile threatening to spill forth. Panic skittered along her nerves, taunting her. The only glimmer of hope was Thomas had been freed.

Meeting his fearsome stare, she stepped forward, fully prepared to meet her death.

Chapter Five

"The temper of a Fenian Warrior can become as volatile as an erupting volcano."

~Chronicles of the Fae

Rory kept his head bent as the waves of pain receded within his heart and soul. Finding it difficult to speak, he willed every ounce of his energy to seal what had been spoken in this chamber. Images from centuries ago were forced back into their places within his mind, but he found himself unable to close the door. He knew they waited for him to speak. Yet, Rory had to control the blinding pain that accompanied his memories.

He battled the tremors coursing through his body as he unclenched his hands.

"Drink," ordered Conn, pressing the mug against his palm and folding Rory's fingers around the solid object. "It's an herbal tonic."

Taking a hold with his other hand, Rory lifted the mug to his mouth and guzzled deeply. Healing and stimulating herbs were mixed with ginger and lemon water, and the cool liquid seeped into his weary body. Wiping his mouth with the back of his hand, he dropped the mug to the ground. Soon, his body relaxed. Strength infused him with each inhale of breath, and he lifted his head to meet the anguished gazes of all gathered around him.

"Erina MacIntyre was accused of witchcraft in the year 1605 and burned at the stake," he stated gruffly. "I witnessed the event and was instrumental in her death. My instructions were to steer the course of another, yet, my focus shifted during my time with her." Rory swallowed and stood. Leaning against the wall for strength, he continued, "Erina died because I failed to save her."

"Her thread on the loom of fate should not have made a difference. If it was her time, then there was nothing for you to do. Saving this woman was not an option," Conn pointed out.

Rory's breathing became labored. "Her *thread* mattered. Her *life* mattered. I *loved* Erina!"

Silence descended within the room. Rory pushed Conn aside and went to the opposite end of the chamber. Shoving aside the tapestry, he flooded the room with light from the window. He gazed out into Loran's vast herb garden, a bountiful space reminding him of Erina's. "To love a human is forbidden. We trained decades to seal off our emotions to them. But for reasons I cannot explain, I fell in love with the woman. It is a curse I shall carry with me until I cross over to *Tir na Og.*"

"Did you recite the binding vows or link yourself by blood?" asked Conn softly.

Rory grumbled a curse and glanced over his shoulder. "If I had done so, Erina would still be alive. I may have been foolish to love, but I was not irrational to destroy both our lives with vows and blood. The king would have seen to our deaths."

Conn frowned, but kept silent.

Bracing his hands on the ledge, Rory could almost smell the combined scent of lavender and roses, mixed with cloves—one of her favorite mixtures. *I loved her completely.*

Turning around, he folded his arms over his chest. "Do what you must—decree your sentence. I grow weary of this torment. Perhaps now that I have freed the words, the dreams will end."

"If only it were uncomplicated," argued Conn. The prince stepped toward him. "The past remains undone. You cannot continue in this realm until you mend what has been torn from your soul. You are a Fenian Warrior, and you must complete what you have left unfinished."

"I have no unfinished business," snapped Rory. He eyed the prince skeptically. "Should not Loran be questioning me?"

"I am only present to oversee this conversation and proceedings," offered Loran.

Rory's gaze never wavered from Conn's. "Then why are you here, *my prince*?"

Conn flinched, but quickly composed himself. "If you are to remain within the Brotherhood—"

"*If,*" echoed Rory, moving away from the window and placing his hands on Loran's desk. "I am a Fenian Warrior, always!" Again, Conn avoided his question, and Rory tried to calm the fury.

"As I was saying, in order to continue within the Brotherhood, you must remove the past and bind the wound you have created. It has left you weak and vulnerable. In your current condition, you are perceived as a threat to both human and Fae."

"How dare ye!" Rory pushed away from the desk

and approached Conn. His hands longed to rip out his tongue. "Who are ye to tell me what I am?"

"I am your prince, and now leader of the Brotherhood," replied Conn.

"*Leader*," he spat out. "I presume ye had naught to lose by stepping into another role, aye? How strange that I am here, yet, ye are now one of the highest ranking members of our people."

Conn's eyes blazed in anger. "You are a fool, MacGregor. You know nothing. Even your language betrays you!"

How could he expect Conn to understand his love for Erina? The man was devoid of emotions. Nevertheless, he was willing to try anything, so he could resume his life within the Brotherhood. Rubbing a hand over his brow, he asked, "And how do you propose I bind the wound?"

Conn waved his hand outward, and a giant silver orb appeared inside the chamber. Lights shimmered around the globe, their brilliance dancing off the walls of the room. "There is only one way," he uttered softly.

Uneasiness washed over Rory, and he took a step back. Glancing at the door, he noticed Taran and Ronan had fully blocked any attempt he might enact to flee. He shook his head and clenched his hands. "Do *not* ask this of me."

Sorrow reflected in Conn's eyes. "You must return and seal the wound left open from the past."

Rory's heart pounded. "Return? *Nae*," he growled. "I will not watch her suffer again."

"There is no other choice, my brother."

The orb fractured, and images from another time reflected back toward Rory. The green hills of Lindane

51

stood out in vivid colors. Every detail of his time spent there came back in a tide of flowing emotions. How could he face her again knowing how their lives would end? But what if he could alter the past? Prevent Erina's death?

As if reading his thoughts, Conn spoke, "The timeline cannot be changed. Events shall remain as they were, for the threads have already been woven in the future."

Rory snapped his gaze to Conn. "So I do this only for me." Bitterness laced his words. "I have to endure watching her torment all over again?"

"Either you mend, or you will surrender your soul to the shadows."

Conn's words resonated in the far reaches of his mind. The shadows had been calling out to him ever since he was confined in prison. He could not continue on this deadly path, and a small part of him understood. Pieces of his soul were splintering away. Nonetheless, he regarded returning to Lindane the same. His soul would be crushed, once again.

Drawing in a shaky breath, he exhaled it slowly and stepped forward. He longed to return to the Brotherhood and resume his life. The shadows of the past had to be eliminated. "I shall return to Lindane."

Conn nodded slowly. Waving his hand upward, Rory was magically dressed in clothes form the early 17th century, specifically the MacGregor tartan. His sword was belted at his side, along with a dirk and *sgian dubh*. "When you are ready, you may touch the images within the orb. Furthermore, once there, recall your training as a Fenian Warrior. Harness all your emotions. Any questions?"

Rory placed his hand on the hilt of his blade. "None, but hear my words well, Conn MacRoich. When I return to this realm, our friendship shall be terminated. *If* you can allow me to stay within the Brotherhood on those terms, then I accept my position as a Fenian Warrior under *your* command."

Not waiting for a response from the man, Rory turned and touched the glittering sphere, vanishing in an array of colors.

Loran approached Conn. "Why did you not relieve him of his powers?"

Conn rubbed a hand vigorously over his face. "Because he must be the same warrior as the one in 1605. There can be no doubt in his mind when he walks this desolate path again. If I had stripped him of his powers, he would have wondered if he ought to have saved the woman. A predicament I did not want to place him in. He must draw upon his training. Contain the emotions this time. Seal the door for all time on this memory and progress forward. I cannot accept him as an elite warrior until he rids himself of this dark smudge on his soul."

Arching a brow, Loran asked, "And if he attempts to alter the timeline?"

Conn's shoulders slumped as he leaned against the desk. "Death shall follow swiftly."

****

"Ye might as well put your blade through my heart, since I will not let ye touch me!" shouted Erina.

A sinister smile formed on his misshapen face. Stepping forward, her captor backhanded her across the face, sending her reeling into the arms of one of the men behind her.

Tears smarted her eyes, but Erina was determined not to show him her fear. "Bastard," she hissed out, pushing away from the other man.

This time, he punched her in the stomach, and she dropped to the ground. Gasping for air, she fought the wave of hysteria. *Please help me, Goddess.*

He grabbed a fistful of her hair, forcing her to stand. "'Tis a shame I have to bloody such a beautiful face."

Erina spit in his eyes and was rewarded with another blow to the face. Dizziness clouded her vision as the vile man shoved her back to the ground onto her stomach. Terror gripped Erina, and she tried to fight him. Placing his knee against her back, he lifted her gown to expose her bottom.

"Nae! Help me!" But her efforts only inflamed his anger, and he pushed her head into the dirt. Her breathing labored and terror engulfed what little sanity she had left.

Leaning near her ear, he snarled, "When I am done, my friends will enjoy taking their fill of ye."

"If ye dinnae remove your hands from her, I will rip them from your shoulders with my blade," ordered a voice all too familiar to Erina.

The bastard took his time removing his bulk from her back. Erina immediately shoved her dress down and rolled away from the monster. Standing, she brushed away the dirt and leaves from her mouth.

Thank you, Goddess! Help had finally arrived in a wondrous vision. Her half-brother, Graham, and his guards stood baring their swords at all four men.

Graham motioned her forward, and Erina skirted around the loathsome other men to his side. "Are ye hurt?" His eyes barely held the fury within as he took in her appearance.

Her lip trembled, but she replied, "Nae."

"Darren, please escort my *sister* to the horses and guard her well," he ordered.

The guard gave a curt nod. Placing a gentle hand on Erina's elbow, he led her away from the others.

"If I had ken she was your kin, I would not have bothered with the lass," stated her attacker.

"Even if she was not, I despise men like ye," argued Graham and added, "Taking women forcibly and leaving them spoiled. Ye taint the air and foul the ground ye walk. I should not let ye leave this place alive."

Halting her steps, Erina turned around. As much as she wished them all dead, she could not let her brother have the blood of these men on his hands. Her troubles were not his, and any attempt to assist her might bring harm to his clan. She twisted her hands together, trying to think of a solution.

Fear showed in the man's eyes when Graham leveled the blade to his neck. "Mayhap, I shall remove the offensive part of your body that ye were trying to use against my sister."

The blood drained from the man's face, and he visually swallowed.

Graham inclined his head. "Ahh…I can see 'tis a part ye favor."

After leveling a blow to the man's groin with his fist, her brother stepped back. He picked up her captor's sword and tossed it to one of his men, ignoring the pitiful moans behind him.

"What will ye do to us?" asked one of the other

men.

He lifted his sword, studying the glint of steel in the sunlight, and Erina held her breath. "I have determined it best to let ye live. I should not want to tarnish my blade with the blood of unworthy men who are so vile. Furthermore, ye shall make a pilgrimage to a shrine in the far north hills of Clardon near Thurso to reflect on your sins."

Erina let out a sigh of relief.

Graham waved over one of his men. As the guard approached, he clamped a hand on his shoulder. "Remove all weapons and leave them only with their plaids. Secure their horses with ours as well."

"Ye cannot mean to have us wander the land with only our plaids?" complained her attacker, slowly attempting to stand.

"I am leaving ye with your *lives*," countered Graham. "Ye should be grateful, since the alternative would have been death!"

The man clenched his fists, but he offered no retort.

Erina waited while Graham issued several more orders before making his way to her. Sheathing his sword, his hands shook when he took her into his arms. "Sweet Mother Mary, it took all my control not to run my blade through his heart," he murmured against her ear.

She let the tears fall freely and reveled in his strength. After composing herself, she leaned back. Wiping the moisture from her cheeks, she spoke up, "I have nae wish to see ye take on my troubles, Graham. However, I am grateful ye came along when ye did."

He grasped her arms. "By the saints, ye are my kin! If ye were under my roof, ye would not have these burdens." Releasing her, he raked a hand through his hair. "Ye refuse to take shelter within my castle, so ye only bring harm to yourself by living alone. Moreover, your troubles *are* mine, Erina MacIntyre. Ye live on my land!"

She jabbed a finger into his chest. "Ye ken why I will not live in your home, Graham. Need I remind ye of your own father's words? Did he not mention that any offspring of my mother—meaning me, would not be welcome?"

"God's blood! The man is dead! And he was *your* father, as well."

Erina fisted her hands on her hips. "He wrote it on parchment, and a priest witnessed his last dying request."

"I dinnae care if there were a hundred priests present, the man is no longer laird, and I demand ye gather your belongings and come home."

She lifted her head to the sky. How many times did they suffer the same argument? All she ever wanted was to live peacefully in her cottage—one where she grew up under the watchful guidance of her grandmother. Her gratitude turned to bitterness. Silence was the only response she had left to give to her brother.

Gazing back at him, she noted the deep lines of worry etched across his forehead and relented. Walking to him, she placed a kiss on his cheek. "Thank ye, truly." Turning around, she went in search of her horse.

"I shall send a guard with ye to collect your possessions!" he shouted.

"Dinnae require one," she muttered and kicked a stone out of her path.

Darren approached, falling in step beside her. "My lady."

Erina almost snorted. "Thank ye, but I shall not require your services, Darren."

The man ignored her and added, "Ye will gather only the important items from your cottage. We will return in a few days with a cart and two other men and remove the remainder."

Weary and frustrated, Erina halted. "Did ye not hear my words, Darren? Have ye lost your hearing?"

His mouth twitched in humor. "My hearing is fine, my lady. Nevertheless, my orders are clear. I have retrieved your *sgian dubh*." Handing the blade to her, he added, "Wait here and I'll go fetch the horses."

The guard gave a small nod and left her standing among the trees. Gritting her teeth, she was going to spout that it was *her* orders he should be listening to, when movement to her left interrupted her thoughts.

She blinked and shielded her eyes as sunlight pierced the thick canopy of trees, illuminating the giant Highlander within. Erina was about to yell for aid when the air warmed around her, and she fought to breathe. The stranger took a hesitant step forward, and her eyes widened in disbelief.

He was the most magnificent man she had ever laid eyes upon. Dark hair curled around his face—one surely chiseled by the Gods. Detailed perfection, even in his stance, and she pondered if he was a vision. Yet, when their gazes locked, his eyes flashed with the radiance of a thousand stars. Erina gasped, but not from fear. Nae, she yearned to learn more.

"Do we ken each other?" A flicker of familiarity wove a thread inside her thoughts.

Beauty and sorrow reflected back at her within his eyes, and she frowned in confusion. Why did she sense his pain—his torment? A shadow of a smile came forth from his lips, and she ached to run her finger across them. Slowly, she moved toward him.

Too late to stop him, Erina watched in stunned horror as Darren slipped silently behind her Highlander and bashed him over the head with the hilt of his sword.

Chapter Six

"The song of the Ancients can be heard in the whisper of a snowflake."

~Chronicles of the Fae

"For the love of Brigid! Did ye have to hit him so hard?" Crouching down next to the giant, Erina inspected the wound on the back of the man's head.

"I thought him to be with the others who attacked ye," argued Darren.

She glared at the guard. "Take a good look at his plaid. 'Tis a MacGregor, not Ferguson like the others"

Darren shrugged and nudged the man's leg with his boot. "For now, I dinnae trust *any* stranger in these parts."

Erina could not find fault with the guard's words. There were many strangers passing through who were known to thieving. Even the current Campbell laird found it difficult to maintain control over the wandering travelers, since he had issues with reivers on his own lands to the north of theirs. He considered it wiser to let the other nobles handle the situation. Those who argued for support from him then became frustrated with his lack of justice. She had often heard many a villager seek counsel from her brother. Though his lands were small, he ruled with an iron fist and did not tolerate injustice.

"Is there another threat?" demanded Graham, unsheathing his sword as he strode forth, along with the rest of his men.

Erina let out a sigh. "Nae, Brother. 'Tis only an injured man."

Darren leveled his blade against the giant's head. "'Tis a man traveling alone, and that be nae good in this part of the Highlands."

Pulling out her *sgian dubh*, Erina lifted her gown and slashed a portion of her chemise to bind the man's head. "Do ye have any fresh water in your flasks?" She lifted her gaze to find her brother glowering at her.

"Only ale and I will not let ye waste one drop on him."

"A wise decision," agreed Darren.

"Stubborn men," she muttered, and did her best to bandage the giant's head. After finishing the task, she stood. Erina pointed to Darren and another guard who had stepped into view. "Can ye place him over my horse?"

"By all that is holy, ye are not going to take him back to your cottage," Graham demanded.

She threw up her hands in frustration. "Then pray tell me where do ye wish me to take him? All my healing herbs and supplies are in my cottage."

Her brother sheathed his sword and motioned for the other guards to lift the giant. "Darren will go with ye to fetch what ye require. Ye can tend to his injuries at Kileburn Castle."

"I am…nae going there," she sputtered. "If ye worry about my honor, then let Darren stay behind. Furthermore, I have my sheep to care for." Erina dared not speak of her recent problems of unlatched gates and missing animals, or it would give her brother more reason to have her come and live with him.

Graham dismissed her with a wave of his hand and walked away. "Darren will return with ye to your cottage to fetch what ye require. And in the morn, I will send two men to bring your sheep inside the keep." He glanced over his shoulder. "There will be nae argument, Erina. If ye wish to see the man live, then ye can tend to his wounds at Kileburn. Or I can order another to see to his injuries."

She was not about to leave the wounded man in the care of a healer who insisted on bleeding everyone, regardless of their injuries. Tapping her foot to temper her anger, Erina blurted out, "Dinnae forget my dog, as well."

"Ye mean that large beast. Aye, he is welcome," Graham shouted back.

Brushing past Darren, she gave a short whistle and Oberon trotted forth from the trees. Reaching for the horse's reins, she mounted quickly and took off down the path along the river. It did not take long for her brother's guard to catch up with her. Keeping her focus on the trail to her cottage, Erina breathed in deeply the cool air and tried to relax her shoulders. Brushing aside the horrific skirmish from earlier, she made a mental list of items to take back with her. The head wound would require comfrey, marigold heads, salves, and clean linen. "He'll most assuredly awake with a pounding headache," she whispered, and prayed she had enough willow bark for tea.

As she approached a dip in the path, Erina maneuvered her horse through a thicket of birch trees and descended the hill toward her home. Thane lifted his head and barked in greeting.

Dismounting, she quickly went to her pen of sheep. After making certain all were present, she then ruffled the fur on Thane's head. "We are taking a journey, my friend," she said, moving along toward the cottage.

She quickly entered and pulled forth her box of herbs and salves from the wooden cabinet. Reaching for fresh linen and a few more items, she removed her satchel off the large hook on the side and placed the wooden box securely inside.

Darren stood motionless outside her front door, reminding her of the stone statues her brother had described once on his journey to Rome. She rolled her eyes, trying hard not to laugh. Did the guard fear stepping inside? Mayhap her heathen ways offended him. Graham often chided her for not seeking out the church. He once blamed her troubles on her lack of devotion to the Catholic religion. Moreover, she argued that Queen Mary and Queen Elizabeth could not agree on which religion was the wisest, which inevitably ended in heated debate about loyalty to the rightful queen.

Approaching the man, she tapped him on the arm. "Ye may take the wooden chest. I shall go change and fetch some clothing to take with me."

"Aye," he clipped out.

His stern look frightened her, so Erina smiled to break the tension. "What troubles ye, Darren?"

The man waved his hand outward. "Your brother is correct. Ye should not be living here alone. 'Tis easy for any to take advantage of ye."

First her brother and now his guard. How many more felt the same at Kileburn? Erina leaned against the door. "I have never feared living here, Darren. This has been my home since I was a wee bairn. Did ye ken I was born in the forest?"

Darren snapped his attention toward her—one of horrified shock. "*Nae.*"

Arching a brow, she continued, "Och, aye. My mother fled the laird's home—my father's, in terror after she sought him out near her birthing. She wished to appeal to him one last time. If the babe was a boy, she requested he take him into his care. When first she told him of her condition, he became furious and banished her. He claimed she enchanted him with lustful images of her body. She left, her heart torn, and sought refuge with my grandmother." Erina backed away from the door and folded her arms over her chest.

"However, as the months passed, my mother hoped he might have softened his heart. For ye see, it was more than the one time in the laird's bed, and she truly believe he cared for her. Especially, since he had requested only her after his wife's sudden death. Against my grandmother's wishes, my mother went to see him. His mood had not lessened over time, and he beat my mother. In pain and grief, she could not make it back to my grandmother. Giving birth beside an old oak, my mother wrapped me in her frayed plaid and took her last breath."

"Sweet Mother Mary," muttered Darren, raking a hand through his hair.

"Aye, I believe Mother Mary *and* the Goddess Brigid were there, since I lay in my dead mother's arms for two days. If not for my grandmother searching for my mother, I would have been food for the wolves. So ye see, Darren, why I have nae yearning to live at

Kileburn. My grandmother recanted the tale to me only once, but it was enough to put the fear of the place into my verra bones."

He straightened and placed his hand on the hilt of his sword. "By my honor, all shall welcome ye at Kileburn, or suffer the wrath of my blade."

A smile curved her lips, and she quickly turned from his intense stare. "Have nae worries. I have nae plans on staying long at my brother's home. Once the giant awakens and is in good health, I shall take my leave."

No sooner did she utter the words than a fierce wind slapped at her face, taunting her. Dead leaves swirled in the air, and she tried to sense their meaning. Out of all death comes rebirth. Would the injured man die? She glanced down at her hands. What if she caused him grave harm? Yet, the omen could be for her. Did the ancients mock her words? Once inside the castle, would she be trapped inside the cold stones of Kileburn, only to have her brother marry her off to a neighboring clansman?

Ignoring the fear and sudden doubts, Erina made her way back inside the cottage, silently making a vow she would stay no more than five days at Kileburn.

****

Jumbled images flashed through Rory's mind, and he tried to separate one from the next. Laughter, rich and warm, coursed through his veins, followed by violent screams. A kaleidoscope of the past unfolded in a blur, yet, he was unable to grasp them for long. They eluded him, like a feather on the wind. Only one vision remained fixed within his mind. Erina walking toward him before someone bashed him over the head.

Her beauty undid him, and he found himself spellbound. How could he forget such loveliness? In truth, he had not. He had merely kept it hidden, tucked away, safeguarded. And when she stepped into his view, the world could have dissolved and Rory would have never noticed. He remained rooted within the trees, as if seeing her for the first time.

Nonetheless, he tried to grasp a fragment of another time—their first encounter. And it did not begin in the woods.

The more he attempted to sort the order of their past, the more the pain intensified. He gritted his teeth, fighting back the shadows that teased him on the outer reaches of his mind. What was wrong with him? Groaning, he rolled over onto his side—trying to open his eyes.

"Shh…" Her soothing voice brushed against his face.

Soft fingers traced along his forehead, and Rory flinched. As he fought the deep abyss, he grasped her hand and opened his eyes, squinting in the soft daylight streaming inside the chamber. Shimmering pale blue eyes stared at him. She tugged at his firm hold, and he released her hand.

Her steps swiftly crossed the room.

"My apologies," he muttered as he made an effort to sit up. The room spun, but Rory managed to settle his feet on the cold floor and braced his arms on the bed. "Where am I?"

"Ye are in my brother's home," she replied, wringing out a cloth in the basin.

Kileburn Castle? How could this be? Not once did he visit the keep. During his time with Erina, her brother had been away in the northern Highlands, and they never ventured near his home. "Does your brother have a name?" Though he knew the answer before she spoke.

"Graham MacIntyre, Laird of Kileburn," she responded. Moving to his side, she surprised Rory by placing the cool cloth on the back of his neck.

The scent of rosemary and lavender filled him, and his heart beat rapidly with her nearness. Gone was the torn, dirtied, and bloody gown he recalled earlier. It was replaced by a tawny material with hues of gold, which accentuated the vibrant colors of her rich auburn hair. The gown clung to her in places he had long buried within his mind. They returned with a vengeance— memories of their lovemaking under the night sky and another that was spent by the river near her cottage. He had traced his tongue over every inch of her body. Aye, those he could summon, but the other memories were fragmented, elusive. Her fingers deftly examined the back of his head, and he fought his growing lust by digging his hands into the furs on the bed.

"Ye are healing faster than I would have thought," she declared, continuing with her examination. She leaned back and eyed him with curiosity.

"Or perhaps it is the skill of a good healer," he uttered softly. When he noticed the fading bruises on her face, his anger surfaced. Rory reached out and gently traced a path along her cheekbone with his fingers. "Who dared to touch ye?"

Erina grimaced. "Vile men, intent on having their way. Thankfully, my brother and his guards arrived. Graham banished them by sending them on a pilgrimage to the North—minus supplies and horses."

"I would have *beheaded* them."

She smiled, and his heart stopped. "Would ye? And what is your name?"

He leashed his inner beast, although, he longed to kill the men who had hurt his Erina. "Rory...Rory MacGregor. And who do I have to thank for tending to my injuries?"

Arching a brow, she responded, "Erina."

Reaching for her hand, Rory lifted it to his lips, his gaze never wavering from hers. "My thanks, Lady *Erina*."

Her mouth parted, and her eyes widened. "Only...Erina," she murmured.

Rory ached to pull her onto the bed. To feast on her tempting body and sate appetites from long ago. A blush stained her neck, and he knew how far it extended. Slowly and with great effort, he released her hand.

Removing the cloth from behind his neck, she walked back to the table, folded the item, and placed it beside the bowl. "I shall have someone bring ye some broth and bread. I assume ye will want to continue on your journey come the morning."

"And wine," he added.

"Nae, willow bark tea and honey." Erina moved toward the door.

"Wine would help ease the pain," he argued.

Erina turned around. "Humph! Not according to my healing practices. And ye are in my care until ye venture out of Kileburn."

Curious, he asked, "How long have I been asleep?"

"Two days," she answered.

Blessed Danu! He'd slept soundly without the

dreams. But why so long?

"Now ye can understand why I cannot fathom your wound healing so quickly. I was worried when ye did not wake. Aye, Darren has strength, but ye should have awakened within hours, or even a day."

She shook her lovely head. "I feared I would have to break my vow and remain longer."

"Vow?" he asked in amusement.

She bit her lower lip. "I had nae desire to stay here any longer than five days."

Rory leaned forward and braced his arms on his knees. "Why, may I ask? Are ye not welcome in your brother's home?"

Erina glanced swiftly around the room and a frown marred her features. "This is *not* my home, and the sooner I depart, the better for everyone. Though, my brother would rather see me safely hidden within the walls."

In all their time together, Erina never mentioned her dislike for the place. And she spoke little about her brother. Was it possible she feared him? "Are there nae healers here?"

Her smile lit up her entire face, banishing the sorrow. "My brother trusts only me and another. However, Brother Michael is away in Edinburgh. Though I do hear he is returning soon."

She turned to leave and then paused. "I am happy to see ye are awake and healing. If our paths dinnae cross again, I wish ye a safe journey."

Stunned by her words, Rory stared at her retreating form, wishing he could stay far away from the enchanting Erina MacIntyre.

Raking a hand through his hair, Rory made to

stand. Dizziness plagued him, but he would not spend another moment lying vertical. Questions continued to surface as he slowly made his way across the chamber to the arched window. His chief concern was the timeline. Something went horrifically wrong. Did he enter too soon? Or too late?

Uncertainty taunted the warrior. Decades of training had not prepared him for an alteration in the timeline. No! He was the one to set the events in order.

Duty demanded Rory return to the Brotherhood, and desire beckoned him to remain and see where the path would lead.

A choice. Another chance to save the woman he loved. Yet, this time, he'd seal off his emotions from the siren who tempted his soul. Fates be damned. If they saw fit to send him to a new dimension within the loom of Erina's life, so be it. Rory no longer cared about the risks involved. None of this was his doing. Did they not order him to return and mend the wound within his soul?

And this time, Rory would do all in his power to see Erina live. Nonetheless, he must determine the month. Convinced he'd arrived in the correct year, he had to obtain the month. His length of stay determined with the necessary information. His initial time in Lindane consisted of a mere three months.

He prayed his presence here would be short.

Rory leaned against the cool stone wall. "We did not meet in the woods, Erina MacIntyre, therefore, ye are safe from my charms. Pressing his palm over his heart, he tried to ease the pain of their first meeting—one that unfolded in glorious details.

"For the love of the Goddess, stop your barking,

Thane. I have nae wish to scare all the fish away."

The animal kept glancing at him and back at his mistress.

Rory chuckled softly while he continued to watch the beguiling lass near the banks of the river. Standing barefoot on a smooth rock, she attempted to harness a fish to her rod. She had taken a portion of her gown and tucked it inside her belt, exposing a fair amount of her shapely legs.

He found her to be intriguing as she continued her attempt at catching a fish. Unable to stop himself, Rory stepped forward from the pine trees and caught the attention of her dog.

A low growl ensued from the animal, and Rory halted his stride. The deerhound posed no threat, considering his age, and he knew him to be blind in one eye. He reached out to the animal within his mind, but was rewarded with a sharp bark.

"For the love of Mother Danu, what now?" Erina shifted her stance to glance over her shoulder. Her mouth gaped open and then losing her grip, the rod slipped into the river. "Bloody hell!"

"Do ye not think it wise to fetch your rod from the water?" asked Rory, arching a brow at her language.

She turned her back on him. "Ye should, since ye were the cause of my misstep."

Rory crouched down on one knee. "What do ye think, Thane?"

The dog gave a bark and then dashed over to edge of the river.

Standing, Rory smiled. "Then I shall retrieve the lady's fishing rod."

Erina let out an unladylike snort, but continued to

keep her back to him.

Stripping free from his plaid, Rory hesitated on removing his linen shirt. Unsure of what the lass's reaction to the tattoos covering his upper body might be, he deemed it best to keep it on. Instead, he opted for taking off his trews. He despised wearing them anyway. The material was too confining in this century. Tossing them aside, he strode toward the river's edge and removed his boots.

Keeping his eyes fixed on the water, Rory bent down. Thane took his place beside him, and he gently ruffled the fur on his head. "Watch and learn," he whispered to the animal.

Taking two fingers, he dipped them forth and swirled them around.

"Is it too cold for ye?" she teased, looking at him over her shoulder.

He gave her a sideways glance and then stood. "I had to warm it a wee bit."

"Ye daft man."

Ignoring her comment, he dove into the river, and heard her gasp. Opening his Fae senses, Rory instantly spotted the rod buried at the bottom. He quickly retrieved the object, and swam to the surface.

Her face lit up in the most glorious smile Rory had ever seen on a human.

"Ye are my hero, my knight!" Clasping her hands together in glee, Erina slipped on the stone and fell head first into the water.

Dropping the rod, Rory dove back under. Bringing her into his arms, he cradled her against his chest and brought her to the surface. Erina gasped for air, sputtering out water and wrapped her arms around his neck. He gently brought her to the side of the river where they could stand.

"Can…cannot swim. How can I thank ye?"

Rory was helpless. Desire drummed into every cell of his body. He longed to lick the water from her berry-red lips. To tease his tongue inside the warmth of her mouth and give her pleasure.

"A kiss from the maiden?" he asked in a low voice.

Her lips parted, and he feared her response.

Slowly, she brought his head down and Erina placed a kiss on his cheek. "Thank ye, Sir Knight."

As she leaned back, she gave him another one of her radiant smiles, and his soul was lost to Erina MacIntyre.

Letting out a curse, Rory shoved the agonizing memory away. It was lost among the stars—a fragmented piece of history that would never befall either of them again.

Chapter Seven

"If a Fae dreams, he risks the danger of walking between the realm of reality and hidden dimensions— lost forever in a cavern of bleak despair."
                                    ~Chronicles of the Fae

Royal chambers of Prince Conn, Fae Realm

"No, no, no!" His voice shook with rage, and Conn slammed the doors to his outer garden with a crash.

"I am sorry to be the one to deliver the news, but 'tis the truth." Ronan's grim expression told Conn how dire the situation had become.

"How did this happen?" Conn paced the length of his library, frustrated with the news.

"We are…unsure."

Conn's fury rose with the warrior's response. "*Unsure*? A Fenian Warrior has altered the timeline—"

"Nae. Rory has not done so," Ronan quickly interrupted, and then added, "If it was by his hand, Rory would now be dead."

Halting, Conn frowned in confusion. "And yet, the threads on this human have been affected?"

"Aye," he confirmed, shifting his stance.

Unable to fathom a reason behind this unnatural occurrence, Conn resumed his pacing. "How did you come upon this news?"

"The Keeper of Knowledge sent a message to the Brotherhood."

Conn let out a groan. "Archie McKibben."

"Aye. He sensed the shift in wisdom and facts. Soon thereafter, he consulted his tomes, noting the date and time of the deviation."

"Did you attempt to consult the seer?"

"She has refused to see any from the Brotherhood, including ye."

"Interesting," Conn muttered. "So I am now on the list of those not permitted to obtain information? Why do I sense a conspiracy against the Fenian Warriors?"

"She has also forbidden ye to speak with your mother, as well," added Ronan.

Leaning against his desk, Conn folded his arms over his chest, trying to gleam a solution from an impending disaster. "Do you believe any in the Brotherhood countered my orders to stay away from Rory?"

Ronan placed a fist over his heart in respect. "All are loyal to ye, Prince Conn."

Conn winced and shoved away from the desk. "Please do not call me prince."

The warrior exhaled softly. "Ye are our prince, and as such, we are honor bound to call ye by your royal name."

Deciding it best not to argue with his friend, Conn resumed his pacing. "Then if none are responsible, how did the timeline change?"

"I can give you nae answers. Even Archie is baffled."

Striding toward the window overlooking his lush garden, Conn watched his wife, Ivy, stroll among the wildflowers. She was heavy with child, and his heart soared each time he cast his sight on her lovely face. His love for her grew each day. He recalled previous conversations with the seer on his own path. Even the mighty one could not see his own future with accuracy. Was there another path for Rory? One they did not predict, because they were unable to see his journey clearly? "Did the seer mention anything about Ivy?"

"Nae."

"Then I shall consult the *future* seer—my wife. She understands the situation regarding Rory, but not the details."

"Ahh…a shrewd plan."

Conn turned from the window and smiled. "Is Archie still entrenched at Aonach Castle in Scotland?"

"Aye. Ye ken he favors the Dragon Knights there."

"Good. Return and ask him to be on alert to any more changes within the timeline. If this is Rory and the human female's new path, I do not want *anyone* interfering. And bring me any news regarding the younger Dragon Knight, Jamie."

Ronan placed his hand over the hilt of his sword. "Who would dare meddle?"

Shrugging, Conn replied, "Any from the Fae council. They are requesting a meeting, which I keep delaying."

"Wise, but dangerous."

Conn arched a brow. "You forget, they now answer to their prince."

In a flash of light, Ronan vanished. His roar of laughter lingered long after he left Conn's chamber.

Strolling out of the room, Conn went to greet his beloved. Embracing her, he kissed her soft, warm lips.

"You are a vision, *mo ghrá*."

Ivy leaned her head against his chest. "A tottering, huge vision."

Cupping her chin, he swiped his thumb over her pouting lower lip. "One who I adore *and* desire."

She pushed away from him. "You are too kind."

He reached for her hand and pulled her back to him. "Remember, I do not jest, only speak the truth."

Shaking her head in mirth, she cupped his face. "I love you beyond words, but I can't help having these moods."

"What can I do?"

Wrapping her arms around his waist, she replied, "Continue to seek me out during the day. You always know what to say to make me smile." She let out a sigh. "Even our daughter, Sorcha has gone silent."

His smile vanished and releasing Ivy's arms, Conn dropped to the ground and placed his ear against her womb. His daughter's heart beat strong. She merely slept.

Ivy splayed her fingers through his hair. "Yes, I've spoken to the Fae midwife. She assures me the time is drawing near, since Sorcha has taken to sleeping most days."

Relief coursed through Conn and he stood. Lifting his wife into his arms, he carried her to a bench. As he cradled his wife, he took in the lush foliage. "Are you ready?"

When Ivy remained silent, he glanced at her sharply and found her studying him. "I'm more than ready," she reassured. "However, I sense you are the one troubled with concerns."

His laugher was unsteady. "I never fathomed

becoming a father. It…frightens and delights me. And though I have faith in our healers, I fear for the birthing."

Ivy reached out and attempted to smooth the crease from his brow. "All will be well. In truth, you are not alone in your thinking. All expectant fathers go through these times of fear and trepidation. It does not matter if they're human or Fae."

"I love you, Ivy," he whispered against her lips.

"And I you." Leaning back, she asked, "Would you care to ask your burning question?"

"I have none. Only to seek your counsel."

"Am I to assume you have been banished by the seer?"

Conn shrugged. "Why would I bother her when I have you?"

Ivy smacked his arm. "There are days when my head throbs trying to keep up with your wit and sarcasm."

"Do I cause you headaches?"

"I'm teasing." Ivy pointed to the rose bushes growing together over a trellis. "Each year the roses rebloom, correct?"

"Yes," he answered slowly.

"Nevertheless, they don't bloom in the same fashion. You clip a vine and it alters the path or direction of the flower." She returned her attention back to him. "Rory has traveled back to the same time period—the rose. However, it is now growing, expanding in a different direction. The vine or thread has been woven on a new path. An introduction, no matter how small, weaved its way along the course."

Confused, he asked, "Can you not explain in

78

simple facts?"

Ivy straightened. "My vision was presented to me in this way. And from my deductions, someone or something introduced a variant in the timeline."

"They tampered with his past?"

"Not exactly. They wove a new thread."

Frustrated, Conn removed Ivy from his lap. Standing, he ran a hand through his hair. "Who?"

"Does it matter? For now, you have given him an assignment. Let the Fates guide him."

Glancing over his shoulder, Conn's gaze traveled the length of his wife's body. Wisdom, beauty, and motherhood radiated from her. "Enough talk about the Fenian Warrior." Turning around, he swept her into his arms.

"Are you not returning to the Brotherhood?"

"No. I wish to spend time loving my wife."

Her rich laughter filled him as he entered his chamber.

****

Rory perused the laird's extensive library. Sunlight filtered inside, and he sought out the solitude. Unsure of his next step, he judged it wise to stay on at Kileburn. The morning brought the knowledge of the same month and year he had traveled the first time he came to the village. However, the events appeared different and distorted. He believed it was an earlier time period.

The cook appeared agitated after his apparent lack of belief in her declaration of the date. He left without taking the meal she presented. Confusion and irritation were his constant companions, and he longed to sort out the continued fragmented images from the past.

As he traced a finger over volumes of Homer, he

studied the gilded writing on the leather-bound tome. Pulling forth a book, he went to an arched window and began to read.

"Do ye enjoy the story, or are ye learning the art of war from the Trojans?"

Rory lifted his gaze to meet one filled with questions. Holding the book aloft, he replied, "The Greek language has always fascinated me. The story is adventure—epic."

The man entered the library carrying a bottle tucked under his arm. "I am happy to ken another who shares the same interest in Homer. I am Graham MacIntyre."

Rory inclined his head. "I thank ye for your hospitality, Laird MacIntyre."

Graham waved his hand dismissively. "Nae, only Graham. My father preferred everyone to call him accordingly, but I have nae wish to strut about with formalities." Walking to a cabinet, he removed two glasses and moved to a desk near Rory. "Brother Michael arrived this morning bearing gifts of whisky." Opening the bottle, Graham poured the amber liquid into the glasses. Passing one to Rory, he then lifted his. "*Sláinte mhath.*"

Rory inhaled the peaty aroma, and took a sip. The fiery liquid speared throughout his body and left a sweetness lingering on his tongue. After downing the rest, he licked his lips in satisfaction. "A fine malt."

"Aye!" Graham poured him another and walked to the chairs by the hearth. Gesturing for Rory to take a seat, he settled himself. "'Tis a remarkable batch he has made."

"I tasted honey," offered Rory.

Graham leaned forward. "Brother Michael is known to keep many bees. I've often heard him speak as though they are his good friends. God chose wisely in placing Brother Michael at the healing institution in Grafton. His medicinal learning has brought about this wondrous liquid."

"At Brunley?"

"Then ye have heard of it?"

Rory took another sip of the whisky, recalling past visits. Those were recalled in vivid detail, yet, his time with Erina, skewed. "Often."

Graham studied him over the rim of his glass. "Why are ye traveling alone?"

He almost burst out in laughter. The man was shrewd—filling a man with whisky and good conversation, and then aiming forth the real question. Rory expected nothing less and bided his time, realizing the MacIntyre was assessing him. His mind sought out the only fragment from the past he could easily recall. Rolling the glass between his hands, he replied, "I am traveling ahead of Laird Ewan MacGregor. I am procuring a place for him to stay near the coast."

Graham arched a brow and leaned back in his chair. "I have heard he is looking for a husband for his daughter. He makes the journey at this time of year?"

Rory finished the whisky and set his glass on a nearby table. "I am one not to ask questions."

"Do ye journey without a horse or supplies?"

"I have one, but apparently the animal is lost due to a misfortune with one of your men," Rory lied, making a mental note to call forth a stray horse the moment he could steal away from the keep.

Scratching the side of his face, Graham nodded. "I

did have the area searched, but my concern was for ye and seeing my sister safely back to the castle."

"And I am in your debt," responded Rory. "As ye can see, I am now fully healed and will take my leave."

Erina stepped inside the room, and glared at them. "Sweet Brigid! The man has only just now recovered and ye are filling him with drink? And I have heard from Darren ye have brought my sheep into Kileburn, including the lost ones. I thank ye, but there was no need."

Standing abruptly, Rory stared at the beauty in front of him. The light from the window shimmered off her skin, highlighting the smooth contours of her neck. His fingers ached to trace a path from her ear to the valley of her breasts. An image of Erina writhing beneath him came unbidden, along with intense pain. Rubbing a hand over his brow, he tried to ease the burning torment and shoved the fragmented memory away.

"No doubt, ye have not broken your fast, so 'tis a wonder ye can manage to stand," she chided.

Rory clasped his hands behind him. "At the time, food was not what I desired."

Graham remained seated. "If ye so wish, ye can fetch us some bread and cheese, Erina."

Her fury rose, and she pointed a finger in Rory's direction. "Obviously, the man is fit to resume his journey, which means I can now return to my cottage."

"Not exactly," Graham countered.

"Explain," she gritted out, fisting her hands on her hips.

Graham tossed back the rest of his drink and stood. Clamping a hand on Rory's shoulder, he said, "Ewan

MacGregor is traveling here with his daughter, and they seek to break their journey here for a few weeks. I require your aid with his daughter."

"Ye need to find yourself a wife," she uttered flatly, glaring at him.

"Careful, sister, or I may find a husband for *ye*."

"Here?" demanded Rory, seething at the knowledge Graham had already known about the MacGregor. However, in the distorted events of the past, Ewan never set foot inside Kileburn. Instead, his travels led him south to England.

"What? Ye did not ken?" the man asked in astonishment.

As he fought to maintain control, Rory stepped out of his grasp. "Apparently, my laird *altered* his plans."

Shrugging, Graham retrieved the bottle of whiskey from the table and steadily made his way out of the library. "Break your fast, MacGregor!" he shouted from the corridor.

"I am now trapped," uttered Erina softly. "He'll never let me leave."

Hesitation filled Rory. "Why do ye not wish to be here with your brother?"

"I have my reasons."

"Is he cruel to ye?" demanded Rory and stepped near her. *By the Gods, he would slay any who dared to touch her.*

Laughter bubbled forth, and Erina cupped a hand over her mouth. Composing herself, she sighed. "Nae, nae…he only wants the best for me. He cannot fathom a woman living alone, especially one who is kin."

"Ye should consider his offer."

Arching a brow, Erina folded her arms over her

luscious breasts. "And why would this concern ye?"

The reality of the situation prickled along his mind. *Do not get involved with Erina MacIntyre!* Taking a step back, he gave a slight bow. "My apologies."

As Rory made to leave, Erina touched his arm. "This place holds bad memories of what the previous laird—my *father* did to my mother."

Rory did the unthinkable. Taking her hand, he brushed a kiss over her knuckles. "Ghosts pose nae threat and memories fade over time, especially if joyful ones replace the sorrow."

Releasing her hand, he quickly departed the lovely lass who continued to weave her spell within his soul. Nevertheless, determined to rid himself of his feelings, Rory considered it best to steal himself away. His new task would be one of protector and guardian, not lover.

And with each step, he tightly wove the chains of steel and stone around his Fenian Warrior's heart.

Chapter Eight

"Once the door of love opens for a Fae, only death can seal it shut, binding the lovers for all eternity."
~*Chronicles of the Fae*

Erina twisted her hands together, furious over her brother's declaration that she remain at Kileburn to help with his guests. He immediately put her in charge of overseeing the preparations for the laird's daughter. A chamber had been chosen next to Erina's, and though she tried to argue once again with her brother, she judged it wise to be present when the woman appeared at Kileburn and kept her tongue.

She scanned the room and believed it would suit the woman and any maid traveling with her. Word had arrived this morning from a messenger stating the MacGregor would be at Kileburn by early afternoon. After adjusting lavender, bluebells, and marigolds one more time inside the vase on the table by the window, Erina brushed her hands down her gown and left the chamber.

Making her way through the corridor, she paused. Her attention drifted toward the training field, and she spotted her brother and Rory MacGregor. Both were shouting while they attempted to do bodily harm to each other. Her brother preferred to keep his training outdoors, not like some of the English or French, who had created large rooms to foster their skill with blades. Leaning against the window arch, Erina watched the masterful way Rory deflected her brother's blows. It was akin to watching a hawk go after its prey. Many a time she had witnessed Graham sparring in the lists. His was one of strength and speed. Whereas, Rory struck in a slow, methodical pattern with accurate precision. Her brother wiped his brow, and she noted his heavy breathing. Yet, Rory remained calm.

Her skin tingled watching the man. What was it that drew her to him like a moth to a flame? For two days, he had remained absent from the banquet hall, leaving her in a sullen mood. She did not know the man, yet, she yearned to catch a glimpse, hear his voice, or see him striding forth.

"Ye are pitiful, Erina," she whispered. "Gawking at the man like a forlorn sheep."

"But even sheep ken a good-looking ram when they see him saunter by," commented Mairi as she peered over Erina's shoulder.

Embarrassed, she composed herself and stepped away from the woman. Curious as to why she was wandering in this part of the castle, she asked, "Did ye require my assistance in the kitchens?"

Mairi's face flushed, and she bit her nail. "Aye, but 'tis not in the kitchens." She blew out a breath and continued, "Ye might consider my request daft and if ye do, pray forgive me."

Erina softened her features and gestured for the woman to sit on a nearby bench. "What can I do to help ye, Mairi?"

The woman tapped her hand on the bench. "I can only speak in hushed tones."

Concern filled Erina, and she took a place beside her. "Is this better?"

Mairi fisted her hands within the folds of her smock. "Many have whispered ye ken the secrets of binding a man to one's heart." She glanced sideways at Erina. "Is it rumor or truth?"

What Erina feared had come to light, though she was not surprised. The old laird most likely wove a horrific tale about her heathen practices to all within his clan. Choosing her words carefully, she replied, "I have no special knowledge, Mairi. Why do ye ask?"

Shaking her head, she muttered, "Ye were my last hope…"

Erina placed a gentle hand on the woman's arm. "There is always hope, so speak your mind."

"Nae, I must not concern ye with my problems. Ye are the laird's sister." Mairi twisted the material on her smock.

"And yet, ye were willing to seek my aid in securing a man's heart."

"It was Larena's fault. She told me to come seek ye out for a charm," Mairi blurted out, and then quickly added, "She kens the old ways and told me ye do as well. Dinnae worry, I can pay ye."

Ahh…the light of truth reveals itself with the cook, Larena. "Tell me about this man who burns within your heart, Mairi."

The woman gaped at her in stunned silence. Finally collecting herself, Mairi whispered, "His name is…*Bryson.*"

"I will require more information to create a love charm," urged Erina, realizing she stood on a dangerous path. Nevertheless, she grew tired of hiding behind fear and superstitious beliefs.

Mairi clasped her hands. "Ye will help me? Ye ken the secrets?"

Nodding slowly, she replied, "Aye."

For the next several moments, Mairi gushed on about the man she longed to claim as her husband. Quiet and reserved, he worked in the kitchens as the butcher. He came to Kileburn soon after the old laird passed. As he was a hard and able worker, Mairi deemed him to be a good choice for a husband.

"And ye believe he has feelings for ye?"

"Most assuredly." She leaned nearer. "Often times, I find him staring at me. As if, I was a lamb and he the lion. Have ye never had another leave ye breathless?"

Only one. Ignoring the woman's question, Erina brushed a hand over her gown. "If he desires ye, then why do ye require a love charm?"

Standing abruptly, she responded, "Because I have nae wish to see him with another. I want him for my verra own."

He is a wanderer with women, and ye are a fool. Folding her hands in her lap, Erina nodded. "I have all the essential information and will bring ye what ye seek on the eve of the full moon."

Mairi hugged her fiercely. "Thank ye, my lady."

"Erina, please." Her voice muffled within the embrace.

The woman glowed as she darted away, and Erina leaned back against the wall. Discontent filled her. Perchance she should abandon bringing the hope of love to couples. Most demanded her charms for all the wrong reasons. Did they not comprehend that love can be fickle? Even the strongest lure can suffer severe consequences.

"Two charms in a week. I shall have to bind them well." Standing, Erina glanced out of the window. Her brother and Rory were no longer in the lists, and she quickly banished all thoughts of the tall giant with mesmerizing eyes.

After retrieving her cloak from her chamber, she made her way to the kitchens. Snatching a basket off a hook from the wall, Erina briefly glimpsed the man, Bryson, hacking away at a carcass of some poor dead animal. Stunned to find him older than the way Mairi described him, she made a mental note to weave the charm firmly for long life.

Turning around, she traveled along a corridor leading out into the back herb garden. The sun splintered through the gray clouds, and Erina lifted her head to the glorious warmth. Moving toward an area filled with yarrow, marigolds, violets, and pansies, clustered in the center, she knelt down. The simple task relaxed her as she relied on her senses for the right colors, scents, and most interesting mix for a charm.

She smiled and held her hand outward. After saying a silent prayer of thanks, she plucked a few and dropped the flower heads in her basket. Snipping off a couple of the long vines with leaves, she considered using them in the charm, too. Standing, she shook out her gown and headed for the vervain. As she brushed her hand over the flowers, she hesitated. This particular item would have to wait until the sun set, since one could not harvest any for charms unless the sun and moon were not in the sky.

Erina continued to stroll along the path and admire her brother's garden as she added more flowers and herbs to her basket. Humming a tune, she tried in vain to search for foxglove—an essential flower. Birds darted in and out of the garden, oblivious to her movements. Approaching a stone archway, Erina pushed against the wooden door and was surprised to see the path led down to the river.

A cluster of foxglove beneath a few rowan trees caught her eye, and she quickly made her way through the brush. The flowers she sought were close to the river, and the gently flowing water beckoned to her. After quickly collecting what she required, Erina walked toward the soothing water gently lapping over the stones.

After placing her basket on the ground, she slipped off her cloak. Stretching out her arms, she tried to work out the knots in her shoulders. The past few days had made her tense and wary. She treasured this time alone. If only her brother understood, but no, Graham was determined to keep her at Kileburn. She prayed Laird MacGregor would not be staying long. As soon as he and his daughter departed, Erina would be on her horse and gone from this place.

Bending down, she dipped her fingers in the cool water. Dead leaves drifted, landing in the river. A reminder that winter would soon follow. Nevertheless, Erina watched their beautiful golden colors swept up within the dark current.

Startled by a loud splash, she stood abruptly and almost tumbled into the river. As she shielded her eyes, she stood transfixed. This was the second time Erina found herself in awe of Rory MacGregor. His back was to her as he stood staring off into the trees. Water trickled down his back to places that remained hidden beneath the surface of the water.

Her face heated as she continued to admire his naked upper body. Strange markings covered most of his back, and Erina grew curious. She tried to recall where she had seen them. Was it with her grandmother?

The man lingered in the flowing river, oblivious to her intrusion. Finally shifting his stance, he ran his hands through his dark locks. Biting her lower lip, Erina tried to calm her racing heart. As a lady, she should look away. But as a woman, desire compelled her to prolong her gaze over his magnificent body.

A hawk's screech startled Erina, and this time she slipped on the smooth stones and tumbled into the river. Cold murkiness descended all around her. As she struggled to stand, Erina's gown held her fast in the flowing current. She fought for air, but only managed to swallow great amounts of water. Her arms flailed about in an attempt to keep her steady, but the water was stronger. And the more she fought, the more the darkness descended all around her.

"Erina!"

She could hear Rory calling out to her from afar. His voice demanding a reply, but she was unable to acknowledge him. Suddenly, powerful arms surrounded her, lifting her against his chest. He glided effortlessly through the water until they reached the ground. There he released his hold, and she dropped to the ground onto her knees.

Gasping for breath, Erina coughed and turned her head. Great spasms wracked her body, and she heaved the contents of her stomach onto the ground.

Rory knelt beside her. His fingers wiped the matted hair away from her face and massaged her neck. He spoke in soothing words Erina did not comprehend, and her chest burned with each inhale of breath. But soon, her breathing slowed, and he settled her onto his lap.

"Thank ye," she mumbled, coughing from the effort. "Ye…ye have great strength to bring us both from the water so quickly."

"Ye should not be by the water, if ye cannot swim. Furthermore, 'tis dangerous to be near the water in heavy material," he chastised, though his voice held concern.

Stunned by his comment, Erina glanced outward, trying to compose herself. Being in his arms caused her to become flustered. Heat radiated off the man, and she fought the urge to place her head on his shoulder. Her face continued to burn even more, as she noted his appearance. The man wore nothing but a plaid wrapped around his waist, obviously snatched the moment he brought her to the riverbank. She swallowed. "I dinnae fear the water. I have always longed to learn, but sadly, my grandmother was not an expert at teaching me this particular skill."

When Rory remained silent, she stole a glimpse at his rugged profile. A muscle twitched in his jaw, and she sensed frustration seething within the man. He refused to meet her gaze.

"Will ye teach me?" she asked softly, stunned she said the words out loud, and fearing his answer.

He snapped his attention to hers. "Why not ask your brother?"

"Ahh…but then it would give him recourse to keep me longer at Kileburn. Whereas, ye might be able to show me a few lessons before ye depart."

Arching a brow, he shook his head. Yet, Erina did

not know if it was in answer to her question or something else. Deciding to change the subject, she asked, "Do the blue markings on your back have meaning? Were they put there by your clan?"

He chuckled softly. Rubbing a hand over his face, he replied, "Aye, by my brothers. They denote my heritage among my people. Are ye feeling better?"

Erina was lost in his silver blue eyes. There were times they mirrored a stormy sea, and other moments when they shimmered, reminding her of a summer sky. Reaching up with her hands, she brought his head down and kissed him lightly on the cheek. Rough whiskers grazed her lips. "Aye." Averting his intense gaze, she made to stand. However, Rory's strong arms were once again around her waist, aiding her movement.

"Thank ye." Trying her best to straighten her gown, Erina finally gave up and twisted her mass of hair around to the front.

"I fear your brother will not be pleased when he takes in your appearance." He plucked a soggy leaf from her hair.

Laughter bubbled from within her, and Erina was helpless to contain the emotion. "Nae. And I can hardly expect ye to accompany me back inside."

Rory's eyes widened. "He would surely have my—"

"Sweet Brigid!" she gasped, bunching her sodden gown within her hands. "What a sight I will present if the MacGregor and his daughter have arrived. I have nae wish to bring disrespect to Graham. Though I disagree with him for keeping me at Kileburn, I will honor his request to assist with his guests. And knowing my brother, 'tis best I return before he sends out all his guards." She glanced around the bank of the river, searching for her basket and cloak.

As if reading her mind, Rory darted off along the path. He returned shortly, and she let out a sigh of relief noting he held her items. Taking her elbow, he guided her upward through the trees. "This is not the time to worry. Is there another way through the kitchens and to your chamber?"

Erina groaned. "If there is, I dinnae ken the way. This is only my second time at Kileburn."

"Truly?"

Rory pushed aside tree limbs, and Erina ducked under. "Aye. The previous laird requested my presence on my tenth birthday. A guard had taken me from my grandmother's cottage to the castle. I sat in the kitchens of Kileburn for hours, until summoned to my father's solar." Erina slashed her hand through the air. "Not one soul offered me food or drink, and the same guard escorted me back to my home."

Rory grumbled a curse. When he reached the wooden door to the gardens, he stood and blocked her from entering. "Wait for me in the kitchens. Fabricate whatever story to the servants. I will escort ye safely to your chamber."

Erina nodded, grateful for his aid. "Ye have a plan?"

His eyes glittered with amusement. "Always."

Chapter Nine

"Within the veins of a tree, the heartbeat of a Fae can be heard."
                                        ~*Chronicles of the Fae*

As soon as the gate closed behind him, Rory waved a hand over his body and clothing magically appeared over his form. He had no time to consider the recent events with Erina as he rushed down the path to the front of the castle. Although, his thoughts battled for control, and his steps slowed. Did not he save her from the drowning river once already? When he tried to bring forth the first image of their meeting, shards of excruciating pain sliced within his mind, and Rory slammed against a tree in agony. Distorted images blurred, and he was unable to sort them out in a chronological order.

Wiping a hand over his brow, he tried to fight the shadows emerging. What the bloody hell was happening to him? He understood the timeline was vague, yet, why was he losing control? A part of his mind roamed in the present, and the other resided in shattered windows of the past.

Rory slumped to the ground. As he placed his palms upon the cool ground, his voice shook. "Help me, Mother Danu. Help your warrior."

A breeze lifted the hair off his neck, soothing the

battle within his mind and body.

"Do not fight against the inevitable. You will lose."

His breathing calmed, and he tried to sense some clarity in the Goddess's words. Unable to find a meaning, he slammed the door on the past. Standing, Rory settled on solving only one dilemma. Getting Erina to her chamber.

Racing down along the path, he quickly made haste through the portcullis. He bit back a curse as he spied the MacGregor's horses and men. Darting to the left, he steadily made his way to the gardens. After ducking under an archway, he came upon the back entrance to the kitchens. Straightening, he pushed open the door and walked inside. He swept his gaze around the place, and found Erina huddled in a corner by the fire. The place was devoid of anyone else.

She stood immediately. Rushing to his side, Erina whispered, "The MacGregor laird has arrived. All the help are filling the hall with food and drink. My brother is asking for my presence."

"Did anyone mention your appearance," he asked looking around the place.

"Aye, Mairi. I told her I had a mishap and begged her to keep silent."

"Can ye trust the woman?"

Erina swiped at her nose. "If she wants the requested item she has asked for, then I believe she will keep her tongue."

Rory eyed her skeptically. "Did ye not think to ask her if there was another way out of the kitchens?"

"Do ye think me daft? Of course I did, but the woman claimed there was none."

Wandering away from her, Rory opened his Fae senses, searching beyond the wood and stone for another passageway out of the place. Smiling, he stepped beyond the drying herbs hanging above a long table. As he moved toward a cabinet, he studied the paneling on either side. Part of the wood was darker on one side. Noting the wolf carving, his fingers traveled along the wood. Rory pressed the image and was rewarded when the panel opened.

"Ye are amazing," whispered Erina behind him.

Musty smells, darkness, and cobwebs greeted him. "Stay here," he ordered. Fetching a bone carcass from the butcher's table, Rory grabbed a cloth. Wrapping the material around the bone, he touched it magically with special oils and brought it near the flames by the hearth. Fire blazed forth on the torch, and he quickly returned to Erina.

Entering the passageway, he held the torch aloft. He turned halfway, and placed a finger over her lips. "Not a word. I dinnae ken where the corridor ends. It might lead us straight into the banquet hall and your brother."

Erina eyes widened, but she complied.

Rory reached for her hand. Moving forward slowly, he concentrated his Fae sight beyond the firelight. Shadows danced off the stone as they continued to travel through the damp passageway. Approaching a division in the corridor, he turned his head to the right. Closing his eyes, he traveled along the path within his mind. Loud voices greeted him.

As he turned toward the left, Erina tugged on his hand. Her breath warm against his cheek as she leaned near. "How do ye ken?"

He rested his forehead against hers. *Trust me.*

Rory heard her gasp and regretted what he had done. What possessed him to speak within her mind? She was a human.

She narrowed her eyes in the fading light of the torch. However, they did not hold fear, only questions.

"Trust me," he repeated out loud.

She lifted her chin. "Do I have a choice?"

Ignoring her response, Rory led them down the path on the left. The corridor twisted and turned until they came to stairs leading upward. After handing Erina the torch, he took the stairs two at a time until he came to a door. As he tried to open the latch, Rory found it would not budge. Raising his hand above the wood, he whispered words of magic and it released with the slightest touch. The door opened with an eerie screech, and Rory peered inside the room. By the grand appearance of the tapestries and furniture, he would have sworn it was Graham's chamber. Seeing the MacIntyre emblem on a shield above the mantel, only confirmed what Rory believed.

Leaving the door open, he descended the stairs. Taking back the torch, he said, "I believe this leads to your brother's room. Can ye manage to get to your chamber safely?"

"Aye. I am along the corridor on the right." A frown marred her features.

"Are ye worried someone will see ye leaving his chamber?"

Nervous laughter came forth. "Nae, but my hair is a mess. I shall have to do my best to comb and braid it." She shook her head in obvious displeasure. "If only Graham had let me return to my cottage."

Rory hesitated, deeming it best to keep silent. But the words tumbled free from the man and this time the warrior let him speak. "Go change and I shall help ye with your hair."

"I...'tis not proper. What if..." she sputtered, trying to form her words.

"Trust me," he urged once again and smiled.

"Sweet Brigid," she muttered and ascended the stairs.

Rory extinguished the torch and sealed the door magically. Erina waited for him, and he pulled her behind him. Cautiously, Rory opened the door of the chamber leading to the outside corridor. As they departed Graham's room, he gestured for Erina to take the lead. She quickly made her way to her chamber.

Upon entering, Rory closed it behind him and leaned against the oak door, staring at the beauty before him.

Erina kept her back to him. "You must help me with my laces."

As he stepped away from the door, he reached out with hands that shook. Clenching them, he fought the tide of desire. Erina was not his to claim. *Ever.*

Unclenching his hands, he worked swiftly on her laces. Within moments, he had freed the garment from her shoulders. Turning around, he walked to the window and leaned against the stone. Staring out at the valley below, he waited.

The rustling of fabric and Erina's soft sighs of exasperation were the only sounds in the chamber. Moments ticked by and he tried not to imagine her with nothing on. Quickly chastising his thoughts, he kept his focus on several deer wandering along through the trees. Letting the land soothe his inner demons, he barely registered Erina calling his name.

After giving her his full attention, his mouth opened like a besotted lad. The ivory and gold material made her auburn hair shimmer in the afternoon light. Aye, it was a tangled mass, but a crown of stunning colors.

Her face took on a rosy glow. "Can ye help me, please?"

Rory blinked, bringing his focus to their situation. "Turn around."

Complying, she gave him a glorious sight of her back, and he swallowed. Tugging at her laces, he made haste. Erina hastened toward a table and picked up a brush and combs. Soft tapping on her chamber door caused her to drop one of the items onto the floor.

"Erina?" called out the feminine voice behind the door.

"By the hounds," he grumbled.

"Give me a moment," she responded.

Rory glanced in all directions. There was no place to hide. The wardrobe was far too small to hide his massive bulk. And he couldn't vanish in front of Erina. He'd prayed there was another solution hiding within the walls. If not, he would magically create one.

Moving quietly to her, Rory grabbed her arm. "Go to the door."

"What are ye going to do?" she whispered.

"I'm going to look for another way out. If your brother has a secret passageway inside his chamber, surely there must be one in here. I'm thinking Kileburn is full of them."

Biting her lower lip, she waved him away.

"Hurry."

The pounding on the door intensified, and Rory feared the woman would come charging forth. Erina pressed herself firmly against the wood as a precaution. Discreetly waving a hand outward, he sealed the chamber and moved near the hearth. After he promptly ran his hands over the paneled walls, he then shoved aside a gilded tapestry and smiled. Using considerable strength, he forced the door open.

Erina gasped, but he was gone before he could utter a reply, and silently closed the door. With a snap of his fingers light glowed softly in the musty area. Waving his hand outward again, he unlocked the door to Erina's chamber.

"Where have ye been? Your brother fears ye have taken ill, or worse," inquired the woman.

"Please assure him I will be joining him shortly. I am trying to comb out my hair."

Rory could hear the other woman clucking her tongue.

"Ye should have called for me earlier."

"Oh, Janet, ye are a wonder. But I beg ye to deliver the message to the laird."

"Humph! He can wait. He's enjoying the company of the MacGregor laird and his daughter. Though I fancy he favors the latter more. Come now, sit by the fire, and let me see what I can do with this mess."

Rory's shoulders relaxed when he heard Erina comply. And with a single thought, he vanished from the passageway.

****

After adjusting his tartan, Rory made his way down the stairs to the Great Hall. Upon entering, he strode toward Ewan MacGregor.

"By the saints, there ye are," bellowed the laird. "Did ye not think to be present when we arrived?"

Rory fought the urge to counter with a retort. He knew the man well in his travels and considered him one of the few human friends he had. Apparently, he had not altered the timeline with his dealings with Ewan, though he could not recall any conversation about the home of the MacIntyre. In the previous timeline, Rory had visited with Ewan and his daughter in Edinburgh before departing for Lindane. The fragmented memory now a vague whisper within his mind. "My laird." He gave a slight nod.

The man gestured for him to take a seat across from him, placing him next to his daughter, Catherine.

"We had thought to send out the hounds," Catherine teased, reaching for the pitcher of wine and pouring some into a cup. She held it outward for him.

"Ah, but then I surely would not have returned," he chided, winking at her, and taking the offered item.

Her mouth twitched in humor. "How foolish of me. We all ken how much ye love the animals, and how ye would have favored time in the hills with them."

"Have ye found your horse?" asked Graham.

"The animal remains hidden," replied Rory. He took a sip of the wine. "No doubt he will venture forth after foraging for food and finding none."

"No doubt," echoed Catherine.

Ewan shifted in his chair. "As I was saying to Graham, we were fortunate to meet in Edinburgh, and he was generous to suggest breaking our journey here at Kileburn."

Rory swirled the contents of his cup, trying to

remember the details of another discussion. Did not he mention Graham's name in passing? "If I recall, ye thought the MacIntyre to be making his way to England."

"I did have plans," offered Graham, leaning forward in his chair. "The Campbell and I considered it wise to present our petitions to the king, praying he would hear about our troubles here in Scotland." He waved a hand about. "Yet, has the king returned? Made an attempt to visit any of the lairds or nobles?"

"Why should he concern himself with our affairs? He's more English than Scottish," grumbled Ewan.

"Hush, Father. Ye speak treason."

Ewan shook his head. "I *speak* truth."

"Regardless, I was sent a missive from the Campbell stating he had taken ill and could not venture with me. I judged it wiser to return to Kileburn and make the journey another time." Graham frowned and added, "If we had not returned, I fear my own sister would have come to great harm. We have been plagued with thieving and travelers seeking to rape and pillage from our lands."

"I have heard rumors 'tis the English planting men to stir the wasp's nest among our clans," suggested Rory, trying to suppress his fury over what had happened to Erina.

"Aye!" agreed Ewan, smacking his hand on the table. "How can we fight this madness?"

"By stating our grievances to the king," suggested Graham.

"Do ye think he will grant ye an audience?" asked Catherine.

Shrugging, Graham replied, "Perhaps. If we do

nothing, then we shall never ken, aye?"

Catherine leaned forward. "Is your sister well? I pray she did not suffer too greatly."

"Only bruises, but nae harm was truly done," answered Erina, stepping inside.

Silence descended in the hall as everyone watched the vision of beauty approach. Rory immediately stood and pulled out a chair for Erina. She gave him a small smile and took her place next to him. Gone was the lass in a tangled mess and sodden clothes. And in its place, a woman with poise and elegance.

"My sister, Erina," introduced Graham.

Catherine inclined her head. "I am happy to hear no true harm transpired."

"Thank ye. I was indeed fortunate my brother came upon me when he did."

Ewan rubbed a hand over his beard. "I must confess, Graham, your sister was blessed with all the beauty in your family." He leaned near her. "Why have ye hidden this gem from us?"

By the hounds, the man was flirting with Erina. Rory leveled a warning gaze at his friend. However, the man refused to back away and uneasiness settled within Rory.

"Ye wound me, MacGregor," chided Graham. He turned to Catherine. "Do ye find my face offensive?"

The woman laughed and reached for a nut from a bowl on the table. Popping it into her mouth, she shook her head.

Erina reached for the jug of wine. "'Tis my own decision to remain secluded, my lord. This is not my home." Before she filled her cup, she asked, "More wine?"

"Aye," interrupted Rory and handed her his cup.

She arched a brow, but complied, and then returned her attention back to Ewan, who continued to stare at her as if she was a feast to be devoured.

Rory drained the entire contents of his cup.

"Please call me Ewan, and ye must remain here during our stay," he encouraged.

"Aye," agreed Catherine. "I have been without the companionship of a young woman to converse with for some time."

"How long are ye thinking of staying here at Kileburn?" interrupted Rory, his question directed at Ewan.

The man leaned back in his chair and fingered the knife on the table. "We can stay the month, if that is in agreement with *your* plans."

Shrugging, Rory replied, "Ye are the laird. My plans are yours."

"His *plans* include finding a husband for me," scoffed Catherine.

Graham wiped a hand down the back of his neck. "One which I should entertain for my sister, as well."

Rory glanced sharply at Erina and noted the color draining from her face. Fury and indecision battled for control within him. Should he not be elated her brother wished her to marry and find happiness? Erina was not destined to be his, so why could he not find joy in this new possibility? Regardless of his emotions, he had to forge a new path. He lifted his cup. "'Tis a grand idea."

Erina gave him a scathing look. Standing abruptly, she inclined her head. "Would ye like to see the gardens of Kileburn, Catherine?"

The woman laughed and stood. "I would be

delighted."

Reaching for another jug of wine, Rory refused to watch the lovely Erina MacIntyre saunter out of the hall.

Chapter Ten

"Often times, Fae men can be as obstinate as their mortal counterparts."

~Chronicles of the Fae

Plucking the velvety rose petals from the bush, Erina rubbed them between her fingers and let them fall gracefully to the ground. Frustration seethed within her. Was she to be bartered off to some man like a pawn in a chess game? Even Rory agreed, which troubled her immensely. She thought him to be different, but he had proven her wrong. Men would continue to side with each other when it came to the marriage bed, leaving their women standing on the side like a herd of sheep.

"At least I treat my sheep with respect," she muttered. Wiping a hand over her brow, Erina walked under a trellis filled with more roses, but their blooms were fading. Soon, they would wither until next spring. Though she had a dislike for Kileburn, Erina found the gardens to be lush and overflowing. They were a soothing tonic from her current situation.

"Are ye feeling ill?" asked Catherine, touching her gently on the shoulder.

Erina sighed and motioned her to a nearby bench. Sensing a kinship with the woman, she replied, "Do ye ever wonder when ye speak your mind that no one listens to your words?"

Catherine laughed and tilted her head upward. "If ye are referring to certain men, then aye, I ken your meaning. I have given up arguing with my father over his persistence on finding a suitable man to marry." She directed her attention back to Erina.

"So ye are resolved with his wishes?"

"Goodness, nae." The woman leaned near. "I ignore him and nod occasionally. I reckon he thinks he has worn me into submission."

Confused, Erina asked, "Yet, why are ye making this journey with him?"

Catherine's eyes sparkled with mischief. "Because I realize I must marry, and therefore, I will choose my own husband. If I refused, my father would seek out some old, rich laird for me."

"Ahh…so in truth, ye are in control."

The woman nodded. "Always. Though my father has no idea."

A squirrel scampered past them, and Erina smiled. "If it were only so simple with my brother."

"If I may ask, why do ye not live at Kileburn?"

Pursing her lips, Erina looked away. "It has never been my home. Graham and I share the same father, but not mother. I was never welcomed here after my mother died." She stole a sideways glance at Catherine, seeing only compassion and not judgment in the woman's eyes.

"I am grateful ye have decided to remain here until we depart, though I cannot imagine how it must pain ye to stay."

"Thank ye," whispered Erina. "I have a lovely cottage beyond the hills in the valley, where I keep a few sheep. 'Tis not much, but I am content. During the last harsh winter, Graham would often send someone with food, supplies, and a strict message, 'Return to Kileburn.' And I would thank the messenger and send him on his way with my regrets to my brother."

Catherine nudged her. "Your brother has kind eyes, so I am sure he will listen to ye after my father and I have departed."

Chuckling softly, Erina shook her head. "Ye have only witnessed his good humor."

"Humph! It is in the timing of your approach. All men have a dark side," declared Catherine, smoothing the folds in her gown. "All ye have to do is watch the shift in their eyes. However, there are those who the coldness reflects all the time."

Instantly, Erina's thoughts turned inward and to one man. Rory MacGregor. *A traitor with shimmering eyes.* She had witnessed the compassion and something more within his depths. Keeping her focus on the flowers, she said, "Rory and your father have kind eyes."

"Now there is an interesting man."

Erina glanced sharply at the woman. "Your father?"

Catherine waved her hand in the air. "Nae. *Rory.*"

She swallowed, trying to keep her voice steady. "How so?"

"My father is laird, but Rory can enter a room and command all. I have seen women almost swoon over him." Catherine cupped a hand over her mouth to stifle the giggle. "I must confess he's one gorgeous man."

Stunned, Erina asked, "But is he not your kin?"

Arching a brow, she responded, "*Nae.* His grandfather was taken in my by great-great grandfather.

At least this is the story told to me by my father. There are times when I suspect another truth to the tale."

Erina quickly glanced away. Mayhap her newfound friend had eyes for Rory. Her heart beat faster, and her stomach clenched. Why did she care? Furthermore, the man would leave when his laird was ready, so she should banish all thoughts of him. But the idea of Rory MacGregor wooing kisses from Catherine twisted her insides like a mass of snakes.

"Do not tell me ye have not noticed the man's looks?" questioned Catherine.

Erina blinked, bringing her focus to their conversation. "He is only a man like any other."

"Hmm...I sense a lie within your words."

Shielding her eyes from the afternoon sun, Erina was about to object when Thane came bounding toward them. Unable to stand for fear of him crashing into her, Erina opened her arms. Something or someone had caused her cherished dog to become excited.

"Sweet Mary Mother of God and all the saints!" exclaimed Catherine, and then cupped a hand over her mouth. She tried scooting off the bench, but Thane had trapped part of her gown with his giant paw.

Erina looked at the woman. Her choice of words had revealed a secret. She ruffled the dog's fur and shoved him aside. "Dinnae fear, Thane is a gentle beast, unless provoked by mean people."

"'Tis good to hear." Catherine slowly pulled the material free and stood. "I hope ye dinnae mind my outburst."

Standing, Erina straightened her gown. "Not at all. And your secret is safe with me."

The woman's face drained of all color. "I dinnae

understand."

"Ye are Catholic."

Catherine stood motionless.

Erina took her cold hand into hers. She did not mean to frighten the woman. "I will share one of my own. I have no religious side. I choose to believe in the old religion. Call me a…heathen. There, I judge my secret is far worse than yours. 'Tis one that many ken well here."

A flicker of warmth returned to Catherine's eyes, and she squeezed Erina's hand. "Ye are a true friend, indeed. My father fears naught what others think. But I have heard the rumors how the new king follows the path of Elizabeth and wishes to bring Scotland under the Protestant belief." Dropping Erina's hand, she continued, "He sees our pope as evil *and* the devil. I pray I never have to meet this king."

"'Tis a shame we cannot follow our own path to light and love, aye?"

Nervous laughter bubbled forth from the woman. "Or for husbands. And speaking of men…" Catherine nudged her.

Following the woman's gaze, she focused on Rory striding with purpose toward the other end of the garden. Almost as if he sense their presence, Rory slowed down and turned. His gaze lingered on hers— powerful and something else she was unable to fathom. Though fleeting, she tried to capture its meaning. Her earlier anger at the man dissolved, and she longed to join him.

"Rory reminds me of those Greek statues of Gods a traveling monk spoke of last winter," whispered Catherine. "They were extremely tall and beautifully carved out of marble. Some even bore no clothing. When I urged the monk to tell us more, my father bade him to speak no more of them in my presence."

A vision of Rory unclothed appeared within her mind, and Erina found it difficult to breathe. Giving them a short nod, the man smiled and continued along the path. Placing a hand on her chest, she tried to calm her racing heart.

"Ye should go speak with Rory," encouraged Catherine.

After snapping her fingers for Thane, Erina moved away in the opposite direction. She was not about to go chasing after the man, regardless of her attraction to him. When her dog refused to come to her side, she patted her side. "Thane?"

The animal angled its head at her and then dashed off in Rory's direction.

Catherine arched a brow. "He seems to have found a new master."

"*Both* are traitors," muttered Erina, glaring at the retreating form of her dog.

"What did ye expect? They're both *male*."

As Erina made her way out of the garden, she could hear Catherine's laughter mocking her along the path. Shaking her head in an attempt to rid her thoughts of Rory MacGregor, she stumbled on a log. "Ye are behaving like a dolt."

At least her sheep remained loyal. She headed in the direction of the enclosure where her brother had assured her the animals were safe. She brushed past a rowan tree filled with berries, and birds darted out in obvious displeasure at being interrupted from their feast. The path ended abruptly, and she found herself staring in two directions.

"Left or right?" Unable to recall her brother's words, Erina decided on the left and tread forward. Sunlight filtered through a canopy of trees, their golden beams dancing off the ground, and she bent to pick up a leaf. She twirled it within her fingers, studying its shape and color. Smiling, she let it drift back to the ground and continued on in her search.

Instead of the soft bleating sound of her sheep, Erina was greeted with loud pounding noises. As her steps hastened, a steep path beneath the shade of an oak tree led her to a bramble and bracken stone structure.

Letting out a frustrated sigh, she stepped into view of the smithy and halted.

Her mouth dropped open at the sight before her. Rory MacGregor stood over an anvil, hammering away at the steel, and without a tunic covering his upper body. His corded muscles rippled with each blow to the metal, and Erina was captivated. Beads of sweat traveled down his back, glistening in the afternoon light. Raw masculine power poured out of the man.

She leaned against the oak tree for support. Once again, she was drawn to the mysterious markings on his back and shoulders. They traveled down and around his waist. Their pattern reminded her of something she fought to recall. And then a glimmer of recognition flitted through her mind. She had seen them on the ancient standing stones her grandmother had shown her years ago during a harvest festival. They had traveled north with others who believed in the old ways. It was a time of feasting, telling bardic tales, and bartering for goods.

When her grandmother stood before the massive

stone giants, she spoke with reverence about the ancient people who had carved the symbols. Erina remembered how her fingers traced inside the curved grooves on the stone. She told her these people were extremely tall with glittering eyes and the power to change the elements. Though they no longer lived amongst them, her grandmother had heard whispers of those who had witnessed seeing one or two of these great people wandering the land.

Her new friend was incorrect. Rory was a Celtic God, not Greek. Was he descended from these ancient people? Even though she believed in the magic of the land, Erina found it difficult to consider ancient gods roaming the land.

Pushing away from the tree, Erina strolled casually toward him. His focus was intent on the blade he was fashioning—commanding and bending the metal to its desired shape. Thane lifted his head from his warm place near the fire.

Rory paused in his movements and raised his head. Eyes that mirrored a tempest at sea stared back at her. His chest rose and fell with each breath. She noticed the stubborn set of his jaw, and his brow lifted in challenge. Others may have feared him, but Erina found him intriguing.

"Have ye lost your way?" he asked, the rough edge of his voice sending shivers across her skin.

"Obviously, since I am here at the smithy, instead of finding my sheep."

He pointed toward her dog. "And here I thought ye came to claim your animal."

She looked at Thane. "Is he bothering ye?"

Chuckling softly, Rory lowered his hammer and

doused the blade he was working on in a bucket of water. "Nae."

Erina studied the man as he went to the animal. "He has never taken to another, before now."

He ruffled the fur on the animal's head. "He is a wise dog." Thane thumped his tail in obvious approval.

"I am happy he has found another friend." She leaned against the cool stone.

Rory wiped his face with a drying cloth, and then tossed it aside. "What about your sheep?"

"What about them?" she asked, her eyes growing wide as Rory stepped near her.

"Should ye not be on your way to find them?"

Once again, Erina found herself tongue-tied and unable to move. She tried to move away, but he loomed over her. "Aye, but I am lost."

Placing a hand on the stone behind her, he cupped her chin. "Ye have never been lost, Erina MacIntyre."

"How can ye be so sure," she whispered, noting the shift in his eyes. "We have not known each other for verra long."

Rory leaned close. His breath was hot against her neck, and she shuddered. His lips grazed the soft spot below her ear. "Because I am certain. I have a keen intuition."

Closing her eyes, she turned her head. All she sought was one kiss—to taste the man on her lips. Rory stirred desires within her Erina had never known. She burned in places that required release.

"Open your eyes, Erina."

Her lashes flickered open and raw desire gazed back at her. *Kiss me, Rory MacGregor.*

His groan echoed within the far reaches of her

mind as he captured her sigh with his mouth. The touch of his lips was a delicious sensation, and sent her body into a wild swirl of pleasure. She reveled in the feel of his mouth on hers and passion drove her onward for more. As she wrapped her arms around his neck, he angled his head and deepened the kiss. When his tongue demanded entry, Erina opened fully. It was a kiss for her tired soul to melt into, and she was shocked at her own eager response. Emotions whirled and skidded as she caressed the tendons in the back of his neck.

Rory's fingers trailed across the skin above the lace on her gown, and she shivered, aching for more. Erina felt confined in her gown, longing to strip the material free from her body. She ached to have his skin against her own. His lips seared a path down her neck, and her knees weakened. "More," she pleaded, splaying her fingers through his dark locks.

Releasing her, he placed his hands above her against the wall. His breathing came out in short gasps, and she saw the battle he fought, since Erina had to battle her own personal restraint. She lowered her hands to her sides. She dared not move. Confused on what to do next, she barely heard his words.

"Leave," he ordered, clenching his eyes shut. "And never seek me out again."

Without a word, Erina ducked under his arms and darted off along the path. The ache in her chest was like a lodestone, pressing against her heart. Tears stung her eyes, and she fought to control them from spilling forth. Tree limbs smacked her face, and she welcomed their sting. Coming along the fork in the path once again, she veered around the bend and collapsed against a pine tree. The anguished cry tore free from her throat as she sobbed into her hands.

Where only moments earlier, Erina had experienced utter passion in a kiss, she now felt ashamed and humiliated by her wanton behavior. What possessed her to even approach the man? Why was she drawn to him? She hated herself for this weakness—yearning for a touch, a word, or a kiss from the man. She wiped her lips with the back of her hand, trying to banish his taste.

A warm nose nudged her hand, and Erina glanced upward. "Dear, sweet Thane," she mumbled. The dog sat regally next to her, and she leaned against him. After wiping the tears from her cheeks, she tried to calm her fractured nerves.

Lifting her head, Erina allowed the swaying branches and the warmth of her friend soothe her. A gentle breeze kissed her cheeks, and she shook her head. Standing slowly, she brushed the leaves and dirt from her gown.

Her lips still burned in the aftermath of Rory's fiery possession, but Erina quickly slammed the door on the memory. Placing a fist over her chest, she vowed never to be led astray again.

"Before the Goddess, I recite my solemn pledge—this day, this hour. Ye will never get under my skin or thoughts again, Rory MacGregor. I am finished with folly and nonsense. If I have to harden my heart, so be it. No man shall claim me. No man shall I love."

Taking a deep breath in, Erina released it slowly and strode with the purpose of being able to return home to her cottage. And soon.

Chapter Eleven

"Love is like a thorn on a rose. Once pricked, it is difficult to stop the flow within your heart."
~*Chronicles of the Fae*

The dying sunset spread out beyond the tree covered hills, and Rory paid reverence to the last ray of light. Striding toward the well, he hauled up a bucket of water and dumped it over his head, removing the sweat and grime. The cold water helped to ease the burning heat within his body and mind.

Raking a hand through his hair, he stared outward. Guilt plagued him after Erina fled, and he fought to close the door on all his emotions. Anger, guilt, confusion, lust, but most of all, *love*.

He had no right to claim a kiss. He had no right to rouse her passion and his. He had no right to love the woman. And yet, he found himself constantly drawn to her. His vision blurred, and the air warmed whenever Erina came near him. She was wild, untamed, and had a passion for the land—qualities he loved about her. Rory continually lost control, and his anger intensified. He should have never returned. He risked putting them both in danger.

Rory slammed his fist into his palm. "Erina deserves better." And he would give her this second chance of happiness. A life filled with joy and children.

His heart hardened further. He must attempt to spurn Erina. Keep his distance. Prove himself unworthy in her eyes.

Yet, his resolve to carry out his plans to fruition always faltered. Rory became conflicted. He ached to possess her again. But time was their enemy. In order to keep her from suffering the same tortured road, he had to lead her to a new future. A destiny without him.

Rory knelt on one knee and tore his troubled gaze upward. "Hear me, Mother Danu. Place your shield of protection over Erina MacIntyre. Show her a new path of light and love." He hesitated and then added, "If ye must, take away this love I have for the woman. Let me return to being only her guardian. Let me right this injustice."

Dropping his head forward, Rory waited for some message or sign from the great Goddess. Moments slipped by in silence, and his shoulders slumped. Grabbing a handful of dirt, he brought it to his lips and then flung it outward.

Standing, he made his way over to the new blade he had forged. When he held it up, the last rays of sunlight glinted off the cold steel. Tomorrow he would construct a hilt and present it to Graham when completed. This would be his parting gift to her brother. Graham should be Erina's protector, not him.

As he gently laid it back on the shelf, Rory walked out of the smithy and through the thick canopy of trees.

His steps slowed as warm air brushed across his face.

"You are her guardian. You are her shield. Mend the two and become one."

Rory's fists clenched. "I cannot undo the past."

"You cannot walk two roads at once. Remember, you are a Fenian Warrior."

"What if I choose not to be?"

A deafening sound reverberated around him, and the ground rumbled beneath his feet. Stumbling forward, Rory slammed into a tree. As he waited for several heartbeats, he realized the Goddess would say no more.

Pushing away from the tree, he strode with purpose to the castle and dismissed the words she had imparted to him within his mind. He had no time to dissect their meaning.

Rory nodded to a passing guard upon entering the bailey. When he entered the castle, his steps hastened up the stairs. He had no desire to dine with anyone or to sit and make idle chatter. Unfortunately, Ewan came forth along the corridor.

He acknowledged the man and steadily kept on walking toward his chamber.

"Will ye be joining us shortly?"

Rory's hand stilled on the oak door. "I shall take my meal in my chamber." Without waiting for a response from the man, he entered his room.

"If I may have a moment of your time, *Fae Warrior*?" demanded Ewan, closing the door.

Biting out a curse, he faced the man. Though Ewan was a friend, Rory deemed he overstepped by calling him thusly. "This must be serious if you're calling me a Fae."

Ewan folded his arms over his chest. "What is wrong?"

"I dinnae ken your meaning."

"If my memory serves me correctly, I dinnae recall

ye mentioning traveling to Kileburn. Ye were making your way to Ireland. Why are ye here?"

Frowning, Rory crossed to the table in an attempt to sort out his mixed thoughts. Unable to bring forth any conversation with the man, he lifted a pitcher. He sniffed the contents and poured the wine into two mugs. Handing one to Ewan, he went to the arched window and sat on the ledge. He swirled the dark liquid. "I am here to see an injustice made right."

"With the woman, Erina?"

Rory downed the contents of his mug. "'Tis none of your concern."

The man stepped forward. "I have never interfered, but this time I will ask ye to step aside."

"Are ye challenging me or are your words a threat?"

"I am still your laird," argued Ewan.

Rory flung the mug across the room, and the pottery shattered against the stones. "And I am a Fae!" Rory stood and stalked over to the man. "Or have ye forgotten?"

Placing his mug on the table, Ewan glared at him, showing no fear. "Ye are not the *Fae* I ken. When did fury and distrust replace friendship and conviction?"

Once again, Rory found it troublesome to rein in the shadows and anger. How could he explain to his friend—a *human*—what he was experiencing? How he had once loved Erina and watched her die? He longed to seek out the counsel from within the Brotherhood, specifically his brother, Liam. By the hounds, he missed his brother.

Walking to the hearth, he braced his hands above the mantel and gazed into the flames. "Forgive me."

Glancing over his shoulder, Rory continued, "I am unable to discuss the dilemma."

Ewan came to his side and clamped a hand on his shoulder. "Come dine with us. Whatever the problem or issue, ye can settle it come the morn. I ken ye are not able to share what ye do, but can it not wait?"

Rory nodded. Regretting his next choice of words, he said, "Ye have an interest in the Lady Erina?"

His friend shrugged. "Undecided. Do ye?"

Rory chuckled softly and pushed away from the mantel. After picking up the shards of his mug, he tossed them into the fire. "Nae. She is meant for the marriage bed and not a quick tumble."

His friend rubbed his chin in thought. "I concur. Though I cannot take a bride who believes in the old heathen ways. Yet, there are those in the church that would burn us both if they knew the truth of who and what ye are."

Startled by his declaration, Rory asked, "How did ye come to this knowledge of Erina?" He feared anyone having this information.

"When I showed an interest in the woman, her brother shared Erina's beliefs." Shifting his stance, he added, "Graham is protective of her, and he took a risk in telling me. Did it sway me toward the lass? Somewhat, and then I had to consider she might view me as too old." He laughed and then added in a more somber tone, "But I also harbor my own secrets."

Rory clasped his hands behind his back. "As do many."

"Aye, *aye*," muttered Ewan. "The priests would surely damn my soul." He strode toward the door. Reaching for the handle, he paused. "I will not speak of your true name again, my friend. And whatever injustices ye seek to make right, I wish ye all the best."

"Thank ye, Ewan. Though if I might ask, have ye mentioned my particular bloodline with Catherine?"

Ewan's hand stilled on the handle, and he glanced over his shoulder. "I honor the sacred vow my Grandfather gave to ye many years ago and will only tell my daughter if I have no heirs." Opening the door, he added, "I shall see ye in the Great Hall. I hear the cook has prepared a dish of wild boar and onions."

Rory grimaced. "Mayhap I shall take my meal elsewhere."

His friend's laughter echoed down the corridor long after he left.

Pinching the bridge of his nose, Rory pushed the pain of their conversation to the far recess of his mind. He had no desire to have the man claim Erina for his wife, but if he could choose a husband for her, Ewan MacGregor would be the one.

And the shadows within Rory mocked him.

****

Boisterous laughter greeted Rory when he entered the Great Hall. Graham was regaling those around him with a tale of how he hunted down a boar several days ago. It was a story honoring not only the hunter, but also the prey. Ewan apparently had his doubts, since he argued over the bow and arrows used on the animal.

Rory almost decided to take his meal in the stables until his gaze came upon *her*. Sitting regally next to her brother, she shook her head and grimaced.

Erina touched her brother's arm. "Did ye kill him swiftly and say a prayer afterward, giving thanks?"

Graham narrowed his eyes. "Aye, most definitely.

Do ye take me for someone who gives nae regard to my food?"

Indecisiveness battled for control inside Rory. Leave or stay? Finally giving in, Rory slowly made his way to the table and took a seat across from her. "Lady Erina."

Her smile vanished, and she darted a glance at him. "Rory."

He barely acknowledged her as he reached for a bowl of cabbages, onions, and wild mushrooms. Scooping out several spoonfuls, he placed the bowl back down. Grabbing some bread, he tore off a chunk.

The conversation continued between the men, and Rory ate in silence. Turning his attention to Erina, he noted the blotched redness on her face. He could sense her fury from across the table, and his food soured in his gut. Pushing aside his meal, he reached for a jug of wine and filled his cup.

"Do ye not care for the boar?" asked Graham, skewering a portion from the platter.

"Rory does not like meat of any kind," interjected Catherine, taking a seat beside him. Picking up her cup, she handed it to Rory. "Would ye be so kind?"

Almost choking on his food, Graham pushed his cup toward Rory, as well. "Truly? Nae meat? How does one survive without it?"

After filling both cups, Rory handed them back respectfully. "I have never acquired the taste."

"Nae, but ye have other ones," mentioned Catherine, smiling demurely.

Erina snorted, but remained silent. She refused to meet his stare, and pushed her food around on her plate.

"Ye have heard too many tales, Catherine." Rory

all but guzzled his wine.

"My daughter listens when she should not," grumbled Ewan.

"Ye wound me, Father. These are stories from the women and not ye."

Ewan gave her a warning look. "Do ye want to shock Lady Erina?"

"And now ye insult me." Catherine placed her cup down. "I am a lady, too."

"There is naught ye could tell me about Rory MacGregor that I probably would not have guessed," stated Erina, placing her hands upon the table.

Rory leaned back in his chair. "I judge it wise to pick another topic of conversation."

"Why?" prodded Erina, giving him a scathing look. "Are your conquests even too embarrassing for your ears?"

Graham dropped his knife. "*Erina.*"

Keeping his hands clenched by his sides, Rory leveled his gaze at her. "Nae, never. But I will not entertain my bedroom adventures in the presence of ladies."

Erina snickered. "Is that what ye call it? *Adventures?*" Stabbing a piece of the boar's heart, she added, "Do ye leave their hearts broken after ye are finished?"

"Enough!" shouted Graham, slamming his hand onto the table. He glanced at Rory. "Pray forgive my sister. Living alone has made her tongue sharp. She often speaks her mind, when it would be best to keep silent."

The lady shot daggers at Rory, and her anger seeped into his skin. Turning his attention to her brother, he said, "There is nae need for apologies. And I find it refreshing to hear honesty over flowered words."

"Aye, aye," agreed Graham. "Regardless, we shall not be entertaining this topic again."

Catherine bowed her head near Rory and whispered, "Do forgive my goading."

Smiling, Rory reached for her hand and placed a kiss along her fingers. "Never change who ye are, dear lady. However, there are some subjects I will not entertain."

She laughed and reached for her wine.

Releasing her hand, Rory stole a glance at Erina. Raw hurt had replaced her anger, and he fought the urge to flee the hall. He hated himself for what he was doing. But it had to be done. They would never become lovers again.

Lovers. The very word sent his mind in search of any memory of their time together. Brief flashes of images flickered within the dark corners. Each day brought less and less, and he could not fathom the reason. As he continued to concentrate, the blinding pain returned inside his head. Blinking back the agony, Rory fought for control. Bringing his focus to the present, he tried to calm his breathing.

He reached for the jug and filled his cup. As he swirled the wine, he tried to listen to the bits of conversation around him as the pain subsided to a dull ache. Draining his cup, he placed it down and rubbed his forehead.

"Does your head pain ye still from the blow by Darren?" asked Graham.

Rory glanced at the man. "On occasion," he lied.

"Erina could make ye a tonic," suggested Graham,

pushing away his plate.

He was not about to ask for Erina's assistance. Rory would seek out his own herbal remedy, if needed.

"I dinnae believe the man wishes for my aid," Erina offered quietly.

"Then if he has nae desire to seek your help, mayhap he will let me tend to his pain," interjected a young man striding forth into the hall.

Erina stood abruptly. "Brother Michael!"

Smiling, the man went and embraced her. Brother Michael inquired, "Is there a reason the man refuses your healing tonics? Ye have great skills."

Rory folded his arms over his chest, tempering his irritation. "Ye do understand I am sitting here?"

The monk directed his attention toward him. "My apologies. Though I must ask, are ye not accustomed to women healers?"

"Since ye have only arrived and were not privy to the entire conversation, I can assure ye I have nae issue with women healers. The lady Erina, assumed I would not welcome her help, before I had a chance to reply."

"This is Rory MacGregor. He is traveling with Laird Ewan MacGregor and his daughter, Catherine," acknowledged Graham.

Brother Michael gave a slight bow to all. "Greetings. He turned back to Erina. "'Tis good to see ye here, though what has brought ye to Kileburn?"

Graham muttered a curse as he poured wine into a cup and handed it to the monk.

"A tale for another time," she offered. "Please sit and tell us of your travels."

After taking the offered item, Brother Michael took a sip and took his place next to Erina. "When last I saw

Graham, I had nae desire to leave Brunley. Yet, with the arrival of a new administrator, I considered it wise to take a sabbatical and travel back home."

"Are they making more changes at Brunley?" inquired Rory. The hospital was known for its healing practices, but with any place governed by a religious order, they often insisted in blending the two—science and the law of religion. Those who refused to follow their belief were ousted or accused of malicious practices.

Brother Michael's face lit up. "Ahh…so ye have heard of the place? Was the hospital one of refuge or treatment for ye?"

"My brother, Liam, often sought out the Brothers for their healing herbs. And I have visited on occasion."

The monk tapped a finger to his mouth. "Liam MacGregor, aye?"

Rory nodded slowly.

"I am acquainted with the man. He comes to the hospital several times a year. His knowledge is far superior to any I have come across." The man leaned forward. "Ye must speak with him and urge him to consider joining the order. And ye must consider my offer, too."

Rory almost choked on his wine. "My brother and I follow a different path. But I will forward your message to him." *If I ever see him again.*

Erina snorted softly, but Rory refused to engage her in conversation. No doubt, she would turn the tables, and they would once again be discussing his conquests in the bedroom. If only she knew how he once had feasted on every inch of her body. Tasted her satiny skin and traced his tongue along places that drove her into depths of yearning. His hand tightened on his cup.

Brother Michael sighed. "As I was saying, the arrival of the new monk and his associates has left uneasiness within Brunley. We fear they will not accept those outside of the order or hospital."

"What about the healers and the midwives in the villages?" asked Erina. "Ye cannot expect everyone to travel for medicinal help to this hospital."

Brother Michael rubbed a hand over his chin. "'Tis a great time of fear. They have spoken of ridding those who practice the heathen ways. Whereas, there are others who suggest a gentler approach to bring these healers into the fold."

Rory swallowed the bitterness in his throat. "They fear those that are different. Who use their gift combined with the magic of the old beliefs."

"Aye," whispered Brother Michael.

A cloak of silence descended over the table.

Erina was the first to break the tension. She gazed around those gathered. "So as a healer with no regard for their—*your* religion, I would be an outcast? And here I regarded the hospital as a place of great learning." Fear showed in her eyes as she added, "What can they do to me? Send me away?"

"Nae. Burn ye as a witch," interjected Rory.

Chapter Twelve

"When the song entered the land through a shaft of light, the birth of a new day gave hope to the lovers."
                    ~*Chronicles of the Fae*

Clutching her basket to her chest, Erina waited on the cold boulder until the last ray of light slipped beyond the horizon. After Rory made his chilling pronouncement last night, she had fled the banquet hall without a word to anyone. Furthermore, she had spilled her secret in front of the MacGregor men. She longed to take the words back, but anger at Brother Michael's own words made her curious. Erina was not one to hide in the shadows. No, she only wished to be left alone. To practice her own beliefs. To tend to those who required healing. Or to assist those seeking love. What harm could that bring?

She had spent a sleepless night tossing and turning within the covers of her bed. Try as she might, Erina was unable to clear her mind of Rory. Chastising herself did not ease the pain inside her heart either. When the first light of dawn broke through the gray clouds, she bounded out of her bed and quickly dressed. The day was spent tending to her charms, reading in the library with Catherine, or wandering among the gardens until she knew it was time to gather the final ingredients for her charms.

Rory's words came back to haunt her during the day, and her fingers dug into the basket. "Burn me as a witch? Ye are horrid men to burn people," she muttered. Erina longed to pack up everything and flee to her cottage.

Thane lifted his head, and she ruffled the coarse fur behind his ears. "'Tis only rubbish. I am of nae concern to those monks. At least we have a friend in Brother Michael."

Shaking her head, she stood. Brunley was far away. Surely their reach could not extend to this side of the country.

With a sigh, Erina went in search of the final ingredient for the love charms—the vervain flowers. Thane followed closely, and she let the beauty of the gloaming descend over her. The land and the Goddess would heal her. Humming a tune, she roamed through the garden until she came upon the beauty. After pulling forth only a few of the flowers, Erina placed them in her basket. Onward she traveled—past herbs, shrubs, flowers, and vegetables. The gravel path led out beyond a cluster of birch trees and past the stables.

The early autumn evening was brisk, and Erina tugged her cloak more firmly around her shoulders. Opening a gate, she moved aside to let Thane take the lead. Erina quickly secured the latch and hastened down the narrow pathway to her sheep. After consulting her brother once again on where the animals were located, Erina was determined to see how they were faring.

Soft bleating directed her and soon, she came upon their pen near an enclosure. Smiling, her steps hastened. Thane let out a sharp bark, and placed his front paws on the top of the fence. Her shoulders sagged in relief as she entered the area. Graham had definitely prepared something suitable. Erina feared he would let them wander the nearby hills and forget about them.

She dropped her basket on a side bench. Greeting each of her sheep in the twilight brought a sense of peace. Glancing quickly inside their small enclosure, she noticed fresh grass and water. "Are ye aching to roam the hills?"

Her favorite, Tam, nudged her leg. "Aye. I ken how ye long for freedom. I, for one, yearn to return home, too. Be patient."

Grabbing her basket, Erina left the place and retreated along the same path back to the garden. Her steps slowed as she watched the first star enter the night sky. The area on the hill opened up, revealing the loch below. Though the water was cloaked in darkness, the moon would slowly make its appearance. Leaning against a pine tree, she realized in five days the full moon would be upon them. She had promised a love charm for Betty Timmons, which meant she had to be back at her cottage within four days. She chewed on her bottom lip in thought. She would be there, regardless of what her brother had decreed.

"I love ye, Graham, but ye can do without me for one day."

A sharp gust of wind blew past Erina, and she blinked her eyes. After checking to make sure her flowers did not take flight with the wind, she lifted her head. Light shimmered along across the loch. Why would someone take a torch out to the water? Were they searching for something or someone? However, the light didn't flicker or waver in the breeze. It remained steady. Curious, she pulled the hood of her cloak over her head and descended the path.

Thane charged on ahead, and Erina fought the urge to shout at the animal. Carefully making her way through the trees and brush, she halted. Rory stood silently by the edge of the loch. She would have known that stance from any distance—day or night. Proud and fierce.

She glanced around and spied Thane sprawled out near a tree. The man must have extinguished the light she had witnessed earlier, and Erina had no wish to disturb his solitude.

Painful memories of his words slammed into her. As she turned around to make her way back to the castle, Erina tripped, spilling the contents of her basket.

Grumbling a curse, she snatched her basket and tried to search for the scattered flowers.

"May I offer ye some assistance?" The soft burr of his voice skimmed across her skin.

Erina refused to look his way. "Forgive me. I saw the light…" Her hands brushed over leaves, rocks, and dirt. "I did not mean to intrude."

Rory crouched down beside her. "If ye tell me what ye are searching for, I can help."

Her heart pounded at her foolish predicament. "Vervain flowers."

"Ahh…a rare beauty," he disclosed.

The man was so close, the heat of his body surrounded hers. Yet, humiliation filled her. Once again, she had approached him. Scooting away, Erina tried to find at least one flower. Her hand brushed over something sharp and she hissed in pain. "Ouch." Wetness trickled down her fingers.

"What did ye do?" Rory reached for her hand, and

Erina tried to pull it free from his embrace.

"'Tis nothing. The bleeding is slight." The harder she tugged, the more he held her hand firmly. Finally lifting her head, she gazed into his mesmerizing eyes. They glimmered in the night. Swallowing, she glanced outward at the water. "Please release me. I have caused ye enough trouble. I will tend to my hand when I return to my chamber."

"Ye are nae trouble, Erina."

Anger replaced her humility, and she snapped at him. "Must I remind ye of your own words from yesterday?"

A frown marred his features, and he sighed heavily. "Forgive my harshness. An error on my part. I was angry with myself. I should have never taken advantage of ye."

Erina angled her head to the side, studying him. "I was wrong, as well," she uttered softly.

His smile came slowly. "How does your hand feel now?"

He released his grip, and Erina held up her hand, flexing her fingers. Gone was the pain and any trace of blood. "Goodness. 'Tis better. What did ye do?"

Without answering her, Rory helped her to stand. Retrieving her basket, he held it outward. "I managed to find your flowers."

Taking her basket, she mumbled her thanks and turned to leave.

"Erina?"

"Aye," she responded, turning back toward the man.

He took a hesitant step near her. "Forgive me?"

She sighed. No matter what the man's previous

conquests had been, Rory MacGregor was an honorable man. Or mayhap, he truly did not desire her and regretted the stolen kiss. Regardless, their paths were heading in separate directions. And Erina had sealed her vow with a prayer to the Goddess. "I will, but only if ye can forgive me. Let us call a truce?"

Rory clasped his hands behind his back and leaned near her ear. "Aye, most definitely."

Though the man had not touched her, the warmth of his breath along her cheek sent tremors coursing through her body. Heat flooded her insides, and she turned to leave. With her back to the warrior, Erina snapped her fingers for Thane, and quickly made her escape from the enticing Rory MacGregor.

Upon entering Kileburn, Erina's steps led her past the Great Hall and up the stairs. Lively conversation and laughter followed her along the corridor. She knew her brother was expecting her to dine with the others, but she had to put away her basket and examine her appearance. Stepping inside her chamber, she placed the basket on a table by the window. However, she gaped at the contents in disbelief. How was it possible there were so many flowers? Erina had only gathered a few, not half a basket. Her mind tried to fathom the possibility. "Ye are a wonder, Rory. Did ye wave your hand over the ground and they appeared?" As she shook her head at the absurdity, Erina undid her cloak and tossed it over a chair.

Erina inspected her hand. No traces of her cut were evident. She glanced down at her gown, and at her cloak. No blood droplets anywhere. "I did not imagine my injury," she whispered. "Maybe the ground was wet? Aye, that must have been the reason. Thankfully, there is nae bruising."

Thane yawned and sprawled out in front of the hearth.

She pointed a finger at him. "Ye are the lucky one, my friend. I shall have to endure another evening listening to the men talk of politics, crops, and drink. What a blessed relief I have Catherine to converse with, or I deem I would go mad."

After casting a swift final inspection of her gown and hair, Erina left her chamber. One more day to cross off, and one more day closer to when she could return home.

****

One day bled into the next, and Erina was trying to deduce a solution to her current situation. Her love charm for Betty was completed, but therein was another problem. How was she going to deliver it to the woman? Maybe she could go out riding for the day? "Aye, I can just hear Graham's retort," she mumbled, descending along the corridor.

The delicious smell of bread teased her senses when Erina made her way to the kitchens. She had no desire to dine in the hall, since Catherine had mentioned she would be out riding early this morning. The woman had encouraged her to join her, but Erina had to return to her cottage. After giving her apologies last evening, she promised to ride another day.

When she entered, Larena was bent over a table chopping vegetables. A few other women were tending to various duties, and she smiled at them in passing. "It smells wonderful."

Wiping her hands on her smock, Larena stepped to the hearth. "Did ye require something, Lady Erina?"

"I wish to break my fast in here, if ye have nae objections."

The woman's eyes grew round. "Your brother will not be pleased."

"Then we will not tell him, shall we?" Smiling, Erina moved toward her. "Please let me prepare my own meal. Show me what I can have to eat. I have nae desire to cut into anything ye are preparing for a later meal. Besides, ye are busy with your soup."

"Stew," corrected Larena and gestured toward the far end of the table. "There is an onion tart, some bread and cheese, along with berries."

"Perfect." Erina grabbed a wooden plate from the shelf and took a seat. Slicing the bread and cheese, she reached for a small pot of honey and put a generous amount on her bread. "Where did ye find the berries?" she asked, plucking one into her mouth.

Chuckling, the woman replied, "Didn't. I thought I had scoured the area and taken all of them, but the MacGregor brought them to me, saying he understood they were my favorite."

"Which MacGregor?" Though, Erina believed she already knew the answer.

Larena winked. "Och, the tall, dark, and handsome one."

"Rory."

Larena stepped back to the table and scooped a portion of vegetables into her hands. Making her way to the pot over the flames, she dumped them inside. "So he has charmed ye, too?"

"Nae," she lied and reached for a ewer of ale and poured some into a cup. She did not want to discuss the man's charms with another woman. Erina had fought to banish him from her mind, especially after he had been absent from the hall for the past few days.

After arching a brow at Erina in disbelief, the woman went back to her work.

While eating her meal in silence, Erina relished the peacefulness in the kitchens and began to devise a plan. If everyone was gone for most of the day, perhaps she could journey to her cottage and back without anyone noticing her absence. A few hours there and back? What would be the harm? If Betty didn't show, she could always leave it tucked away with a note for the woman.

Finishing the last of her meal, she brushed her hands off and stood. She pointed to the rosemary strewn about on the table. "Are ye using the herb for the bread?" she asked one of the women.

"Aye, a few will be added. And some will go into a conserve for my husband."

"With sugar?" Erina leaned forward to inspect the process.

The woman chuckled. "'Tis the only way I can get him to take a tonic."

"Ahh…does he suffer from pains in his chest?" Erina picked up a sprig and twirled it between her fingers.

"Aye."

"Try adding honey, instead of sugar. Or mix some with his wine," suggested Erina, making her way out of the kitchens.

"Thank ye kindly."

Mairi emerged carrying several baskets of onions, turnips, and cabbages. Startled, she almost dropped her items. "Did ye require something, Lady Erina?"

"Nae, nae. Here let me help." Taking one of the heavy baskets, she moved back inside to another worktable.

The girl dumped the contents of her basket onto the table. "Do ye have it?" she muttered, glancing over her shoulder at Larena.

Brushing the dirt from one of the onions, Erina replied softly, "In my chamber. I have placed your charm inside the box on my table. Leave what payment ye deem ye can manage. Secure the charm someplace on your body and keep it there for the next three days."

Biting her lower lip, Mairi leaned near. "And afterwards?"

"Bury the contents and pouch by a yew tree."

She gave a curt nod and went to her task.

Erina steadily made her way out of the kitchens. Walking along the narrow passageway, she heard footsteps and turned around. "Is something wrong, Mairi?"

The woman grasped her hand. "Thank ye. She placed a coin inside her hand. 'Tis all I can give ye."

"Is this all ye have?"

"Aye…bu…but I will promise to pay ye more later," Mairi stammered.

Erina was not about to take the last bit of coin from her. Reaching for her hand, she placed the coin inside and closed her fingers over the item. "Dinnae worry. Let me do this one for ye."

Her eyes lit with delight. "Och, Lady Erina, I promise to repay ye one day."

"I pray ye find love, Mairi."

"I ken I will with your charm." Smiling, she moved away.

After retrieving her cloak, gloves, and a small pouch from her chamber, Erina hurriedly left the castle. Glancing upward, white puffy clouds dotted the blue sky. The air was brisk, but a perfect day to accomplish her task. When she entered the stables, she froze.

"Good morn, sister," greeted Graham as tended to his horse. He dropped the brush on a nearby bench, and surveyed her clothing. "Are ye going somewhere?"

Erina's hands tightened around her pouch. "I must return to my cottage for a few hours."

Graham narrowed his eyes. "And why am I finding this out now? Did ye leave a note or message with anyone?" He waved a hand in the air. "Or were ye thinking of sneaking out?"

She lifted her chin in defiance. "The latter."

He pinched the bridge of his nose in obvious frustration. "Ye could have asked me, Erina."

"Truly? And ye would have let me go, aye?"

Retrieving a cloth, he replied, "Nae."

"Can ye now see my predicament?" She softened her tone and stepped near him. "Before ye came to my aid in the woods, I was returning from a friend's home. She had asked me for some herbs for a special day. I told her to seek me out before the full moon. I'm only dropping them off at my cottage, though I might stay in hopes of seeing her."

Graham wiped a hand over his brow. "Can ye not wait until Darren returns? The woods are not safe. Or take Catherine with ye and one guard?"

Her shoulders slumped. "Did ye not hear me, Graham? The full moon is tomorrow. I cannae wait another day. Besides, Catherine is out riding and I do not ken when she will return."

"Sweet Mother Mary! Do ye wish to draw attention to yourself? Many fear those who practice the dark arts."

"And ye ken I am not one of those." Irritation laced her words.

"Aye, Erina, but these are troubling times."

Rory entered the stables and nodded to Graham in passing. Erina saw her brother's eyes alight, and before he uttered a word, she shook her head. "Nae. I will not have *him* escort me. Give me another guard."

Graham folded his arms over his chest. "Did I mention the MacGregor? But now that ye have, I consider it a fine idea."

Halting beside one of the horse's stables, Rory glanced over his shoulder. "Excuse me?" He turned fully toward them and arched a dark brow.

Her brother gestured to her. "Erina has an urgent package that must be delivered to a friend. Would ye be so kind as to escort her to her cottage for the day? 'Tis less than an hour's ride to her home."

Nae! Her chest constricted. "I dinnae reason why I cannot go by myself. Furthermore, Rory might be needed by his laird. Or ye can ask another guard. Or…*or* one of the women. Aye, that would be most helpful."

"Nonsense. Ewan has gone hunting with some of his men. He will not be returning until late," argued Graham. Giving a pat to his horse, he added, "I would be most grateful for the assistance, Rory."

"I will go and search for Brother Michael. Surely we have much to catch up on regarding herbs and such," she protested.

"Nae, he is gone until evening. I deem he went in

search of mushrooms," stated Graham. "Ye can have the MacGregor escort ye."

Rory's hands were fisted by his sides, and she noted the conflict within his gaze. He wanted nothing to do with her, and she hated her brother for putting him in this situation. It was enough for Erina to change her mind, and regret filled her at the loss of more coins. "Dinnae worry, I won't trouble ye. My friend will have to wait until next month."

Making her way to leave, Rory's words made her pause.

"I would consider it an honor to escort Lady Erina."

Chapter Thirteen

"Love and laughter will bind the heart. Whereas, hate and tears can cement the pain within the soul."
~*Chronicles of the Fae*

Not one word came forth from Erina's luscious lips as they traveled through the dense forest. Gone was the woman Rory once knew and adored. She no longer laughed in his presence or chatted incessantly about the land and animals—from a bird flitting by to a rabbit skittering past.

He had done this to Erina. And Rory hated himself.

Every waking moment was spent trying to crush his feelings for her. It was a continual battle—one that left him weak and frustrated at the end of the day. He kept his body and mind busy during the daylight with as many tasks that he could possibly do, but the nights left him bitter and longing to have her by his side.

Rory should have fled eons ago. But he had a mission to oversee. And he was determined to right the injustice of Erina's death. He continued to fight the shadows, but with each new dawn, a piece of his memory of their time together slipped away. Undeniably, there was something wrong. Sifting through all of his training and knowledge did not bring forth anything he could use.

Light splintered through the canopy of trees above

them as they moved parallel to the stream. Usually the music of nature was a soothing balm for him, but Rory could no longer stand the silence between them.

"'Tis a fine autumn day. No threat of rain or snow," he mentioned, lifting his hand upward.

Erina looked startled, as if she had been in deep thought. She ducked under a heavy pine limb. "Aye," she uttered softly.

He maneuvered his horse around a bend in the path. "'Tis my favorite time of year."

"I prefer the spring," she declared, keeping her focus ahead.

"Ahh…one of rebirth. The land awakens once again."

She stole a glance at Rory. "A rare observation."

"Why?"

Turning her horse down a narrow path to the river, she replied, "Because men pay nae heed to the changes of the land. Unless they are farmers or have cattle."

"Yet, I am neither."

The road opened up, and Rory could see Erina's cottage in the distance. Fragmented memories of their time together flashed within his mind.

She halted her horse and shielded her eyes. "And what are ye?"

His mouth twitched in humor, and it was his turn to shield himself from her intense stare. "A man on a journey."

"Hmm…one who never stays long in any place?"

Rory snapped his gaze to hers. She had read him exactly, slicing through to reveal the Fae. She studied him from pale blue eyes and thick lashes. Waiting to see if she was correct in her observation. When the corner of her mouth lifted slightly, Rory knew she had guessed correctly.

He glanced upward. "There has been nae reason." Returning his attention to her, he added, "*Yet.*"

Erina turned away. "My cottage is across the stream. We can cross farther along the path."

As the door to their conversation ended, Rory pursed his lips and watched as she nudged her horse onward. At least she was speaking to him. Honestly, what did he expect? "More," he uttered softly, giving a pat to his horse.

When they arrived at the cottage, Erina quickly dismounted and reached for her satchel. She didn't bother asking Rory if he wanted to come inside her home. No. She simply walked inside and closed the door behind her.

Grabbing the reins of her horse, he led both animals to a small pasture in the back. After retrieving a bucket, he went and filled it with water from the well. Approaching the horses, he let hers drink first, before letting the other take his fill. Dumping out the rest, Rory placed the bucket back near the well and went to sit beneath an elm tree.

As he stretched out his legs, he glanced around the area as if seeing it for the first time. Her place was a simple stone cottage, but the beauty of the land took its hold within the crevices. Vines of ivy snaked upward, framing the windows. A variety of flowers on both sides of the entrance greeted any visitor. The path was a mix of gravel and thyme, weaving a pattern Rory found intriguing. He knew her garden faced south toward the stream, but that's where his memory ended.

He no longer fought to retrieve the lost images.

Instead, Rory forged ahead. He would make new memories with Erina. When the time came, he would see her happy and leave. Regardless of his depth of emotions for her, he had to see her on another path. Once again, the shadows teased and ridiculed him. Placing the heel of his palms over his eyes, Rory groaned. It was as if he was doing battle with two different men, and he grew weary of the fight.

"I have brought ye some food and drink," offered Erina. "'Tis from the kitchens at Kileburn, since I have none here for ye."

Rory lifted his head. The gentle breeze blew tendrils of hair free from the braided mass around her head. "A kind gesture and welcomed."

Erina bent down next to him and handed him a plate. "Eat the food first." Placing a mug alongside him, she added, "The drink is a healing brew to help with the headaches."

He smiled and started to reach for her hand, but Erina quickly stood. Clenching his fist, he responded, "Thank ye, but I can assure ye, there is no more pain from my injury."

"Then why do ye scowl and touch your head?"

What could he possibly say to her? That he was conflicted every waking moment? Just being in her company soothed and pained his heart and soul at the same time. "I am dealing with a dilemma which has no solution. At least none that I favor."

She bit her lower lip. "Would it help to let another listen?"

Her generosity and kindness undid him. "Not at present."

She started forward and then hesitated. "There is a

stone boulder around the back of the cottage which overlooks the garden and stream. Ye might be more comfortable there. I find it a place of solace when I have troubles on my mind."

He angled his head toward her. "I am enjoying the view from here."

She laughed, and Rory found the sound delightful. "'Tis also a favorite spot for my dog, Thane. At least when he's not keeping a watchful eye on my sheep."

"A wise animal." Rory picked up one of the small pastries and sniffed the contents.

"Aye, there is nae meat inside. I do remember the conversation," clarified Erina as she made her way back to the cottage.

Rory glanced at her retreating form, marveling at the woman. He stuffed the entire contents into his mouth, relishing the intense flavors of the vegetables and spices. After finishing the other two, he licked his fingers. Reaching for the mug, he quickly downed the contents of the cool liquid mixed with herbs. Wiping his mouth with the back of his hand, Rory closed his eyes and let the meal and land help ease his mind.

Hours passed without any sign of Erina's friend, and Rory grew concerned. He had no wish to travel in the dark. If this friend did not present herself soon, he must urge Erina to leave. Standing slowly, Rory brushed the leaves and dirt from his plaid and strode toward the cottage.

Knocking softly, he called out, "Erina?"

When she didn't answer, he knocked harder and waited. Frowning, Rory opened the door and glanced inside. "Erina? Are ye all right?" He steadily made his way to her small kitchen. Glancing inside, he noted her satchel on the table, but no indication of the lass. Checking her storeroom, Rory inhaled the fragrant herbs drying on pegs along one side of the wall. A candle sputtered in its holder on a worktable. Waving his hand outward, he extinguished the flame.

There was only one possibility left. As he cautiously entered her bedroom, Rory paused at the entrance. Leaning against the frame, he gazed at her sleeping form. One arm was draped over her forehead, and the other flung out to the side. A light breeze wafted inside from the open window. He did not have the heart to wake her. She mumbled a word and turned on her side. Desire rolled through him, and Rory stepped away from the room.

Walking to the entrance of her cottage, he clasped his hands behind his back and let his sight roam the land. Why did she tempt him beyond reason? To offer the light of happiness, when none should tease him? The lure to stray outside his training and warrior skills was a heady potion. Erina had no idea the power she held over him.

Rory had not understood his love for Erina the first time, nor did he comprehend its appeal this second time. And truth be told, he no longer cared. His memories were now fading of their first time together. Each time he tried to recall a fragment, Rory had to endure agonizing pain. Closing the door on the past seemed to be the only solution. The Fates had decreed another path.

A falcon made lazy circles above the trees, and Rory watched its flight. The bird flew with fluid precision—dipping and swaying with the wind. Stepping outside, Rory held his arm outward and waited.

Within moments, the falcon dove and landed on his arm. As he uttered soothing words of greeting, Rory gently stroked the bird's breast with the back of his two fingers. "I am in need of a favor, my friend."

The falcon eyed him with scrutiny.

"Can ye search for any lone female travelers? I would be most appreciative."

Sensing Erina's presence behind him, Rory continued to speak to the bird in his ancient language. Rory lifted his arm higher, and the falcon flew off toward the south. He fisted his hands on his hips and waited.

"That was amazing. How did ye command the bird? And what language were ye speaking?" Stepping alongside him, Erina tilted her head to the side as if assessing Rory's worth.

He shrugged. "'Tis the old speech of my people."

"From what land? Would ye care to share more?"

"Why?"

"Are ye always so stubborn?" Erina folded her arms over her chest and lifted her gaze to the sky.

Rory barked out in laughter. "My family would concur."

She gaped at him. "Ye should laugh more often."

"Aye, another point my family would agree upon." Turning his back on her, he bent and cast his hand over the ground. Plucking forth a violet, he turned around and held it out to Erina. "I shall endeavor to laugh more, but only with ye."

Erina glanced at the offering. "What a beautiful shade of lavender." Taking the flower from him, her fingers brushed over his, and Rory's heart raced. "I don't recall seeing any along the path."

"They are a beauty," he uttered softly, though his meaning was meant for her.

She clasped the flower against her breasts. "Thank ye."

They stood silently together. Clouds drifted by. A doe and her fawn ambled among the trees, uncaring of their presence. Leaves flutter down from the oak trees, and time moved forward with no sign of Erina's friend.

Erina broke the quiet serenity with a heavy sigh. "I fear Betty will not be coming here today."

He glanced down at her. "Do ye believe the lass will attempt to travel at night?"

"Goodness, nae. But I have to consider how badly she requested this item."

"Which is what?"

She averted his gaze. "Only a small pouch of herbs."

A love charm. "For?"

When she lifted her head toward him, he noted the red splotches on her cheek. "They are herbs to attract the man she wishes to marry."

"Ahh...'tis a shame the lass cannot let her heart guide them both."

"Aye. Love can be fickle. I did tell her this." Erina waved her hand about. "Though did she listen to my words? Nae. Mind ye, when I have had others making the same request, I always try to counsel them first." She held the violet out in front of her. "Love can be as fleeting as the flower I hold. One moment it enters your life with its beauty, and the next, it withers and dies."

The twilight danced off her auburn locks, and Rory ached to take her into his arms. How he wanted to bring love into her heart once again. "Are ye speaking from experience?" He stepped nearer, her scent filling him.

"Me?" She shook her head. "Nae," she whispered.

Rory brushed his hand against the side her gown. *Ye deserve to love again.*

Erina glanced sideways at him. "And ye? Has love ever claimed your heart?"

Aye. Ye have captured my heart and soul. 'Tis yours until the end of my days, Erina. No other will I take. No other shall I love. "Nae," he lied.

Smiling sadly, she tucked the flower in the bodice of her gown. "I assumed with all your conquests ye would have found love."

Regret filled him of her knowledge of his bedroom liaisons. They had meant nothing to him. Rory longed to shout his love for her. He withdrew his hand from near her side and stepped away. Raking a hand through his hair, he said, "None have captured my heart."

When she said nothing further, Rory glanced over his shoulder. A frown marred her features.

"Ye are a man on a journey, aye? Love will find ye one day, Rory MacGregor."

His breathing became labored, and he slowly made his way back to her. He brushed the back of his fingers across her cheek. "I might be on a journey, but love is not on the path."

"Why?" she asked, trembling from his touch.

Rory placed his hands on her shoulders. "I am destined for another destiny in life. One where there is no room for love."

"So ye rather give your body, but not your heart?"

Her words slashed viciously at his soul, and he hated himself. How true she spoke. Never once did he

151

Mary Morgan

consider what he had been doing when he took others to his bed. "Mayhap one day I will share a truth with ye."

Sadness filled her eyes. "Soon ye and I will depart. There are nae truths to be told. Ye owe me nothing. Though, I have a question for ye."

"Ask me anything."

She arched a brow. "Only one. Do ye regret kissing me at the smithy?"

Unprepared for her question, Rory remained silent. The air warmed around them, and he brought her closer to him. Unable to stop the tide of his affections, he replied, "Aye."

"Oh…" Erina bent her head.

Rory cupped her chin, forcing her to meet his gaze. "Since that day, I have thought of nothing else, but the taste of ye on my lips. It was wrong, Erina, for I crave *more*."

"May I ask one more question?"

His mouth twitched in humor, though he knew his eyes held desire. "Anything."

"Will ye kiss me one last time, Rory?" She placed her hands upon his chest and quickly added, "Only one."

Grabbing her around the waist with one hand, he crushed her to him. Rory leaned near her ear. "Then let this last kiss be my parting gift to ye, Erina MacIntyre." His mouth grazed her earlobe and traveled a path down the side of her neck. "When your nights are filled with longing, recall the fiery claim of my lips."

Erina moaned, and Rory sought her mouth, taking fiery possession. The touch of her lips on his sent a shock wave coursing through his body. His tongue sought entry, demanding hers. Rory devoured the taste of all she had to give. Blood pounded in his brain, and his cock swelled. He held nothing back, giving Erina all his passion.

One kiss would never be enough.

The world spun around them, and the more he deepened the kiss, the more Rory ached to profess all to the woman who held his heart *and* future.

Chapter Fourteen

"A Fenian Warrior is honor bound by a code of ancient laws. If broken, a schism can fracture the foundation of the Brotherhood."

~Chronicles of the Fae

Erina fought the desire to toss off her cloak as they made their way along the path near the river's edge. Though the late afternoon contained a biting wind, her body burned in places she had never imagined. Rory kissed her for what seemed an eternity. When he had finally released her, his eyes glowed in the soft fading light. Never before had she witnessed such color. Did the Gods gift him with the light of the stars? She was sorely tempted to ask him, but found herself tongue-tied and weak after his passionate kiss. Each time she licked her lips, Rory's taste filled her.

"How can I want another, when ye have showed me such desire?" she whispered.

As she ducked under a heavy limb, she let out a sigh. Though they were attracted to one another, their journeys were leading in two different directions, and she must close the door on her feelings for this man. He had granted her one last request, so now it was time to move forward.

Yet, each time she glanced at him, she yearned to ask what journey he was on that would not include love. "A life without love is only half a life," she muttered.

An owl hooted in the distance, bringing Erina's focus to her surroundings.

"Mocking me, wise one?"

The owl took flight from one of the trees, and she watched its ascent. With no one to talk to, Erina was often spouting her problems into the trees for any animal—fur or feathered—to hear her troubles. Why she thought they cared was a wonder. However, it did bring her comfort.

"What would ye do, Grandmother? Can ye show me a sign? Speak from the veil?"

Erina brought her horse to a halt. Looking around the woods, she waited and listened. The rustle of leaves swirled around her. She removed one of her gloves and clutched her pendant beneath her cloak. Closing her eyes, she slowed her breathing and allowed herself to become one with the land and spirits.

Oberon snorted and pawed the dirt, but Erina kept still.

Something touched her face, and she opened her eyes to find Rory staring at her.

"Where are ye?"

"I…I was thinking of my Grandmother," she stammered, frustrated with his intrusion.

"Has she crossed over?"

Erina lowered her head. "Aye. In early spring."

Rory reached out and squeezed her hand. "Yet, her spirit surely is with ye."

Smiling, she lifted her head and nodded. "Most do not speak in this manner. I find it refreshing to ken another."

He drew back. "And 'tis rare to encounter someone who embraces all the land has to offer, including the ancients."

Erina stared at him, the stubborn set of his jaw, the way his brow lifted in challenge. She noticed others feared him, but she found Rory intriguing. "I wish ye could have known my grandmother. She spoke as ye do, and believed in the old ways."

Charming creases framed his smile. "So, she was your teacher."

"Everything I am is because of her."

"What about your mother?"

They rode along, side by side, and Erina shifted in her saddle. "I never knew her. She died giving birth to me."

Rory halted his horse. "My apologies. I did not ken."

Erina stole a glance at him. His expression was one of shock, and she could not fathom the reason. "There is nae need."

He returned to her side. "Then 'tis fortunate ye had a loving and wise grandmother to teach ye."

"Aye, but 'tis fear that rules the land. Even my own brother worries." She blew out a frustrated breath. "Why can't we follow our own hearts when it comes to a certain belief? Nae, we must be ordered to obey one over the other. So many cower with each new queen or king, changing their religious convictions as surely as they change their clothing."

"Are ye fearful of the new king?"

Erina waved her hand dismissively. "The man is many miles away, so I am not troubled. Although, I am nae fool either. There are many here who would point a finger at their neighbor, accusing them of some foul deed."

"People are ignorant of what they cannot understand," acknowledged Rory, leading his horse upward and in front of hers.

"Aye," agreed Erina.

As they came in sight of Kileburn, they journeyed once again side by side, and she was saddened their time together was ending. The sun slipped silently behind them, and she wiped her nose on the back of her gloved hand. "What about your family? Do ye visit them often?"

He gave her a dubious look and remained silent.

She reached out and touched him on his arm. "Forgive me if 'tis too painful to speak about."

Rory glanced down at her hand. "Nae," he uttered softly and then lifted his gaze to hers. "Sadly, I have not seen my mother in some time. My father passed to the other side many years ago during a battle."

"Nae siblings?"

His smile was one filled with sadness. "Only a brother. Our paths have not crossed in many months. I pray one day I shall see him."

Smiling, Erina squeezed his arm and pulled away. "Your words are filled with love when ye speak of them. When ye take your leave, I suggest seeking out your mother. Time is precious. Here today and gone tomorrow."

He gaped at her, and Erina laughed. "Forgive me. I have an inclination to speak in odd ways. So my brother keeps telling me."

Rory stunned her by leaning forward and brushing a feather-like kiss on her mouth. When he broke free, he whispered, "Never stop."

Nudging his horse, he galloped on ahead, and Erina urged her mount to follow.

As they entered the portcullis, Darren strode forth from the bailey. He cast his sight to Erina and then to Rory. A frown marred his features as he approached her.

"Let me assist ye," he offered, reaching his hands out to her.

"I am stunned to see ye here, Darren. I assumed ye would be returning tomorrow," she stated, allowing him to help her dismount.

"I was able to conclude my business earlier." His tone gruff.

"Are ye cross with someone? Or is your tone directed at me?" asked Erina, taking the reins of her horse and leading him to the stables.

"Both."

Erina halted her stride and looked at the man. "Since I have not seen ye in several days, please explain."

Darren approached and gently removed the reins from her hands. "Forgive me for saying, but why did ye not take Catherine and another guard with ye? Ye barely ken the MacGregor. We grew—"

"*We?*" she interrupted. She tapped her foot in frustration. "Did my brother happen to tell ye I argued against having Rory escort me? Or that I wished to have another one of his men? *Or* that it was his suggestion to have Rory come with me?"

Darren bowed his head. "He shared none of this with me."

"Humph! I reckon my brother is trying to stir the

pot and cause friction. I suppose he grew frantic when the day grew late."

The man snapped his gaze to meet hers. "For what purpose would he do this?"

"One can only guess, Darren. Ye will have to ask him."

"He is my laird. I dinnae question his orders."

Erina shook her head and turned from him. As she walked away, she tossed out over her shoulder, "And he is your friend, so consider my words."

Her brother was most likely seeking suitors for her and considered Darren to be one of them. Furthermore, her brother was a fool to even think of the man. His guard was more like a brother to her and not husband material. If she didn't love Graham so much, she would disregard his orders to remain and depart in the morning. She was sorely tempted to make a love charm for her brother, so all the women would become besotted and drive him mad.

Upon entering the castle, Thane bounded toward her. After greeting him with a gentle pat, Erina hurriedly swept past the Great Hall. As her foot landed on the first stone step, her brother's words made her pause once again.

"Come walk with me to my solar, Erina."

Fighting the barb on her tongue, she turned and followed him along the corridor. The glow from the candles flickered, and their shadows followed her. She shivered slightly and pulled her cloak tighter. No matter how many years had passed, she always dreaded walking back into this room. When Graham opened the door, he stepped aside to let her enter. Erina hesitated, but lifted her chin and went inside.

Though the room was warm with a blazing fire, her body trembled. Memories of her father standing at his desk flooded her mind, and Erina gripped the back of one of the chairs.

"Ye are as ugly as the one who bore you," sneered her father. *"Do ye practice the dark arts like she did?"* He pointed a finger at her. *"I ken she bewitched me, luring me to her bed with chants. I should banish her from the lands."*

Erina stood rooted to the floor. The man in front of her could not be her father. He spoke evil, and his eyes were one of a monster.

"Can ye not speak? Has the devil taken your tongue?"

Her chest tightened from fear. "I am Erina Mac...MacIntyre."

"Nae!" he bellowed. "Ye are not mine. No claim shall ye make on my name or lands." He stepped from his desk and loomed over her. "From this day forward, do not show your face at Kileburn. Ye are naught. Take that message back to your mother."

She swallowed the bile coating her throat and turned to leave. Throwing the door open, she glanced over her shoulder. "Your message will die in this room, since my mother has been dead these past ten years."

"Erina? Erina, what is wrong?"

Graham's soothing words and touch banished the cold and fear she once held for the room. Their father was dead and buried. She would not allow the ghosts of the past to haunt her. Lifting her head, she blinked back the tears. "This was the place where I had the one and only conversation with our father."

Her brother wrapped his arm around her shoulders.

"And did he spout pleasantries?"

Nervous laughter bubbled forth, and Erina coughed into her hand. "Nae, quite the opposite." Letting out a sigh, she added, "Did ye ken I was only ten?"

"Since this is the first ye have mentioned the conversation, nae. Our father was a cruel man, Erina. None of this surprises me." He led her to a chair by the hearth and went to a side table. "At least ye only suffered his bruising words—once. I had to endure the lash and his verbal outbursts many times."

"Goodness, I did not ken."

Graham reached for a pitcher and poured some wine into two cups. Handing one to her, he then took a seat across from Erina. "Ye and I have not spoken of the cruelty of our father. We have kept it locked inside us. Your scars are inside your mind and heart, whereas, mine are on my back." He swirled his wine and gazed with intent inside the cup. "After the first lashing—at five—I made a vow that when I had bairns I would never take a hand to them. Nor would I let his words put fear into my mind. When the lashing began, I thought of other things. Not once did I cry out, which only made him seethe with fury."

Placing her cup down, Erina extended her hand and he grasped it. "I believe we both made vows to not let our blood rule us. Ye are a much wiser, kinder, *and* generous laird, Graham. Ye will never be like him."

"In truth, we have the blood of our mothers to guide us," he offered quietly.

Erina withdrew her hand and picked up her cup. "I'd like to believe my mother is guiding me, along with my grandmother." She took a sip of the wine, letting the warmth settle within her. "Why did ye wish to speak to me?"

Graham chuckled low. "To give ye yet another lecture. But I can see that bringing ye to this room was an error on my part."

She twirled a finger in the air. "Mayhap, our mothers are warning ye not to speak your mind."

He downed the contents of his cup and leaned forward. "I deem I must always speak truthfully with ye, Erina."

Worried and confused, she asked, "Is this about my journey today? Are ye concerned because Rory and I returned late? Or do ye not trust me? Because if so, be warned, I did argue for another." *Stop rambling, Erina or the man will become suspicious.*

From the furrow of his brow, she thought she'd struck a nerve. "I think," Graham said carefully, "that ye should consider what ye are doing. Making *love* charms is seen by the church and others as devil's work."

Erina gripped the side of the chair. "*How*…did Rory speak to ye? Did he run to your side with this knowledge the moment he stepped foot inside the castle?" Traitorous man. She thought they understood each other. *How dare he!*

"Nae, sister. Do not blame Rory. Remember, the walls here at Kileburn are rife with ears listening everywhere. Eventually, all is revealed, even to the laird."

She tapped her foot in irritation. Who could have been listening? Did Mairi mention anything to Larena? "This is why I cannot stay here. Everyone is fearful of the other. "

Sighing, Graham stood. "Regardless, ye must

remember that as the sister to the Laird of Kileburn, ye are subject to more scrutiny. All eyes will be on ye, be it here, or at your cottage. They may call ye the White Healer, but in truth, the verra name can bring about your downfall."

Chapter Fifteen

"A Fae's love is as brilliant as all the stars in the universe."

~*Chronicles of the Fae*

The tune was a mournful one and Rory knew it well. It was one played on occasion, leaving many weeping at the end. Countless would gather at feasts and listen to the story of how the star-crossed lovers were ill fated. Though their families objected to the union, they still held firm in their love. When the young man was sent away, he was seized upon and killed. His body dumped into the ocean. The young lass waited for his homecoming, even though she was told he was dead. Her love had blinded her to the truth. And as the years passed, she grew bitter. One day, when the ache in her heart could not be soothed, she stripped her clothing and ventured out into the sea in hopes of reuniting with her lover. They say if one listens in silence on a summer twilight, you can almost hear her mournful weeping within the ocean breezes.

Yet, the voice Rory heard singing the melody was one of hope and not sadness. As he followed the beautiful sound, Rory emerged near Erina's chamber. Her door was partially ajar, and he pushed it open further. His heart pounded against his chest as he watched her fingers glide over the harp near the window. Morning sunlight streamed down around her, encasing her in golden light. She was an ethereal vision, and he was held captive.

Her singing ignited something within Rory. He longed to join her in song, and he stepped forward. When she ended the second verse, he lifted his own voice.

"May the light of my love surround ye always. 'Til ye return and bring me your heart, so I give ye a piece of mine to carry. As the tides ebb and flow, so shall my love for ye. From one season to the next, I pray ye do not tarry and come home to my embrace."

Startled, Erina stopped playing and looked up at him.

That gaze, both hungry and confused, had ripped him apart. Had turned him inside out with a need so fierce, it took all his control as a warrior to keep it contained. "Continue," he encouraged.

Her smile lit up her face, and her fingers took up the strings upon the harp. Not once did her gaze waver from his as she continued to play.

Clasping his hands behind his back, he wove a single thought within his mind, and a rose magically appeared inside his joined hands. The thorn bit into his palm, but Rory gave no care. Her voice banished the shadows and brought light to his weary soul. A peace centered inside and he held it firm.

When she finished the last note, Erina folded her hands in her lap. "Ye have heard the song before?"

"Aye," his voice sounding hoarse to his ears.

She stood and straightened the creases of her dress. "I've heard it played several times at the market fair. Ye have a good voice. Do ye favor singing?"

"When the mood strikes. Though sadly, it has been a long while since I lifted my voice in song." He brought forth the rose. "A flower for the lady."

Her eyes lit up with joy. "How kind of ye, but where did ye find a white rose? There are none among the others."

"Away from the main garden," he lied.

"'Tis a rare beauty," she exclaimed, fingering the petals. "Although, fragrant and stunning, their thorns leave a nasty bite." Erina took his hand and inspected the wound, which was now mending.

I would endure a thousand thorns to see your smile each day.

"'Tis naught."

"Let me put some salve into the wound."

Rory nodded and slowed the healing process within his palm. After following her to a side table, he watched as she concentrated on finding the small jar she required. Pulling one forth from the back, she opened it and dabbed a small amount with her finger. He held his hand outward, and Erina dotted the healing ointment onto his palm. Rory stood transfixed, watching her every movement.

She reached for a cloth and wiped her finger off. "If ye would like, ye can have this jar. I have another. Ye should apply a small amount in the evening."

Taking the offering, he asked, "Why then?"

"Because I hope ye would have washed after a day doing whatever men do." She laughed and backed away from him.

"Thank ye."

Erina picked up the rose. "And thank ye for the lovely flower."

Rory risked her reputation if any should come passing through the corridor, but desire propelled him toward Erina. Reaching for her hand, he placed a lingering kiss along the vein in her wrist. "Until we meet again."

She gasped, and her eyes darkened with desire. Thank the Gods her door was open, or Rory would have ravished her mouth. Taking a step back, he bowed and left the chamber, only to be met by Catherine along the corridor.

The woman tapped a finger against his chest. "Ye should be more careful," she warned.

"Jealous?" he teased.

"Rory MacGregor, ye wound me. Am I not like a sister?" Her tone took a more somber tone. "Tread carefully. Kileburn has spies everywhere."

"And here I thought ye were warning me against the Lady Erina."

"Humph! I fear more for *her* heart than yours."

Rory swallowed. How untrue Catherine's words were, and he gave her a curt nod.

Unfortunately, in trying to depart, the woman linked her arm through his and propelled him back inside the chamber. "How unexpected that I should run into ye and Erina. I have some glorious news to share with ye both."

Erina looked up in surprise, her cheeks stained with red blotches. "Good morning, Catherine."

"My how lovely ye look in that lavender gown. The color brings out your rosy complexion."

Erina darted a quick glance at Rory, but quickly recovered. "What is this *glorious* news?"

Catherine released her hold on Rory and went to

Erina. "Today is Thursday Market and truth be told, I am looking to purchase some cloth for new gowns and ribbons. Graham mentioned St. Timmons Square boasts the best market on this side of the coast."

"Aye, 'tis true," agreed Erina. "I am in need of candles and salt for my home."

"Wondrous! Though the day is brisk, the sky bears no clouds. It will be a lovely day." Catherine turned to Rory. "And ye can be our escort."

Rory narrowed his eyes. "I must protest—"

Catherine cut him off with a wave of her hand. "Graham was the one to suggest the outing. If ye must ken, Darren and Brother Michael will be accompanying us, as well. So dinnae regard this as a chore. Ye should take it as a day of rest. Ye can wander with the other men."

He fisted his hands on his hips. "Why do I sense ye have controlled this day, Catherine?"

She pouted. "Once again, ye wound me. Does not a day escorting beautiful women sound appealing?"

Rory couldn't help himself, and he barked out in laughter. "God help the man ye marry one day."

The woman snorted. "And he will be a man of *my* choosing, aye."

"I shall go tend to the horses."

She dipped her head. "Splendid. We will join ye shortly."

Rory quickly made his way out of the chamber, intent on enjoying the day with Erina.

****

The women chattered incessantly during their journey to St. Timmons. Nevertheless, Rory only cared for one voice. *Erina's.* She laughed, pointed out the animals and birds in passing, and challenged Catherine to a game of chess later. His chest had swelled when she approached the stables earlier wearing the white rose pinned to her cloak. When Catherine asked where she procured the flower, Erina lied and stated she found it tucked among the others.

"I can tell by your smile, ye are enjoying the day," commented Brother Michael, coming alongside him.

"And how did ye come to this conclusion?"

Brother Michael laughed. "Ye are smiling. 'Tis a rare occurrence with ye."

Rory rubbed a gloved hand over his chin. "Your observation is correct."

"I've often been told I am a good listener."

"I am not one to favor confessions," Rory replied dryly.

"Nae, nae. I am not in a position to give absolution. That would require a priest." He lifted a finger. "Though, if there was none around, I would be honored."

Chuckling softly, Rory replied, "Do not fear, Brother Michael, for I am not about to confess my sins to *anyone*."

The man adjusted his robe. "Do ye wish to unburden any concerns? Is there something plaguing your thoughts?"

Aye, only one. Erina. "Nae. I am only enjoying the fine day."

"I concur. Yet, I fear snow will soon be here. I might have to extend my stay at Kileburn."

Rory glanced sideways at the monk. "How long have you known Erina and her brother?"

"Most of my life. My mother married a MacIntyre,

though I did not meet Erina until after the elder laird passed. Graham bade me to seek out his sister and urge her to come to Kileburn." He shook his head in mirth. "However, once in her company I grew to understand her solitude and love of the land. She would never be happy at Kileburn. Mind ye, I did try to persuade her for Graham's sake, but the lass is as stubborn as her brother."

His gaze found Erina. "She will never relent. Kileburn is not her home."

Brother Michael sighed. "I heard she was attacked in the woods, so Graham is more insistent she remain at the castle for her safety. I believe he would prefer that until she marries."

He snapped his attention back to the monk, and Rory's mind screamed at him to remain silent. "Has Graham mentioned any suitors?"

The man slowed his horse. "Many, though I wonder if ye should be considered."

Stunned, Rory eyed him skeptically. "Why would ye consider me?"

The monk shrugged. "God works in miraculous ways. I may have chosen a life of abstinence, but any fool can see how ye look at Erina."

Rory blew out a soft curse. "I have nae lands or money, and have pledged a vow to never marry."

"Are ye firm in those convictions?"

"Most assuredly, and I reckon Graham would want someone to give his sister a comfortable life, not one of poverty." However, a small part of Rory wanted to believe he could claim her hand in marriage. Did he dare to have what his own people denied him? A life with a human? The mere idea had his heart racing, and he thought of another Fenian Warrior—Aidan Kerrigan. The elite warrior defied the Fae and married a human. Yet, sorrow filled Rory upon recalling how he was banished from the realm, stripped of his powers, and made mortal.

"Ewan MacGregor speaks highly of ye," countered the monk.

"Then mayhap Ewan should marry her." Regret filled Rory the moment he had spoken the words. He had no desire to see Erina wed his friend. In truth, he did not want to see her with anyone but him. Dark fury burst inside Rory at the mere idea of her bedding another man.

"I believe an offer was extended to your laird, but he politely declined," offered Brother Michael.

"What?" Rory frowned in confusion. Why hadn't Ewan mentioned the marriage proposal? "And how are ye privy to this information?"

The monk laughed. "I was present this morning as a witness and friend."

Rory relaxed his shoulders. "I ken it best to leave the choosing to Erina."

"She has nae wish, therefore her brother must seek one. I reckon he will attend to his other plan."

"Which is?"

"To invite other lairds who are seeking wives to a feast and hunting on his lands."

"And Erina will be the prize?" asked Rory, staring off in the distance. "She will flee the moment the truth is revealed."

The monk shifted uneasily. "Exactly what I told Graham. Nevertheless, he deems it a good time to discuss the growing concern of conflict among the lands with other lairds."

The area opened up, and Rory slowed his horse. The ghostly ruins of a cathedral stood in stark contrast to the green, lush land in the far off distance. A testament to the one God, and he frowned. He tried to recall why the place bothered him, but was unable to bring forth any concrete image.

"'Tis only stones and wood," he muttered softly and moved toward Erina.

The square was beyond the river, and tents dotted the place. Boisterous laughter, music, and gaiety greeted them as they made their way across the bridge. It was a place teeming with a variety of goods and life.

Darren was the first to dismount and quickly made his way to Erina's side. As he did his best to control his emotions, Rory glanced away and removed himself from his horse. He made his way to Catherine and lifted her off her own mount. The lass gave him a wink and strolled over to the couple.

"Why don't ye show me the fabric stalls?" asked Catherine, tugging on Erina's arm. "The men can go seek their own pleasure."

Erina laughed, but she stole a glance at Rory. "Good, for I feared they would consider this day dull."

Rory's mouth twitched in humor. "In the company of such beauty, how could any one of us consider this day boring?"

Darren gave him a scathing look before turning his attention to Erina. "If ye should have need of anything, I will be at the ale tent."

"The only thing we may need is strong arms to help us carry back our wares," Catherine interjected.

The men watched as the women departed in

laughter.

"Are ye buying a tankard for each of us, Darren?" proposed Rory, realizing he was poking a bear. "I require something to slake my thirst."

"How generous," commented Brother Michael, rubbing his hands together to ward off the chill in the air.

Darren grumbled a curse, but nodded. "Then ye can buy the second one, MacGregor."

Rory clamped a hand on the man's shoulder and replied, "And Brother Michael the third round."

The monk lifted his hands. "I have nae coin."

This time, Darren's stern expression turned to one of mirth, and he pointed a finger at Rory. "Ye ken I can drink ye under the table?"

Rory folded his arms across his chest. "A challenge. I accept."

The man snickered and strode down the path with Brother Michael following and again stating he was without funds.

Rory slowly brought his attention to Erina's retreating form. "Look back, lass," he commanded in a hushed tone.

Her unhurried steps lessened, and the breeze lifted a lock of hair from the nape of her neck. As Catherine continued to chatter, Erina glanced over her shoulder.

And the smile she gave Rory tempted him beyond measure. It was one filled with moonbeams of kisses yet to be explored, and the oath he had made many moons ago to not claim her now faded away.

Chapter Sixteen

"Ten times must a Fenian Warrior journey into the silence without food, drink, or companionship. If he breaks the vow, he will be banished from the Brotherhood."

~Chronicles of the Fae

As she twirled the satin ribbon between her fingers, Erina gazed longingly at the color. She had enough coin for candles and her precious salt. She could ill afford to spend money on foolish items. Dropping the item back onto the table, she moved along the other stalls. Catherine continued to do her best on bartering a more fair deal for some lavender brocade, and Erina shook her head. She knew the man well, and he would not part with any coin. He was a shrewd dealer.

As Erina observed a young woman in obvious pain, she made her way toward the woman. "Do ye require aid?"

The woman clutched her abdomen. "Nae. 'Tis always the same when I am with child."

"Do ye find it difficult to keep food down?" asked Erina.

"Aye, but the priest tells me 'tis my punishment as a woman."

Erina held back the argument that threatened to spew forth. Why did the priests spread such dread among their followers? "Each morn brew a cup of mint tea. And then in the evening make a brew of nettle tea. The mint will soothe your stomach pains and the nettle will provide nourishment for ye and the bairn."

The woman gaped at her and then peered around Erina as if beholding a secret. She tugged on her sleeve. "'Tis what my grandmother told me. But I feared going against my priest."

Erina patted the woman's hand and smiled. "Remember, though he is your priest, the man has never carried a child."

"Aye, *aye*." Her eyes grew wide. "Thank ye kindly." The woman dashed off among the stalls, and Erina shook her head.

Smells of food drifted by, and her stomach protested. Spying some toasted hazelnuts, she was sorely tempted to buy a small bag, but turned away from the vendor. As she made her way along the other side of the stalls, Catherine came charging toward her.

"By the saints, are all the men obstinate here?" Her friend asked, taking her arm.

"I take your meaning ye were unable to procure a deal?"

Catherine rolled her eyes. "Not one."

"So ye have purchased naught?"

Pouting her lips, Catherine replied, "I daresay I might have to return and pay the asking price on one portion of fabric in a lovely shade of light blue."

"The color would suit ye and your blonde hair."

Her friend halted their stride. "I can see there will be nae argument from ye. Therefore I must return before someone else snatches it away."

"If I may offer a bit of advice?"

"Please," Catherine pleaded.

Erina glanced around, before turning her attention to her friend. "Seek out the women. Ye will be able to barter a fairer deal, since they need the coin more."

"Sweet Mother Mary," she muttered. "Why didn't I think of that?" She pulled away from Erina. "Have ye not found anything?"

Erina laughed. "As ye can witness, I have not ventured far from this area of satin and ribbons."

"Tempting, are they not?"

"Aye."

"Well, I am going to go make my purchase and return it to the ale tent for safekeeping."

"Then I will go with ye," Erina suggested. "There is naught which I need from these vendors."

Catherine waved her away. "Nae. Go find your candles and salt. I will come find ye, *or* I'll tell a certain man to search for ye." Her voice trailed off among the many others, and Erina was left speechless.

Recovering her senses, Erina steadily sought out the vendors to procure her salt and candles. After giving her thanks, she stuffed the items into her satchel and moved out of the area. Once again, her stomach protested at the lack of food as she continued to wander away from the main market. Several young girls were playing a game of hoops in a circle, and she paused to take in their skill. Their laughter was contagious, and she smiled.

Leaving the gaiety behind, Erina strolled in the soft afternoon light toward a cluster of pine trees. Blissful silence greeted her as she leaned against the rough bark of one of the trees and dropped her satchel. She sniffed the air, deeming snow would soon come to Kileburn.

A squirrel darted out from among the leaves and paused in front of her.

She lifted her hands in surrender. "I am sorry my friend. I could ill afford any nuts this day, or I would gladly share."

"Ahh…but I do have some of what he craves," responded a low male voice behind her.

Startled, Erina turned and met Rory's hard gaze. He stood within the shadows of the trees, the fading sunlight behind the clouds dancing off his features. "Would ye care to share?" Her stomach protesting once again.

When he stepped forth, his smile sent shivers throughout her body. "Always," he responded huskily and then tossed several to the small animal. The squirrel stashed his precious food into his mouth and scampered away.

Rory held out the bag to Erina. "Why have ye not eaten?"

Erina ignored his question and withdrew several hazelnuts. "Thank ye." She brushed away their skins and popped a couple into her mouth, savoring their rich flavor. "Good."

He reached out and wiped a thumb across her lower lip. "Ye missed a piece."

She swallowed and searched his eyes. Waiting. Seeking. Needing some assurance he was feeling the same. "Why are ye here?"

"To make sure ye would not go hungry. Did ye not wish to sample some of these nuts?"

"Ho…*How* did ye ken?" she stammered, wishing for more than the touch of his hand. Recovering her partial senses, she asked, "Were ye following me?"

His laugher was rich, warm, and sensual. "It would be unwise to do so."

Erina's mind screamed to move away. Yet, her body craved more from the man. "Why would it be unwise?"

His thumb continued to stroke gently across her lip. "Because I long to taste ye again."

"Another stolen kiss?" she challenged.

Rory arched a dark brow. "Or given freely, perchance?"

Erina bit her lower lip, wanting to touch and taste the man. She ignored the battle within her mind, warning her to flee. It was dangerous being so close to him—intoxicating. "Always," she uttered softly, echoing his own word.

His groan surrounded her, and he dropped the bag of nuts. Grasping her firmly around the waist with one arm, he cupped her chin with his other hand. "I find I cannot stay away. By the hounds, I have tried." His mouth sought hers, filling the emptiness with his kiss, and Erina wrapped her arms around his neck. Passion hummed in every part of her body, and she yearned to strip her gown free and lie with this man among the trees. Rory brought forth her wildest desires, and she ached to have him touch her in those secret places she had heard others speak about. Erina's desire for him overrode everything else.

When his tongue slipped inside her mouth, her body tingled all the way to her toes. This time she was the one to moan when his hand cupped her breast, and he deepened the kiss. Slowly, Rory walked her backward until she was against the rough bark of a pine tree. After releasing his grip on her body, he placed his hands on either side of her, trapping Erina.

Lust danced within the depths of his beautiful eyes. Slowly, he lowered his head and with his tongue traced a path along the vein in her neck, igniting a firestorm within her blood. The sensation pooled in an intimate part of her body where she longed to have him touch.

"Does your blood burn, Erina?" he asked, nuzzling her neck.

"Aye," she gasped, placing her hands on his hips.

Rory glanced down at her hands. "Do ye see my desire for ye?"

"I want ye, Rory. I crave ye like no other." She closed her eyes, trying to calm her breathing.

"And I ye." His voice so hoarse, she could barely understand his words. He continued to tease her breasts, and all she wanted was to be set free.

"More," she pleaded.

Rory grasped her hand and led them deeper into the woods. By the time he stopped, the echo of voices from the market were a light whisper among the branches.

"Will ye take me here?" she asked, brushing a lock of hair from his face.

He touched her trembling lips with one finger. "Nae, but I promise to give ye pleasure."

Her mouth parted on a sigh as he swept her into his arms and took her to a nearby boulder. Setting them both down, Rory cradled her on his lap. He placed soft kisses on her cheeks and lips, and his hand slipped under her gown. Rory's fingers stroked along her thigh moving upward.

Erina wrapped an arm around his shoulder. "Wh…what are ye doing?"

His gaze seemed to see straight to her very soul.

"Giving ye pleasure, *mo ghrá*."

She couldn't speak. Couldn't move. The air warmed around them, and Erina surrendered to the growing passion.

Rory slipped one finger inside her center. "One day I will taste ye here," he declared, drawing his finger back out before stroking her again.

Erina shook her head, shocked by his words and touch.

He smiled seductively and kissed her lips. "Aye, ye *will* allow me."

When one finger stroked over her sensitive core, colors danced before her eyes, and she arched backward. His hand was doing glorious things to her, and Erina tried to grasp what to do as her body trembled.

"Let yourself go, Erina," he whispered, while he continued to stroke and tease her in a place that was driving her into an unknown abyss of pleasurable delights.

She squirmed and gasped, trying to capture an elusive sensation she did not understand. His mouth covered hers hungrily, and when she thought she couldn't go any further, Erina shattered into a million tingling pieces. She soared, floated, and a scream of pleasure ripped through her.

Time dissolved around them, and she broke free from Rory's mouth. She leaned her head on his shoulder as she tried to calm her breathing. She'd never known such pleasure, and Erina tried to fathom what it would feel like with Rory deep inside her. Would there be pain? Or would the pleasure be greater than what she had just experienced? She shuddered and closed her eyes.

Rory removed his hand and attempted to smooth her gown, but he made no sign of wanting to leave their trysting place.

"I ken there is more between a man and woman," she uttered softly and looked up at him.

He wrapped his free arm around her waist, and she snuggled more against him. "Aye, but I will not take ye here."

Erina cupped his cheek. "The trees will keep us safe."

Rory chuckled softly and kissed her palm. "Agreed, but when I take ye, I want ye for an entire night."

She bit her lower lip. *Would there be many nights? Or only the one?* "A night?"

He leaned his forehead against hers. "I was speaking of our first time."

Good, Rory MacGregor, because ye will be mine. Her lips sought his, and the kiss made her weak all over again.

After finally removing his arms from around her, Rory brought them to standing. Erina's legs wobbled, and Rory placed her hand in the crook of his arm. "Ready?" he asked.

"Not really, but we must."

When they stepped out of the protection of the trees, Rory released his hold on her hand. "Go onward, and I shall follow shortly."

Erina nodded. Striding toward the market area, she was unprepared for the assault that came barreling toward her in the form of Betty Timmons. She clasped her hands together and attempted to smile in greeting.

"Betty, what a lovely surprise to see ye here at the market."

Fury glittered in the woman's eyes. "How dare ye! I came to your cottage, only to find ye gone! Furthermore, I waited most of the night."

Frowning, Erina replied, "I left ye a note tacked to the door, Betty, telling ye where to find the love charm I made for ye."

She shook her head vehemently. "There was naught."

Erina placed a hand on the woman, but she jerked out of her grasp. "I can assure ye that I did. In truth, I have a witness."

Betty folded her arms over her chest. "'Tis a lie."

"Nae, lass, Erina speaks the truth," argued Rory, stepping forth from the trees, carrying her satchel. "She did indeed leave ye a note."

Erina swallowed, but kept silent.

Betty darted a glance at Rory and then swept her gaze back to Erina. "I have missed my chance because of ye." She pointed a finger at Rory "Were ye with him that night? Is this your lover?"

"Ye dishonor the lady," warned Rory, taking Erina's elbow.

A tremor of unease trickled down Erina's spine. "There is still time, Betty."

"Nae," she spat out. "The moon is full this night, and my Fergus is gone."

"*Gone*?" echoed Erina.

She took a step forward. "I followed him to the market and then watched as he took coin from a man and left. When I approached the man, he laughed and told me Fergus was leaving to return home to his kin in the north. If I had the charm yesterday, I would have prevented him from leaving. I did not ask much from ye, only sought out your help. I deemed ye were my friend."

"I am sorry, Betty."

The woman's lip trembled as she spoke. "Nae, Erina MacIntyre, ye should be the one who is sorry. I curse ye where ye stand that love never finds ye."

Erina watched in horror as the woman turned and stormed away. Betty's words spread like poison inside her, and Erina clutched a fist to her chest. *Foolish woman, ye have cursed your own self.*

But when she turned to look at Rory, his expression was one of cold steel, and his eyes were shards of dark crystals.

Chapter Seventeen

"When the Dragons assisted the Fae, great miracles occurred and peace was attained between the worlds, until fear drove a wedge between them, killing the dragons."

~*Chronicles of the Fae*

With each blow of his hammer to the anvil, Rory took out his frustration on the steel. Sweat and grime beaded along his brow, and trickled down his face. Though the day was brisk, his body burned from the work. Picking up the blade, he submerged the metal into a bucket of water and held it up for inspection. Tossing it back onto the anvil, he wiped a hand across his forehead.

Betty Timmons' words remained a lodestone around his heart, and he could not shake the opinion the woman posed a dangerous threat to Erina. When they had returned from the market, Erina swiftly excused herself and took her evening meal in her chambers. How he longed to give her comfort, but Rory stayed away that night, and the following ones. He remained steadfast in his belief to guard and protect her.

A leaf fluttered past him, and he held up his hand. Blowing across his palm, he whispered, "May the winds warn ye of any danger, Erina MacIntyre. Let this be a message to ye."

Rory leaned against a post. His previous memories of Erina were now only tiny bits of images, dissolving with each day. If the Fates had given her another chance, why did they not strip his love for her as well? His previous oath was now shredded and another one took its place. A vow of love, honor, and protection.

"Are ye hiding from me, Rory MacGregor? Or have ye become the new blacksmith for Kileburn?"

Erina's words startled him, and he glanced over his shoulder. Her lips twitched in merriment, and her gaze bore into his. He became a flustered youth in her presence and often times found he could not utter one single word.

She cradled a basket over her arm. "I thought I'd seek ye out and tempt ye with some food. Or will ye banish me once again?"

'Tis not food ye are tempting me with, lass, and by the Gods I have missed ye. "Do not remind me of my earlier rude behavior. What fare are ye presenting?"

She laughed, the sound filling Rory, and he placed his fists on his hips waiting for her to approach. When she neared him, Erina lifted the cloth from the basket, and he inhaled the hearty aroma of warm bread mixed with herbs. "Larena has been teaching me to bake."

"So the woman has softened to ye? How did ye manage the task?"

"It was simple," replied Erina, walking past him and disappearing beyond the forge.

Curious, Rory grabbed his tunic and followed the alluring woman through the trees. As he ducked under a cluster of birch and yew trees, he approached her standing near the stream. Bending on one knee beside her, he splashed some water on his face and chest. The brittle sting did little to douse the fire inside his body as he slipped on his tunic. He darted a glance at Erina, noting the blush staining her cheeks, and her hands clutching the basket tightly.

"I did not think to bring a covering for the ground," she protested, looking around the area.

Rory took her elbow and steered her toward a fallen log. "The forest will provide. Now, do share how ye managed to persuade the cook."

After regaining her composure, she took a seat and placed the basket on the ground between them. Tearing off some bread, she handed him a portion. "I merely stated I wished to learn, since one day I might have to for a husband."

"*Husband*?" He croaked out between the bite of bread he had just devoured. By the hounds, had another stepped forward and made an offer of marriage? Ewan? No, he had declined. Darren? The other lairds?

She waved him off dismissively. "Aye. It was the—"

Rory tossed the bread into the water, and stood. "Who has spoken for ye?"

Her eyes narrowed to slits as she glared up at Rory. "If ye would let me finish…"

Wiping a hand over his face, he sat back down. "Pray forgive my outburst and continue."

Erina tore another piece from the loaf and held it out to him. "Please dinnae throw this one away. As I was saying, by telling the woman I intended to learn for a *future* husband, she positively beamed and agreed to assist me." Pursing her lips, she added, "Though, she did quickly add I would most likely have a cook to prepare all my meals."

Rory leaned his forearms on his thighs. "So ye lied."

Erina shrugged and retrieved another pouch from the basket. "Not really. Mayhap there is a husband out there for me."

He glanced outward at the stream. "How many other lairds have arrived?"

She looked aghast at him. "Ye *have* been hiding. They arrived two days ago."

"I have nae desire to go hunting."

"But do ye not want to aid your laird when he is tending to the hawks?"

Rory shook his head. "My laird understands me well, and he would not want me around his birds."

"Oh. How many did he bring?" she asked, handing Rory some berries.

"Two. Both females and I would surely set them free to soar over the land. No bird is happy being chained to a master."

She brushed the crumbs from her gown. "I mean no disrespect, but ye eat nae meat, and do little to help your laird, so why would he bring ye along? Ye even appear like ye dinnae have any desire to be here. Ye are not an ordinary man."

Rory blinked and then burst out laughing. He popped the berries into his mouth, savoring their sweetness. "My *laird* has other needs for my services. Ye are a keen observer, Erina."

"Sometimes," she uttered softly, and turned away from his heated gaze. "To answer your earlier question, there are three other lairds from the neighboring lands. I have been *ordered* by Graham to appear at the feast tonight, since I have done my best to avoid everyone."

"So ye have been hiding as well."

Her mouth twitched in humor. "Aye. Catherine is furious with me for leaving her to the wolves."

"Wolves?"

Nodding, Erina added, "Those are her words. She states they are naught but groping men with bad teeth, and a taste for lewdness. She's shocked Graham would invite them as possible suitors and told him so in his solar this morning. Then she promptly informed me that if I did not show a sign of unity with her this evening, she would bring all the men to my chamber, no matter my appearance."

Rory stood slowly. "Then ye must attend the feast."

"Aye," she grumbled in protest and kicked a rock away.

"But ye have naught to fear."

"Words spoken by a *man*," she contested and dropped the berries back into the basket.

Rory grabbed her hand and brought her to standing. "As ye have already stated, I am nae *ordinary* man."

Her eyes grew wide, and her lips parted in an invitation. "Nae…nae ye are not."

He released her hand and took a step backward. Stripping his tunic free from his body, he tossed it aside. Erina's gaze traveled the length of his chest, and Rory fought the yearning to take her into his arms. "I thank ye for my meal, but now I must prepare for tonight's feast."

Her brow furrowed, and she angled her head. "Feast? Ye…ye will be there?"

As he removed his boots, he winked at her. "Aye." Loosening his trews, he paused. "Unless ye are joining

188

me in the water, 'tis best ye leave now."

She gasped. "Oh…aye…I mean…*aye* I shall leave ye to your bathing. Ye can return the basket when ye are finished."

Rory waited until she was safely gone and then stripped free from his trews. As he started forward, he shook his head and glanced over his shoulder. There standing among the trees was Erina. Raw passion glittered within the depths of her eyes, and it took all of his willpower to remain rooted to the ground. Ever so slowly, she turned and slipped into the darkness.

****

"Wolves have better manners than these men," he muttered, studying the gathered group at the table.

"On that we can agree," acknowledged Brother Michael, coming alongside Rory.

He gestured for the monk to precede him into the hall, but the man shook his head. "I must tend to my prayers. I agreed to stay until ye arrived." Brother Michael made a slight bow. "My duties have been fulfilled, and I reckon ye can deal with those men and their barbs far better than myself."

Rory inclined his head. "A good evening to ye."

Upon entering the banquet hall, Rory searched for Erina or Catherine—both apparently absent. As he strode toward Ewan, the man eyed him with curiosity and motioned for him to take a seat next to him.

His laird quickly made the introductions and Rory nodded his greeting to all. He reached for a jug of wine, promptly filling his cup and extending the courtesy to Ewan. Drinking deeply, he kept his focus on the doors to the hall and the conversation of the men.

"I am honored ye would show your presence this

evening," Ewan muttered, attempting to pull a leg free from the roasted pheasant on a trencher.

"Rumor reached me there were *wolves* attending the feast. I am here to make sure no harm comes to anyone."

Ewan choked on a piece of the fowl and reached for his cup. After recovering, he glared across the table at the other men. "Ye have spoken to Catherine."

Rory rubbed a hand over his chin. "Nae. Erina. Though, she did profess her source as your daughter."

The man grumbled a curse and then drank deeply. Wiping his mouth with the back of his hand, he continued to eat his meal. "Mind ye, though they lack certain manners, these men are powerful in their own rights."

Rory eyed the man skeptically. "And ye would consider them a possible husband for Catherine? She will flee," offered Rory quietly.

Ewan placed his cup down. "She can try. However, the only place I reckon will be suitable for my daughter would be a convent. She has defied me long enough. I have given her until the new year to accept a marriage contract. In truth, none here are deserving, but I shall wait out their visit."

Rory was about to argue further, when both women entered the hall. The din of noise settled as they made their way to the table, and Rory was held captivated by the lovely vision drawing near. Erina's tresses trailed in soft curls down her back. The radiance of the gentle candlelight shimmered off her features, and his hands itched to twirl a lock between his fingers. Her emerald green gown highlighted far too many curves, and he swallowed. Casting his sight around the table, he noted several empty places between the visiting lairds.

Standing abruptly, he gestured for Catherine to take her place beside her father. Ewan muttered a curse, but nodded in agreement.

As Rory moved around the table, he pulled out a chair for Erina and then promptly took his seat next to her.

The man to Rory's right, Laird Ranald Cameron, let out a belch. "Ye have hidden these treasures from us MacGregor and MacIntyre."

"I believe, *Laird* Cameron, ye were hunting for several days," scoffed Rory, refilling the man's cup.

The man ignored Rory's offering and asked, "What is your name, lass?"

She gave him a tight smile. "Erina MacIntyre."

"This is my sister," said Graham. "And the other is Catherine MacGregor."

Ranald chuckled and opened his arms wide. "'Tis a shame ye have no more hiding, since we might be fighting for both."

The other lairds laughed, but kept silent.

"I daresay, one dance with each will not be enough," Ranald suggested, leaning an arm on the table.

Erina looked at the man in stunned horror and then glanced at her brother. For her part, Catherine leveled the man a look of contempt over the rim of her cup.

Rory leaned forward, doing his best not to burn the man's tongue from his mouth. "They are *not* cattle to be bought."

Ranald looked at him in disgust. "And who are ye to speak in this manner?"

"Enough!" shouted Graham, smacking his hand

onto the table. "Ye dishonor my guest and the other women at the table."

Ranald held up his hands in surrender. "Ye are correct. I will speak privately with ye regarding your sister." He took his cup and held it upward. "To the lovely women who have graced us with their beauty this evening."

Erina paled, and Rory slipped a comforting hand over hers beneath the table. She stole a glance at him, giving him a weak smile.

"Have ye spoken with the Campbell?" asked Ewan, poking at his meal. "There are many who seek to banish the thieving in these parts, but he refuses to listen."

Ranald wiped his nose and reached for his cup. "I did not ken there were any problems." He waved a hand about. "Aye, a few missing sheep, but I put blame on the lads tending to the pens."

"I have had sheep gone missing," blurted out Erina. "In truth, I deemed someone was unlocking the gate and setting them free."

The other men halted their conversations and stared at her.

"My sister is fond of her sheep," interjected Graham. "Pay no heed to her. I am sure it was merely a prank played on her by some foolhardy lads."

The Cameron narrowed his eyes. "Are ye the one who lives in the cottage near the south fork?"

"Aye," she responded, lifting her chin.

"And the one they call the White Healer?"

She kept her gaze level with the man. "I dinnae ken what they speak about."

"My sister tends to the sick and makes garments from her wool. I find it admirable how she helps those in need," Graham stated. "Ye ken how the old folk talk and spew tales across the lands."

"Agreed," interjected Ewan and pointing a finger at Ranald, he added, "But what I find distressing is your lands seem to be unscathed from these attacks."

The man shrugged, but kept his focus on Erina, and Rory found the man shrewd and calculating—one who could not be trusted.

Ranald snorted and looked at the other lairds gathered. "Do ye seriously consider this more than lads seeking mischief?"

"Aye," responded another man. "I dinnae care about the thieving of sheep, but a few of my cattle have been taken. 'Tis a serious crime. Others have come to me, complaining their grain has been stolen, as well."

After downing the contents of his cup, Ranald said, "Then when the Campbell returns in the spring, we shall *all* go and speak with him."

"Or we can take charge of the problem ourselves," insisted Graham and gestured to the bard near the hearth to begin playing, hence ending the heated debate.

The music helped to soothe the festering tension in the hall, and the discussion turned to one of the harvest. However, Rory sensed uneasiness within Erina. Religious wars were rife over the years—each battling over the one true belief or version. Many healers were accused of witchcraft, and an icy tendril of fear snaked through Rory. He'd thought Erina safe at Kileburn—free from those who would do her harm. What if he was wrong again?

Rory was on a path of no clear direction. He was conflicted by his emotions. Unsure if he was protecting or bringing harm to Erina. Nevertheless, he could not deny the link of destiny with her. He no longer fought against the tide of emotions, instead choosing to embrace them all.

For the first time in his existence, Rory MacGregor, Fenian Warrior, broke the chains of training around his heart and freed all guilt, including the past.

Chapter Eighteen

"The heart of the Fenian Warrior lies in his conviction to honor both—Fae and human."
~Chronicles of the Fae

Erina slipped behind a chair, doing her best to avoid any dancing with Ranald Cameron. The man was an insufferable ass, and she refused to suffer his boring discussions any longer. When the dancing started, both she and Catherine complained of headaches. However, her friend informed everyone that there would be dancing after the next evening meal. Erina fought the scream of protest and glared daggers at the woman. Catherine was not dismayed and gave her a passing wink as she fled the hall.

By the Goddess, how she despised taking her meals with everyone, except one. *Rory MacGregor.* His name invoked images of his half-naked body and the kisses of fire he traced along her body. In trying to deny her feelings, Erina busied herself in the kitchens or tending to her sheep. What a foolish notion, for it did nothing to squelch a scorching need to know more about the man.

She placed a finger to her lips as she walked along the corridor near the stairs. Recalling the other places he had explored on her skin, ignited a passion so fierce, Erina found herself moving toward the front entrance of Kileburn for cooler air.

As she stole out the front door, the icy blast of air slapped at her face and for a moment, Erina regretted not retrieving her cloak. The waning moon hung gracefully in the inky black velvet sky as she made her way across the bailey and toward the stables. Stepping inside, she picked up a lantern and walked to her horse's stall.

"There ye are, my friend." She slipped the lantern on a peg and turned toward her horse.

Oberon snorted and drew near, and Erina held out her hand in greeting. "Forgive me for being absent these past few days." When he refused to acknowledge her greeting, she withdrew an apple from a nearby basket.

The horse let out a soft whinny, but refused to accept her offering.

"Ye offend me. Will ye not accept my apology?" She waved the fruit in front of his nose. "I promise to take ye out tomorrow. Ye ken I dinnae make promises I cannot keep."

"Even if there's snow?" asked the familiar male voice behind her.

Erina's heart fluttered as she tried to steady the apple she held. Longing for cooler air, she chided herself for running into a firestorm. "Aye, even if there is snowfall."

Rory bent near her ear. "Then Oberon will take your gift."

His lips grazed the soft spot below her ear, and she shuddered. He stepped to the side and leaned against the stall. Erina wanted to toss the apple onto the ground and devour the man. Instead, she turned her sight to her horse as he took hold of the fruit.

Erina could feel the heat of Rory's gaze along her skin. "Are ye looking for a new position as stable master, instead of blacksmith?" she teased, glancing sideways at the man.

"Nae. I followed ye."

She bit her lip and looked away. "Ahh…again. Ye have stealthy moves, Rory MacGregor. I did not see ye *or* hear ye."

"Your focus was on the moonlight."

"Then I should be more aware," she countered, brushing her hands off and giving Oberon a gentle pat.

"On that we can agree, *mo ghrá*." Rory stepped near and tugged a lock of hair free from its comb.

Erina's heart pounded fiercely within her chest. Once again, the man used words of endearment, and she was held mesmerized by his eyes. "What do ye want?" The question tumbled free, and she feared his response.

His presence was intoxicating as he pulled gently, twisting the hair around his finger. "*Ye*."

She closed her eyes on a sigh. Erina desired him more than anything, but indecision left its thorn within her thoughts. "Ye will leave soon with your laird, and I dinnae want to be a passing fancy."

Rory kissed her softly on the forehead. "Ye could never be a passing fancy. Sleep well, Erina."

When she opened her eyes, he had slipped out as silently as he had approached, and her lips trembled. Choking back a sob, Erina hugged her arms around herself. "What am I to do with ye, my chivalrous knight?"

After brushing back a lone tear, she took in a few calming breaths and departed the stables. She ran into the castle and dashed up the stairs. Entering her chamber, she closed it softly and leaned against the door.

The blaze in the hearth had died to embers, and Erina had no energy to add more peat or wood. Walking slowly to the window, she sat on the cushioned ledge and gazed at the glittering stars. Her mind battled with her heart, and she leaned back against the cold stone. It was times like these that she ached to talk to her grandmother. How she truly missed the woman. She always knew the right words to help her see clearly. "What am I to do? Everything is twisted like gnarled vines and I can't think." Blowing out a frustrated sigh, Erina rested her chin on her bent knees.

Her grandmother tapped a finger to her head. "Stop making decisions with only your mind."

"Humph! Then what do ye suggest? Tossing them out there for others to tell me what to do?"

"Tsk, tsk, child. There is another part of your body ye are forgetting."

Erina rolled her eyes. "Do tell."

"Dinnae take that tone with me," warned her grandmother. Walking toward her, she grasped Erina's hand and placed it over her heart. "Do ye feel it beating?"

"Aye," she uttered solemnly.

"Then listen to it, as well. Ye keep fighting against your emotions."

"How can it help me to make a decision?" Erina protested.

Her grandmother smiled and cupped her cheek. "If it feels right, then ye have your decision. However, if there's a tiny spark of indecision, then settle your thoughts. Reach out for the Goddess to guide ye."

"I'm scared."

Shrugging, her grandmother released her hand and plucked a rose. "There is always fear when walking an unknown path. Furthermore, if ye let it rule your life, then ye are not living." Holding out the rose to her, she added, "Though a rose has thorns, it will not prevent me from admiring its beauty within my hand."

Erina smiled and took the flower. Inhaling deeply, she said, "What would I do without ye, Grandmother."

"Live your life, as ye have been doing. Now make your decision."

Erina moved off the ledge and placed her palm over her heart. "It feels right, Grandmother. My soul leapt for the first time when our gazes locked. I guess I have found my answer."

****

Rory braced his hands over the hearth and stared into the flames. Sleep was elusive, and his mind troubled. How he yearned for Erina and yet, her words halted him from taking her into his arms inside the stables. Did he truly expect to love *and* leave her? If he made love to her, Rory longed to tell her everything about himself. He had to give her not only his body, but also his soul as a Fae. Would she be horrified? Reject all that he stood for? Mayhap this was his greatest challenge.

"The truth, she must ken the truth," he uttered softly. No matter how hard he tried to stay true to a new path, his heart and soul belonged to Erina. The past gone—vanished. And this new road would not end in her death.

Smacking his hand on the stone, he backed away

from the hearth. Reaching for his plaid on a nearby chair, he wrapped it around his body and strode to the table. Picking up a jug, he poured a hefty amount of wine into a cup, wishing it were a good bottle of single malt. He drained the contents in one gulp and wiped his mouth with the back of his hand.

As he grumbled a curse, he poured more into the cup and walked to the window. Lifting it, he spoke in the language of his people. "May the stars guide my Fae brother and sisters, for I deem they no longer speak to me. From this moment forward, I walk this path alone. Forgive me."

"What does it mean?"

Startled, Rory swiftly turned around, spilling a portion of the wine on the floor. He, a trained warrior, and this mere slip of a lass had entered his chamber without his knowledge. His heart leapt with joy at seeing Erina standing in front of the armoire with nothing but a white chemise and shawl wrapped around her shoulders. "I was making a toast to my people."

She twisted the edges of the shawl within her fingers. "Are they gone?"

"Nae," he uttered in a low tone.

"Then mayhap one day I can meet them."

Nae, mo ghrá. They will never accept ye. And I am already an outcast. He deposited the cup on the table as he strode toward her. Grasping her around the waist with one arm, he trailed a thumb over her bottom lip. "Ye have found another secret passageway?" he asked peering inside the dark interior.

"Aye," she whispered softly. "There is one in the back of your wardrobe cabinet."

He closed the door softly, backing her against the

armoire. "'Tis dangerous to be here with me. *Alone*. Is there something ye want?" *Or desire?*

Taking his free hand, she placed it over her breast and let the shawl fall to the floor. "*Ye*. All ye have to give."

"Erina, *mo ghrá*," he groaned, taking her mouth with savage intensity. She tasted of honey and spices, filling him completely and easing the torment that continually plagued him.

Breaking free, he placed his hands on either side of the door. Giving her all of him required something more from Erina. Without the assurance of accepting him for what he was, Rory would be a lost man. "Are ye certain ye want to ken all of me? I want ye as sure as the sun rises and sets over the land each day, but ken this, Erina—there is more to me than a simple bedding. There are things about me that might frighten ye. What I'm about to share with ye may cause ye to question my existence, or worse, my sanity."

Her laugh was seductive and soothing as she wrapped her arms around his neck. "From the moment ye stepped through those trees that first day, I realized ye were not like any man I had encountered. It was as if the trees parted and ye came forth from inside them." She brushed her fingers along his brow. "For one, ye have the most mesmerizing eyes *and* they shift colors."

"And the second?"

Her face turned a rosy glow, yet, she held his gaze. "I thought your body chiseled from the old Gods, especially with all the markings on your back and arms."

His gaze swept over hers. "I am nae God, Erina, though some would call me a demon."

She traced a finger down along his arm and shook her head. "Ye are not a monster, but I am nae fool. Ye are not like other men, Rory. I have seen the markings on your body elsewhere." Her finger curved around his shoulder and he trembled. "They are similar to the ones on the standing stones carved by the ancients."

Rory fought the tide of emotions sweeping through him. She had come to the conclusion all on her own. "And ye would not flee if I told ye I was one of those ancients? One where the bards wove tales of giants who lived thousands of years ago among your own people? Others would call the story incredulous and filled with heathen words." He held his breath, fearing her reply.

The smile she gave him speared straight to his soul. "Nae. I would not flee."

Taking her hand, Rory led her to the window and pointed upward. "My people came from the stars, *mo ghrá*. We settled here in Ireland and Scotland thousands of years ago. However, over time, we deemed it necessary to create another realm to live."

"Why?"

Rory sighed and brought her close to him. "Your people grew fearful of mine. The path of a new religion spread and some judged us to be demons because of our power over the land. When the wars began, my people fiercely considered it unwise to use powers against yours, and a decision was finally made to leave."

Erina wrapped her arms around his waist. "Where did ye go?"

"Beneath the Hill of Tara in Ireland."

"Hmm…a magical place, indeed."

"Ye have heard of the land?"

She leaned her head against his chest. "Many times

from my grandmother. She told me the Fae folk live there."

Rory cradled her in his arms. "I would have liked to meet this wondrous woman."

"Aye. She would have warned me against ye, though."

Rory cupped her chin, forcing her to meet his gaze. "Truly? Why?"

"She often cautioned me against any man with alluring eyes, saying it might lead to sorrow. Although, she did state once that the man might also be one to bring happiness, but he would be fraught with troubles."

Smiling, he released his hold. "Was she a seer?"

"Goodness, nae. But a verra wise woman. She taught me everything about the old beliefs and knowledge of the land—from healing herbs, plants, flowers, trees," Erina waved her hand outward, adding, "including the stars. Whenever she was disturbed or troubled, she'd go out at night and look upward at them. Afterwards, she'd return with an answer to some problem she was trying to solve."

"The stars are a marvel in themselves."

Erina twisted in his arms and placed her hands upon his chest. "So ye are…ancient?"

He brought his hands to her shoulders. "I am a Fenian Fae Warrior for my people and far older than ye can imagine."

Her eyes went wide. "Oh. Are ye important?"

"Aye."

"Why me?" she asked in a hushed tone.

"Because your soul called out to mine, *mo ghrá*, and no one ever has in my entire lifetime." Rory brushed a delicate kiss along her lower lip. "Once I take ye to my bed, ye will be mine. There will be no turning back. I want ye now *and* forever."

Erina looked away, and he could sense the battle of indecision within her. "If I give myself to ye, I am fearful of what tomorrow might bring."

"There will be nae doubts, or fears between us, Erina. I have recently learned that tomorrow can be as fleeting as the next day. Each moment, each *second* should be a treasured memory. I wish to have those that were stolen from me." He ached to tell her how they first met, but there was nothing he could draw from within his fragmented memories.

She glanced sharply at him and cupped his face. "Then let us make new ones, starting with this night."

How her words banished the ugly past and sparked a hope for the future. For new beginnings. Rory lifted her, treasuring the feel of her in his arms, and with a single thought sealed all the doors and passageways to his chamber. Striding with intent, he made his way to the bed.

After gently placing her on the edge of the furs, he knelt in front of her. "Your feet are cold." Trailing a path from her toes to along her thigh with the back of his hand, Rory watched her eyes widen, and her breathing hitched.

"Are they?" she murmured. "I did not notice."

"Aye, but I'm positive they can be warmed." As Rory's fingers neared her nest of curls, she tried to push his hand away.

He arched a brow. "I thought ye enjoyed my touch?"

Bright red splotches appeared on her cheeks, and

she bit her lower lip. "I do, but I…dinnae want ye…" She looked away. "'Tis wanton."

"The pleasure it brings ye?" he asked, slipping a finger between her soft folds.

She nodded and let out a gasp.

His hand stilled. "Do ye wish me to stop?"

"Nae!" she blurted out and returned her gaze to his. "But, ye are down there…I want ye near me."

Smiling, he complied and settled her on his lap. "Is this better?"

"Aye. But I wish to feel ye." Surprising Rory, she removed her chemise and tossed it to the floor.

The blood pounded in his veins—in his soul. Her innocence and passion to learn fueled his own desire. "Ye are so beautiful." He brushed his fingers across her breasts, and she trembled. He noted the stunning necklace she wore and lifted the amethyst to study its radiance. "Where did ye come upon this gem?"

"From my grandmother. The stone has been in our family for many generations."

Rory gently placed it back between her ivory breasts. As he nuzzled her neck, her intoxicating scent filled him. Erina moved against him, and his cock swelled more. He longed to sink deep within her body. He trailed a path down to her breast with his tongue, capturing the taut nipple between his teeth, lavishing one and then the other.

"*Rory*," she moaned, placing an arm around his shoulders.

Lifting his head from her silken globes, he took her mouth in a searing kiss and thrust his tongue deep within. He wanted all of her—reclaiming what was once lost. His hands roamed over her skin, committing to memory every single touch. Each kiss, each sigh, each moan resonated deep inside him.

When Erina slipped her hand beneath his plaid, her hand swept across the top of his cock, and he almost spilled his seed. "Nae," he uttered in a guttural cry and pushed her back onto the bed. Her legs parted, giving him a view of what he longed to taste.

Standing, Rory removed his plaid and watched as Erina's gaze darkened further. Her tongue darted out, tempting him to bring her head down upon his erection. He ached to have her succulent lips descend and devour him.

Erina held out her hand. "Let me touch ye."

"I cannot hold back."

Her smile was provocative. "One touch," she whispered.

His legs shook as he stepped forward and crawled across the bed to her. Lying on his side, he took her hand and placed it over his cock. He gritted his teeth as her fingers slid delicately down one side and up the other. Rory felt his control slipping with each touch and with a growl, he rolled her onto her back and kissed the pulsing hollow at the base of her throat.

"Ye smell of spices and the woods," he murmured, as he continued to ravish her body with kisses. His hand slipped down across her abdomen, until he reached her sensitive core. Erina whimpered when he flicked a finger over and around, rousing her passion and igniting a firestorm within him.

"*Please*," she begged, arching against his hand and digging her hands into his scalp. "Ne…need *all* of ye."

Rory recaptured her mouth and slid on top of her, slowing bringing the head of his erection to her entrance. Her heat surrounded him, along with the scent of her passion. He tried to force himself to go slowly, but when Erina wrapped a leg around him, he lost all sense of purpose and thrust deeply.

Letting out a hiss, Erina dug her nails into his shoulder and closed her eyes.

He stilled. "Have I hurt ye?"

Her eyes fluttered open. She swept away a lock of hair from his eyes. "Only slight. Dinnae stop."

Slowly, he withdrew and then entered her again—her full breasts rubbing against his chest in a seductive dance. He continued to move in and out in long, intense strokes. Rory delved deeper into a wave of ecstasy more powerful than anything he had known. With each thrust, kiss, and moan, he brought them closer to the flame, and when he thought he could no longer maintain control, Erina arched against him. The moment his mouth covered her lips, his own pleasure exploded forth from him. The power of Rory's release vibrated all around them and for a moment, the stars surrounded them as he emptied all he had to give into the woman he loved.

A wave of euphoria swept through him as he rolled onto his back, bringing Erina with him. Cradling her soft body within his arms, he tried to calm his breathing. And in those quiet, tender moments, Rory spoke the words in his ancient language to link his soul forever with Erina's.

"Blood to blood, I am yours. Heart to heart, ye are mine. Soul to soul, we shall be joined as one. I bind ye with these words for all eternity."

Erina lifted her head and kissed the tears streaming down his face.

Chapter Nineteen

*"A Fae's love is similar to a butterfly. It remains in
its protective cocoon until it's ready to present itself."*
~*Chronicles of the Fae*

In an attempt to seek the warmth of his body, Erina
brushed a hand over the furs. Yet, the more she tried
searching, the more frustration seeped within. Forcing
her eyelids open, she blinked in confusion. Sunlight
danced through the glass in a room that was not what
she last remembered. Did she imagine being in Rory's
chamber? Was their lovemaking all a dream? Her mind
was fuzzy, and she tried to focus.

As she propped herself up on her elbows, she
winced from the pain. Tossing aside the fur covering,
she lifted her chemise and saw the evidence of blood
staining her inner thighs. "Definitely not a dream," she
muttered and smiled. Flopping back down against her
pillow, she cupped a hand over her mouth in glee. The
man must have carried her back to her own chamber.

Her body ached in wondrous places she'd never
experienced. Rory's touch was divine pleasure, taking
her over and over again. Her face heated at all the
wonderful things he had done to her, as memories of
their lovemaking came back in a rush of images. Her
nipples hardened, and Erina longed to have his mouth
on her once again.

Startled by the tapping on her door, Erina bolted upright. She glanced around the room and spied her wrap on a chair by the hearth. Dashing out of the bed, she darted across the cold floor and reached for the material. "One moment," she ordered, placing the garment around her shoulders.

Thane lifted his head, but made no attempt to leave his warm spot by the dying embers in the hearth.

She paused before the door and tried to steady her jumbled nerves. Uncertain how she looked, she asked, "Who is it?"

"Open the door, Erina. It's Catherine."

Letting out a breath, she opened the door.

Catherine swept past her. "Sweet Brigid. Do ye ken the hour?"

Erina glanced out into the corridor and then quickly closed the door. "Well, the sun is high in the sky, so I reckon late."

Her friend whirled around and studied her. "All these weeks and I have never known ye to sleep past the first ray of dawn, Erina MacIntyre." She pointed to Thane. "Even your dog rises early."

She glared at the animal. Traitor. Ye could have awakened me, unless Rory took ye out earlier this morn. Clasping her hands in front of her, Erina responded, "Aye, but I fear it was nae lie when I professed I had a headache last evening."

Catherine continued to survey her. "Forgive me. Ye do look like ye have a fever, too." She wandered over to the cushioned window bench and sat. "In truth, I have suffered the same. I even dismissed riding my horse today for fear one of those men would want to escort me."

"Ranald Cameron is the worst," complained Erina and walked to the hearth. Tossing in some peat, she turned back around.

The woman shuddered visibly and fingered her gown. "He was horrid. I swear if my father makes a marriage agreement, I shall flee north."

"Ye have kin there?" Erina asked, and took a seat on the opposite side of the bench.

"Aye. My aunt on my mother's side," replied Catherine and gazed out the window. "Though I hear she wanted naught to do with my father after my mother died. Therefore, my stay there might be fraught with troubles, or she could turn me away."

Erina leaned forward and placed a comforting hand over hers. "Then let us pray ye dinnae have to find out. I am confident your father will listen to your concerns."

The woman laughed and returned her attention back to Erina. "I hope I can persuade him. We depart for home tomorrow."

"So soon? I will miss ye, Catherine."

Sadness replaced mirth on her friend's features. "Aye. Father deems it best before the snows. He did mention we should return in the spring, so he and Graham can take their concerns directly to the king. Furthermore, ye are welcome anytime, especially if ye need to flee from a certain brother."

Erina gave her a weak smile as she leaned back. "Mayhap we should remain in our respective chambers for the day."

"A grand idea, but I refuse to cower in my room." She angled her head at Erina. "Ye look different. Should I send for the healer?"

Swallowing, Erina shook her head. "I have nae

210

wish to have a healer bleed me."

"Hmm…ye are correct. 'Tis a messy process, as well." Pursing her lips, Catherine stood. "Shall I see ye at the evening meal?"

"Only if ye promise there will be nae dancing."

Catherine laughed. "Aye, I did promise the offensive man. But only to divert him from last evening." She tapped a finger against her lips and then her eyes lit up. "I have it! We will dance with each other. Or better yet, ye can dance with Rory, and I will take a turn with Graham."

Erina's face heated at the mere thought of being in Rory's arms once again. "I like the first idea."

Shrugging, Catherine made her way to the door. "As long as ye are at the meal, it makes nae matter." Pausing, she glanced over her shoulder. "Are ye sure I cannot send for anyone?"

There's only one person I long to see, but I shall not utter his name. "Nae, but I thank ye."

As soon as the door closed, Erina rushed over to the basin and dumped some water inside the large bowl. Splashing cold water on her face and arms, she reached for a bar of lavender-scented soap and scrubbed her face, arms, and thighs as best she could with a cloth. Her hair was a knotted mess, but she managed to braid a large portion and weave it around her head.

After hastily dressing, Erina grabbed her cloak and opened the door. She glanced over her shoulder. "Out ye go, Thane. Ye can return later."

The animal stretched and shook himself. She gave him a pat when he sauntered past her and out of the room.

Her nerves were twisted, and anticipation danced

along her skin at the thought of seeing Rory. As she left her chamber, her hands shook. Pausing, she tried to calm her racing heart. A door along the corridor opened, and Brother Michael stepped outside.

"Erina, 'tis good to see ye have left your bed. I feared your pain from last evening would leave ye inside your chamber all day." The monk shifted his stance. "Are ye breaking your fast? I can fix ye a medicinal brew."

She fidgeted under his scrutiny. "Nae. But some food will be welcomed."

He nodded and gestured her forward. "If ye dinnae mind, I would like to give ye something."

She glanced at him sideways as they made their way along the corridor. "I can assure ye, the pain is gone."

"My gift is one ye requested through Graham."

They halted by the stairs, and she took his arm. "Ye have brought some rose flower syrup?"

He chuckled softly. "I am surprised ye have not asked me."

"In truth, I had forgotten." How could she explain her fixation on only one man?

"Then I am happy ye are surprised. I have placed the bottles in the kitchens."

Erina took his arm. "Thank ye. How kind of ye to remember. Most of the roses have faded at Kileburn. My brother did let me harvest some during the summer, and I made lovely soap."

"Graham spoke to me of extending your own garden to include roses."

Stunned by this revelation, she asked, "Graham does not wish me to live at the cottage, so why would he aid in my garden?"

The monk squeezed her hand. "Mayhap, this was *before* the trouble started festering across his lands. Now, he judges it wiser to have ye remain here."

As they descended the stairs, a tremor of unease settled inside her stomach. Ranald Cameron stood off to the side speaking with another one of the lairds. They both halted their conversation as she and Brother Michael approached.

"Lady Erina," greeted Ranald.

Giving both men a slight smile, she nodded and kept moving in the direction of the kitchens. She hated how the quiet one followed her with his eyes— menacing and dark. At least Ranald voiced his thoughts, but the other laird made her stomach churn with uneasiness.

"I do hope to have a dance with ye this evening," he called out.

"I have promised them to another," she lied and continued down the passageway.

The man grumbled a response, but his words were lost to Erina.

"Ye tempt fire with that one," muttered Brother Michael.

Removing her hand from the monk's arm, she countered, "Then provide me with a pitcher of water, so I can douse the beast."

Brother Michael coughed into his fist. "Amen."

When they entered the kitchens, Mairi gave her a tight smile and brushed past her without an acknowledgement. Bryson stood over one end of the hearth, tending to some meat. His features were strained, and Erina judged he and Mairi had already had a lover's quarrel. Or worse, the charm did not work.

"All I have is porridge for ye, Lady Erina," stated Larena, and she pointed to a small pot hanging over the fire. "Unless ye are here for more cooking instructions?"

"Porridge is fine, Larena." Retrieving a bowl, Erina went to the hearth and scooped out a small portion. As she took a seat in the corner, she looked around for any berries or honey to sweeten the bland meal.

Brother Michael sat down across from her and proceeded to hand her a bottle of rose syrup. "I have put the other bottles high near the box of salt and spices. Ye have four and I have given the cook a couple to use in her dishes."

"Ye are too kind, Brother Michael. Thank ye." Erina took the syrup and squeezed his hand. Opening the top, she dipped her spoon inside and poured some over the top of her porridge.

His eyebrows rose in mischief. "So ye cannot stomach the fine fare in your bowl?"

"I'd rather have a stale bannock," she muttered, watching the sticky liquid trickle across her meal. She resealed the jar and set it down. Taking a bite, she savored the sweetness, letting the food linger on her tongue. "Divine."

The monk folded his arms over his chest. "I am happy to hear of your enjoyment."

"When I return to my cottage, ye must come for a visit and teach me how to prepare this delectable treat."

A frown skittered over his brow, but he kept silent.

"Regardless of what my brother wishes—*demands*, I am returning to my cottage."

"I will pray on the matter." Rising, he added,

214

"Enjoy your meal."

As she watched him depart, Erina had no desire to finish her meal. She grew weary of the same battle with her brother. Not one man would stand beside her in support. "Mayhap we'll both flee together, Catherine," she uttered softly. She picked up the bottle and tucked it inside the pocket of her cloak. Standing, Erina went to a large bucket filled with water and placed her bowl nearby. She waved farewell to Larena and left the kitchens.

A blast of brittle air greeted her as she left the castle. Rubbing her hands together to ward off the chill, Erina darted through the bailey, dodging past a couple of stray cats. As she entered the warmth of the stables, she went directly to Oberon's stall and halted. Apparently, someone had taken upon himself to prepare her horse for riding.

Erina leaned back to peer inside one of the other stalls. Excitement skittered across her skin. "Do I have ye to thank?"

Rory smiled as he led his horse out of the stall. "Aye."

Oberon nudged her, but she kept her focus on the man in front of her. "Are we going somewhere?"

"I hear there is a faery glen called Reeves Grove deep within the forest, where a cave dwells filled with shining stones." He took a step forward, and his heat invaded her. "Take me there."

She placed a hand on his chest. "Why do I sense ye ken of this special place?"

Rory's lips twitched in mirth as he bent his head near her ear. "Aye, but I have never visited."

The touch of his breath sent tremors down her

spine. She trembled with desire, and turned her head to meet his lips. Hot and demanding, he devoured her mouth in a searing kiss. By the time he broke free, heat had entered every pore of her body.

"Let us take advantage of the fine day, before the snow descends," he suggested and moved aside.

Erina could only nod and follow as he led both horses out of the stables. He glanced around and then turned to help her mount her animal. After adjusting her fur-lined cloak, she waited for Rory. Soon, they both galloped through the portcullis and headed for the hills.

The glen was over the first ridge of hills, and the higher they ascended, the more the wind slashed at them. The terrain became treacherous at times, and Erina had doubts about continuing farther. She glanced upward as ominous gray clouds gathered and uttered a silent prayer to the Goddess to hold back the threat of rain, or worse, snow.

"One moment the sun graces us with its beauty, and the next, the sky opens and unleashes its torrent of rain upon the land. How could I forget your wise words about the land, Grandmother?" she uttered quietly.

Unexpectedly, a shaft of sunlight pierced through the dismal sky, quickly banishing the impending threat of doom. Erina smiled, and nudged her horse onward along the narrow path. As they made their way to the top, the view opened, and she could see the area beyond a group of oak and yew trees.

Smiling, she pointed. "Do ye see north across the river?"

Rory gave his horse a gentle pat. "Aye, though strange to see the trees woven together."

"The bards mentioned that the druids blessed the

area many centuries ago. Only those with a pure heart may venture inside. Many of the villagers stay away from the place, for fear the priests will judge them as heathens."

"Nae, I dinnae believe the tale."

Erina noted the stern look of concentration on his face. "Then do ye ken the real reason?"

"I sense another purpose for the Fae, although, I cannot fathom the motivation. The area is shrouded in mystery, yet 'tis sacred to our people." He turned his attention to her. "Even with my Fae senses, I am unable to fully understand."

"My grandmother took me, once. She made me recite all the favorite flowers of the Fae inside the glen. Afterwards, I left a gift of honeyed bread." Sighing, Erina cast her sight once more on the trees.

"When did ye visit?" asked Rory softly.

"Two months before her death."

He reached out and grasped her hand. "A fond memory. Now, let us make another one."

The warmth of his touch spread throughout her body, and Erina nodded. "Aye."

After releasing her hand, Rory urged his horse forward, and Erina followed along after him. The land became a blur as they descended the hill and galloped across the land toward the trees. Clouds parted and the sun danced all around the special area. Her heart reveled, and all her worries were cast aside the moment they both entered the glen.

A sense of awe and peace descended over Erina, and she slowed her horse to a light canter. Bird song greeted them as they slowly made their way through the thick cluster of trees. At times, the path narrowed and leaves fluttered down as they passed. As they went deeper, the air warmed considerably. Onward they traveled over bare tree roots, moss, and aging leaves.

When they passed the last oak tree, Erina brought her horse to a stop. A curved path beneath the shade of a yew tree led to a bramble-and-moss-covered entrance to the cave. Rory had already dismounted and was kneeling on the ground. His head was bent as if in prayer. Holding her horse back, she waited. This was his land. Somewhere inside her, Erina sensed the knowledge. She glanced around in all directions. The lush foliage was like no other she had encountered, or remembered. Vibrant wildflowers burst forth from the ground and surrounded him. She blinked in awe and dared not move.

After some time, Rory stood. He reached backward and held out his hand to her. Dropping Oberon's reins, Erina rushed to his side. He wrapped a strong arm around her waist, and pressed his mouth to hers. She succumbed to the forceful domination as his tongue swept inside. Heat pooled in places she remembered from their lovemaking, and her knees weakened. He showered kisses around her lips and along her jaw, whispering words Erina did not understand.

Sweeping her into his arms, he strode toward the cave. She leaned her head against his shoulder and placed a hand upon his chest. His heart beat fierce against her palm as she closed her eyes. There was no doubt what he wanted, since her blood burned with desire for him as well.

As they entered the cave, Rory placed her down. Holding his palm outward, he blew across his skin. Light from the stones illuminated the place in a soft glow. Even the ground they stood upon glittered in soft hues. Water trickled down the stone wall into a small pool and lapped gently over other smooth stones. Erina's mouth dropped open in awe. This was not the same cave she had visited with her grandmother. Yes, then it had a sheen to the place, but never this intense or luminous. It was as if Rory had captured the moon glow and starlight and brought it inside. She turned her gaze to him. His eyes shimmered like stars, and Erina yearned to learn more about him.

"Are ye afraid?" he asked in a hushed tone.

She reached upward and touched his face. "How can I fear such beauty?"

Rory wrapped his arms around her waist. "I dinnae deserve ye, *mo ghrá*, but my love for ye expands to the stars and beyond."

Her lip trembled, and tears misted her eyes. "And I love ye, Rory. I never thought to hear or say such words to anyone."

Taking his thumb, Rory wiped away a tear that trailed down her cheek. "From this day forward, ye are mine, Erina. There will never be another." His last words were smothered on her lips, teasing, coaxing, and sending her senses spiraling.

As his lips seared a path along her cheek, eyelids, and down along her neck, his hands removed the cloak and lacings of her gown and tossed them aside, until she stood in nothing but her shift. Releasing her, he stepped to a polished boulder and without breaking his gaze with hers, removed all of his clothing, including his boots.

Erina feasted her eyes on every inch of the man. "Dinnae move."

He arched a brow mischievously, but complied.

Slipping out of her shoes, she let her toes curl into the soft ground. The air smelled of herbs, intoxicating and heady. Removing her combs and pins from her hair, she shook the mass free, and watched Rory's gaze darken, along with his growing arousal. The power of seduction filled her, and she became brazen.

She moved toward him in unhurried steps. When she stood mere inches in front of him, Erina slipped out of her shift and brushed her fingers across his muscled chest, marveling at the firmness of his body. As she continued her path of exploration, she walked around him—her hands never leaving his hot skin. She heard the indrawn hiss, when she trailed one finger across his bum.

"I will not tolerate much more," he ordered in a hoarse voice.

She chuckled softly and stepped back in front of him. Leaning forward, she swiped her tongue over his nipple.

His growl echoed all around them. When she teased the other one, he grabbed a fistful of hair and tugged gently. As she tried to utter a protest, he covered her mouth hungrily. The kiss was urgent, demanding, and Erina pressed her body against his. Slanting his mouth, he thrust his tongue deep into her, while his hands roamed over her body. With each stroke, her passion grew.

As his hands grasped her bottom, he ordered, "Wrap your legs around me."

When Rory lifted her, Erina complied, and this time she grazed her teeth along the vein in his neck. She had no idea of where he was taking them, but she continued to tease and torment him with her own kisses. When the first splash of water hit her bottom, she moaned. The warm water caressed her body. Without releasing her hold on him, she showered his face with slow, lingering kisses.

"Ye are a temptress," he murmured against her cheek.

"Is it wrong?" she asked.

"I find it…*stimulating*." Rory placed her on the edge of a flat, smooth rock with her feet dangling in the pool. The water hit him below the waist as he stood before her with his hands on her thighs.

His smile raked over her body in delicious sensations. "I have longed to taste ye."

Erina bit her lower lip. Was he really going to taste her? Down below? She shook her head.

He brushed her thighs farther apart. "Aye."

She tried to scoot away, but he held her firm.

"I wish to give ye pleasure." His eyes never left hers as he brushed his hand over her curls.

"*Rory*," she uttered his name on a sigh. "Ye are tormenting me."

Her body quivered from his touch. As she braced her hands on either side of the stone, she was completely under his control and watched in a sensual haze as he trailed kisses up her thigh. When the heat of his mouth touched her most private area, the touch sent a pulsing tremor burning through her body. Erina never imagined such pleasure as his tongue teased and coaxed the flame of desire. She was caught in a spellbound haze, and found it difficult to breathe as the passion grew within and then shattered into thousands of tingling sensations. Erina screamed his name, as he brought her into the water with him. Turning her away from him, he entered her in one thrust—deep and powerful, and she clutched onto the stone for support.

"I take ye here, on the land I can call home," he growled into her ear and squeezed her taut nipple between his fingers.

Erina arched against him, wild and free.

Withdrawing again, he entered her again, and again, each time tracing a sensuous path with his lips over her ear, neck, and along her shoulders. The water slapped all around them, intensifying their need. His body imprisoned hers in a web of growing arousal, and her breathing became labored.

Over and over, Rory proclaimed his love for her and on the last thrust, lights danced in an arc of jeweled colors, and she splintered into a pleasurable abyss.

Rory's cry of release was so powerful, the land shook under her feet, and for a moment, Erina thought she had flown to the stars.

Chapter Twenty

"With each new millennium, the realm of the Fae is bound to shift. If not, then we become as stagnant as the world we left behind."

~*Chronicles of the Fae*

Rory skimmed his fingers in a loving caress along her lower back, treasuring the peace that surrounded them within this sacred place. Erina did not know how unique this haven was for his people. Though the Fae no longer dwelled below, their mark was left in this glen and cave after they made the Hill of Tara their permanent home. Only the echoes of the past Fae whispered among the stones here and something else he was unable to grasp.

Sighing softly, Erina snuggled deeper against him and propped her head upon his chest. "Where are ye?" she asked, tapping a finger between his brow.

He reached for her hand, pressing a kiss into her palm. "As I stated earlier this place is honored among my people."

"Agreed. But can ye share more?"

"When we first arrived thousands of years ago, there were two groups. One settled in Ireland and the other here in Scotland. This place was used for the Fae herbalists to study."

"'Tis more beautiful than I remember."

He kissed the tip of her nose. "Only because I used magic to lift the veil that was hiding its inner beauty."

Erina glanced around. "My grandmother told me tales of how special this area of the land was to the Fae. It was the only knowledge she imparted to me."

Rory propped his arm beneath his head. "Did ye ever ask your grandmother how she came to this knowledge? She was a woman of vast wisdom."

Laughing softly, she replied, "Aye. And do ye ken what she answered?"

"Do tell," he encouraged.

"The Fae spoke to her."

All traces of humor vanished from Rory and he made to sit up. Hugging his knees to his chest, he reached out again with his Fae senses, probing, searching, and seeking an answer. Silence greeted him in return.

"What is wrong?" Erina placed a gentle hand on his back.

Rubbing a hand vigorously over his face, he turned back to her. "There is nae reason the Fae would speak to your grandmother. Dinnae take this wrong, but she posed nae value to our people."

"Humph!" She poked him in the chest. "And mayhap ye are wrong."

He roared with laughter and brought her to his chest. "It would not be the first time, *mo ghrá*."

She ran her tongue over her bottom lip, and desire shot through his veins.

"Why did your people come here?"

Rory sighed. "To share and find new knowledge. Our home world was dying. Our sun was fading, turning our opulent world into a frozen land mass. This world was chosen for its abundant landscape. We thought the people were similar to our own, but once we arrived, we found it quite unexpected. Their minds were like those of our children. Yet, over the years, we helped them to grow, learn, and prosper. Our dragons—"

Startled, Erina squeezed his arm. "*Dragons*?"

He nodded slowly. "Aye. They were benevolent beings. Sadly, all but one was killed in the battles."

"I am sorry." She wiped a hand over her brow and looked away from him.

Gently, Rory cupped her chin. "I sense your uncertainty of my words."

"Nae. 'Tis hard to fathom your world exists, but I do believe ye." She cupped a hand over her mouth to stifle the nervous laughter. "Goodness, if any heard our conversation, we both would be burned at the stake."

Images of Erina's body bound at the stake ripped through Rory's mind, and he crushed her body to him. He would kill any who harmed her. "Dinnae speak those words, nor think them."

"Sorry." Her apology was muffled against his chest.

"There is nae need to apologize. But words have a way of drifting onto the winds for others to hear."

Erina leaned back and studied his features. As she brushed away a lock of hair, she shivered. "Ye are correct."

Rory reached for her cloak and wrapped it around her shoulders. His hand encountered a hard object within the folds and he withdrew a jar. "Is this a special medicinal ointment?"

"A gift from Brother Michael. Rose syrup. He

brought several with him."

He lifted the item, noting its rich hue. "Can ye not make the syrup? I have seen your garden and the stunning roses."

Snorting, she took the jar from his hand. "Do ye ken the cost of sugar? Sadly, I am unable to make do with the short supply I have."

"And the monk is able to procure a great amount of sugar?"

Smiling, she replied, "Nae. He has found a way to mix a small amount of sugar with his special honey. 'Tis delicious."

Rory cocked a brow in amusement. Retrieving the jar, he opened the lid and dipped a finger inside. After scooping a small amount of the sticky syrup, he pushed the cloak from her shoulders. "I must sample this fare."

Erina's eyes grew wide. "Wha…what are ye doing?"

Ignoring her question, he wiped his finger over her pert nipple. She gasped as he cupped her breast. His mouth descended, and he savored the sweetness of the syrup mixed with her own scent. Desire tore through him, and Rory craved more. This time, he used two fingers to scoop out more of the delectable treat. Smearing it on the other breast, he caught her gaze— hot, seductive, and he bent his head to lavish and feast on the other breast.

His hands shook to be on her body, so Rory placed the jar on the ground. However, Erina surprised him by pushing him back.

Reaching for the jar, she was the one to take some syrup using her fingers. "My turn," she demanded. "If ye will permit me."

He fought the urge to toss her backward and thrust deep inside her. "And where shall ye begin?"

The blood pounded in his ears when she lowered her gaze to his swollen cock. How he longed to have her luscious lips over him.

"Lean back," she ordered.

"Why not," he suggested and pointed to his ribs.

She shook her lovely head. "Nae. Ye put your mouth on my intimate area—"

"Ye did not like it?"

Placing a finger over his lips to silence him, she replied, "Aye, most assuredly. This is why 'tis my turn to give ye the same pleasure. Is it not what ye wish, too?"

Ye have no idea my thoughts. "Then let us not keep ye."

Resting his forearms against the ground, he watched as she lightly smeared the syrup on his swollen cock. By the hounds, Rory thought he was going to spill his seed right then and there, and he hissed.

"Did I hurt ye?"

"Nae," he gritted out. "Do what ye must or I will take ye now."

Her smile turned wicked, and slowly she descended over him, teasing him with pleasurable strokes of her tongue. The electric shock scorched through his body, and Rory thought he was going to die right there. The pure ecstasy of her hot mouth, combined with her hair brushing against his thighs had him spiraling to another plane. His fingers dug into the soft ground, fighting the urge to take her swiftly as she continued to explore and give him pleasure.

She was a seductive siren. A temptress who rivaled

none in his existence. A vixen who made his blood boil, and he was hopelessly out of control.

As the desire reached a fever, Rory growled, "Nae more."

When Erina lifted her head, her eyes blazed with desire. He grasped her around the waist and brought her down upon his thick cock. They both cried out in unison as their bodies joined in a fusion of heat and passion. With each thrust, Erina found her own rhythm, and Rory grasped her hips, grinding harder into her. He tried to maintain control, enjoying the vision of her riding him. Yet, the raw act of possession overtook him, and his body began to vibrate with liquid fire, finally succumbing to a powerful release that sent them both spiraling to rapture.

Erina collapsed against his chest, and he wrapped his arms around her quaking body. Time slowed inside the cave with the only sound of the water lapping over the stones. Wetness grazed his neck. "Are ye weeping? Did I hurt ye?" Concern filled him, and he cursed himself for taking her again so soon.

She refused to lift her head. "What now, Rory?"

"Look at me, lass."

Slowly, she met his gaze. Her lips trembled. "Are ye leaving come the morn with Ewan and Catherine?"

"Nae!" He cupped her face tenderly. "When we return, I will speak with your brother privately."

"Ye will?"

"*Mo ghrá*…have I not professed my love for ye already? Ye are mine. Nae other shall claim ye." He brushed away a lone tear that had escaped. "Will ye marry me? I have nae lands and cannot return to my own people. All I have to offer is my body for protection, my mind to offer ye wisdom, my hands to earn a living, and my love. Will it be enough?"

"I, Erina MacIntyre, take ye, Rory, as my husband. Here in this sacred place, ye are mine. What I have is yours."

His heart burst with love for her, and he took her hand, placing it in the middle of his chest. "A Fae's heart is centered to his body. This is where we are joined. Nae other can remove what has been sealed for all eternity."

Removing her hand, Erina bent and kissed where his heart beat for only one—her. "Then I seal my love with a kiss over your heart. May we walk *together* on this journey."

Rory rolled her onto her back and captured her sigh with his mouth, further sealing their love.

****

The wind slapped at the lovers as they hurriedly made their way back toward Kileburn. Darkness slipped through the sky, and Rory feared the elements would open and deluge them with a torrential downpour. He wanted to remain safe and warm inside the cave with Erina, but sadly, they had to venture back to civilization.

By the time they entered through the portcullis, the first drop of rain splattered the ground. Bringing their mounts to the entrance, Rory quickly dismounted and helped Erina off her horse.

"Let me help ye," she argued, trying to take Oberon's reins.

"Go to your chambers," he ordered, and silenced her with a kiss—not caring if they were caught.

She grumbled a protest, but complied.

Rory made his way to the stables and tended to the animals. One of the lads jumped down from a bale of hay and handed him a brush.

"Were ye the one with Lady MacIntyre?" he asked, wiping his nose on his sleeve.

He gave him a passing glance. "Was someone asking for her?"

"Aye, Laird Cameron."

Bastard. "Hand me some fresh hay." Tempering his fury, Rory moved aside.

"He acts as if he owns Kileburn," grumbled the lad and handed Rory some hay.

Dumping some in the corners of both stalls, he asked, "What is your name?"

"Stephen, sir."

Rory smiled, handing the boy the brush. "Can ye finish tending to both the horses? Or am I asking too much of ye?"

Stephen puffed out his chest. "'Tis an honor for ye. I can also keep an eye on the Cameron, if ye reckon."

"Am I to pay ye coin for this service?"

The lad jumped onto a nearby bench. "Nae. I am well taken care of here at Kileburn."

Rory's admiration grew for Graham. He placed a firm hand on the lad's shoulder. "Seek me out anytime."

"Thank ye, sir."

As he strode forth from the stables, Rory swiftly made his way into the castle and to his chamber to prepare for a feast. In truth, he had to mull over the right words to present to Graham come the morning. They would be the most important of his life. Would he give his blessing to the union with his sister?

Upon entering his room, he closed the door and leaned against the wood. "Forgive me, Mother Danu, for this is the only path I ken is true. My home is now in this world." If only Aidan Kerrigan were here to give him counsel. How did the greatest Fenian Warrior accept a life among humans? Without his powers? Yet, his mentor did forge a life with the woman he loved and cherished.

Rubbing a hand over his brow, Rory hastily changed into fresh clothing and left for the banquet hall.

Unruly laughter reached him as he descended the stairs. Darren stood off to the side of the entrance of the hall, a frown marring his features. Approaching the man, Rory gave him a curt nod.

"What is the source of the amusement?"

Darren shifted uneasily. "Laird Cameron has taken it upon himself to alter the bard's tale with bawdy words."

"Are there any women present?" Rory glanced inside the hall, noting the Cameron was already deep into his cup and staggering.

"Lady Catherine has retreated to her chamber, and some of the other women have departed the hall."

"And Erina?"

Darren glanced sideways at him. "Not here…yet."

"He should be removed from the feasting," suggested Rory, and folded his arms over his chest.

"Along with the other two lairds. They remain silent, but encourage him with drink and laughter." Darren bit out a curse. "And to think Graham had thought them possible suitors."

"We are in agreement," Rory muttered.

Darren kept his focus on crowd when he said, "A

word of caution, MacGregor."

"Aye?" Though Rory surmised he knew what the man was going to state.

Straightening his tunic, Darren turned his attention to Rory. "If ye ever bring harm or hurt Erina, I will take my blade to your heart. Do ye ken my meaning?"

Ye are not her protector! "Dinnae worry. Her safekeeping is my concern." Without waiting for a reply from the man, Rory stepped around him to greet the vision descending the stairs.

Smiling fully, she took his outstretched hand, and he placed it in the crook of his arm.

"Darren? Are ye not joining us?" Erina asked, pausing just inside the doors.

"Another time," he replied, and walked away.

"He seems distressed."

Rory shrugged. "Apparently there is trouble already festering with Laird Cameron."

She sighed and glanced around the hall. "I look forward to the day he and the others leave Kileburn."

"If ye are searching for Catherine, she has already retired for the evening."

Erina tugged on his arm. "She and I made a pledge to—"

He placed a finger over her lips and bent near her ear. "Her father thought it wise when the Cameron took to his lewd singing."

"Then mayhap I should leave."

"Have nae worries, I shall remain at your side. Let us go greet your brother, and then I will escort ye to your chambers."

He noted the rosy glow spreading across her face and neck. "Will ye join me?"

"Nae. I shall let ye get some rest."

She halted their progress and looked aghast at him.

Rory fought the smile forming on his lips. He knew her body was sore from their lovemaking, and he battled the urge to recant his words. After removing her hand from his arm, he gestured her forward and nodded to others in passing. "Dinnae fear, *mo ghrá*, I will come wake ye before the first ray of light dances across your chamber's floor. Will that suffice?"

Her eyes flashed with azure fire. "Then it will be a *verra* long night for both of us."

Chapter Twenty-One

*"Within a mirror a human can see their own
reflection. But when a Fae glances inward, they are
able to witness a lifetime of failures."*

~Chronicles of the Fae

Erina wandered aimlessly in the garden, hugging
her arms around herself. She sighed, recalling earlier
memories of Rory sneaking into her chamber and
waking her with heated kisses. It was torture having to
endure the long night without him by her side. How she
had been tempted to make her way to his room and be
the one to surprise him. But she fought the desire, and
when her eyes could no longer remain open, she had
drifted into an abyss of pleasurable dreams. Only the
dream became a reality when she woke with him doing
glorious things with his mouth on her skin.

She paused under a trellis. Her love for Rory
consumed her. Now, her nerves skittered as she waited
for him in the garden. He had requested to speak with
her brother in private and reassuring all would be well.

"There ye are." Catherine came striding toward
her, a smile on her face. Quickly embracing Erina, she
whispered. "I ken 'tis a wondrous match."

Confused, Erina leaned back. "To what?"

Her friend poked her on the arm. "To your
marriage to Rory."

Erina blinked. "Ye have heard the news?"

"Aye. Rory spoke with my father last evening."

Moving away from her friend, Erina plucked a dead leaf from a nearby branch. "I love him with all my heart." She let it flutter to the ground and turned back toward her friend. "It might not be the match my brother wanted, but I pray he welcomes this one."

Catherine grasped her hands. "Trust me, I believe I ken your brother these past few weeks. He has spoken nothing but kind words about Rory. And why would he object to your happiness? Dinnae fret. Besides, ye have a voice as well. Tell him your heart. At least ye will not be chained to one of those horrid men we dined with these past few evenings. I for one, was delighted to see them depart this morning."

"Aye. There were moments when I thought I was being hunted as prey."

"The Cameron was the worst!" snapped Catherine and released her hands. "He tried to pinch me in passing."

"And I did not care for the silent looks from the other two lairds. In particular, one whose smile never reached his dark eyes." Erina shivered slightly.

"They are gone. If our paths do cross, at least one of us shall be a married woman."

Erina stared at her. She would always treasure their time spent together. "I will miss ye, my friend."

Catherine embraced her. "Ye must promise to send me letters with all the details."

"I promise," she reassured.

"Lady Erina! I have found ye!" A young lass scampered toward them. "Ye must bring your herbs," she begged as she tugged on Erina's gown.

"Goodness, child. What is so urgent, Clara?" asked Erina, clasping the child's hand.

"My brother cut his hand and is wailing like a banshee. 'Tis naught but a wee scratch, but mother bade me to seek ye out."

"Did ye run all the way from your home?" asked Catherine.

Clara nodded, her golden locks bouncing in the soft light.

Erina placed a comforting hand on her shoulder. "Go tell your mother I will bring her some comfrey and other healing herbs."

"Aye." She started forward and then turned halfway. "Thank ye."

"I think I'll go fetch those herbs. Their home is near the river and not far." Erina rubbed her hands together to ward off the chill. "Be well, my friend."

Catherine stepped back. "Do ye want me to pass along a message to your brother where ye are going?"

"Oh, aye. Thank ye."

"I wish ye much happiness." After blowing her a kiss, Catherine walked back toward the castle.

Smiling, Erina continued on the garden path, which led to a small stone cottage she had used for collecting her herbs. Smoke from the hearth floated into the brisk morning air, and her steps hastened. Upon opening the door, she spied Brother Michael tending to a pot over the flames. He was singing a song about a lost maiden, and she chuckled softly.

He glanced over his shoulder and waved her over to him. "Thank the saints 'tis ye."

"Were ye expecting another?" Erina asked, closing the door behind her.

"I am making a batch of mead and dinnae want to be disturbed." He gestured to the pot. "I had to procure this vessel from the kitchens and had nae desire to be questioned by the keen eyes of the cook."

Erina peered inside the pot. "I thought she was your friend."

"Aye, but if she suspected what I was planning on doing, then the woman would demand to watch me like a hawk. Furthermore, I would rather have a peaceful time of reflection while I'm tending to the brew."

She reached for a basket and began to peruse the herbs hanging on pegs. "Is this how ye make mead? I considered the manner to be more laborious."

"'Tis only the beginning. I have to boil the honey and water together. The finished product will not be ready for tasting for a few days."

"Do your plans include staying at Kileburn through Midwinter?"

The monk eyed her with curiosity and stepped away from his pot. "Should I?"

She turned away. "It was only a question."

Brother Michael tapped her shoulder. "I approve of the union of ye and Rory."

Erina gasped. "Does everyone ken? He is only now speaking with Graham."

Laughter bubbled forth, and he gestured her toward a chair. As he settled down across from her, he placed his hands on his thighs. "I am nae fool. Simply because I choose to live a celibate life as a monk does not mean I am blind to the ways of love. I have seen the way he looks at ye. And ye at him."

Her face heated, and she wove her fingers around the basket handle. "He is a good man." *What would ye think if ye knew he was a Fae? Would ye call him a demon?* "Do ye think my brother will object?"

Brother Michael sighed and leaned back in his chair. "He has only wanted your happiness. In truth, does the MacGregor have lands? Money?"

"None," she blurted out and placed the basket on the table. "But we can live at my cottage."

"Do ye love him?"

"Aye. With all my heart."

"Och, there is your answer, and one ye can state. Furthermore, I am positive Ewan spoke well of Rory to your brother—"

The door crashed open, startling both of them. Abruptly standing, Brother Michael stepped in front of Erina. "Can I be of service to ye?"

As she twisted in her chair, Erina clutched a hand to her chest. The man's bulk blocked the entrance, and his look was one of hatred. He stepped aside, allowing another man to enter, and this time icy tendrils prickled her skin. She couldn't recall his name, but she would never forget the face. He was one of the visiting lairds. A man who uttered very few words, yet, his eyes haunted her whenever she entered a room.

Standing slowly, she tried to keep her voice calm. "Did ye not leave with Laird Cameron?"

Brother Michael narrowed his gaze. "Ahh…ye are one of the lairds traveling with the Cameron. Greetings. Pray forgive me for not remembering your name."

The man snarled. "'Tis Sinclair." He leveled a dirk at the monk. "Are ye working with the *witch*?"

Erina gasped and took a step backwards. Her pulse began to beat erratically at the threatening in his deep voice.

"I can assure ye, Lady Erina is not a witch. If ye have nae other questions, I recommend ye take your leave," protested Brother Michael.

Instantly, Sinclair took a fist to Brother Michael's face. Blood gushed forth from his nose, and the monk staggered.

"Ye bastard," hissed Erina, reaching for a cloth off the table. "How dare ye harm this man."

After pushing the monk out of the way, Sinclair grabbed her forearm. "Anyone who protects ye will suffer the lash." He gave a curt nod to the other man. "Bind the monk. We shall take him along. Bishop Stewart will judge what to do with him. And make sure her brother is placed securely somewhere."

A cold knot formed in her stomach, and the man's grip tightened. She clenched her hand until her nails bit into her palm. "What do ye want?"

"Ye are to be brought forth for your crimes."

She swallowed, trying to loosen the lump of fear in her throat. "Nae," she mumbled.

"Cease this!" Brother Michael ordered.

Sinclair again leveled the tip of his blade against the monk's throat. "If ye speak another word, I will be forced to remove your tongue."

Erina shook her head at her friend, pleading with him to remain silent. Lifting her chin in defiance, she said, "Then let me meet my accuser."

The man's laugh was sinister. "Trust me, ye shall meet them *all*."

As he shoved her forward, Erina's heart constricted with terror.

****

Clasping his hands firmly behind his back, Rory

waited patiently for Graham to speak. He had spoken his heart to Erina's brother, telling him he would protect and cherish her always. At first, the man glared daggers at him when he professed his undying love, but as he continued pouring out his soul, the man's features softened. Never in his entire existence did Rory sense an unsteady path or future. He needed the assurance and blessing from Graham.

Yet, within his heart, he held fast to the one truth—his love for Erina.

If Graham prohibited the union, he worried what risk he would dare to take to persuade her to leave this part of her home. They might have to flee to Ireland—live among the lush hills near Tara. His mind sought to find another solution, since a life without his beloved was not an option.

Graham braced his hands on the window ledge. "What will ye do for coin? How will ye survive?"

"I can work the land. Furthermore, I can build a smithy away from the cottage."

The man snorted and pushed away from the ledge. "Why would anyone seek ye out? There is already one here at Kileburn."

"Currently, ye are without a blacksmith," countered Rory. He moved toward the table and picked up the leather sheath containing a sword. Striding back, he presented the blade to Graham. "I have fashioned this for ye. It has been forged by the fires and waters from Kileburn. 'Tis my gift to ye."

Taking the sword, Graham unsheathed the blade and held it up to the light. "Magnificent. Where did ye find the stone?" Bringing it closer for inspection, he ran a finger over the gem on the hilt.

"A token from my home. I considered it wise to bind the union with a blending of both families."

Graham nodded slowly and returned the blade to its sheath. Securing it against his side, he beamed with pleasure. "Ye honor me, MacGregor. Nevertheless, I do have my concerns with this marriage."

Rory started to interject, but Graham held up a hand to stay his words.

He grasped Rory's shoulder. "Ewan has shared how his family gave protection to yours centuries ago. In addition, he declared how ye have always been loyal to the MacGregor clan—a quality I admire. Therefore, if my sister is truly in love with ye, I can find nae more objections. Ye ken I must speak with her?"

The tension he had been holding in check eased and Rory smiled. "There is nae argument from me."

"Good." Releasing his hold, Graham went to a cabinet. "Would ye care for a dram of *uisge beatha*?"

"Most definitely."

"'Tis a fine bottle from Ewan." After pouring some into two cups, Graham handed one to him.

"Then it will be one worth tasting," Rory commented.

"He has not shared it with ye before?"

Rory took a sip, savoring the amber liquid as it slipped down his throat. "Aye, aye."

Soft knocking interrupted any further discussion and Graham moved to the door. Rory listened as one of his men handed him a missive. He waited as Graham opened and read the note. After giving thanks to the messenger, Graham closed the door and tossed the letter on a nearby table.

"Apparently, Erina's healing remedies are required

from one of the villagers."

Rory tossed back the rest of the drink. "She is a gifted healer."

Graham looked at him skeptically. "Did ye ken they have given her the name of White Healer?"

A flash of memory entered his mind. He recalled someone calling her thus. Rubbing a hand over his brow, he tried to bring forth the person, but with little success. "Nae," he lied.

"I cannot find fault in what she does for the people, but the land is rife with fear over the old beliefs." Graham refilled his glass and held the bottle outward. "More?"

Nodding, Rory strode over and placed his cup on the table. "There has been strife over religious beliefs since the beginning of time."

"How true," murmured Graham. "There are times when I worry they will come after her."

Rory retrieved his cup and leaned against the table. "Never, while I breathe."

Graham pointed a finger at him. "On that we can concur. Nevertheless, ye may want to consider lands farther north. I have nae desire to see Erina leave her home, but I deem she'll be safer there."

"Or in Ireland," suggested Rory, draining his cup.

"Do ye honestly reckon the situation less volatile over there?"

There was one place Rory once considered taking Erina. Yet, his own world was forbidden to humans. And now, to him as well. Placing the cup back down, he walked to the hearth and gazed into the flames. "Regardless of the conflict, life shall go on. Seasons pass, crops flourish, and people continue to dwell, be it in harmony or turmoil."

"Ye sound like Brother Michael."

Or a druid. Rory glanced over his shoulder and shrugged.

"Care to join me in the lists?" Graham started for the door.

Rory turned around. "Are ye sure ye can take the force of my blows after a few drinks?"

Graham roared with laughter as he opened the door. "'Tis fire for the battle."

Shaking his head in mirth, he followed the man. "Your confidence will be your undoing, MacIntyre."

When the man remained silent, Rory continued, "I have often heard such words from—"

As he came to a halt in the corridor, his eyes blazed with fury when a blade was swiftly leveled against his side. Another man held a dirk to his friend's throat and another stood off to the side.

"What do ye want?" demanded Graham.

"Move," ordered one of their captors.

Rory clenched his fingers, waiting for the opportunity to take down his foe. The blade dug into his backside as they steadily made their way along the corridor. As they entered another section of the castle, he frowned, unsure of where they were going.

"Again, I ask, what do ye want?"

"Silence," hissed the man behind Rory.

As they approached a narrow archway, another man stepped forth and opened the steel door.

"Ye seem to ken your way around my home." Graham's voice grated harshly.

They descended a stone path, which was dimly lit. Ducking under an archway, Rory grumbled a curse as he looked around the dank place.

"Welcome to the dungeons of Kileburn," snapped one of the men. He removed the sword from Graham's side and flung it across the stone floor.

Their captors shoved them inside and slammed the iron gate. The sound reverberated all around them, and Rory fought the wave of power. He could not risk Graham witnessing who he was, and tried to center himself.

One of the bastards moved forward. "Ye are hereby ordered to remain locked inside here."

"Whom do ye take your orders from?" demanded Graham. "Surely, ye are not their leader."

The man smacked his blade against the bars. "Laird Sinclair *and* Bishop Stewart."

Graham gripped the bars. "*Roger* Sinclair has just signed his death warrant. But I cannot fathom why the bishop is involved with capturing me and my friend."

"We aim to cleanse the land of the evil and heathen practices. Some would claim ye give sanctuary to them." Turning, the man made to leave.

"Ye are a dead man. Heed my words!" shouted Graham.

Rory swept his gaze over each of them as he braced his hands on the cold steel. His lips curled in disgust, and he committed to memory every detail of their pathetic features. For when the time came, Rory would see them all die.

As the main dungeon door slammed on them, Rory glanced sideways at Graham. "Where *exactly* is Erina?"

His friend wiped a hand over his brow. "Not far enough." He let out a bark of nervous laughter. "Though for once, I'm grateful she's outside the grounds of Kileburn."

"We need to find her and quickly."

"Aye, agreed. But first, we must free ourselves," stated Graham.

In that silent moment, Rory made a solemn vow the past would not repeat itself. He would do all in his power to make sure his beloved came to no harm.

This was his pledge as a Fenian Warrior.

His oath as a Fae.

His right as her future husband.

Chapter Twenty-Two

"The light of a Fae's love can alter the stars."
~Chronicles of the Fae

"For the love of God, I beg ye to let the lady ride one of your horses," pleaded Brother Michael.

Erina shook her head. "Dinnae waste your words on the man. He cares nothing for me."

"Your shoes will be in tatters soon. This is an outrage. I have nae objection to being pulled along by a horse over the rough terrain, but ye are a woman."

"Regardless, if ye continue to lash out with words, the man has threatened to remove your tongue. I have nae desire to see ye come to harm."

Her friend fumed and gave her a curt nod. "Be warned, the moment I come upon this Bishop Stewart, I shall state my grievances. By what right does he fetch a lady from her home? Ye are nae more a witch than I am. They continue to fear those who have the healing ways. Instead of learning from them, they would rather banish them."

Erina stumbled over a tree root, but quickly righted herself. "Do ye ken this bishop?" She tried to keep her focus on the road ahead of them.

"Nae. He might be new to the area. In truth, many are appointed to oversee these rash accusations by the villagers. Dinnae fear, I tend to object to any who accuse ye of being a witch."

An ache of despair wove a thread inside Erina. As much as she felt comforted by the monk's words, there was doubt any would listen to him. If Laird Sinclair did not believe him, why would a bishop? How did her life turn upside down in one day? The day had bloomed with hope and love and now looked to end in fear and anguish. A lump of sadness settled in her throat, and tears misted her eyes. The wind slapped at her, ripping away the fragile threads of hope Erina was desperately struggling to keep close to her heart.

She lifted her head to the stark bleak sky. *Hear me Goddess. Send out my plea for help to the man who holds my heart. Let Rory come to my aid. I deem ye can send this message. Bring him to me as the man I love.*

Once again, she tripped, and this time fell to the ground. The horse and rider continued to drag her along the arduous path. Erina struggled to stand, but the effort proved futile.

"Stop! I beg ye!" Brother Michael shouted and yanked on his bindings.

Sinclair held up his hand to halt their progress. Giving a quick glance over his shoulder, he barked out orders to help Erina.

One of the younger guards dismounted and came to her rescue. "Are ye hurt, Lady Erina?"

She wanted to scream at the man, but held back when she noted concern in his eyes and voice. "Nae, I shall be fine."

The man helped her to standing, and she winced. "Ye are in pain."

She wiggled her foot, trying to ease the discomfort. "These shoes are not meant for walking over rough land."

Brother Michael stood near her. "Unless ye are prepared to drag her to the bishop, I suggest ye place her on a horse, Sinclair."

The man glowered at them. Pointing a sword at the guard, Sinclair ordered, "She can ride your horse and *ye* can walk."

"Aye," mumbled the guard.

As the man started to remove his dirk, Sinclair yelled, "Nae! Undo the rope from the saddle, but keep her hands bound together."

After quickly complying, the guard led Erina over to his horse. Taking a hold of the pommel, he eased her onto his animal and made sure the rope was secure.

"What is your horse's name?" she asked.

He assessed her before answering. Stroking the nose of the animal, he replied, "Ryden."

"A good Norse name. And yours?"

The guard swiftly looked away. "I reckon it would do nae harm, but I have been ordered to give ye none."

"Can we proceed?" Sinclair bellowed, and gestured for the group to continue onward.

Giving her a slight bow, the guard moved away.

Brother Michael approached from the side. "Apparently, Sinclair has put in them the terror of even speaking their names to ye."

Erina snorted in disgust. "What a foolish man. I have nae magic over a *name*." Biting back her next words, she recalled the love charm she wove for Betty and Mairi. Did she not utter the names of each, along with the men they desired over the herbs? Aye, she had. Did that make her a witch? "Nae," she mumbled.

"Dinnae worry, Erina. Your brother and Rory will

find us. Rest assured, they will come to our aid, and God help these men when they do."

His words did little to comfort her. Time receded as they continued on their journey. Hours had already bled away. How would they know where to begin their search? And what if harm had come to Graham back at Kileburn—or even to Rory.

As if hearing her unspoken words, Brother Michael said, "If I ken your brother, he has already plotted out a plan of escape. They cannot keep a MacIntyre secure for verra long, and they said nothing about Rory. Therefore, I'm confident help is arriving soon."

She tried to remain hopeful and gave him a weak smile.

As they trudged along the road, Erina noted their surroundings. When they emerged from the wooded area, her last tendril of hope faded away. In the distance, the imposing stone cathedral loomed before them. A place where only a few years ago, several women and men were burned at the stake for witchcraft in the courtyard. She was not a seer, nor a witch, but the signs were there for her to witness.

"Calder Cathedral," she uttered softly. "It will be my place of death."

Lightning splintered the gray sky, and the first drop of rain slashed across Erina's face.

****

Rory paced their small prison in an effort to calm his fury. With all the power at his fingertips, he was duty-bound not to use magic to free himself or Graham. Precious hours had slipped by and yet, his friend remained composed on the cold stone floor.

"I do wish ye would take a seat," suggested

Graham.

Coming to a halt before him, Rory fisted his hands on his hips. "Ye seem mighty calm for what has transpired."

The man shrugged. "I am merely counting down the minutes until we can depart."

Rory dropped his hands. "Would ye care to share this grand scheme of how we can break free?" *If ye don't, I shall break down the walls of this prison, regardless the cost of revealing who I am to ye.*

Standing, Graham went to the far back wall and pointed upward. "Do ye see the lion's head?"

Narrowing his eyes, Rory angled his head. A sliver of light bounced off the wall, reflecting the carved animal embedded on the stone. "Aye."

"If ye push on his mouth, the wall will open."

He snapped his gaze to the man. "Then why did we have to wait? We could have fled hours ago."

Graham rubbed a hand down the back of his neck. "The passageway leads to the Great Hall, and I judged it best to give our captors time to search for Erina. I did not want to risk entering the hall surrounded by more of the enemy." He tapped a finger to the wall. "My great-great-grandfather had them build this passageway after he was imprisoned by a raiding clan." Chuckling softly, he added, "He vowed never to be imprisoned in his own dungeon again."

"Ye have many secret corridors within Kileburn." Rory surveyed the man.

Graham's features hardened. "Explain."

"There is one in your kitchens, the wolf marks the entrance."

"Which leads to my chambers," snapped Graham.

Rory gave him a cool regard. "If ye must ken, I was assisting Erina on the day we both found the passageway. She had fallen into the river on the day Ewan and Catherine arrived. She did not want to arrive the way she looked and bring disgrace on ye." He moved away from the intense gaze of Graham. "We did not remain long inside your chambers."

"Any other ones ye have found?" Graham's tone almost a growl.

I have nae desire to have my head served on a platter, if ye knew Erina and I had been using them to go back and forth between our chambers. Pressing his palm onto the lion's mouth, Rory replied, "Nae, but I am confident there are many more." The wall opened with a groan, revealing a dank, dark cavern. "And yet, another obstacle."

Graham pushed him aside. "God's blood! How are we going to make our way through?"

"With cautious steps," suggested Rory and peered over his shoulder. "Let me lead the way."

"If ye stumble and break a limb, Erina will take my head."

"And if ye break your neck, your sister will never forgive me. Trust me, I can see well in darkened surroundings. I am used to traveling at night."

After finally relenting, Graham gestured him forward.

Rory stepped inside the narrow entry and let his eyes adjust magically. He swept the surrounding area. The walls glistened with moisture and rats scurried out of his way. As he extended his eyesight beyond the walls and corridor, he came upon the Great Hall. The path curved and dipped, but nothing hazardous to mar their way out of the prison.

"Are ye praying for light?" asked Graham.

Rory fought the urge to knock the man out, dump him over his shoulder, and magically transport them both out of the dismal cell. "Follow closely."

Taking small, steady steps, Rory waved his hands over the ground, absorbing the moisture. He had no wish to have Graham slip and injure himself.

"Bloody hell," hissed the man.

"Agreed, though I believe Hell is hotter."

Graham snorted as they continued to move along the passageway. The area narrowed considerably and several times, they were forced to bend low, making it more difficult for them. When they approached the wall leading to the hall, Rory placed his hands along the stone edges.

"Is there another animal's head?"

"Fortunately, I have never ventured down this path, so I cannot say," Graham responded dryly.

Rory grumbled a curse and searched with his fingers and eyes. Frustration gnawed at him, so he whispered ancient words, and the wall opened a fraction. Light splintered through, and he diverted his sight to the right ledge and smiled. When he pressed both his hands on the raven's head, the wall opened up fully. The passageway exited next to the massive hearth.

Both men remained rooted in the darkness while Rory scanned the hall. Tables, benches, and chairs had been tossed without regard. Food, drink, and broken pottery littered the ground, and the doors leading out left open. Yet, not one soul was present.

Rory cautiously made his way into the hall,

continuing to sweep his gaze for any sound or movement. He glanced over his shoulder. "Let me check the outside corridor. Stay here."

"I am not a meek lass," Graham argued.

Clenching his jaw, he pointed to the exposed entrance they had emerged from only a few moments earlier. "If we close it now, we risk someone walking in here and witnessing our escape. I want to clear the way first."

"Go, then."

Rory ran swiftly to the entrance. He examined the corridors, taking note of the silence and then came upon two slain guards. Closing his eyes, he let his Fae senses search along the perimeter of the castle until he could go no farther. Rory stepped back inside and nodded to Graham to seal the passageway.

"Too quiet," Graham commented as he walked past Rory and headed out of the castle.

Rory followed and surveyed the area. The guards were missing from their posts, and a chill of foreboding slipped through him. He brushed past Graham as he sprinted to the stables. When he entered, a cat hissed at him in passing. All the horses were in their stalls, including the one he had hoped was gone. Oberon.

Wiping a hand over his brow, he left the stables. Graham met him halfway. "What is wrong?"

"All the horses are accounted for."

The color drained from Graham's features. "Erina's horse, too?"

"Aye! Would Erina venture without her horse to the woman's home?"

A muscle twitched in Graham's jaw. "Nae! The cottage is too far to go on foot. If they took a blade to two of my men, then I fear for anyone else who defied them."

Rory stormed past him and entered the castle. Not caring who now heard them, he began shouting and opening doors. Taking the stone stairs three at a time, he continued searching out any living soul at Kileburn. Empty silence greeted him. His frustration, along with the dark shadows within his mind grew. He had thought her safe—far away.

He barely registered Graham's shouting and shoved away the turmoil within his body and mind. After retracing his steps along the corridor, he ran down the stairs. He followed the sounds of voices beyond the kitchens. As he rounded the bend in the corridor, Rory came across one of the guards as he stumbled free from Kileburn's cellar. Blood seeped from a wound to the man's head, but he gave a weak smile to Rory in passing.

Graham was assisting one of the women, reassuring her that the threat of danger had passed.

"Did anyone witness Lady Erina leaving the castle?" Rory asked, trying to keep his voice calm.

Many shook their heads solemnly as they made their way out of the cellar.

"Not one soul?" He raked a hand through his hair. Someone tugged on his plaid, and Rory glanced down at the wee lass.

"I saw Lady Erina walking along the path to the herb cottage."

Bending down on one knee, he took her hand in his. "Was this earlier in the morn?"

She shrugged. "Right before the bad men came."

"Thank ye." Rory placed a kiss across her knuckles

and stood.

"The cottage is at the eastern end of the garden," offered Graham. "Let me account for everyone and speak with my guards. Afterwards, I shall meet ye in the stables."

He gave the man a curt nod and took off toward the herb cottage. His steps slowed as he approached the structure, and his hands shook, fearing what he would find inside the place. When he placed his hand on the door, thunder rolled in a deafening echo.

Paying no heed to the elements, he stormed inside the cottage.

His heart pounded furiously as he tried to control his emotions. As he took in his surroundings, he slowly made his way around the room. Several items were strewn across the floor, and the fire in the hearth had dwindled to embers. The scent of honey, herbs, and blood assaulted him, and Rory staggered. *Must not be hers*.

He clenched his jaw and lifted his palm outward bringing the scent inside him. There was only one person he could recognize from the blood, and he prayed with all his might that it was not Erina's.

Immediately, relief coursed through him, and he leaned against the table. "Thank the Gods." He was unable to determine whose blood it belonged to, but it did not belong to his beloved.

Making one final pass over the area, Rory then proceeded toward the stables. Before he entered the bailey, he snapped his fingers. His sword appeared magically belted at his side, along with a dirk secured to his back.

Bending down, he scooped up some dirt into his

hand. "Help me to find Erina, Mother Danu. Lead a clear path for me to find her. Until I reach her, I beg ye to keep her safe from harm." Standing, Rory leveled his gaze outward. "If ye are unable to do so, then turn your face from my wrath. For there is no one who can stop me, if any harm comes to the woman who holds my soul."

Rory waited for two heartbeats and then tossed the dirt out into the air. "I am coming for ye, *mo ghrá*."

Chapter Twenty-Three

"A tiny spark of hope can illuminate the Fae soul with light from a trillion stars."
~*Chronicles of the Fae*

Regardless of the frigid, dark cell, sweat beaded across Erina's brow. The place reeked of bodily fluids, and rats continued to scurry past her and Brother Michael as they sat on the cold floor. One torch flickered outside their prison, casting ominous shadows. They slithered across the stones, as if seeking to wrap their tendrils around her neck and relieving her of all air. Between the stench, darkness, and her unknown future, Erina found the walls closing in around her.

"I believe I am going to be ill," she uttered in a weak voice, and turned away from Brother Michael. After heaving what little she had in her stomach, Erina leaned back against the stone wall. "Forgive me."

Brother Michael placed a cool hand on her forehead. "I understand the foul smell is making ye queasy, but ye need to breathe. Taking in shallow breaths only increases the fear ye are holding back and will make ye weak."

"'Tis vile."

"Agreed. But ye are strong, *Erina MacIntyre*."

"Aye, how could I ever forget I am a MacIntyre," she uttered with mock severity. She wiped the spittle from her mouth on the back of her sleeve. Taking a deep breath in, she released it slowly. And then took in another.

"Good, lass," Brother Michael encouraged and dropped his hand.

She drew her cloak more firmly around her. "How is your nose?"

He chuckled low. "'Tis broken. But it isn't the first time."

Surprised by his confession, she asked, "Someone has taken a fist to your face before?"

"Definitely. Once, by my older brother. Then there was the time when a traveler did not approve of my remarks on his wares. I merely pointed out to him that some of his items were not what he was presenting to the villagers. He was offering miracle ointments and tinctures to cleanse the body. They were nothing but water from a nearby stream and marsh grasses stuffed into goose fat."

"How awful. Ye are perceptive."

"I caught him earlier in the morn by the stream making his ointments. The man definitely was out to get his coin, even if it meant deceiving good people."

Another rat squeaked past them, and Erina gritted her teeth. "How much longer are they going to keep us down here?" She huddled more against Brother Michael. "Usually I dinnae fear the small animals."

He patted her hand. "Ye are anxious, and the darkness only makes them more menacing."

"I ken," she whispered, and placed her head on her knees. "I only want to end this. Meet my accusers. How have I wronged anyone?"

Erina longed for answers. What crime had she

committed against another? When Brother Michael remained silent, she lifted her head to look at him. Fear clutched her heart, yet, she had to know the answer. "Do *ye* believe I am a witch?"

Sighing, he replied, "Nae, Erina, ye are not a witch. But in truth, ye walk a path that others will say is heathen. And for all accounts, I dinnae reckon any will listen to what I have to say. I dinnae ken this bishop and I have defended ye."

Hurt infused her heart at having her friend involved with her predicament. "Ye should have remained silent."

"Why? I merely defended a noble and good woman."

"Your church would disagree."

"There is only one which I follow. Our Lord Jesus Christ. He tended to many outcasts by taking meals with them to treating their ailments of the body and soul. I do his work, Erina. Remember my words."

Glancing upward, she smiled. "Do ye ken there are certain heathens who call Jesus their druid?"

Brother Michael shifted and stretched out his legs. "I have heard this tale from travelers returning from their pilgrimages in the north. I find this…encouraging."

Erina swallowed, and she glanced at the monk. "Do ye reckon your Jesus would have found me at fault?"

He angled his head toward her. "There is nothing to find fault in ye. The good ye do for others is a testament to your character. In truth, he already loves ye."

"Ho…how do ye ken?" she stammered.

Brother Michael took her hand. "Because he loves us all. We are his children. His flock."

Smiling, she nodded. "Since ye are on speaking terms with this *Jesus*," she hesitated, and then continued, "will ye offer a prayer to him for me?"

"Och, Erina. He hears all prayers, even ones from ye."

"Truly?" Her question echoed within their tiny prison. She was unable to fathom how his God would want to have anything to do with one who believed in the old Gods and Goddesses.

Her shoulders relaxed, and she leaned her head against the wall. Peace and calm entered her body, and for the first time since taken prisoner, Erina let herself drift. However, her respite was brief. The scraping of an outside door brought her fears back to the front. Brother Michael helped her to stand as they waited.

When the guard entered the light, Erina clutched a hand to her chest. The young man was the one who had assisted Erina and given her his horse. "Have they sent ye to bring us forth?"

The guard unlocked the prison door and stepped inside. After placing a finger over his mouth, he glanced over his shoulder and then returned his focus to them. "If ye want to live, keep your voices low. Aye, I am to escort ye to your trial, Lady Erina, though I dinnae agree with what they have planned and refuse to take part."

Erina's stomach lurched, but she quickly fought the rising panic inside her.

"What are they planning?" Brother Michael demanded tersely.

"She is accused of witchcraft and will be burned at

the stake."

She gasped. "I haven't even had a trial."

"There is nae time to argue. I am here to help ye. When we leave the main part of the dungeon, I will set Brother Michael free." He turned his attention to the monk. "Ye must take a fist to me, so it looks like a skirmish happened."

"I will not leave Lady Erina—"

"Aye, ye will." She grabbed her friend's arm. "Ye must go find help. They will not care about ye, but if *I* escaped, they would surely come swiftly and retrieve me."

He groaned. "*Erina…*"

"I beg ye, please do this."

"Lord help me," he uttered softly.

"And say a prayer to him for me," she added, and released her hold on Brother Michael.

She straightened and turned toward the guard. "I am ready."

He gave a curt nod and gestured them forward.

As they steadily made their way up along the narrow corridor, moans from the other prisoners echoed around her. She shivered, wanting desperately to free them all. When the area opened, the guard pointed in the direction of another set of stairs on the right leading downward.

"This is wrong," she protested softly and tugged on the man's arm. "Why are they keeping people in the dungeon of a cathedral that is half in ruins?"

The guard cast her a sharp look. "The bishop would like to be recognized for his good in this country. He seeks to gain favor with Rome and hopefully to rebuild those that were destroyed by King Henry VIII."

"Someone must put an end to this barbaric torture."

"Agreed, but for now I must save ye. I will release the others later. Take this path, Brother Michael. It leads to an area used for rubbish. Ye will have to wade through the stench. Turn north and ye will come upon a path outside the cathedral. Be wary, often times, some of the guards take their wenches out by the trees. At least ye will have the cover of darkness, but dawn will be here soon."

Brother Michael nodded. "I will be on alert."

"Good. Now, hit me in the face."

"God forgive me," Brother Michael muttered and landed a fist to the man's jaw. The guard staggered and fell to the ground. Shaking his head, he slowly made to stand.

"Again," he demanded.

"By all the saints." This time, the monk punched him in the stomach and then landed another blow to his face. He stumbled, but remained standing.

Erina placed a fist against her mouth to squelch her cries.

Blood oozed from a cut near his brow, and the guard blinked. Wiping his hand over the wound, he winched. "This should be sufficient."

"'Tis already swelling," Erina confirmed.

Brother Michael shook out his hand. "Pray forgive me. Nevertheless, I shall always remember your act of kindness." He turned toward Erina. "May our Lord watch over and protect ye." Making the sign of the cross in the air, he moved swiftly away.

"May the Goddess watch over ye," she uttered softly in return.

"We must leave," ordered the guard and placed a

firm hand on her elbow.

Erina glanced sideways at him. "Before I take another step, ye will give me your name."

He inclined his head, and his mouth twitched in humor. "Malcolm. Malcolm MacKay. May we now proceed?"

After taking her elbow once again, they moved silently along the passageway. Curious about her new friend, she asked, "Where do ye hail from, Malcolm?"

He glanced at her briefly. "The Great Glen, specifically, Aonach Castle."

As they emerged outside, she drew her cloak more firmly around her shoulders. The rain had turned to light showers and for a moment, she wished for the skies to continue their deluge upon the land. Recalling her grandmother's stories about the MacKays of Aonach, she said, "I have heard the tales of the MacKays and why they fled Urquhart."

Malcolm halted, giving her a sad smile. "Stories filled with magic, aye? Now ye understand why I must help ye. We, too, are going through troubled times."

Erina shrugged out of his grasp, stunned by his declaration. "Then why are ye here? With them?"

"I came with the bishop from Arbroath Abbey. The place has significant meaning to me. One of my ancestors helped to build a portion of the abbey. I was unaware of the bishop's plans until recently." He rubbed a hand down the back of his neck. "I was on a pilgrimage of sorts. To forge the past and future."

Her eyes grew wide. "Then the tales are true? The Dragon Knights do exist?"

"I stand before ye, a Dragon Knight, descended from Stephen MacKay. Though my powers are not as strong as my ancestor, I will do my best to assist ye. My vow to ye."

Tears misted her eyes. "Ye must promise me, if this plan of yours does not end well, ye must flee. Ye cannot risk being exposed."

Malcolm snorted in disgust. "Generation after generation of MacKays have suffered. Mine will be nae different. If I must die to save a life, then I will do so honorably. We shall have strength in numbers, if Brother Michael brings back aid."

"Then let us finish this mockery of a trial," stated Erina.

****

By the hounds! Where did they take her? The dizziness which plagued him weeks ago, now returned with a vengeance. The shadows mocked Rory, and he fought to banish them to the far reaches of his mind. As he scanned the area, he was unable to determine which direction they had taken Erina. The land refused to show him any sign, and his irritation grew with each hour.

He cast his gaze to the stars. "Give me something. Anything, Great Guardians of the Sky."

Waiting patiently, he held his breath and clenched his jaw. Even the stars remained silent, and the great dragons that had passed and ascended into the stars refused to help him. He pinched the bridge of his nose, trying to ward off the growing unrest within his soul, and let out a frustrated breath.

Bitterness and despair became his new companions. Regardless of the consequences, Rory would bend the wheel of time to prevent her abductors from taking her.

A force of power slammed into him, and he fought to remain standing. His horse whinnied in obvious fear.

"You are forbidden to tamper with the Veil of Ages for your gain. Do not think you can control the Fates, Fenian Warrior."

Rory raised an eyebrow in amused contempt. Glancing upward, he noted the blazing outline of one of the dragons against the night sky. "And now ye choose to answer me?"

A blow of power leveled him across the ground, and he slammed against a tree.

"Is death what you seek, Fenian Warrior?"

Wiping the blood from his mouth, he stood. "To save her life, I'd do so willingly."

"You are walking into the abyss. Banish the shadows."

He held out his hands in aggravation. "Then show me another way."

"The answer lies within your heart."

Turning around swiftly at the sound of a horse approaching, Rory waited and withdrew his sword.

Graham emerged through a cluster of trees. As he dismounted, Rory met him and sheathed his sword.

"I am unable to find any trace or direction. I hate to admit it, but we must camp here for the night. I've sent other riders to the neighboring village in hopes they have heard anything relating to Sinclair or this bishop. They will gather at the entrance of the forest come the morning." Graham fisted his hands on his hips. "I fear we are losing precious time."

Rory's hands shook as he tried to remain in control. Finally taking a step toward his friend, he took the reins of his horse. "If Erina is going to be put on trial, it will come in the morning. Even those men must require their rest."

Graham wiped a hand over his brow. "Aye, ye are correct." He removed the satchel from his horse and strode to a small open area within the trees.

Rory led the horse to a nearby tree and then went to retrieve his own horse. He made sure both animals were secure for the night and headed back to their camp. Graham had started a fire. Though the blaze remained small, it was a beacon of warmth for their dreary moods.

After pulling out a pouch with dried beef and cheese from the leather satchel, Graham settled across from Rory on a boulder. Removing the food, Graham tossed some to him.

Both were content to eat in silence with their thoughts. A cold breeze settled around them, and Graham bent to retrieve a flask. He took a swill and then handed it to Rory.

Taking the offered item, he asked, "Do ye ken where this bishop resides? Or Sinclair?"

Graham leaned his forearms on his thighs. "We are heading south in the direction of the Sinclair's lands. Although, I sense he is *not* taking her there."

Taking a sip of the whisky, Rory let the heat invade his body. "Why?"

"He spoke of problems with his own people. He worried there were those who still practiced the heathen ways and feared they would poison his food or drink."

"And ye considered him a suitor for Erina?"

"I came upon this news only recently." He shifted back. "Did he take Erina as an example for others? Is he doing this as a way to garner support from the church? I dinnae have the answers. Nevertheless, we will continue to journey toward his lands."

Rory handed the flask back to him. "I shall take the first watch. Go get some sleep."

"Sleep?" Graham stretched and slumped down against the boulder. Wrapping his plaid around his shoulders, he continued, "Nae, until Erina is found and put into safekeeping, I won't rest."

"Regardless, do try. I will wake ye in a few hours."

Graham grumbled a curse, but closed his eyes.

Rory tossed in another piece of kindling into the fire. The flames hissed and embers danced upward—reminiscent of what had happened to the woman he loved in the past. Whispers of Erina's past haunted him. They echoed of a wronged injustice. No longer could he bring forth the other memories of his time with her, but he did know the outcome.

And this time, the past would not be repeated.

He stood and moved away from the fire. Clasping his hands behind his back, he let his gaze roam the night. Nocturnal animals called out to him, and he in turn, sought their aid, appealing for their sight. Come daylight, others of the animal kingdom would join their cause. He would use their sight over the land to assist him in any way.

Rory knelt on one knee. Placing his hand upon the ground, he drew forth the energy from the land and absorbed as much as possible. The ground rumbled in protest, but he continued to draw forth from her bounty.

Standing quietly, he sent out a single whisper on the breeze. "Show me where ye are, Erina."

Chapter Twenty-Four

"Time has many colorful layers. Yet, there is always a beginning and an ending."
                                              ~Chronicles of the Fae

Erina huddled upon the stool, trying to fight the panic coursing throughout her body. Many people filled the large room, their hushed whispers echoed all around her. She glanced around, trying to see if she recognized anyone. None would meet her stare, but Erina was not about to recoil in shame. She had done nothing wrong. Some of the stone columns had been battered, scars of previous battles a swift reminder that the belief in any one religion was like changing your garments.

As she clutched the amethyst around her neck, she brought forth the image of her grandmother. Her breathing slowed, and she straightened and leaned against the wall. Feeling comforted by the memory, she dropped her hand.

Malcolm had swiftly departed after bringing her inside the room, and she worried he had taken her advice and fled. She would have found no fault if he had, but MacKay had brought a sense of calm to her trembling insides. She lifted her head, scanned the area, and saw him standing off to the side of the entrance. Reassured by his presence, she then went on her search of finding anyone who would dare to accuse her of witchcraft.

The crowd fell silent as a short, robust man in long, flowing robes entered the room. He was followed by Laird Sinclair and several of his guards. As they made their way to the front, she stood to get a better view. However, the guard next to her shoved her back onto her stool. Biting back the barb she wished to release, she remained silent.

The man in the flowing robes lifted his arms upward. "Lord, give us the strength and courage to cast out the devil's mistress who sits in our presence. Bind her power, so she cannot wield a curse or cause further harm to those she has enchanted."

Erina fidgeted. Did the man's words pertain to her?

"Bring the woman forward," he demanded, pointing to a place directly in front of him.

The guard grabbed her arm, yanking her to her feet. As he shoved her forward, he continued to prod her along like cattle. Erina kept her focus steady and met the glare of the small man. She refused to show her fear and kept her hands clasped together to prevent them from shaking. Coming to a halt in front of the man, she waited.

He leveled a gnarled finger at her, and she recoiled. "By all that is holy, ye shall speak words of truth. Do ye understand, witch?"

"My name is Erina—"

Laird Sinclair stepped forward and slapped her across the face. Her body stiffened in shock, and she heard the crowd gasp. Blood trickled from a cut to her lip, and she attempted to blot it with her sleeve.

"Ye will hold your tongue, unless Bishop Stewart calls upon ye." Sinclair made a fist with his hand. "If ye do not comply, I can find other means of silencing your words."

Anger and hurt infused Erina. She wanted to rake her nails over his face. Giving him a curt nod, she watched him step back.

"As Laird Sinclair aptly pronounced, I am Bishop Stewart. Ye have been found guilty of the crimes of witchcraft. Do ye deny these charges?"

"Aye," she declared. "I am nae witch."

"Silence!" he shouted, his face twisting in disgust. "Just answer the questions."

Erina battled the words she wanted to hurl at the horrible man. She clenched her jaw so tight, she feared it would snap, but she held her tongue silent.

Bishop Stewart snapped his fingers. The crowd parted farther back along the walls as the side doors opened. She glanced over her shoulder, and her heart froze. Entering the room were Betty Timmons and her parents; Bryson, the butcher; and one of the men who had tried to attack her many weeks ago. She gave no care about the man, but the others were people she knew well.

Betty refused to meet her stare as she made her way past Erina and stood off to the side of the bishop. Yet, Betty's parents sent her scathing looks in passing. Graham's words came back to haunt Erina. Did they not once call her the White Healer when she tended to a sick Betty?

The bishop gestured toward Bryson. "Ye may give your account."

The man stepped forward, refusing to look at Erina. "I found this in my bed one evening." Pulling forth the pouch of herbs Erina had given to Mairi, he tossed it on the floor in front of her.

The crowd murmured their objections, and Bishop Stewart held up his hands to silence them. He then redirected his attention to Bryson. "How do ye ken it belongs to the witch?"

"I saw her with the vile charm."

Liar! Ye found it on Mairi. Either she has told ye, or ye are protecting her. Erina fought the wave of panic and tried to settle her breathing.

"We find ye speak the truth. Ye may leave."

Do I not have a say? Erina screamed within her mind.

Without a word, Bryson swept past her.

"The others may come forth," the bishop ordered.

Betty's mother reached for her daughter's arm and proceeded to move forward. Her father stepped around them and stood near Sinclair.

Bishop Stewart placed a hand on Betty's shoulder. Her lip trembled as she kept her focus on the floor. "I ken ye are scared of the witch, but ye must speak the truth. 'Tis not your fault what has transpired. Afterwards, ye can be cleansed of your sins."

"I…" Betty coughed and lifted her head. "I told Erina—"

"The witch," corrected Bishop Stewart.

"Aye," she mumbled. "I spoke of my…feelings for a man." Her eyes went wide as she turned swiftly to her mother. "She said she could give me something to make the man love me. I realize I should not have taken the charm, but she…*threatened* me."

Her mother's mouth thinned in disapproval. "She was working for the devil, child." She turned her heated gaze to Erina. "We should have never let ye touch our daughter when she was with fever." The woman leveled a finger at her and continued, "Ye have enchanted her with the devil's words."

Betty collapsed into her mother's arms. "'Tis true, Mother. I have not been the same since ye let her into our home."

Erina could no longer hold back. "Ye were my *friend*. I would never bring ye harm."

Instantly, Sinclair took a fist to her stomach, and Erina crumpled to the floor. The room became a blur of voices and colors as she fought to breathe.

Sinclair stooped down next to her. "I warned ye. Now get up."

After regaining her strength, Erina stood on shaky limbs and hugged her arms around herself. She glared at Sinclair with burning reproachful eyes.

"Enough! If ye cannot keep your voices down, I will have the guards usher all of ye out of here," commanded Bishop Stewart.

The crowd quieted.

He turned toward Betty and her parents and held his hands in the air over them. "Ye have spoken the truth. Though I deem your actions were unwise to let the witch into your home for healing, ye were kind people and did not see the error of your judgment. The witch lured your daughter with the devil's words, and hence, she became corrupted." The bishop inclined his head to Betty's father. "See that ye come faithfully each day to wash the sins away."

Betty's father bowed his head and then led his family away.

Erina's resolve was quickly fading. She'd thought the Timmons family her friends. Never did she fathom such betrayal and lies.

"This man came on a pilgrimage, seeking forgiveness for his sins and to enter into our Lord's service. If not for him, we would not ken the full extent of the witch's powers. Let the last accuser give his account," ordered the bishop.

When her attacker stepped forward, Erina shot him daggers. *Ye vile creature.*

The man snarled and pointed. "She bewitched me with her body, tempting me one day many weeks ago. I came upon her bathing in the stream with nothing but the skin she came into the world with. She sang a song and wove her seduction."

A woman from the crowd shrieked. "Burn the devil's mistress! She carries the Blackthorn rod and made me lose my bairn!"

The bishop snapped his fingers at a guard, who then went to remove the ranting woman.

"Continue," he encouraged. "Tell us how ye escaped."

"I recited the Lord's prayer."

"And what happened?"

"She twisted upon the ground, spouting loathsome words, and I took off through the trees."

"Not true!" Erina snapped. "He tried to force himself on *me*."

When the blow came, Erina's head snapped back, and she fell backwards. Darkness clouded her vision. The bile in her stomach came unbidden onto the pallid floor. Panic ensued all around her as the room erupted into a hysterical mob.

Someone pulled her to standing. His strength soothed the turmoil within her, and she twisted to get a glimpse of the man. *Malcolm!* She blinked trying to focus. Malcolm kept a steady hold on her arm, and his gaze fixed on the bishop.

"Ye may step away from the witch," Bishop Stewart ordered and then took a step toward her. "Ye have met your accusers. Do ye deny knowing these good people?"

"Nae," she mumbled as a sense of coldness enveloped her the moment Malcolm walked away.

"Do ye deny using herbs to create love charms?"

"Nae."

"Do ye deny treating those who are sick without the aid of a true physician?

"Nae."

He slowly moved around Erina. "There is a remedy to rectify to the crowd ye are not a witch and to appease the church of your sins."

The bishop returned to face her. His mouth twisted in a malicious grin.

One of her eyes was now swollen as she swept her gaze over him. Waiting.

He tapped a finger to his mouth in thought. "If ye can recite the Lord's prayer to those present here, your punishment will go lighter."

A shaft of light pierced through one of the arched windows, and Erina lifted her head. Swallowing, she realized her fate was sealed. She did not know this prayer. Yet, in her heart, she judged that if Jesus were in this room, he would not ask this request.

She directed her attention back to the bishop. "I was never taught this prayer ye speak of."

"Then by the decree of our Lord, I hereby sentence ye to burn to the stake for witchcraft."

Taunts and shouting spilled forth. This time, the bishop did nothing to squelch the people. He let them spew obscenities at her. Sinclair thrust her forward and she stumbled. Numb, confused, and defeated, Erina moved through the crowd. Some spat at her and others held up wooden crosses.

When she stepped out of the room, she swept the area for one last remnant of hope. The throng of people continued to engulf her as Sinclair pushed her along the corridor and out into an open space in front of the cathedral.

She doubted Malcolm had remained, but she held on, praying, seeking his presence. And then her eyes came upon her end. Her execution. A hideous stake surrounded by so much wood. Once, the large pieces of wood were beautiful trees. Now, they resembled her funeral pyre. She shuddered visibly, and her heart clutched in terror, but one thought remained fixed within her mind.

I love ye, Rory. Farewell, my Fenian Warrior.
****

As he nudged the sleeping man with his foot, Rory waited for him to wake.

Graham grumbled a curse and blinked. After tossing his plaid aside, he rubbed at his eyes and stood. "God's blood! Why didn't ye wake me?"

Shrugging, Rory dumped more dirt over the dying embers. In truth, he required little or no sleep. "The first light of dawn is arriving. Do ye need to break your fast?"

"Nae. And I can see 'tis almost daylight."

Rory handed him a flask. "Drink."

When Graham took a sip, he spat out the liquid in

disgust. "*Water?*"

"Our minds and bodies need to be clear and focused."

Graham approached him. "Do ye hear yourself?"

"Indeed."

Shaking his head in dismay, he handed the flask to Rory. "I shall require a moment, and then we can depart."

Understanding the man's need to piss, Rory gave him a curt nod and secured the flask to the side of his horse.

As soon as Graham returned, they mounted their horses and proceeded across the open fields. Training his Fae senses all around him, Rory listened with intent to any movement other than the animals. He inhaled deeply, trying to capture anything with Erina's scent. A flower, a broken branch, or a torn section of her dress. Again, he received nothing. Not even the birds had noted her direction.

When the first light of the new day shimmered over the hills, he pressed onward with more urgency. The fingers of time were slipping away, along with Erina's life. His desire to find her increased a manic ferocity inside him he had never experienced.

Then he saw the whisper of movement in the trees to the left. As he led his horse in the new direction, Rory ignored the heated shouting from Graham. He prayed with all his might it was Erina. As they galloped across the land, his hope soon faded when Brother Michael emerged forth.

Bringing his horse to an abrupt halt, Rory jumped down and ran to the man. He swept his gaze over him and stumbled. Erina's scent clung to the man. His voice shook as he grasped the monk's robe. "Where is she?"

"Ye…*ye* must save her."

Graham ran over to his side. "Release him, MacGregor. Can ye not see he is injured?"

Complying, Rory took a hesitant step back. "Forgive me."

Brother Michael wiped a shaky hand over his brow as Graham led him to a fallen log. "Can ye explain?"

He shook his head. "I am sorry, Graham. We were seized upon at the herb cottage by Laird Sinclair and his guards."

"Dinnae worry. I ken ye did all that ye could. How did ye escape and not Erina?"

"We encountered unexpected help from a man named Malcolm MacKay." He chuckled softly. "The Lord works in wondrous ways."

Rory stiffened. *Dragon Knight, Malcolm MacKay was with Sinclair?* "Why did the man help ye?" he asked. "Surely, he is one of the Sinclair's guards."

"Apparently, he had nae desire to be a part of this mockery of a trial."

"*Trial?*" Rory's hands clenched.

"The MacKay set me free, in order to find aid for Erina. When I left her, Malcolm was taking her to be tried for her crimes of witchcraft."

"Sweet Mother Mary, nae!" Graham moved away from the man.

Rory's vision blurred. It had all been for nothing. He had returned to this century, and found it altered, trusting in the Gods and Goddesses that Erina would not suffer the same fate as before. A second chance, he deemed. Now, the past collided in a torrential blur into the present. Upon the very ground he stood.

He staggered, unable to control the emotions overtaking his soul. They slashed into his heart, ripping through at dagger like precision, and the pain bled out of him.

"Where is she?" His question came out as a growl, and both men gaped at him. "*Where?*"

Brother Michael stood slowly. "The ruins of Calder Cathedral. Not far from St. Timmons Square."

Chapter Twenty-Five

"Within each Fenian Warrior, is the capacity to call upon the power of the cosmos. If used unwisely, worlds will collide."
~*Chronicles of the Fae*

The land blurred past Rory as he urged his steed faster toward the forest near the base of the hill. Once there, he would use magic to transport them to Calder Cathedral. He'd disregarded the words of Graham and Brother Michael, urging him to wait for the other guards, and left without the men. How could they understand that the trial would be swift and unjust? Each minute was one spent waiting for a future already plotted and threaded on the loom. And he sought to alter *her* destiny.

There was no other alternative.

As he approached the trees, Rory slowed his animal. Glancing over his shoulder, he quickly scanned the area to make sure no one was behind him. The trees surrounded him, and Rory let his horse slow to a light canter. He placed a hand over the mane, and whispered quiet words of what he was about to do. After he lifted his hand, the air shimmered.

When he appeared by the edge of the river outside of St. Timmons Square, the mass hysteria had already begun. The taunts of the people reached his hearing, and he tempered his fury. Though the cathedral was well over five miles north of St. Timmons, he could witness everyone—each word, each intake of breath, and their movements with his Fae senses. He urged his horse onward.

He searched for a place at the side of the ruins and swiftly dismounted. As he smacked his horse on the rump, he watched the animal galloped toward protection among the oak trees. Rory turned his attention to the one area he sought to find her.

The blood pounded in his ears when he caught sight of her bound to the stake. The scent of smoke filled him, and as her first scream ripped through the air, the blinding rage surfaced. It could no longer be denied. He had waited for this day to right an injustice—one that happened because of him.

His training forbade him to change fate. Yet, his heart demanded he save her life. The decision was made. The oath sealed with a whisper.

In a single thought, Rory magically appeared behind the manic crowd. The flames licked at the wood, and he followed their path. When his eyes rested on Erina's swollen face, pure rage exploded inside him.

After removing his plaid, he then stripped his tunic free from his body. Removing his boots, he stood with only his trews on. He chanted the ancient words of battle, words that had not been uttered from his lips in a millennium, and he held his arms outward. The markings on his arms and back blazed with the power they possessed, infusing Rory with strength. His voice rumbled across the land, and the power built with each word.

The ground shook violently, and he judged his time

was limited. Soon, his people would come for him. He had to seal the door on time around them. Prevent the other Fae who would seek him out and remove him from her world.

Closing his eyes, he called upon the ancients and from the guardians of long ago. The energy swept through him, piercing every cell in his being, and he snapped his eyes open when Erina's scream tore through his heart. Her eyes were wild with fear as they met his.

"I am here, *mo ghrá*!" he shouted. The wind slapped viciously at his face, and the cries of the others soon filled the air.

"The devil has come for the woman!" screamed a woman and ran back into the ruins of the cathedral.

"'Tis only the MacGregor!" Sinclair shouted, ordering guards to put a blade through him.

As the men lunged at Rory, he waved his hand outward, flinging them across the courtyard. More followed, and he did the same with each attempt, until fear drove the rest of the guards to scurry away like rats.

Sinclair moved toward Erina, his dirk raised. The wind howled like a banshee, and Rory could still hear the taunts of the man.

"I will rip her heart out before ye can even attempt to save her. Let the fire cleanse her soul. Or are ye under her spell?"

"Leave or I shall kill ye, Sinclair!" he roared, and the force of Rory's words caused the man to falter.

Sinclair held his arm higher in an attempt to toss his blade.

"Leave devil's spawn," screamed a man in flowing

robes. He charged at Rory, waving a cross in front of his body.

With precision thoughts, Rory tossed the man against a tree and magically removed the dirk from Sinclair's hand.

When he turned his attention back to Sinclair, the man's eyes grew wide in disbelief and dread. Rory steadily approached him, letting the power flow. Sinclair foolishly reached out to touch him and cried out in pain. He collapsed to the ground, and Rory stepped over him and made his way to the burning pyre.

Terror and screams continued to sweep around him, but Rory gave no care. Holding his hand upward, the skies darkened and rumbled. Lifting his hand higher, the swirling mass of clouds gathered.

"Let me help ye, Fenian Warrior," someone shouted from the mass hysteria.

Rory cut the man a swift glance. "*Dragon Knight.*" His words came out in a guttural growl.

"Aye. Call forth the rain, and I will direct it *all* onto the fire." The Dragon Knight coughed and moved closer to the flames.

"Nae, *nae*, Rory. Di...dinnae show who ye..." Great coughing spasms racked Erina as she pleaded for Rory to stop.

He heard her words, but the power flowing through his veins blinded all clear thought. Rory circled his fist over and over, and the air crackled with the force of his power. When the first drop slashed across his face, he opened his fist.

Time froze, sealing out the other world. The universe was as one entity. The shredded loom of fate would be rewoven.

And the skies opened fully.

****

Conn staggered when the first blow rumbled under his feet. "Shit!" He pushed away from his desk. As the second wave of energy slammed into him, he let out another curse.

His hands clenched as he breathed heavily. "Damn you, Rory MacGregor!"

He raked a hand through his hair and paced back and forth. This was his fault for leaving the warrior unattended. He trusted in the Fae, and now the consequences were dire for his friend. The moment he was brought back into their realm, death would swiftly follow.

Ronan was the first to appear in Conn's chambers inside the halls of the Brotherhood. "We have a conflict in the mortal realm."

"How many have felt the abuse of power?"

"All," announced Taran, entering from a side entrance. "The Fae council is demanding all Fenian Warriors to seek out the disruption and bring forth the violator. The entire kingdom felt the force."

"*Violator*," Conn hissed. "He is our brother!"

Taran shifted uneasily. "He has called upon the power of the old ones. Do you believe he has crossed over to the Realm of Sorrows?"

"If he isn't there already, I deem he will be there soon." Conn's voice heavy with sarcasm. "Though it would seem the council is unaware it's Rory, correct?"

"Yes," Taran affirmed.

One by one, more warriors entered the chambers of the Brotherhood. Each took a stance around Conn as if in protection. He realized they were waiting on him for orders. None would ever willingly do the bidding of the council, and Conn smiled inwardly. One of the warriors sent him a single thought letting Conn know the outer fortress was sealed. No other Fae would be allowed inside.

Did the warriors believe he was going to bring Rory back here for safekeeping? Duty or friendship? Sworn vows to a kingdom? What choice did he have? Conn had no clear answer.

Ronan stepped forward, placing a fist over his chest. "Whatever ye decide, we will support your decision."

And if I choose to hand him over to his death? Will you continue to follow me?

Conn narrowed his eyes and went to the fount in the middle of the chamber. He placed his hands on the ledge and directed his gaze outward. He waited patiently, coaxing the mortal world open to reveal Rory. What was the warrior doing? Conn required answers. The water rippled, but the image of the other world refused to part. Smacking his hand on the stone, he looked around the room.

"Who has tampered with the Veil?"

"As I have stated, no one—"

Conn slashed his hand in the air to halt Ronan's words. "I am asking all within the Brotherhood at this precise moment. The warrior entered an alternate time, and if I find anyone has lied, my wrath for that someone will be far worse than my anger for Rory."

The chamber remained silent, and Conn bowed his head.

"Clear your chambers." His father's order pierced his thoughts.

Lifting his head, Conn returned his gaze to Ronan and Taran. "Assemble the strongest and most experienced warriors and wait for me at the south entrance to the mortal realm. I shall join you shortly."

Both men gave a curt nod and left.

He turned to those remaining. "You have pledged your loyalty to the Brotherhood. One of our own is in jeopardy. I need warriors to maintain a vigil around Rory's home and that of his mother. Seal off the area. Let none of the council or their guards enter. If they refuse to accept your orders, you can tell them these orders came from their prince."

Each responded with a fist over their chest and then vanished in a flash of brilliant colors.

When the last of the warriors had left, Conn made his way back to his desk. Folding his arms across his chest, he said, "My chambers are cleared."

King Ansgar appeared within seconds. Storming past his son, he went to the fount and waved his hand over the water. "Release the shroud which masks the truth."

Confused, Conn stepped over to his father. "Why is Rory cloaked?"

"To finish what he began many centuries ago."

"Which is?"

His father pursed his lips. "In order to save his soul, he had to rescue the human female."

Anger burst inside of Conn. "You are my king, but I am the *leader* of the Brotherhood. Even you do not have the right to tamper."

King Ansgar turned abruptly and jabbed a finger into Conn's chest. "How do you know I have tampered?" His voice reverberated around the chambers.

Conn leaned forward, challenging his father. "Because if you desired to help him, you would have made me aware of the assistance. Or offered your knowledge."

His father's eyes blazed. Regardless, Conn sought to find the truth.

King Ansgar turned away and paced in front of the fount. "The Fenian Warrior has been on a path of destruction since the day he let the female die." Halting across from Conn, he added, "I had no wish to see him cross over to the Realm of Sorrows."

Realization dawned, and Conn sneered. "You're the one who altered the timeline."

"Yes." His was tone resigned, and he wandered back toward the fount.

"I sent him through to witness and heal—"

"Albeit with full powers," King Ansgar interjected. "I must admit, I am stunned you did so, considering how he felt for the female and the danger he posed to both worlds."

Conn grumbled a curse, growing frustrated with the conversation. "I am not following your meaning. And the *female* has a name. She is called, Erina."

A glint of humor passed briefly over his father's features. "Rory MacGregor was in *love* with Erina MacIntyre. Not only did he hide his pain from the Brotherhood, but his love for the human."

"If I may ask, how did you come upon this knowledge?"

"The Seer. I sought her out for my own concern." His father narrowed his eyes at him.

Doing his best to temper his anger, Conn turned

away. "Yet, you did not think to alert me?"

"I am telling you now. However, you sent him back in the most cruel way ever. To witness the woman he loved die all over again."

Your timing is a bit off, Father. Conn pointed to the water. "I sent him back to seal what he left open. I understood he loved her, but," he paused and then continued, "I assumed it was one of his lustful conquests that had gone too far. His amorous liaisons over the centuries are well known. He deemed there were too many to love."

"Has he ever mentioned he *loved* any of them?"

Stunned by his father's question, Conn took a moment of reflection and recalled everything about his friend. Yes, he was a lover, but never once did he profess loving anyone. In truth, Rory deemed he would never marry, since there were so many women to please. He barked out in laughter and moved away from his father. "I never asked why she was different. I only sought to heal the warrior—*my friend*."

When his father approached, a look of sadness creased his brow. "What if you had to witness Ivy dying all over again? And what if she did indeed pass over. In addition, what *if* you had to endure living with this knowledge—these emotions for centuries, only to be told to witness them all over again? What would you do?"

Conn exhaled slowly. "I would do all in my power to save her, regardless of the consequences."

"There is more I must share," added his father, wiping a hand over his chin. "When I spoke of what happened to my brother, I did not speak of my pledge I made on the day he died. I vowed no other Fenian

Warrior would ever walk into the Realm of Sorrows again. In order to rectify the past, I snapped a thread from the loom of fate and changed the moment he and Erina met for the second time."

"You do realize the predicament he had to face? He was ordered to close the door on his feelings. His past."

"This was his greatest challenge. The shadows were gripping him more each day, especially after his time in the Room of Reflection." King Ansgar gestured to the fount. "Here is your warrior."

Conn cast his attention to the water, and his mouth gaped open. "By the Gods! He has gone too far." He watched the scene unfold as his friend wielded the power of the ancients. "Are you positive he has not crossed over to the Realm of Sorrows?"

"Yes. Though there are injuries, Rory has not killed anyone. He is in control, which says a great deal about the warrior. Although, his restraint is weakening and soon he'll give in to the emotions."

Glancing sideways at his father, he asked, "How are we going to bind his energy? In addition, what am I to do about the Fae council?"

King Ansgar lifted his palm outward, and a crystal scepter magically appeared. Holding it in front of Conn, he said, "Do what you must to contain the power. Afterwards, bring Rory to my inner chamber. As for the council, I will take responsibility and order the guards to stand down."

Taking the glittering scepter from his father, Conn inclined his head, and in an arc of light, he vanished.

Chapter Twenty-Six

"Even in the darkest moments of a Fae's life, a whisper of love can pierce through the bleak despair."
~*Chronicles of the Fae*

Rain battered Rory's body as he continued to call forth the water from the sky. Stretching his arm farther, he drew out everything the elements had to offer. He heard the whispers of those long gone guiding him. The power lifted him, urging him to defy those who had dared threaten to kill the woman he loved. The humans were a pitiful species. Insignificant. Inferior. Mere mortals without forethought of their actions.

Death should come to them all.

The shouting began, but it was stronger, intense. Did he recognize these voices? Or had the enemy rebuilt? Did they send for reinforcements?

"Rory."

Her soft plea stabbed at his heart, and his hand wavered.

"No more, I beg ye."

Even through the blinding haze, her words bloomed within his mind.

He shook his head, dazed by the intensity of so much power. Rory slowly turned his attention to her. The fire had been squelched, but the rain continued its angry deluge across her body and the land. Malcolm

289

had since dropped to the ground, weary and ashen.

"Erina." Rory's words came out in a garbled mess.

Her head was bent forward and concern filled him. As he dropped his hand, Rory stumbled forward. However, movement to his left alerted him to another, and he swiftly turned toward the intruder.

Conn leveled a blow to his jaw, and Rory staggered, but remained standing.

"Fenian Warrior, I hereby order you to release your energy."

Rory fought the uncertainty, a raging battle locked within his mind and body. His temples throbbed, and he glanced down at his hands. They shook as he lifted them upward. The battle for justice was not over. Who was he to demand Rory release his power?

"I will not ask you again, *Fenian Warrior*!" shouted Conn.

Indecisiveness wavered within his mind. Slowly he cast his sight all around him. Why were so many from the Brotherhood here? Then he noticed Graham and Brother Michael gaping at him in fear from the side of a cart.

It was done. Finished. He had succeeded in his mission to rescue her. Time had now resumed, and all his memories returned in a torrent of images. The water from his body dripped in slow methodical drops onto the ground as he tried to calm his breathing.

He snapped his gaze to Erina. "Does she live?" he asked in a hoarse voice.

Graham approached from the side and climbed through the charred debris. He gently lifted her head, and a moan escaped from her lips. "Aye."

A guttural cry of relief tore through Rory, and he

collapsed to the ground onto his knees. The energy he had held contained within his body released in a violent flow back into the cosmos. His breathing was labored as he attempted to calm his racing heart. Lifting his head, he watched as Graham and Brother Michael freed Erina. They carried her to a nearby bench and wrapped a plaid over her.

Footsteps drew near from behind him and he waited. Conn crouched down in front of Rory. "You are done here, Rory. No one was killed. The Brotherhood will wipe the memories from those who have witnessed this destruction."

He narrowed his eyes at Conn. "What about Erina and her brother? Their friend?"

"It is entirely up to you. I will follow your orders."

Stunned by Conn's words, he wiped a shaky hand over his brow. If he removed her memories, Erina would have another chance with someone else. She wouldn't be plagued with the horrors from the past. But then he might as well erase all knowledge from Ewan MacGregor and his daughter, Catherine, too. He laughed at the irony. He had no right to tamper further with any of their lives. "Nae. Let them keep their memories."

"Done."

Conn held out his hand, and Rory grasped it firmly to stand. "The crystal scepter? Would you have used it against me?"

"Yes."

"Good." Rory raked a hand through his damp hair. "Give me a few moments alone…with my friends."

"I see you had help from an unexpected source."

"Aye, the Dragon Knight."

Conn shifted his stance. "Malcolm is on his own quest. But this brings to mind of another Dragon Knight I wish to discuss with you after you return. First, I must warn you, King Ansgar has demanded you appear in his inner chamber. Taran will accompany you back to the Fae realm. There will be no objection to this order."

Rory nodded. "I will do so immediately after I am finished here."

Conn started forward and then paused. "If you still want to become part of the elite group of warriors I am gathering, seek me out in the chambers of the Brotherhood."

Rory swallowed. "First, there is something I must attend to after I speak with the king. Will this be acceptable?"

"Granted."

After Conn stepped away, Rory retuned his gaze to the woman lying on the wooden bench. His beloved lived. But his heart now cleaved in two at the decision he was going to make. His steps moved slowly toward her and instantly, Graham unsheathed his sword and stood in front of Erina.

"What are ye? And who were the others? Are ye demons?" Graham demanded. The tip of his blade aimed directly at Rory's heart.

Rory hesitated. "I bring ye no harm." He glanced over his friend's shoulder. "Nor to ye, Brother Michael."

His friend's voice grew tense. "That is not the question I asked ye."

"I cannot give ye the answers ye seek, except to say we are a peaceful people who live among ye. We are *not* demons. 'Tis your belief, not ours. I was sent to right an injustice and my task has been completed. Furthermore, I love your sister with all my heart and soul." Tapping a finger to his chest, he added, "She shall always remain here, even when I return to my own homeland."

"You offered marriage, MacGregor. Now ye wish to withdraw your claim? *Why*?"

Rory blew out a frustrated breath. "At the time, I judged my former life over and sought to make a new one with your sister. In all honesty, my heart will always be with her. However, I broke the laws of my people by saving Erina. By rights, my life might be forfeit upon my return."

Graham slowly lowered his sword. "And what am I supposed to tell Erina when she wakes?"

Deep sorrow filled Rory. "Tell her…" He cleared his throat and continued, "Tell her I will love her until the stars fade from the night sky."

Unable to say anymore, Rory turned and strode toward Malcolm. As he approached the Dragon Knight, he held out his arm in a gesture of friendship. The man grasped his forearm firmly. "Whatever journey ye are on, if ye ever require my assistance, ye may call upon me. I am honored to call ye my friend. I knew your ancestor, Stephen MacKay, well."

Malcolm smiled. "I am returning to Aonach. I reckon my time spent away has taught me important lessons regarding life and family."

"Thank ye for your aid, as well," stated Rory.

After releasing his grip, Rory turned to leave and then halted. Glancing over his shoulder, he uttered in a firm voice, "Graham, visit Ewan MacGregor. He holds the answers ye seek."

Shock registered across the man's face, but Graham nodded.

Rory swept his gaze one last time over Erina. *Be well, mo ghrá. Look for me in the soft whisper of a morning breeze, and on the caress of a flower petal. My love for ye spans the cosmos. Dinnae forget.*

When he finally lowered his gaze, Rory turned and walked away. With each retreating step, his heart splintered into a million shards of pain.

****

Rory watched the golden sphere suspended high within the darkened forest of the king's inner chamber. Nine multicolored dragons hovered in various positions around the globe. Their light shimmered in a rainbow of colors off the trees, creating an alluring environment. Inhaling the scent of the rich earth and heady floral spices, he tried to settle his thoughts.

He'd never been allowed this deep within the royal palace. Instead of sensing fear, Rory found himself filled with questions. Apparently, Conn still considered him to be a part of the Brotherhood, and the death he thought awaited him, no longer applied.

He shifted his stance and clasped his hands behind his back. His body and mind were battered and weary from the battle. His heart was another situation entirely. The pain so intense, it took all of his willpower to seal the ache when he stepped into the king's chamber. This was not the place to let the tide of his emotions overtake him.

Nevertheless, Rory was home. The whisper of the land reached out in healing to him. Would he accept the soothing curative to his heart? In truth, he deemed it would never come. Whatever plans Conn had for him, he hoped they were ones to remove him to the farthest reaches of time. Even being sent on a mission five hundred years away from Erina's century was not far enough. He'd demand at least a thousand years back.

One of the dragons swirled in a pale blue haze around the sphere. It reminded him of another dragon. The last remaining one that dwelled in the waters of Loch Ness in Scotland. Recalling Conn's words about another Dragon Knight he wished to discuss with him, Rory pondered a visit to the Great Dragon was in order.

The air warmed around him. One of the massive trees blurred, its giant limbs lifting, and King Ansgar stepped forth. It was as if seeing Conn, except the king had kept his hair cropped short. Both had a way of commanding a room when they entered. However, this was his king. Bending on one knee, Rory placed a fist over his heart in reverence and bowed his head. "Greetings, my king."

"Rise, Rory."

Stunned by the king's familiar use of his name, Rory stood and faced King Ansgar. Once again, he clasped his hands behind his back out of respect.

The king surveyed him. "Walk with me."

Unclasping his hands, Rory kept stride alongside King Ansgar. The chamber opened to reveal a moss-covered pathway descending even deeper within the realm. Water trickled from afar, and his body urged him to find the source. The air was potent and warm, and he fought the alluring calmness centering into his being.

"Do not fight the land, Rory." The king continued to walk along, keeping his direction on a bubbling brook in the center of a patch of wildflowers.

Rory halted a few feet away. He had no desire to

be near any flowers. They reminded him of *her*.

King Ansgar snapped his fingers, and an obsidian bench appeared. After taking a seat at one end, he placed his hands on his thighs. "Are you prepared to stand there during our conversation?"

"Why am I here?"

The king narrowed his eyes at Rory, but remained silent.

The battle between Fenian Warrior and King of the Fae brushed over the land. The flowers faded as they slipped into the ground, and the air cooled.

"Is this more acceptable?" asked King Ansgar.

Rory exhaled softly and took a seat on the opposite end. "Forgive me. 'Tis…it is too soon."

"Are you prepared to live a life without her? Can you now become a *true* Fenian Warrior?"

He leaned forward, letting his shoulders relax. He had no clear answers for the king. His emotions clouded everything inside him. "I am unable to give you an answer. I require some time apart from the Brotherhood."

King Ansgar smiled knowingly. "I recall a certain request to the Fae council many centuries ago, and—"

"It was denied," Rory interrupted tersely.

"*If* I had been present…" The king paused and stood. Walking to the brook, he kept his back to him.

Rory waited for him to continue. He sensed concern from his king, and then he grew curious. Standing, he asked, "I do not believe time away would have healed the wound left open by…*Erina's* death." By the Gods, how it ached to even speak her name out loud.

"You may fully never know." King Ansgar turned

back around.

"If I may ask, why would you interfere? For me? Surely death is my punishment."

King Ansgar smile held sadness. "Because I made a pledge—a vow no other Fenian Warrior would succumb to the Realm of Sorrows. There have only been a few, but when the last warrior was put to death, I judged it wiser to devise a plan so others would not fall prey to follow the dark path. Part of you had already entered the realm of misery and sorrows when Erina died. When you were placed in seclusion, your dreams began. As a warrior, there is one power you have forgotten. At one time in our history, we stripped this power from our Fenian Warriors. Eventually, we considered it unwise." The king moved forward. "It is the most powerful and one even I cannot control."

Confused by the king's words, Rory shrugged. "You are the King of the Fae. Your power is dominant. Is there another greater than yours?"

King Ansgar's laughter echoed all around the serene foliage and trees. "Not even a king can weave a mightier power than *love*."

His declaration slammed into Rory. Every cell in his being loved Erina. With each breath and exhalation, the emotion filled him. Yet, he was bound by laws and oaths—ancient and unyielding. Though he loved her, it was forbidden. Was he not trained to seal off his emotions around the humans? *Yes, repeatedly.*

"As a trained Fenian Warrior, I understand the laws regarding love with a human."

"And yet you did fall in love!" King Ansgar snapped. "However, this is not why you are here. You have a decision to make, and I wanted to give you my assurance I will stand beside you in whatever path you venture onto. You have found that love can alter even the greatest of warriors."

Aye. The greatest Fenian Warrior ever. Aidan Kerrigan. And look what love did to him. He was stripped of his powers and made mortal, never to return to his own world. I would gladly give up everything to be with Erina. But the time has lapsed.

"What if I want to leave the Brotherhood?" Rory kept his expression neutral.

"The choice is yours, Fenian Warrior. Choose wisely and remember my words from this conversation. You are free to depart."

Rory's troubled spirits quieted. Inclining his head to the king, he left in a sliver of light.

Chapter Twenty-Seven

"The mortals have a saying, 'Time heals all wounds.' Yet, for the Fae, wounds left by love surface with each waking moment. In order to heal, they must find love again."

~*Chronicles of the Fae*

Shielding his eyes from the intense glare of the new dawn, Rory pulled his satchel more firmly over his shoulder. The rose-colored light splashed across the valley below, a beacon of renewal to his fatigued soul. Lush, green grass carpeted the ground for as far as he could see. A river ran adjacent to numerous rowan trees, their giant limbs gently waving to him as if in greeting.

"Home," he uttered softly.

Rory lost all sense of time on his journey back to a place that brought comfort to his soul. It might have been months, or even a year. Instead of magically appearing at his mother's front gates, he had determined to spend the time in quiet reflection on a pilgrimage throughout his world. He longed to soothe and close the door on the past. Erina was gone. When the nights became too unbearable, he drew down the stardust and blew it across the realms, praying she heard his soft whisper of love.

After meeting with Conn, he told him that before

returning to the Brotherhood, he required some time away. Though he was stunned, Conn gave his consent, and Rory left immediately.

His first thought was of his mother. Remembering a certain conversation with Erina about family, he deemed it was time to pay his respects. Secondly, Rory determined it was also long overdue to heal the puckered scar on his side. Even with the altered time, the disfigurement remained. When the healer told him to seek out the Master Apothecary, he found the woman refused to see him. She left a note stating to return when his heart was healed. Frustrated, Rory left the next morning.

Now, his travels became a blur. Decisions he had wanted to make along the way, more confusing. Did he truly want to return to the Brotherhood? Could he live amongst his people serving another purpose? Yet, all he knew was to be a Fenian Warrior. Could there be more to his life? Was he worried? On the contrary, paths and answers often revealed themselves. During his travels, Rory found patience and listened to the land.

As he traveled down the hill, his steps grew swifter, until he found himself running. The spirit of his youthful days teased at his memories. By the time he entered the valley floor, he was lightheaded from the exertion.

The familiar stone cottage with its thatched roof reached out to him in welcome. Sweet peas, roses, and honeysuckle spilled out like a blanket along the path and trailed up along a huge trellis in front of the home. He had forgotten how much his mother loved her flowers. She must have cultivated every seed Earth was known to have upon the land around her cottage.

Butterflies flitted about, filling the air with more beauty. As he inhaled deeply, his smile came unbidden.

"Ye would have loved Erina," whispered Rory as his fingers brushed over a rose petal.

Though his family was from the Royal House of Avieon, his parents enjoyed living outside the confines of the royal court and the Crystal Palace. When he and his brother, Liam were young, his mother sought out the gentle landscape and lush rolling hills that protected the bucolic valley, creating a home filled with flowers and herbs. She had brought all her knowledge to the area. Now, even the Fae healers consulted her for specific herbal and floral remedies.

Rory sensed her thoughts before she appeared at the door. Her greeting within his mind was one of a mother who had missed her son, and he chastised himself for staying apart for so many years.

Striding forward, he choked back the emotions as she approached him with her arms outstretched. Time had not dulled his mother's beauty. Raven hair with only a touch of gray at the temples cascaded in a flowing mass down her back. Her lavender eyes continued to sparkle as those of a youth. He dropped his satchel and embraced her. Closing his eyes, Rory exhaled slowly, letting the past ease out of him.

"I am happy you journeyed on foot," she uttered softly.

As he released her, Rory tipped her chin up with his finger. "How many times did ye order Liam and me to wander the hills when our minds were troubled?"

Her mother chuckled and turned away from him. "Too many times to count." She gave him a passing glance over her shoulder as she made her way into the cottage. "And did it help you?"

"Always," Rory affirmed and picked up his satchel.

As soon as he entered his home, he felt like a soothing balm had been applied to his soul. He had come home. A place that brought him immense joy. The exterior was small, but when you stepped inside a Fae's home, their tastes usually transformed the interior into opulent colors and greenery. In addition, some homes were vast inside. His parents' home was no different.

The main living area was akin to stepping into a painting depicting autumn foliage. Rich in amber, yellow, red, and green colors, the room glittered. Crystals of various sizes and shapes adorned the large table by the huge stained glass window. Overstuffed chairs beckoned him to sit for a spell near the giant hearth. Long ago memories whispered to him, especially those of his father. A man who was a warrior in his own right, but never sought out the Brotherhood. When Rory and Liam both announced their intention to become Fenian Warriors, his father retrieved two armbands from a stone box he brought with him from their homeland on Taralyn. They were ancient and powerful and had passed down from father to the oldest son. However, his father had heard the whispered words from a Seer, stating his sons would become great heroes. Therefore, one was given to Liam and the other to him. After Erina died, Rory removed the armband. Not only did he fail in his mission, but to his family, and he considered himself unworthy.

Rory clutched his upper right arm in remembrance. "Ye left us too soon father, but I will retrieve what ye have given to me. I should not have discarded the family heirloom."

The aroma of honeyed sweet bread drifted past him, and his stomach protested, snapping him out of his thoughts.

Wandering into the massive kitchen, Rory dropped his satchel on a nearby bench. The room enveloped him with the tantalizing scents of hearty soup and bread. He stepped near his mom and peered over her shoulder. "Wild mushroom, leeks, and garlic?"

"Of course. It remains your favorite, correct?"

"Aye. So ye sensed my arrival?" He produced a spoon and attempted to scoop out a portion, yet, his mother smacked his hand out of the way.

"Of course I did. Honestly, where are your manners, Rory? Go wash, change, and do so without the aid of magic."

Feeling ten years old all over again, he banished the spoon, but not before placing a kiss on his mother's cheek. Reaching for his satchel, he darted out of the kitchen and strode along the tree-lined passageway and up the crystal staircase. When he pushed open the door to his chamber, he paused. The room was not unlike the one he kept within the palace, including the polished amber floor. Except here, there were mementos of his childhood placed within the crevices of the trees and stones.

After he stripped free from his clothing, he stepped into his inner bathing chamber. Picking up a pine-scented soap, Rory walked downward over moss-covered stones to the waterfall flowing gently down the side of the hill. When the first drop of warm, soothing water touched his skin, he groaned. Letting his head drop forward, he allowed the water to glide over his body, and he closed his eyes. Moments passed and he stretched his shoulders.

Opening his eyes, Rory lathered his body and washed the grime from a battle he let cling to his skin for months. As he stepped out of the gentle mists and water, his mind became clear. His heart would always ache, but now he saw the path more clearly. Stepping back inside his chamber, he went to his armoire and took out a sleeveless tunic and dark trews. He dressed swiftly. Brushing his hair from his face with his hands, he stole a glance at the door and with a snap of his fingers vanished to the base of an ancient yew tree away from their home.

The place hummed with old energy. From those in his family who had gone before him. When a Fae passed over to the realm of *Tir na Og*, part of their ashes were always scattered on land sacred to the family. Approaching the tree, Rory placed his palm on the rough bark. The tree pulsed beneath his skin, and he acknowledged the wise spirit by bowing his head. After several moments, he crouched down at the base.

"When I sealed ye within, I had no desire to ever come upon ye in my lifetime. I was in error and misjudged. Open the land and wipe away the hatred I placed around the relic when I buried it centuries ago."

The ground rumbled, and Rory stood. Light splintered around him, and the silver armband he had banished from his existence, now floated in the air before him. His fingers trembled when he reached for the item, and when his hand closed in around the armband, he sighed. Bringing it to his lips, he kissed the ancient family artifact. And with a wave of his hand, the armband became attached to his upper right arm.

The power of his ancestors flowed with intensity throughout his body—*his blood*, causing him to stagger. Their many voices traveled all around him, greeting him once again. Strength infused him, and he drew back. He placed his fist over his chest. "May my remaining days be spent in honoring what I have tossed so carelessly away. My oath as a Fae. My pledge as a Fenian Warrior."

****

Kileburn Castle, December 1606

"Stop scratching, Lady Erina," pleaded Larena. "Ye can only cause more harm to the skin."

Erina glared at her, but snatched her hands away. "I used to adore winter, but now the bitter cold leaves my legs aching and itching."

Larena placed a comforting hand on her shoulder. "Ye ken 'tis the scars."

Erina gritted her teeth. She knew she shouldn't complain, understanding it could be far worse. The fire had left its ugly mark on her legs and had hampered her in ways she had never known. After Graham and Brother Michael had returned with her to Kileburn, she had spent many months in horrible pain. Not only to her body, but her heart. And she couldn't determine which one was worse. Both seemed to fight for dominion, almost crushing her with their weight.

When the fever from her burns kept her in its grip, she recalled the vivid dreams of the man—of the Fae she had loved and lost. How she yearned to be swept away in his arms, never to return to the land of the living. But fate was cruel. A dream was only a dream, and when the tide of sickness passed, Erina woke to agonizing pain within her soul.

For days, she refused to take any drink or food. The healing broth Larena made was left untouched, until one day she felt the whisper of his touch across her cheek. It was also the same day that a small bird entered into her chamber and refused to part through the window. Perching its tiny body on a ledge by the window, it kept her company with birdsong. Her spirits grew with each hour, and by the end of the day, Erina vowed to heal. Rory had given up everything to save her, so she would honor his memory and time together by living her life. When the next morning dawned, her feathered friend had departed.

"Would ye like me to fetch your salve?" Larena asked as she retrieved a basket of herbs off the table.

She smiled at the woman and shook her head. "If I require any, I will go fetch it myself. Ye are not my maid, and I am capable of walking. Though I do thank ye for offering."

"Ye have come so far in healing since those first few months."

Thane strolled over from the hearth to Erina and slumped down at her feet. "I had many to give me comfort during those dark days." She brushed her fingers over the animal's coarse coat, recalling how even her dog refused to leave her side. In an attempt to remove the dog from her chamber, many were met with fierce growls and snapping.

Larena chuckled as she proceeded to pull the herbs apart. "How many times did your brother read ye the tale of King Arthur?"

"Which version? I found myself questioning him when he professed the knights were all of Scottish descent and Arthur was kin to the great King Kenneth

MacAlpin." Erina lifted her legs away from her dog. "I swear if I never hear the story again, I shall be eternally grateful. Not only did he go into detail about their lineage, but he would deviate from the story and discuss the animals and weaponry."

After wiping her hands on her smock, Larena patted her cheek. "He knew ye enjoyed the story, and wanted to see the smile return to your face. Furthermore, ye do realize some believe every great king has Scot's blood flowing in their veins."

"It was more laughter than smiles," she snorted and stood. Leaning against the table, she stretched her legs. The pain would lessen come spring and warmer weather. For now, Erina would count the blessing she was able to walk, among the other bountiful ones in her life.

"When do ye leave us?"

Erina folded her arms over her chest. "Do the people still whisper tales within the corridors?"

Larena shrugged and went back to her herbs. "They never stop. And thank the Lord your brother banished those that brought harm to ye here at Kileburn."

Reaching for a rosemary branch, Erina brought it in front of her face and inhaled its pungent odor. The herb always brought a smile to her face. "Early spring," she responded. "Darren and a few other guards will accompany us on our journey north."

"Aye, the isles will be a safer place for ye."

Crestfallen, her smile quickly faded. Erina had no desire to leave her home or Kileburn. Graham and she had bonded more as a family during her time at the castle. The past fears of the stone fortress were replaced with healing and joyful memories. However, Graham judged it wiser to have her journey to a haven where her kin continued to believe in the old ways. Even though the bishop and Sinclair vanished months ago, her brother feared someone else could take their place and come after her.

Erina dropped the rosemary twig. "I fear I shall never return here."

"Ye will be missed." The woman's eyes misted with unshed tears.

Choking back the emotions, Erina squeezed her hand. "Let us not dwell on my leaving. 'Tis not for many months."

"Aye, aye."

She stepped away and grabbed her cloak off a peg. Erina walked slowly out of the kitchen with Thane taking the lead. She left the castle through a side entrance and ambled along the herb garden. This was her daily ritual—a time of peace and solitude. As always, her steps led her beyond the garden and out near the river. Eventually, her gaze would travel outward, and she'd recall the day she spotted Rory standing in the river.

Her pulse skittered, and she placed a hand over her heart. "Sweet Goddess, I pray my love still lives. Can ye carry my words across the winds to his realm?" The biting cold snapped at Erina, tempting her to return inside to the warmth, but she would not relent. This was her only time to mourn—for one more touch, stolen kiss, or a glimpse of the man who would always hold her heart.

No matter the months or the years that might pass, Rory would always be with her. There were no regrets. She was determined to forge a new path. Her Fae lover had given everything for her to live and much more. Honoring the gift he had presented to her was her single focus.

Though it pained her, Erina crouched down. Placing her palm upon the hard, damp ground, she let her sorrow mixed with love pour out. "I will love ye until the stars fade from the night sky, *my* Fenian Warrior."

A lone tear slipped down her cheek as she stood slowly, and Erina retreated to the castle.

Chapter Twenty-Eight

"The veil of reality is often times clouded when a Fae is uncertain of his direction."
~Chronicles of the Fae

Beads of sweat broke out along Rory's brow with each blow of the hammer onto the anvil. He continued to pummel the metal, forging and coaxing the shape he desired. His focus stayed intent on the creation. His desire was to create a perfect sword. The energy hummed around him as he continued to strike blows to fashion a blade. No magic was required. Only his skilled hands and keen eyesight.

His mother was correct once again. Manual labor is always good for what ails you. It keeps you centered to the land. How he'd forgotten those words of wisdom. She had never criticized him when he returned home, especially on his use of the old language from the mortal realm. Her eyes withheld judgment, and her words encouraged him. Each day, he sought out something to do around the cottage for his mother. In a sense, this was Rory's way of healing. He had yet to tell her fully about Erina, but he sensed she knew when one day she placed her hand on his chest, stating his heart required healing. He had no words to tell her otherwise. His love for Erina would always span his life, no matter where he traveled.

No other would he take to his bed. No other would ever claim his heart or soul. Rory had sealed it with Erina's long ago.

Often times, in the quiet moments before dawn, Rory fought the urge to return to her time. Seek her out for reassurance all was well. But he was honor bound by an oath—one he had made when he sought to rescue Erina. This pledge was the only sliver of sanity that prevented him from breaking it and facing total banishment from the Brotherhood.

By the Gods, did he truly want to return to the Brotherhood? Uncertainty continued to plague him. Even the months spent at home hadn't changed his initial thoughts. He longed for the freedom to venture away, but he was trapped with indecisions. One was his relationship with Conn. Would he be able to accept him fully as his leader? The burning rage he tried to contain had surfaced on more than one occasion. If it had not been for King Ansgar's interference, she would have burned at the stake, and he would have suffered Erina's death all over again.

Rory lifted the hammer high and with a curse, he sent it flying across the forge.

The power of another warrior brushed against him. He picked up the blade and doused it in a bucket of water. Lifting it up to the early morning light, he noted Conn's reflection in back of him. As he gripped the partial blade more firmly, he waited for him to approach. The indecision to leave flickered for a brief moment, and then Conn took a step forward.

Rory dropped the blade on the anvil and turned around.

Conn gestured outward, noting the unfinished

pieces of metal discarded in a side corner. "Is there a reason you have built this forge? Are you preparing to make weapons for an army?"

"Greetings, my prince." Shifting his stance, Rory added, "Is there a purpose as to why ye have traveled to this remote part of the realm?"

Conn arched a brow in a display of disapproval. "There is no need to address me thusly. I wanted to seek you out—"

"I am not ready to return to the Brotherhood," Rory interrupted and folded his arms over his chest. "Instead of traveling all this way, ye could have sent a message."

Shaking his head, Conn fisted his hands on his hips. "When are you going to remove this barrier between us, Rory?"

"I do not know."

Conn took a step forward. "Each of us has had to walk a path of injustices, Rory. You are blinded by yours." Jabbing a finger into his chest, he continued, "You were the one to betray the Brotherhood after the first incident with Erina. You should have trusted us— your brothers! But you sealed everything away. Now what? You think you're the only one of us who has suffered?"

"Ye have *suffered*? What do ye ken of the pain of loss?" Rory bellowed, shoving past Conn.

He stormed along the narrow path toward the stream. It took all of his control not to level a fist at the Fae prince. In truth, he deemed he would always find it difficult to be around someone he once considered a close friend. There were times he envied Conn's control. Even when he and Liam approached the Fae about joining them in their quest to assist the Dragon

Knights, Conn had remained steadfast and calm.

But the Fae standing nearby was not the same one he fought with many months ago. Something changed. He had said nothing about his reasons for claiming the seat of heir to the kingdom. In the past, Conn adamantly avowed he would never become king. Why the shift? What did he face in the Room of Reflection? Questions he never thought of, now unfolded within his mind.

A pair of swans glided silently over the water, and Rory envied their peacefulness. He wiped a hand down the back of his neck. *Love is the greatest power.*

"I have come to seek a favor." Conn stood partially in the shadows of an oak tree. "It is important to both worlds, and I require your keen insight on this one."

Rory released the breath he had been holding. He glanced sideways at him. "One condition."

"Name it."

"When I return, ye will answer all my questions."

Conn's mouth twitched in humor. "Done. There is much we need to discuss upon your return."

"Good." He started to move forward and paused. "My mother would greatly appreciate a visit from ye."

"I would not dare take my leave without seeing her lovely face."

Rory proceeded forward with Conn following alongside him. Both remained silent as they approached the cottage. His mother was bent near a patch of wild violets and humming a soft tune. Her face transformed into a radiant smile as they both entered the garden. She stood and brushed her hands on her smock.

"Sweet Goddess, it is good to see you grace my home, *Prince* Conn." She held out her arms in welcome, and he swept her into an embrace.

"Please do not address me in that manner, *Reena*." He drew back and kissed her hand.

Sunlight and mirth danced within her eyes. "Ahh…but you are worthy of the title, and I am honor bound."

"It is one I'm having trouble adjusting to, so indulge me while I'm here, and do not call me thusly."

"As you wish, Conn. Would you care for some apple fritters and a cup of ale? Or are you only here for a brief visit?" She turned her attention to Rory.

"I believe we both would enjoy a cup of ale and meal of your delicious fritters," Rory stated and gave his mother a smile. "We will join ye after I speak with Conn first."

"Excellent." Reena beamed. "When you are through with your conversation, come into the kitchen."

His mother retreated into the cottage, and Rory tuned to face Conn. "What is this favor ye seek?"

Conn frowned and rubbed a hand over his chin. "Have you sensed the shift within the youngest Dragon Knight?"

Leaning against a pillar, he nodded slowly. "Only recently. It's a flicker of awareness, and I gather he is seeking knowledge. Does this bother ye?"

The prince gazed outward. "When I last visited, the young lad's powers were growing at a tremendous speed, along with his height. Though part of him is human, the Fae side is progressing at a much stronger rate. Of all the Dragon Knights, James MacKay MacFhearguis is the strongest to have ever walked the land."

"What are your concerns?"

Turning his attention back to him, Conn replied,

"There is a darkness within his light. I must determine if he requires a guardian to help further his training and keep him focused."

"And for protection?"

"It would depend on whom I'm protecting him from and since I am no longer his guardian, I must trust only the best Fenian Warrior to guide him."

"Why send me?"

Sighing, Conn replied, "Because you, Liam, and I were the only ones who have met Jamie. I trust and value your insight. I sense he'll be more amenable to those he considers friends."

Rory bristled at the mention of his brother's name. "Then I will prepare for the visit."

Conn held out a hand to stop his movement. "I know there's an unspoken question, but I am not permitted to gather any information regarding Liam. Furthermore, I am forbidden to go near him. I have tempted fate on more than one occasion with the Fae council."

Rory glanced sharply at the entrance to the cottage, fearing his mother was nearby. "Why hasn't he had a trial?"

"You better than anyone can fathom the reason. His crime for taking Aidan Kerrigan, another Fenian Warrior, through the Veil of Ages—one who had been stripped of his powers—is punishable by death."

"Not if I can prevent it. Ye ken any one of us would have done what Aidan asked."

"Agreed. But for now, I am ordered to stay away. My involvement with your trial brought the Fae council to my chambers at the Brotherhood. If not for the king, I judge they would have sought to strip me of my powers. In truth, they came to issue me a warning, but I shall covertly seek out how Liam fares. You must remain patient. My interference will only be tolerated so much from the council members."

"Even for a prince?"

Conn shrugged. "I've held back on using my royal status, unless required."

Rory once again looked at the cottage's entrance. "Not once since I've returned has my mother said anything about Liam."

Conn chuckled softly. "My intuition tells me your mother knows exactly how he is doing and where. Her insight and knowledge is second only to the seer's. Remember, she can call out to the land to find him."

"Then I will bide my time and pray Liam will get a fair trial, as well."

"I will alert you the second they release him from his Room of Reflection."

Rory exhaled slowly. "Thank ye."

****

Aonach Castle, Scotland, Home of the present day Dragon Knights

As Rory stood in the shadows of the pine trees, he swept his gaze across the mist-covered hills, past the loch, and finally on Aonach Castle. Conn's words about the young Dragon Knight unsettled him. Did they not vanquish the evil monster, Lachlan last year? If the prophecy were correct, the next battle would not be for a thousand years.

A late autumn breeze swirled around him as he crouched down near the land. A falcon eyed him with curiosity from a nearby branch, and Rory sensed another set of eyes. The power pushed against him, but he remained steady. Was it a warning? Rory was unable to determine the source, and he stood.

His thoughts went out at once to the Great Dragon. She acknowledged his greeting, though the energy he encountered was not hers. It belonged to another—one more powerful than his ancestors. The lad was growing.

"Dragon Knight." Rory acknowledged.

"Why do ye stand in the shadows, Fenian Warrior?"

"There is light even within the darkness."

"True. For those that can see the shimmer. Then there are the others who seek the solitude from the shade."

Startled by the conversation with Jamie within his mind, Rory emerged into the sunlight.

"Ahh...there ye are. I will go announce your arrival to my parents."

The falcon swiftly took flight toward the castle, and Rory fisted his hands on his hips. Conn was indeed correct. The power that brushed against his own was near to those of the Fae. No human since the inception of the Dragon Knights had ever possessed such energy. The young lad had actually manipulated the bird to be his eyes over the land.

With a wave of his hand, Rory vanished from his position on the hill and entered the portcullis. Striding forth, he was met by Dragon Knight, Adam MacFhearguis, Jamie's father.

The man held out his arm in welcome, though worry showed over his features. "Greetings, Rory. 'Tis good to see ye again. We were told of your freedom."

Grasping the man's forearm, Rory frowned in confusion. "By whom? Jamie?"

Adam chuckled and released his hold. "Nae. I dinnae reckon Jamie's knowledge can extend into the Fae realm. Archie McKibben informed us."

"The Bard for the Fae always has his pulse on the realm."

"Aye. He keeps us informed. But what of your brother, Liam?"

"Nothing," Rory answered with staid calmness.

"Let us take this conversation into the Great Hall. Meggie is preparing drink and food. She will be happy to see ye."

As they strode through the bailey, the power Rory had experienced earlier teased at the outer edges of his inner Fae. His steps slowed, and he turned toward Adam. "How is the young Dragon Knight?"

Adam eyed him with curiosity, but kept on walking. "A question ye must ask him. Our son continues to grow and be trained by Archie, the Great Dragon, and me. As I am sure ye already ken, since he has spoken with ye." He halted by the massive oak doors and waited.

"I wish to hear *your* opinion." Rory approached by his side.

Glancing sideways, Adam replied, "The day he tried to battle my inner dragon was the moment I realized my son might require another more powerful to guide him. If ye are here to assist, we shall welcome the aid. By rights, I am the elder Dragon Knight, but at nearly five winters, Jamie speaks like an ancient."

Rory leaned against the door and pondered his next question. Yes, Conn had only desired Rory to observe and bring back his knowledge, but he did not like keeping Adam in the dark regarding his son. "Do ye deem it wise he should have a Fae guardian?"

"By the saints, aye," Adam muttered and raked a hand through his hair. "Meggie frets more over the lad, but keeps silent."

He straightened and placed a firm hand on Adam's shoulder. "This is why I am here. Conn sent me to discern if there was a necessity for a guardian."

"Trust me, Meggie and I are unsure the path he is on. One moment, he is a lad of almost five, and the next, a Dragon Knight wielding his power of fire."

"Has he harmed anyone?"

"Nae, *nae*. As with any power, mine included, there is a need to harness and experiment. Though, I have warned him about using his inner thoughts in our minds."

"His is strong."

"Aye. He often scares his mother by sneaking up on her and then announcing himself within her thoughts."

"Ye do ken, he inherited his stubborn, forceful trait from his lineage?"

Adam wiped a hand down the back of his neck. "He is verra much like his Uncle Angus."

"However, the elder Dragon Knight knew how to control his Fire Dragon."

After nodding in agreement, Adam pushed open the doors and gestured Rory forward. "Agreed. 'Tis a shame his uncle cannae be here to help guide him."

Rory smiled as a seed of inspiration blossomed within his mind. "Nae. But we can always send him to *Uncle* Angus."

Adam snorted in disgust. "Meggie would surely counter the idea, especially since we have been denied the chance to journey back ourselves. The ache of losing her brothers continues to haunt her."

"Forgive me," Rory apologized. "I was not aware of the circumstances at the end of the battle."

Pausing before the corridor, Adam cast his sight over Rory's shoulder. "The only request the Fae accepted from Meggie was the one to spare all of your lives—Conn, Liam, and *yours*. We were not permitted to return home to our time." Taking a step toward Rory, he uttered softly, "I would deem it unwise to send my son back in time to live with his uncle. If a future battle waits, he will need those here in the present to assist him. His army is growing."

"Army?" Rory demanded. "What are ye saying?"

"For one, the MacKay cousins," Meggie interrupted, stepping forth from a side passageway. "And those yet to be born."

Rory bowed his head. "Greetings, Margaret."

"Goodness, are we on formal terms, Rory MacGregor?" Her smiled disarmed him, and she extended her arms outward.

He swept her into his embrace. "Nae, but I did not want to offend ye with our conversation."

Meggie drew back and studied his face. "'Tis a discussion Adam and I have constantly." She gave her husband a small smile. "Jamie will continue to train here. Furthermore, we shall speak more later. Let us go see what my sons are up to in the Great Hall." She linked her arm with his and moved him along the entryway.

Adam groaned. "If the doors are closed, then Jamie is either showing him his prowess with a sword, or he's regaling him with yet another tale of the Dragon

Knights."

"Ye have another son?"

Meggie paused. "Aye. Alexander Conn MacKay MacFhearguis. I'm shocked Conn did not mention the birth."

"As am I," Rory drawled.

She nudged him. "And the next two bairns will be named after ye and your brother, Liam. Apparently, Jamie acquired this information about future brothers from the Great Dragon."

Stunned, he asked, "But why our names?"

Releasing her hold on him, Meggie cupped his face. "Without the help of the Fenian Warriors, none of us would be standing here today discussing our son's future. Death's blow and evil would have surely claimed all of us. Our children will carry each of your names with them."

Emotion overtook Rory. No child of his blood would carry his name, but to know another—a future Dragon Knight would, made his heart soar. Wrapping his arms around her, he whispered, "I am honored."

Meggie broke free and reached for her husband's hand. "Come help gather the food and drinks. Let Rory greet our sons alone. Besides, I believe Jamie will speak more openly without us hovering nearby."

Adam wrapped an arm around her waist and nuzzled her neck. "Sound advice, my love."

Rory watched them depart down the passageway with a sense of pain and loss. Their love spanned centuries and overcame death. As he stood in the half-lit corridor, he envied Adam and Meggie.

Looking away, Rory slammed the door once again on emotions that left him dizzy with longing. For a woman that held his soul and left him without breath. Each day, each month, each year, could not wipe away the love he carried for her.

Turning around, he pushed open the doors to the Great Hall and strode inside.

Chapter Twenty-Nine

*"Often times, the light of wisdom from children is
clouded by stubbornness."*
~Chronicles of the Fae

As Rory stepped inside the hall, he halted. He
listened with intent as Jamie proceeded to discuss in
vivid detail the powers of his uncle, Duncan MacKay,
to wee Alexander. Apparently, the younger son of
Adam and Meggie had inherited the powers of the sky
and storms. Jamie continued to extol accolades on
Duncan, and Rory almost laughed at the absurdity. It
had been Duncan's sword that killed Meggie.
Thankfully, the Guardian of the Fae realm sought
justice by sending her soul forward into the future, but
wiped out all of Meggie's memories. She also was
responsible for sending forth Adam to bind what had
been destroyed.

The threads of fate were snapped and then rewoven
for Meggie and Adam. A bloodline divided. A new
order of Dragon Knights reborn.

But not for him and Erina. Rory exhaled softly, at
least he had saved her. The oath to save her life had
been rewoven, too.

Alexander waved a fist into the air, and Jamie
nodded. "Aye, they were all great knights. Did I
mention I met them?"

The wee bairn made a garbled sound from his basket on the table and Jamie chuckled. "Ye should have seen them standing before the hearth when father and mama were married. I ken one day we shall all reunite."

Rory frowned in concentration. Did Jamie overhear the conversation with his father? Or did he see the future—one that would require the aid of his uncles? He marveled at the young lad. He might be almost five winters, yet, Jamie's stance, language, and height marked him much older.

Alexander sputtered out babble. Jamie responded with a gesture and nod.

Again, Rory watched in awe as the two Dragon Knights communicated with each other in silence and clipped words of acknowledgment. The new Order was more powerful than the Dragon Knights who adorned the tapestries. The blood of the Fae from thousands of years ago flowed more than the human within their veins.

Rory suspected Jamie was waiting for him to utter the first word. He would not underestimate this Dragon Knight.

He proceeded forward. "Greetings, Jamie *and* Alexander."

Both glanced his way, and their eyes blazed with that of their inner dragons. The power flickered, and then Jamie blinked. Jumping down from the table, he ran over to Rory.

"'Tis good to see ye, Rory." The lad hesitated briefly and then embraced him. Breaking free, he smiled fully. "Were ye listening to the tale I was telling my brother?"

"Aye. I favor any tale where there is a mention of a Dragon Knight."

Jamie laughed. The sound so infectious that Rory chuckled, too. Alexander let out a screech and both turned his way. The lad was clutching a wooden sword and demanding attention.

Rory made his way to the bairn's side. Inclining his head, he said, "'Tis good to meet ye, Alexander. How old are ye?"

"Ten months," offered Jamie. He quickly stole a glance at the entrance to the hall. "I must confess, Alexander can speak, but he is choosing not to until he marks his one year birth."

Curious, Rory asked, "How do ye come by this knowledge? And why would he keep silent?"

Jamie hopped onto the table and fingered Alexander's wooden sword. "I ken how worried my parents are for me at times. I have nae desire to see my brother being fussed over by my mama or father. Alexander was speaking to me months ago. He is also good at running away."

Rory placed a hand on the lad's shoulder. "Ye underestimate both your parents. Your mother lived with powerful Dragon Knights. She is *married* to a Dragon Knight and carries her own powers. Ye do them an injustice by not sharing your wisdom. Aye, they have concerns, but they have witnessed evil."

"So have I!" Jamie smacked the sword onto the table and sparks flew outward.

Alexander bunched his fist together and thunder rolled overhead.

With a wave of his hand, Rory pushed the threat of rain away and pointed a warning finger at both the lads.

"The first lesson a Dragon Knight learns is to *control* the beast within. If ye surrender to the fiery temper, disaster can strike. Furthermore, ye must always respect the eldest Dragon Knight, which is your father." He swept his gaze to Jamie. "Remember in your lessons to your brother to inform him what happened when Uncle Duncan let loose his anger. He set in motion a chain of events that were almost disastrous."

Jamie swallowed. "He did find redemption."

"But it cost him and everyone dearly. Yet, he did find love."

The boy narrowed his eyes. "And did *ye* learn your lesson?"

Rory arched a brow in defiance of the remark, and he fought the fury surfacing. The lad might be a strong Dragon Knight, but he was nothing compared to a Fae Warrior. "Ye are not privy to that information. Until ye have experienced your own pain, do not tamper with those of another, *especially* a Fenian Warrior."

Jamie's face transformed into one of a child once again. "Ye are correct. My apologies." As he slid off the table, he reached for Alexander. After placing him on the ground, he took his chubby hand into his. "I reckon 'tis time we mention your ability to speak, Alexander, and that ye can walk fully on your own."

Crossing his arms over his chest, Rory nodded in agreement. "Wise decision."

He watched the young lads retreat out of the hall and then turned his attention to the Dragon Knights gazing back down at him from their respective tapestries. The last time they had all been together was during the great battle against the evil druid, Lachlan. He, Liam, and Conn were instrumental in sealing the realm between time and both worlds—human and Fae. When victory was attained, they found themselves shackled and sent off to the Fae prison, otherwise known as the Room of Reflection.

"There are no regrets, my friends. If given the chance, I would have walked into battle with ye once again." Rory fisted a hand over his heart. "Your deeds are honored in the hallowed halls of the Fae. I salute ye—Angus, Duncan, Stephen, and Alastair."

"Let us not forget Adam," declared Archie, walking up alongside him.

Glancing at the Bard of the Fae, Rory smiled. "Never. However, Adam is here." He gestured to the tapestries and added, "These knights have long since ventured into the land of forever."

Archie pointed to the fourth tapestry. "Ye were his guardian."

A stab of guilt plagued Rory. "Aye, but I ken there are regrets for leaving Alastair so early on his journey."

"If I recall, ye were ordered to do so. His path to redemption did take longer, but in the end, Alastair chose wisely."

"Albeit with help from the Great Dragon," Rory added.

"Thank Mother Danu," muttered Archie and moved away. "When are they sending a Fae guardian for Jamie?"

"Unsure. Though, I will make a suggestion to not wait and to appoint one now."

"Good." Archie leaned against the table. "I am happy to see all is well with ye."

Rory masked his inner turmoil with deceptive calmness. "Thank ye."

"Your appointment to the elite branch of the Brotherhood has not been mentioned. Are ye having doubts?"

The bard was perceptive and inquisitive. "I required time...away. When I return, I will accept the position."

Archie pursed his lips, and Rory deemed there was more he wished to convey.

Both turned as Adam and Meggie came strolling into the hall, their arms laden with food and drink. Jamie and Alexander were following at a distance, as well. And Rory's conversation with the bard would have to wait for another time.

****

Rory stood on the edges of the loch, the water gently lapping at his bare feet as he stared outward. His time with the Great Dragon was one of healing, reminding him that love takes many forms. She never mentioned his broken heart. Yet, she sought to soothe the shards and to remind him that nothing is ever truly lost. The love he held for Erina would always stay with him—for all eternity.

In addition, the time spent with Adam, Meggie, and the children was a joyous reunion. Initially, his plan was to stay for a couple days, but he enjoyed the company and remained for an entire week. When he returned, he would confess his desire to become the young Dragon Knight's guardian. Would Conn accept? Indecision filled Rory, and he doubted his own plan. Rubbing a hand over his chin in thought, he almost missed the approaching brush of power.

"Good afternoon, Jamie."

The lad moved to his side, tossing a rock into the

air. "Did ye ken I can make the stone skip four times across the water?"

"Impressive," Rory drawled. "Is your father showing ye?"

Tilting his head back, Jamie peered at his face, a smile tugging at the outer edges of his mouth. "Aye."

"How many times can your father skip the stone?"

"He has mastered eight."

"Let me guess. Ye plan on surpassing that number one day?"

Jamie roared in delight. "Of course."

"Another word of warning, Jamie. Never underestimate an elder Dragon Knight."

All humor vanished from the lad's face. "I have great respect for my father. He is my hero and I love him. While he is the oldest, he will not lead the army against the darkness. I will. Therefore, I must excel in everything."

The fire dragon's power blazed all around the young Dragon Knight. Rory had questioned him about the growing darkness he had talked about, but the boy refused to offer any more knowledge.

Rory gestured outward. "Do your best, Jamie."

The lad winked and hurled the stone across the water. Rory watched in awe as it skipped across the loch five times.

"Aye!" Jamie shouted and picked up another stone.

Rory placed a gentle hand on his shoulder. "Well done."

Both continued to gaze outward at the serene setting.

"Are ye leaving?"

Rory sighed. "Aye. 'Tis time."

The boy glanced up at him. "Be well, Fenian Warrior."

"And ye, too."

Releasing his hold, Rory strode quietly away. However, Jamie's words within his mind froze him where he stood.

"When ye return to the Fae realm, give my regards to Sorcha."

Confused by the lad's words, he had no time to question him as Jamie ran off into the trees. Bewilderment soon turned to unease, and Rory vanished in an arc of light. As he emerged outside the hall of the Brotherhood, he composed his emotions and went on through the gilded doors.

Several warriors nodded to him in passing as he made his way to Conn's chamber. The doors were partially open. The sound of Conn's laughter drifted out and he froze. Never before had he heard the warrior relaxed and carefree. When he slowly approached the room, his hand gripped the handle.

Conn was nuzzling the neck of a woman and speaking words of endearment. His senses reeled as he fully stepped inside. When had he become involved with a Fae? In all his lifetime, Rory had never known the warrior to openly show affection to anyone. He kept his lovers a secret from all.

The lovely lass lifted her face, and her eyes grew wide. "We have a visitor."

Conn half-turned. "I have been waiting for you, Rory."

She tried to move out of Conn's embrace, but he held her firm. "No, Ivy. It is time to introduce you to my good friend."

Rory's hands clenched. *Friend?* The air hummed of another energy not of the realm, and he found himself fighting the growing fury. Her blood was not all Fae. "*Human?*"

Ignoring his question, Conn placed a protective arm around Ivy's waist. "Rory, this is...Ivy O'Callaghan. My wife."

The room blurred and for a moment, Rory wanted to take a fist to the warrior's face. "Explain!"

Conn arched a brow. "Of course."

Fear showed in Ivy's eyes, and she snuggled closer to her husband. Taking a deep breath in, Rory released it slowly. His anger was at Conn, not the stunning vision before him. After bowing his head in respect to her, he then moved forward. "Forgive me, *Princess* Ivy."

Giving him a weak smile, Ivy removed herself from Conn's embrace. She reached out and grasped his hands. "I have longed to meet you. Please call me Ivy. I hope you can find it in you to forgive Conn for his recent rude behavior. He should have spoken to you sooner."

Conn winced and wiped a hand down the back of his neck. "Regardless, my friend has given me no time to fully divulge the details of our marriage."

The lovely lass clucked her tongue in disapproval. "I am positive you can remedy the situation. You can also invite him to dinner this evening."

Her smile and touch broke the anger within Rory, especially seeing the tiny human female bring out a softer side to his leader. Never before had he witnessed Conn smiling like a young lad. He lifted her hands and placed a gentle kiss across her knuckles. "I would be honored, *Ivy*."

She laughed, and Rory was smitten.

"Wonderful! I will expect you later. For now, I'll leave you to pester my husband with the many questions you have for him. I must go tend to our daughter."

"*Daughter?*" he croaked and looked in bewilderment at Conn.

Ivy beamed. "Yes. She was born three months ago. You must come and see her. She has her father's stunning eyes, unlike the lavender of the Fae women."

"I will see you later, *wife*." Conn kissed her soundly and walked her to the entrance. After softly closing the door, he motioned for Rory to take a seat.

"I believe it wiser I stand to hear everything."

Conn shrugged and folded his arms over his chest. "You accused me once of not knowing any pain of loss. You were incorrect. You assumed I saved my life by agreeing to take my rightful place as heir to the Fae realm. Once again, you were wrong. I made a bargain to save a life. *Ivy's* life. Sadly, I was unable to share this information until after your journey." Pain showed across his features, and Conn moved to a chair.

Rory blew out a frustrated breath and sat down across from him. "What happened?"

Conn placed his hands on his thighs. "Where do I begin…"

"I've found it best to start at the beginning," Rory offered.

"My crime was not what I…*we* did in assisting the Dragon Knights. Apparently, I made an error in an event within the timeline. Changed the course of a generation of people. I was forced to return to the present and correct the mishap in the O'Callaghan clan—Ivy's people. Truth be told, destiny sought to bring Ivy and me together. I fell in love. Plain and simple." Conn stood abruptly. "That mere wisp of a human lass touched my soul. Yes, I fought the love." He sighed and clenched his hands. "When her life was threatened, and I found her near death, I brought her to the only place I knew of for healing."

"The Fae realm," interjected Rory.

Conn turned away. "So I made a deal with my father. A life for a life. My blood so she could live and I would remain here. I willingly gave up the Brotherhood to become *Prince* Conn once again."

"But ye are the *leader* of the Brotherhood. What changed?"

Conn glanced over his shoulder. "After my father granted my request, Ivy healed and returned to the mortal world. Bitterness and resentment became my companions. Over time, darkness would have clouded my judgment and hardened my heart. I deem the king—with urging from the queen—sought to bring Ivy and me back together. They had no wish to see a hardened Fae rule the kingdom. As part of the agreement, I took control from the Fae council and became the leader of the Brotherhood."

Rory stood and began to pace within the chamber. "They let ye marry a human? How many times did they speak of *not* tainting the Fae blood with a human? Only the creation of the Dragon Knights were permitted to have Fae blood." He paused before the massive table and slammed his fist upon the darkened wood. "By the hounds! Look what they did to Aidan Kerrigan for taking a human wife!"

Turning around, Conn came and placed a hand on Rory's shoulder. "Recently, I have witnessed that the Fae and seers are not always correct in their wisdom. They spout rules and edicts, but often times, they are just that. Words. Even the mighty ones are unable to fully see the path destined for a Fae or Fenian Warrior."

And what about Erina and me? "I wished I had known," he uttered softly.

Conn shook him gently and then released him. "Before you take your oath into the new Brotherhood, I give you permission to seek out Erina MacIntyre."

Rory's mouth opened in shock and words failed him.

"Do you love her, Rory?"

"Aye," he affirmed with conviction. "With all my heart and soul."

"Then go after her."

Uncertainty filled him. Would she still want him? There was only way to find out and if Conn was letting him go, Rory would not let the opportunity slip through his fingers. "Thank ye."

As he walked to the door, Rory paused. Turning around, he asked, "Who is Sorcha?"

Conn's expression stilled and grew serious. "My daughter. Why do you ask?"

Trying to keep the smile from forming on his mouth, he replied, "Jamie sends his regards."

The warrior's eyes narrowed to shards of silver. "Shit! He goes too far."

Rory chuckled softly. "When I return, I will give ye my report on the Dragon Knight. I deem it wise to appoint a guardian immediately." He angled his head. "Ye will have to share how he has a claim on your

334

daughter."

Conn grunted another curse and dismissed him with a wave of his hand. "There is no such claim. I'll send her to Abela to become a priestess and my worries will be solved. He's as arrogant as his uncles *and* his father."

Rory continued to watch the great Conn MacRoich, Prince of the Fae Realm, leader of the Brotherhood, pace along his chamber in an agitated state and continue with his rant against the young Dragon Knight.

It was a memory he imagined he would fondly recall for many years.

Chapter Thirty

"Love can bring down even the mightiest of warriors, along with assumptions."

~Chronicles of the Fae

Lindane, Scotland, August 1607

Rory leaned against the rowan tree for support as he gazed at the cottage he knew so well. A warm summer breeze lifted the hair from the back of his neck and bees swarmed about the wildflowers growing in abundance everywhere. Erina's cottage was the same, but the surrounding area was vastly changed. There were no sheep in her pen. The herb garden was a tangled mess, and he wondered if she had decided to remain at Kileburn. He had thought to go there first, but yearned to come to the place she called home.

However, fear kept him rooted in the shade, since he had not realized how many months had slipped through the window of time. In the Fae realm, time moved slowly, and he cursed himself for not realizing his error and misjudgment.

Hearing the soft whinny of horses, Rory moved away from the shadows. His steps led him to the side of the cottage where two horses and a cart were tethered to a post. Trunks filled the cart and he frowned. Was she leaving for Kileburn?

While their love was real, his stomach roiled with doubt, especially with the passing of so many months. Yet, he would not return without her. He would explain everything to her. Bring her to his world. Keep her safe.

A soft hum flitted by his ears, and Rory lifted his head in search of the delicate sound. Making his way down the path filled with flowers and wild grasses, he froze. There in the middle of a patch of foxgloves sat a wee lass. Butterflies danced over her head as she hummed a melody he found enchanting. Her raven hair clung to her shoulders, and he thought her to be no more than a year old. She brushed her hand over the flowers and giggled. The smile came unbidden to his face as he continued to be mesmerized by the scene.

Why was she left unattended out here? And where was her mother?

"Angelica? Where are ye sweet lass?"

Rory snapped his head at the sound of Erina calling for the wee child. His smile vanished, wiped away by astonishment. When Erina emerged from the cottage, he found himself unable to breathe. His heart slammed against his chest, and he quickly shielded himself with magic. Her beauty was even more breathtaking than he remembered. Her mass of hair more glorious as the sun shimmered off of her locks.

She took a small step forward, and he noted the limp. As he brought his hand forward to remove the cloaked veil, Rory stilled the movement. Another approached and grasped Erina's elbow.

"Darren," he hissed out. The air cooled, and he fought to control the rising fury.

The man gestured her toward the cart and helped her onto the seat. Rory's heated gaze followed the guard as he moved past him and toward the small lass. Darren lifted her into the air, and she responded in laughter.

"Och, my child. There ye are." Erina shielded her eyes.

The light of illumination pierced like an arrow to his heart. What Rory had feared had occurred. Erina had found happiness with another man, and this was their child. His world shifted beneath his feet as he watched father and daughter return to her mother's outstretched arms. Deep anguish filled him as he stumbled backwards.

Darren reached for the reins of the horses and gave a quick snap. The cart jerked forward and proceeded to amble down the path away from the cottage.

Rory rubbed his palm over his heart in an attempt to banish the pain. Yet, it was a futile effort. No amount of time would ever heal the hurt of losing her, but at least he knew she lived.

He straightened and took a step forward, keeping his eyes on the retreating family. "Be happy Erina. I shall love ye forever, *mo ghrá*. Never forget."

As if hearing his words, Erina turned in her seat and their gazes locked. In a blur of lights and tears, Rory vanished from her sight.

****

Upon entering the grove, which sat within the Brotherhood, Rory hastened across the stones. He wanted to get the ceremony done quickly and then set out on his new mission. After returning from visiting Erina, he promptly informed Conn he wished to be sent to Aonach and oversee Jamie's training. When the warrior asked what happened, Rory's answer was that

Erina was doing well. She had married and given birth to a child. She had moved on with her life. He judged this was far better for her than a life within a realm she wouldn't be able to comprehend.

For some insane reason, Conn called him a stubborn ass, but relented in the end.

Rory's only request was that the initiation into the elite Brotherhood take place within a day. He had no wish to remain in this world. He sought work, training, and centuries long removed from Erina. The temptation would be far too great to check in on her, and his heart could not stand to see her in the arms of another man. Again, he considered being placed as Jamie's guardian. Many centuries removed from Erina.

Pushing open the massive oak doors, Rory entered the ceremonial chamber. As he stepped inside, he glanced upward at the open sky. Sunlight glistened in a rainbow of colors within a vast room filled with nine giant oak trees. In the center, crystal steps led to a marble dais where the rite would take place. Many other Fenian Warriors had already arrived, and they acknowledged him in greeting.

Rory adjusted his pale blue, sleeveless tunic and made his way up the steps. Conn stood off to the side, conversing with another warrior. He nodded to both and went to approach his friend, Taran.

"I have yet to thank ye for keeping a vigil over me during my trial," said Rory.

Taran shifted his stance. "You would have done the same for me, old friend."

"I doubt ye would have entered the dark abyss."

"We all falter at times, Rory. Even the greatest. I am no fool to think I shall not be tested in my lifetime."

"Then I pray ye never have to endure any pain."

Taran made a dismissive gesture. "If you are referring to the affairs of the heart, I can assure you I will never succumb to any."

Saddened by the warrior's remarks, Rory replied, "Love is the most powerful emotion, bringing ye epic joy and misery. I have nae regrets."

A flash of annoyance briefly crossed Taran's face. "Then I shall leave the wisdom of your words to others."

Rory nodded and watched Taran step aside. He was truthful in his words to the warrior. He had no regrets. His love for Erina would span the cosmos. Forever.

Conn strode forward and motioned him to the center. "Are you ready?"

"Aye."

He arched a brow at Rory's use of language. With a snap of his fingers, a silver dagger, tipped with a green crystal, appeared magically in Conn's hand. He turned toward the warriors gathered and they silenced their conversations. Conn stood quietly, keeping his focus on the doors.

After several moments passed, Rory became agitated. "What are we waiting for?" he whispered.

"We are awaiting more guests."

Rory leaned toward him. "Most of the Brotherhood is in attendance. Is the king making an appearance?"

"No."

Confusion settled like a cloak of nettles. "Can ye share the names of the guests?"

"No."

"Can ye share *anything*?"

Three bells chimed in the distance.

"Open the doors to admit our honored guests," Conn ordered.

Slowly, the oak doors opened and a vision of beauty stepped inside. The breath left Rory in one swoosh, and he staggered as Erina walked down the path with Ronan assisting her. The warriors gave way, each inclining their heads in reverence as she passed them. Her gaze locked with his, and he found them shining with unshed tears. Was he dreaming? Was she really here? Jubilant emotions burst within his soul, and he turned toward Conn.

"How?" he demanded in a strangled voice.

Conn nudged him forward. "Contrary to what you may believe, Erina never married. You were in error."

"But the child?"

"Do you mean *your* child who is now strolling down the path?"

Rory returned his attention to the tiny lass following behind her mother. She hummed as she toddled along in merriment. And in that quiet moment, Rory's heart surged with euphoria. His woman. His daughter. His *life* was walking toward him.

Leaping off the dais, he ran toward the woman who held his heart. She opened her arms for him, tears now streaming down her cheeks. Grasping her around the waist, Rory crushed her against his chest.

"Rory," she uttered on a choked sob.

"*Erina.*" His lips came crashing down upon her sweet mouth. The kiss sang through his veins, healing the ache and weariness of loss. He stole the breath from her sigh and gave it back mingled with his own. His emotions whirled and skidded as he deepened the kiss. Never did he believe he could hold her within his arms again or feel the touch of her skin against his own. The satiny softness of her lips pressed to his.

He broke free and leaned his forehead against hers. "Ye are truly here, *mo ghrá*. How?"

She gave him a glowing smile. "I had a visit from a Fenian Warrior."

"Conn," he uttered softly. He glanced over his shoulder and nodded to his friend.

"Aye. He was extremely convincing." Erina cupped his cheeks and forced him to meet her gaze. "How could I say no to the Prince of the Fae? I *love* ye, Rory. My home is with ye."

"As I love ye. I will always protect ye." Grasping her hands, he placed them on his chest. "Can ye forgive me?"

"There is nothing to forgive," she reassured.

"I abandoned ye afterwards." Rory paused, unsure of what to say next. "In order to save ye, I had to use magic. A great deal of magic. I broke Fae laws and believed death would be my punishment."

"In truth, ye saved two lives." There was a slight tinge of wonder in her voice, and Erina drew back one hand. "Come meet your *daughter*, Angelica."

The wee child grasped her mother's hand and buried herself within the folds of Erina's gown.

My daughter. Rory slumped to the ground on both knees. "Greetings, Angelica. Welcome to the realm of the Fae. I am your father."

She turned slightly toward him. Reaching out with her hand, she placed it centered to his heart and the love poured into him. Her lavender eyes sparkled like those of the Fae, and the air warmed around them. Rory trembled as he took her tiny hand into his.

Moving away from her mother, Angelica settled against him. Rory cradled her hand and closed his eyes. Never did he imagine such joy. He thought his love for Erina was the most powerful, yet, to hold his child in his arms brought another kind of love. After kissing the top of her head, he took her into his arms and stood.

"When was she born?" he asked softly.

Erina brushed aside a lock of hair from the child. "On the first day of August. I feared for her safety and stayed confined at Kileburn." She dropped her hand and looked away. "The fire burned part of my legs and for months I dinnae ken I was with child. They gave me herbs for healing and such, so it was not until mid-spring that I realized I might be carrying our child."

Rory drew her near him with his other hand. Speaking tender words of endearment, he then kissed her soundly. "Ye were brave, my bonny lass."

"As my brother continues to mention. Ye should have seen his face when I announced my plans to go live with ye in your world. I thought he was going to bar the exits to Kileburn."

"So he spoke with Ewan MacGregor?"

Erina laughed nervously. "Aye, most definitely. It took several hours for the shouting to subdue, and I took to my chamber until both ceased trying to talk over one another. Yet, I am here and Graham sends his regards, stating ye must bring me home once a year on Midwinter."

"Granted."

Angelica let out a giggle and patted Rory's cheeks.

Smiling, he wiggled his nose at her. "Ye are a beauty like your mother."

"Another reason we had to leave Kileburn. Our

daughter has a touch of magic within her."

"Truly? I am not surprised. She carries the blood of the Fae. What can she do?"

Erina gave her daughter a wink. "Create flowers to blossoms from the land and call forth the butterflies."

Rory roared with delight. "She inherited the gift from her grandmother, my mother."

Conn approached from the side. "Now that you, Erina, and your daughter have been reunited, can we proceed with the ceremony?"

"Aye. And Conn, thank ye. For everything."

Smiling, he inclined his head.

As they slowly made their way to the steps leading to the dais, Erina hesitated. Worry crossed her features. Noting her injuries were more severe than she mentioned, Rory understood what to do.

He bent his head near her ear. "Close your eyes, *mo ghrá*."

Her eyes went wide.

"Trust me."

She bit her lip and complied. "Always."

Brushing a feather-light kiss over her cheek, he transported them magically to the dais. "Ye may open them."

She let out a gasp and shook her head in amusement. "There is much I need to learn in your realm."

Rory placed Angelica back into her arms. "We have eternity. Will ye marry me?"

Erina touched his face. "Aye, but I already made my vow to ye within my heart when ye made love to me."

He brushed a light kiss on her lips.

Turning around, he strode to the center with elation in his being. He removed his tunic and held his arms out to the side. As the first brush of Conn's words entered his mind, Rory brought forth those who had gone before him—from father to son—each generation entered and touched his soul. They acknowledged the Fenian Warrior, whispering their approval, and the power flowed through his veins.

In that quiet moment of initiation, Rory became fully healed, and the shadows of sorrow passed from his soul.

Chapter Thirty-One

"Even in the tiny dewdrop of water on a leaf, there is hope."

~*Chronicles of the Fae*

Laughter bubbled forth from Angelica as she played in the garden beside her grandmother. She had coaxed the bluebells and pansies to burst forth in wild array as far as the eye could see. Butterflies danced in array of abundance over the petals, and Angelica clapped her hands in glee, along with Reena.

Soon after the ceremony, Rory whisked Erina away to meet his mother, which had turned into a joyous reunion. The woman embraced her and Angelica with tears in her eyes, and stated she had waited for this moment for years.

For several days, Reena asked about her life in the other world, what she liked to eat, and of course her knowledge on herbs and plants. She almost burst out laughing at the last request, since obviously Reena's wisdom was vastly superior.

Each day brought a new sense of wonderment and awe. Erina and her daughter's rooms were a magical paradise—one filled with every flower from the Fae realm. Crystals hung like dewdrops from the ceiling and at night, the roof opened to reveal glittering stars. Even dear Thane was taken in by everyone. One elder

Fae deemed it important Thane be made an honorary ambassador to the animal kingdom.

Joy infused her soul and healed the wounds of loss from so long ago.

However, there was concern, too. Anxious to be in Rory's arms again, Erina was also worried. His kisses left her dizzy and craving his touch, but she held back and sought her own room without asking him to join her. His pitiful, hurtful looks could not sway her resolve.

He remembered her body as free from blemishes, not the ugly scars that covered most of her legs. How could she enter his bed? Would he recoil from the red, puckered skin? She loved him with all of her heart, but was it enough for him to overlook? She hated being vain, especially after everything they had been through.

With the wedding day approaching in the morning, her nerves were twisted like gnarled vines in the pit of her stomach. Everything had been prepared, and the welcome from the Fae people had overwhelmed her. Daily gifts were brought to her and Angelica, some even stooped down to her daughter's level to sing songs of praise and greetings. Her daughter would pat their cheeks in return, and the Fae were enchanted.

Erina let her feet dangle as she sat on the wooden swing. "Oh, grandmother, what am I to do?" Thane lifted his head in a lazy motion and then slumped back down.

The warm breeze touched her cheeks, and Erina listened for any messages. A tiny green bird chirped from a nearby tree, but it wasn't the answers she longed to hear. She dropped her head on a sigh.

"What troubles ye?" Rory's breath caressed her

cheek as he wrapped his arms around her waist.

Startled, she tried to move away. "Did ye appear out of the air again?"

His laughter was rich and sensual, sending shivers down her spine. "Nae. I have been watching ye from a distance." Nibbling on her neck, he added, "Ye are frowning too much."

"I am…anxious."

He came around to the front and lifted her from the swing. "For our wedding day?"

"Nae, not really." Suddenly, his presence was too overwhelming, and she looked away.

"I ken something is bothering ye, *mo ghrá*. Tell me," he encouraged softly.

Returning her attention to him, she blurted out, "I am not the woman ye bedded those many months ago. Ye will find my body much changed."

He kissed her tenderly. "Ye are the most desirable woman I have ever encountered—Fae or human. Your body screams to me. 'Tis like lush fruit waiting to be plucked and tasted."

She pushed at his chest. "But I have *scars*."

Erina found it impossible to understand the words blistering out in a torrent from him. He released her and marched over to his mother's side. Bending down, he whispered into her ear. Reena's cheeks took on a rosy glow, and a smile spread across her face. Rory then placed a tender kiss on Angelica's head and stormed back toward her.

She lifted her head, gazing into eyes that had turned to silver. She gasped when he lifted her into his arms and started to walk down a path to the river. "What are ye doing?" she hissed. "And what did ye tell your mother?"

He kept his gaze focused on the path. "I asked if she could watch over Angelica for the remainder of the day and evening."

"For what purpose?"

"We are long overdue for a proper reunion, Erina MacIntyre."

Tremors of fear and excitement coursed throughout her body. "Explain, Fenian Warrior."

"I am going to make love to every inch of your lush, beautiful body."

"Ye dinnae have to prove anything, Rory," she uttered softly.

He let out a growl and tightened his hold around her body. In a flash of brilliant colors, he brought them under the shade of elm trees by the water's edge and set her on her feet. As he cupped her chin, he pierced her with a searing look of desire.

"Never in all my existence have I known such passion. Your beauty lies within ye, Erina, and I am going to show ye with each touch, taste, *and* word."

Her lip trembled. "I dinnae deserve ye."

His thumb traced a path over her bottom lip. "Aye, ye do, *ghrá*. Never forget my heart belongs to ye and *only* ye."

Giving her no time to respond, his mouth ravished hers with a hunger that set her body on fire. Erina yielded to the passion as his hand slid down to cup her breast. The heat seared through the gauzy material of the gown, and her nipples hardened. Aching for more of his touch, she groaned and moved against him.

As he broke free from the kiss, his fingers pushed the gown from her shoulders, exposing her breasts.

"More beautiful than I remember," he murmured and fondled each.

Erina watched in a lust-filled haze as his mouth descended over her breasts. Thrusting her hands into his hair, she urged him to take more and closed her eyes on the heady sensations. Her body quivered and desire shot through her blood. How she ached to have him deep in her again.

Slowly, Rory brought them to the ground, and he stripped free from his clothing. While she was giddy and light-headed, she tried to toss away her fears. She reached out and traced a path over the new ceremonial markings across his chest. Her fingers tingled as they skimmed over his skin. When she placed open-mouth kisses over his hot skin, his growl resonated deep within her.

Rory shoved her back onto the grass and nipped at her neck. "I will take ye here upon the land that is my home. I claimed ye in your world and now I shall do so in mine."

His hand reached down and gathered the material of her gown and a tiny flare of doubt crept inside her. Swallowing the fear, Erina kept her gaze on his. When his hand touched her foot, she gasped. The touch was tender and warm over a part of her body she hated. And when he bent to kiss her scars, she let out an anguished sob.

"I am so sorry," he said softly. "Ye should not have suffered."

"They do not offend ye?" Erina demanded to know the truth. If there was any hope of a future, she needed to be reassured.

"*Mo ghrá*, nothing about ye offends me."

His hand trailed a path over every inch of her scars on both legs and then with a wave of his hand, her gown was removed magically from her body. "Ye are perfection to me." Without giving her time to complain, he covered her with his body. His lips recaptured hers, more demanding this time, and Erina surrendered. Desire drummed into every core of her body, begging for release. Each touch, each word of love whispered into her ear, sealed the pain of long ago.

His fingers stroked her inner thigh, and she trembled. When one finger flicked over her intimate area, Erina bit his shoulder.

"I ache for ye, Rory. Take me now," she begged, and her thighs parted to receive him.

He entered her deeply, and her fingers dug into the taut flesh on his back. Erina kept rhythm with each thrust, until the flame of passion burst all around her in a dazzling sparkle of light. She sang out his name as she soared over the mountaintops and crashed along the waves by the sea, taking Rory's cry of release into her own body.

Erina basked in the warmth of his arms, sated and content. How she loved this man. This Fae warrior. Her heart was filled with happiness. She sniffed, trying to keep the tears from spilling forth.

Rory placed a tender kiss on her lips. "Why do ye weep?"

"I never thought to see ye again. Or if I did, ye would not want me."

He shifted onto his back, bringing her alongside him. "I never fathomed seeing ye again, as well." He pulled on one of her curls. "Our love was destined. A journey that did not end well the *first* time. My heart was sealed the moment I rescued ye from the stream. The verra first time we met."

Confused and wary of his words, Erina tried to sit up. However, his arm held her firmly against his side. "We did not first meet by a stream."

"Aye, we did, *mo ghrá*. I was sent to assist Ewan and your brother with a mission, but came upon ye trying to catch fish from the stream."

Erina's heart pounded in her ears. "Ye are scaring me, Rory."

He brought her hand up and placed it over his heart. "Remember, I am a Fae. Anything is possible. Will ye hear my tale of how we first met? At the end, I will show ye *my* scar. Inside and out."

She roamed his features, seeing only love, sorrow, and concern. She trusted him with her own scars, now it was time to give Rory her trust. She brushed away a lock of hair from his brow and smiled. "Start at the beginning and leave nothing out of the telling."

He let out a deep sigh and nodded. For the next several hours, Erina listened with rapt attention to the story of how she and Rory first met.

When Rory grew silent, Erina thought he had gone to sleep. Sitting up, she shielded her eyes from the setting sun. The light was a web of silver and gold, with a splash of rose against an azure sky. His world stole the breath from her body with its beauty. Still trying to comprehend his account of their first encounter, Erina glanced sideways at him to ask another question. One arm rested beneath his head and the other was flung out to the side in a careless manner. They both had endured the pain of loss, but Rory had witnessed her death.

She shuddered and propped her head onto her

knees. Her toes dug into the thick grass, warm and soft.

"Are ye cold?" His voice was a gentle caress over her skin.

"Nae," she responded, stretching her legs out and tucking herself by his side. "I cannot fathom what ye have had to witness."

Rory opened his eyes. "In many ways, I have Conn to thank for sending me back through the Veil of Ages, as well as the king."

"Thank ye for sharing." She clasped his hand and intertwined her fingers with his. "For loving me, Rory, and giving me the greatest gift of all."

He brought their joined hands to his chest. "The gift of love is powerful, aye?"

She nibbled his chin. "Especially when a child comes from the union."

His brow furrowed. "I should have been there for ye during your time."

Erina smiled wistfully. "Ye were in my thoughts every waking moment. When I held our daughter for the first time in my arms, I wept tears of joy. It was like seeing a piece of ye again. With Angelica, the healing began. I shall never forget her smile on the day of her birth. I knew she was special, but her tiny grin soothed the ache I had been carrying with me."

"Why did ye name her Angelica?"

"I had thought to name her after my grandmother. Yet, when I held her in my arms, it was as if my grandmother was telling me to give her the name of my mother. Therefore, I whispered the name of Angelica over her face and in return, she gave me the most radiant smile."

"An angel *and* a fae," he offered.

Erina laughed. "My grandmother often referred to my mother as a misguided angel."

Rory kissed the tip of her nose. "And what was your grandmother's name?"

"Aelish, meaning—"

"*Truth teller*," he interjected and sat abruptly. "By the Gods, nae! Could it be? *Impossible*."

Startled by his outburst, Erina tugged on his arm. "What is wrong?"

Rory's answering smile was as warm as the Fae sun, and he cupped her cheeks. "I deem our story is not finished. There is a piece missing which needs to be told, including the light within your amethyst."

She batted his hands away. "Once again, ye are scaring me, Rory MacGregor."

He jumped up, bringing her to stand beside him. Wrapping his arms around her waist, he rocked from side to side. "There is no need to fret while ye are with me, my lovely *wife*."

"Humph! We are not married...*yet*."

His laughter roared across the land. "When I took your body the verra first time, I pledged my soul to yours. In our world, we judge this as a rite of marriage."

She lifted her chin in defiance and countered back, "In *my* world, we speak words pledging our love and devotion for eternity. In front of witnesses. With a morning and evening feast, followed by dancing."

He lowered his head and placed a hot kiss on the soft spot below her ear. "Did I not mention that our vows of commitment last three days in my world?"

Erina shivered from his touch, but recovered quickly and pulled back. "I must endure three entire days of celebration before ye can come to my bed?"

His thumb traced a path over her bottom lip. "The feasting is in our honor. Whether we choose to stay or not, is entirely up to us. With the look ye are presenting me, I can tell we shall only be greeting our guests for a few hours."

Erina wrapped her arms around his neck. "Delightful. Now can ye explain the meaning of our unfinished tale?"

Lifting his head, Rory closed his eyes. When he finally opened them, he gathered her into his arms. "Close your eyes, *mo ghrá.*"

Erina eyed him cautiously. "Where are we going? Need I remind ye, we are without clothing?"

She could feel the rumble of his laughter against her chest, and with a snap of his wrist, they vanished in a ripple of air.

Chapter Thirty-Two

"A life without a loving guardian is a dangerous one to take."

~*Chronicles of the Fae*

For as long as she lived, Erina would never get used to moving from place to place within the air in seconds. Once, she opened her eyes, and cried out in pain from the intensity of the glittering colors. She would never make the same mistake again. Nor would she get used to him removing her clothes and putting them back on her body with one snap of his fingers. There would be boundaries after they were married.

Rory paused before the gate to his mother's cottage. His hand stilled on the wood. Was he afraid? Should she be fearful? He had proceeded to share some bits of knowledge after they returned. He told her the answers to their questions were inside his mother's home. Was she prepared to meet her final destiny?

Brushing her hands down the silk folds of her gown, she let out a sigh. She took a step alongside him and linked her arm within his. "Whatever awaits for me inside, it will not change how much I love ye, Rory."

He drew her closer. "Not only are there answers for ye, but I reckon I need to hear them, as well." After brushing a light kiss along her lips, he opened the gate and moved along the path.

The door to the cottage was left open, and the heady aroma of fresh flowers filled Erina. A prickle of awareness swept through her as they stepped inside the home. Someone else was here—another who whispered to her. Her body began to tremble, and she removed her hand from Rory's.

"Erina, dinnae be afraid," Rory comforted.

"Where is she?" She darted a glance beyond the main living room.

When he refused to answer her question, she ran from the room and followed her senses. She ignored Rory's pleas to wait and ran out the back entrance of the cottage, past the bubbling fountain and into the main garden. Her heart pounded fiercely against her chest as her steps faltered. Coming to a halt by the garden gate, Erina pressed a fist to her mouth to stifle the gasp.

"*Grandmother*?"

There among the rows of lavender and bluebells stood the woman who she believed was dead. Lights sparkled before her eyes as dizziness swamped Erina. Grabbing a hold of the gate, she blinked in an attempt to focus and lowered her head.

Instantly, Rory was there, wrapping his arm around her waist for support. Her mind scrambled trying to discern what she was seeing. "Breathe, Erina." He kissed her temple, and her shoulders relaxed.

When she lifted her gaze, her grandmother was moving toward her. "Is this a dream? An illusion?"

Her grandmother paused. She clasped her hands together and gave Erina a weak smile. "I am not what you believe, my child, and I am very much alive. Will you walk with me among the flowers?"

Erina stole a glance at Rory. He brought her fingers to his lips. "Go hear your *grandmother's* story."

Her lips trembled when she removed her hand from his. Rory opened the gate for her, and Erina made her way slowly to her grandmother. The impulse to rush into her arms was powerful, but fear kept her from reaching out. Erina stopped a few feet away from her.

"How can ye be alive?"

Her grandmother plucked a bluebell and handed it to Erina. "All life withers and dies, only to be reborn, *aye*?"

Though she took the flower, she longed to fling it to the ground. "After everything I have gone through, I have nae desire to stand here and debate the life and death of the land. Ye have taught me well. Now is the time for *honest* answers."

Pursing her lips, her grandmother turned and started down the path. Erina had no choice but to follow. A rabbit skittered across her path, causing her to stumble. "Please stop."

The woman's shoulders stiffened. Glancing over her shoulder, Erina could see the disapproval within her eyes. Her grandmother never did tolerate disobedience or impatience. Her solutions were always sought outdoors among the land or the stars.

"I am leading you to a bench, so you can rest. I thought a leisurely walk among the flowers would help to calm your spirits before I tell you everything."

"Then ye understand how it pains me to walk verra far?"

"I have been told of your injuries." Tears misted in the woman's eyes. "I am sorry I was not there to protect you."

Frustration seethed like bee stings in her stomach. "Ye died!"

"Nae, I did not." She turned back around and proceeded toward a rose-colored bench. After adjusting her gown, her grandmother sat down. Lifting her head to the sky, she closed her eyes.

Erina fought the barb she longed to toss out and approached in slow steady steps. Sitting on the opposite end of the bench, she clasped her hands together, crushing the bluebell's petals. She pursed her lips and studied the woman. She appeared younger than Erina remembered. The lines around her eyes were gone, and there was a youthful glow to her cheeks. Instead of the silver streaks of gray that ran throughout her dark locks, there was only one band of white on the right side. This woman might claim to be her grandmother, but something was different. Even her language was changed.

The light of illumination blossomed within Erina. They were in the Fae realm—a place of magic and beautiful people. She reached for her hand. "Ye are *Fae*," she uttered with conviction.

Her grandmother opened her eyes and smiled fully. "Yes, my child."

"Am I...Fae?"

She squeezed Erina's hand and then released it. "No. I shall always be your grandmother, but not in blood."

Anguish tore into Erina. The woman she cherished, loved, and thought to be her kin was someone else entirely. She gripped the sides of the bench and cast her gaze outward. "I am listening…"

"I am known as the Master Fae Apothecary. I have

been the guardian over great healers and those who wield magic over the land for thousands of years. Actually, longer than I can fully explain or you can comprehend. I came into your mother's life when she was but a wee lass. She had the gift. Her own mother had no interest in tending to plants, herbs, and flowers, so she let me take over in assisting her." She paused and stood.

"As she grew older, your mother was spirited, but refused to listen to my advice when it came to love and men, especially when her own parents passed on to the land of eternal youth. One day, the Laird of Kileburn came passing through. He flirted outright with her, and she succumbed to his charm and flowery words. Refusing to listen to my concerns, she left for the castle and did not return for many months. When she did, she was already carrying his child—you. My heart splintered the day I came upon her in the woods. I spewed out words to the Gods and Goddesses, angry for not sparing her life."

Her grandmother dotted her cheeks as the tears spilled down. "The moment I removed you from her cold arms and bundled you into mine, I fully understood what the Fates had destined. You were meant for the greatest journey of all, and I fell in love with you immediately."

Standing, Erina wandered over to a rosemary bush. She fingered the soft needles, their fragrance more potent in this world. "Rory has spoken to me of my death."

"Bah! It should not have been!"

Erina snorted and pulled her hand away. "So Rory has declared *many* times."

Her grandmother approached warily. "My child, I understand how learning this knowledge has left you with doubts. You have endured great pain and suffering. I am sure you need time to dwell on my words and Rory's."

She wanted to laugh at the absurdity of her response. She wasn't blood, but this woman in front of her had protected, guided, and loved her. Her heart burst with unsaid words and emotions. Did it truly matter if the woman was Fae or human? She had raised Erina and in doing so, had given her so much.

"You're wrong. With everything I have heard, my love for Rory will never change. In truth, it grows each day." Erina gestured outward. "Aye, I find it difficult to process this world, Rory, and now I have ye—*alive* and well. My love for ye both will never diminish." She rubbed a hand over her forehead. "I confess, I'll likely be in shock for some time, but I love ye, *Grandmother*."

The woman opened her arms. "As I love you, Erina."

As she embraced her grandmother, Erina sighed, and the tears she had kept within spilled forth.

For several moments, they held each other. Her grandmother whispered soothing words in her ear and the tension eased. Erina drew back, since one question continued to plague her. "Why your death? Why not stay?"

Her grandmother chuckled and pointed a finger over Erina's shoulder. "Because the Fenian Warrior would have become suspicious and questioned my reasons for being with you. I feared he would have soon left, and I decided it was time for me to depart. If I had stayed, Rory might have deviated from his journey. In truth, it was time for *you* to begin your destiny, as well."

Rory approached them. He wrapped an arm around Erina and kissed her tenderly. "When did you come upon this knowledge, *Aelish*? You died months before my arrival."

Her grandmother shrugged. "The land sent me a message."

"A Fae messenger from the seer?" Rory countered.

"Is it not all the same?"

"Regardless," interjected Erina, "I am happy you are alive. And I must admit, ye look wonderful, Grandmother."

Aelish winked at her. "In your world, one must gradually grow older with each passing year." Turning to Rory, she asked, "When did you realize I was Erina's guardian."

Shifting his stance, he brought forth the amethyst pendant around Erina to the light. "There was something strange when I noticed the shimmer of light in the amethyst in our world. Only gems and crystals from our world capture the radiance." Letting it drop, he continued, "Of course, when Erina mentioned your name, the spark of knowledge entered my mind. When I sensed your presence nearby, I gathered ye were her grandmother."

Erina clasped her pendant, the stone warm in the palm of her hand. "I have had this for as long as I can recall."

Aelish cupped her cheek. "I gave it to you on the day you planted your first flower. You were three summers."

Her eyes lit up. "I remember that day. We stayed in the garden until the moon rose over the trees."

"Yes. And when the moon glow touched your cheeks, I draped the pendant over your neck. I understood there would be a time when your Fae lover would come for you. Your soul was tied to the land and—" Aelish grabbed Rory's hand and placed it with Erina's. "—to this Fenian Warrior."

She took a step back and extended her arms, but her gaze was directed to Rory. "Regardless of what the laws state about a love between a human and Fae, the future was woven. To tamper with the Goddess is forbidden, even in this world, Fenian Warrior. The Goddess blessed this union and not even the king and queen, or anyone else can go against what she has destined."

"I sense a shift in the Brotherhood. Conn is forming a new Order," Rory stated.

Erina leaned into him. "Again, so much to learn."

Her grandmother waved her hand about. "Enough of lessons. This is a time of joyous reunions. I am eager to meet my great-granddaughter. I've heard she can charm the butterflies."

Laughter bubbled forth from Erina. "She has been doing so since the first few days after her birth."

Aelish began to move along the path. "No surprise. She's destined to become the next Master Apothecary."

Erina stared at her grandmother's retreating back, completely stunned by her pronouncement.

Rory brought their joined hands to his lips. The warmth of his touch seared into her body, and she turned her attention to him. "Will I ever *not* be in a state of amazement?"

"I hope not, *mo ghrá*," he whispered and captured her mouth in a passionate kiss.

****

Erina traveled along the length of Rory's library chamber, brushing her fingers over the gilded spines of his books. Some of the titles she recognized, but there were many that were foreign to her. Parchment scrolls were tucked into smaller nooks within the shelves, and she deemed those to be ancient works. His vast collection was a wonder. As soon as they were married and settled, she was going to have him teach her all the different languages.

His rooms inside the Crystal Palace were opulent and spacious as she continued to move from one room to the next. Erina marveled at the lush colors—from tapestries of the Fae realm to the many crystals of various sizes placed on polished maple, oak, and yew tables. Entering his private chamber, her cheeks heated. A massive four-poster bed rested in the middle of the room. Above, light glittered in jeweled tones from a stained glass mosaic of a giant oak tree. Its roots branched outward in various colors. A giant hearth stood opposite, and the mantel was adorned with fresh greenery. The heady scent of pine lingered, along with fresh rose petals that had been strewn across the bed coverings.

Her nerves tingled in anticipation of him making love to her on the golden velvet coverings. She hadn't seen him for two long days. Her grandmother and Rory's mother had ordered him to return to other chambers within the Brotherhood far away from Erina. In truth, they had banished him immediately. She'd never forget the hurt look he gave them both when he vanished before their eyes. Though Erina missed him, she was grateful for the time spent becoming reacquainted with her grandmother. She also enjoyed listening to tales from Rory's mother about his youthful pranks, and having both women fuss over Angelica.

Treasured bonding memories.

She slipped out of the room, closing the doors behind her. Moving to the garden doors, she pushed them open. The warm air kissed her cheeks in greeting.

"My wedding day," she uttered softly.

Turning toward the sound of knocking on the main chamber door, Erina brushed a lock of hair from her shoulder and made her way to the entrance.

When she opened the door, she was unprepared for the vision smiling up at her. "Greetings, Erina." The tiny woman grasped one of her hands. "My name is Ivy. May I come in and wait with you?"

Her speech was one she had never encountered, and then Erina gasped, recalling the name of Conn's wife. "Princess Ivy," she affirmed and curtsied. "I would be honored."

The woman giggled. "Oh, goodness, please don't do that." Ivy released her hand and stepped inside the chamber. "I am still finding it difficult that most of the Fae continue to bow or wait until I speak before they utter a word."

Erina closed the door. "But ye are a princess."

"Yes, but there are times when I just want to have a normal conversation. As I am sure you will understand once Rory takes you around the realm."

Smiling, Erina gestured her forward. "Would ye like to sit with me in the garden?"

"Love to! Oh, and you are stunning, Erina. The

pale green gown is a perfect color for your dark auburn tresses and blue eyes. You are a beautiful bride."

Erina fingered the gauzy material. "Thank ye. 'Tis so soft, but I am not used to wearing such…" She bit her lip, trying to find the right word.

"That there should be more material?" Ivy pointed out.

"Aye!" She laughed and dropped her hands. "I started to protest when my grandmother and Rory's mother presented me with the dress."

"Considering the century you're from, it does seem that way for you. In my time, you would be shocked at the way women now dress. However, I do love the way the material clings to our bodies and seems to float with each movement."

"Ye are not from near my own time?" Rory mentioned Conn also marrying a woman from the mortal world, but assumed it was within her own century.

"Nope. I am ahead of yours by hundreds of years."

Erina staggered. "Sweet Goddess."

Ivy clutched her arm. "No fainting on your wedding day. Rory would have words with Conn, and they are finally on civil speaking terms again. Let us go outside and wait for the High Priestess to come for us."

"Then ye can tell me all about yourself."

After leading Erina to a cushioned chair, Ivy brought another one close to her side. She immediately went into a detailed account of how she and Conn met. Her mind fought to keep up with the woman's conversation and choice of words that were unfamiliar to Erina. By the third attempt at explaining a certain phrase or word, Erina gave up and listened with rapt attention to Ivy. She found the woman enchanting with her short hair and pale skin. Her eyes danced with mirth, and when she spoke of Conn, love infused each word.

"'Tis an incredible account, Ivy."

As she shielded her eyes from the sun, the woman shifted. "I hear your tale was fraught with danger and fire damaged your legs."

Erina let out a sigh. "Aye, but out of the ashes came a spark of life to help me heal. Our daughter, Angelica."

Ivy placed a gentle hand on her arm. "A true miracle. I am so happy for you and Rory. After you are settled, please bring Angelica to visit with Sorcha. It will be good for her to have another half-human to bond with, besides all the Fae children."

Bells chimed in the distance, and both women turned. The air thinned and a rainbow of lights shimmered. Ivy stood and stepped aside. "The priestess is arriving."

Standing slowly, Erina gently straightened the folds of her gown. She pressed her palm to her pendant to steady her nerves as the woman glided through the light.

Her robe of white flowed in gentle waves across the ground. She approached Erina, presenting her with a bouquet of white roses. The woman inclined her head. "These are from the royal garden. A request from Rory."

For a brief moment, she felt the kiss of Rory's lips across her cheeks. Extending her hand, she accepted the flowers from the priestess. "Thank ye," she murmured, inhaling their potent floral aroma.

"My name is Priestess Talena. I shall escort ye along with the princess to the Cathedral of Trees where you will be joined with Rory MacGregor from the royal house of Avieon. I understand it is difficult for you to walk, so I will transport you part of the way."

Joy filled Erina. Everyone had been so kind and welcoming. Her life with Rory was truly beginning.

She pressed the flowers against her chest and lifted her head. "I am ready."

Chapter Thirty-Three

"In any belief...in any world, love will always heal and banish the darkness. For love can illuminate the darkness with hope."

~Chronicles of the Fae

Erina trailed her fingers over the vines of ivy snaking around the pillar before the bridge. She had not been in this area of the realm, and the sight that greeted her was a heady mix of opulent foliage and floral scents. A river flowed under the bridge, its sound similar to tinkling bells. White swans passed by her in a graceful procession, and she marveled at their rose-tipped feathers.

With each step she took, her body tingled with anticipation. As she lifted her head, her mouth dropped open in awe. The Cathedral of Trees was unlike any place she'd encountered—a jewel glistening against the sapphire sky. Banners fluttered in the soft breeze from the four crystal turrets, each depicting a dragon. Her grandmother had prepared her for this vast, exquisite vision, but her words were nothing compared to the glorious view in front of her.

Bells continued to herald her arrival. Reaching the grand staircase, she placed her hand on Priestess Talena's outstretched arm. The woman nodded to her and Erina closed her eyes. In a whisper, she was brought inside the cathedral. Upon opening her eyes, she gazed at the crowd gathered. Inside the darkened interior, giant trees towered to a ceiling that mirrored the night sky. Their branches were decked in twinkling lights, casting a serene glow throughout. Moonlight danced within the cathedral and beauty surrounded her.

Yet, there was only one she longed to see.

Her breath hitched as her gaze swept the area and landed on the man standing on a raised mound in the center. "*Rory*," she uttered his name on a sigh.

His smile was a beacon of love, renewal, and new beginnings, and she moved across the lush ground toward him. Many tossed out garlands and flower petals along her path, offering words of endearment and approval. Her heart swelled in gratitude for these people. They had come to accept her in such a short time, including her daughter and the many gifts they had presented to her.

There was nothing but love in this realm.

Erina's smile grew more when she spied her sweet cherub waving to her from her grandmother's arms. Their daughter would be safe here. There would be no threat because she was different. Hatred did not belong in this beautiful world.

Rory's mother stood on the opposite side beaming at her as well. She stepped forward and took Erina's hand into hers. "Before you proceed, I have a gift for you." Reena lifted her hand upward and a thin circlet appeared inside her palm. Tiny seed pearls wove around the silver band.

"I have nae words. 'Tis lovely."

"This was a gift from my mother. Since I bore no daughters, it shall be passed down to you. It will bind

370

you to the royal house of Avieon." She secured it on Erina's head, and then kissed both her cheeks. "Welcome, my precious daughter."

Erina embraced the woman. "Thank ye."

Reena withdrew a silk cloth and dotted Erina's eyes. "Joyful tears to present to my son. Go forth, dearest."

Before leaving, Erina went and kissed her daughter. "I am so happy ye came into my life, sweet child." Angelica giggled and brushed her nose against Erina's. After giving her grandmother a kiss, Erina drew her gaze to the man who held her heart.

Rory had always made her knees weak and her mouth dry, but the man she was heading toward made her blood burn. Never before had she witnessed him in such finery. He wore ivory trews that shimmered with silver, and his tunic was the same, though, the edges were woven with some of the markings on his arms and back.

Her pulse quickened, and a song of joy poured forth from her lips as he extended his hand toward her.

"Ye are the light that banished the fire and darkness. A ripple across the wave of time, ye sought me out and took me as your own."

Rory's harmonious voice echoed rich and firm. "And with your love, ye quenched my thirst and awakened my soul. A love forged by fate. A love destined to overcome death."

When her fingers grasped his, the warmth spread in a hundred tingling sensations across her skin.

Rory brought her hand to his lips. She tasted of an intoxicating scent of spices, and he found his senses reeling from the touch. The moment Erina had entered the cathedral he found himself motionless, unable to take his eyes from her. Her beauty rivaled any within the kingdom. The gown of silken pale green clung to every curve, and his mouth salivated in memory of feasting on her skin. He made a note to thank whoever had chosen such a delicate material for his beloved. How he yearned to pull out all the crystal pins keeping her tresses atop her head and run his fingers throughout. She radiated a beauty—within and out.

He slowly guided them toward the center of the moss-covered ground. Leaning near her ear, he whispered, "If ye wish, we can ask for Mother Danu's blessing standing."

Erina angled her head around. Her lips brushed against his, sending shards of pleasurable fire through his veins. "With your help, I would like to kneel," she uttered softly.

Smiling, Rory placed a firm arm around her waist and brought her slowly to the ground. Moonlight encased them in a prayerful sphere as they lowered their heads. The air warmed considerably, and the Goddess brushed a kiss over the lovers. Her words of approval resonated deep within Rory, and a final thread of healing wove its way into Rory and Erina's hearts.

As Rory lifted his head, he gazed at Erina. Love reflected in the depths of her eyes, and he realized she had experienced the same touch from the Goddess.

Gently, he brought them both to standing and led her down to the High Priestess.

She lifted her arms outward, and her ancient voice echoed within the cathedral. "Welcome, warrior and healer. Fae and human. You have both come freely to the Mother and the Fae. We, your people, rejoice in your union. May love, light, and wisdom be the strength beneath your feet as you journey together as two, but joined as one for all eternity."

The priestess held her palm upward and blew across, sending stardust over Rory and Erina.

"Walk with me to the fountain of life and love," offered Rory, placing her hand in the crook of his arm.

They descended the path toward a rose quartz fountain. The water bubbled gently forth from the center in various shades of lavender, pink, and rose.

"The water is stunning. May I?" Erina asked, while she held her hand outward.

"Aye," Rory encouraged and took her flowers, placing them on the edge of the fountain.

She let out a giggle when her hand passed through the bubbling water. "'Tis a tingling feeling that is spreading over my skin—warm and soothing."

Rory deemed no one in the realm had ever asked to run their hands through the sacred waters. He could deny Erina nothing. This was her home now. One to explore and learn. He'd grant her anything to bring happiness to her life.

"I ken everyone is watching, but thank ye."

Reaching inside the pocket of his tunic, Rory drew forth the ring he had chosen for her. Taking her wet hand, he said, "I give ye this ring, Erina, as a part of my love for ye. The circular silver band has etchings similar to my armband, and the red stone is from my homeland of Taralyn within the stars."

Her eyes grew wide, and she gaped in awe when he slipped it on her finger. "Beautiful beyond words."

"The ring mirrors your own beauty, *mo ghrá*. Ye are my stardust and moonlight. Ye are my anchor when the world is filled with chaos. My life began when my soul touched yours. The threads of our destinies have been rewoven."

Erina's smile was a moonbeam of promises. Her fingers reached into the bodice of her gown, and Rory's groin tightened. It was his turn to be shocked into silence as she withdrew a gold band with Celtic engravings.

"When Conn came and explained everything, I asked for several weeks to prepare and say my farewells. Everyone thought I was leaving for the islands in the north, which I was going to originally." She twisted the band within her fingers, but her eyes held his as she continued, "I wanted to bring ye something from my world. Graham bought the gold, and Ewan had one of his men fashion the piece to my specific instructions." Taking his hand, she first kissed his finger and then placed the ring on. "I hope ye do not mind."

The ring was warm against his skin, and he held it up to the starlight. On impulse, Rory brushed his hand through the water, sealing their love and bonding the metal to his finger. He cupped her cheeks. "Ye honor me with this gift. 'Tis now sealed forever on me."

Her eyes bore into his as her voice wavered. "Love cannot be found in a simple charm, nor in a casual glance. It requires nurturing like a tiny seedling. Ye have shown me how sacrifices in the name of love are powerful. But I can tell ye this, Rory, the stars shattered the day ye stepped forth—be it on the shore by a river, or between ancient trees. My heart opened to love the day we met. When dark clouds threaten to burst around us, let us seek the shelter of our love for protection. We will fill our home with joy, laughter, and many children."

"*Many*?" he echoed. "I like your idea."

Leaning up on her toes, she nibbled on his chin. "Aye."

Rory had no desire for the final portion of the ceremony to be witnessed by the gathering. It was a private, sacred bonding—one which he had yet to explain fully to Erina. Nevertheless, the rite had to be completed. All he required was assistance from another.

After giving a nod to Conn, he waited for the prince to seal them inside a sphere of golden light, shielding them from the others. Only when the act was done would Rory unseal their enclosure.

Rory stepped back. He removed his tunic and placed it on the ledge near her flowers. "There is one more part of the ceremony. 'Tis one where I was given permission by the king."

Erina eyed him with apprehension. "Ye are not considering making love—"

"Nae," he reassured, and brought her to his side. "I am *asking* your permission to extend your life with mine in the realm. Ye are human, Erina."

A frown skittered across her features. "I never thought…" Her voice trailed off filled with confusion.

"In truth, the aging process will slow inside your body as you dwell here. I wish to *further* your lifeline." As if sensing her thoughts, Rory added, "Our child is already part-Fae. *All* our children shall live long lives."

"Then ye desire to make me part of your people? How?"

"Do ye trust me, *mo ghrá*?"

She laughed and the sound filled him. "Always.

Have I not stated several times?"

Rory burst out in laughter. "*Aye*. A question I fear that will be repeated."

"What needs to be done?" she inquired.

Lifting his hand upward, a small silver dagger with a crystal blade appeared within his palm. He placed the tip centered to his heart and made a tiny incision. Reaching for her hand, he did the same across her palm. Then, Rory pressed her hand to his chest. "Blood to blood, my soul to yours. Blood to blood, my body shall shield ye in this realm and the next. Blood to blood, yours is now mingled with mine, and the Fae people who descended from the stars thousands of years ago. I bind ye with these words for eternity."

Erina let out strangled gasp as the union of their blood forged a greater bond. The ground rumbled beneath their feet and mists surrounded them inside their golden enclosure. She closed her eyes and leaned against him. "I feel dizzy, but oh, so wonderful."

Rory uttered soothing words in his ancient language. He longed to whisk her away to a soft patch of wildflowers and make love to every inch of her skin. Never did he expect the bonding to be so potent and arousing.

"I love *ye*," he declared and swiftly took possession of her lips.

She slipped her arms around his neck, taking the kiss deeper. When she rocked against his erection, he fought to break free. Holding her back, Rory tried to calm his breathing.

Her eyes glowed with desire. "I dinnae think I can endure three days of feasting."

With a groan, Rory released her and stood back.

"Though we are shielded, we are not alone."

Erina's cheeks turned a rosy glow, and she grabbed his tunic, handing it to him. "Please dress, before I change my mind. Ye are too tempting standing there partially clothed."

"What are ye tempted to do?" As he started to pull the tunic over his head, she halted his progress.

"Wait!" She reached out and traced a finger over his heart, where only moments before he had made the incision. "'Tis already healed."

"Of course, as well as your hand."

She snapped her gaze to her palm. "Astonishing!"

Bringing her back to his side, he nuzzled her neck. "Welcome to my world, *wife*."

With a flick of his wrist, Rory let the golden shield shimmer back into the ground, and he turned them toward the crowd. Trumpets blared and those gathered sang out as one. Their song echoed throughout the cathedral and kingdom.

Epilogue

Leaves swirled in a magical dance around his beloved as she splashed her feet in the water. Laughter bubbled forth from her as Thane bounded down the edge of the stream, barking at the swans. Her treasured animal thrived in the realm and this made Erina happy. Rory would do anything to keep her contented. No more pain. No more tears of sorrow.

A new beginning.

He was held captivated by the scene. She filled his heart with joy, along with their wee daughter.

After the ceremony, the feasting began in earnest. Nonetheless, Rory had made a promise to Erina they would endure no more than one full day. The tension, private looks, and stolen touches between them almost undid him. After Conn informed him he'd ordered the entire Brotherhood to appear and swear their allegiance to Erina, Rory considered it wise to whisk his wife away from the feasting. The warriors could swear their loyalty of protection over her another time.

He had magically created a banquet along the stream. It wasn't far from the royal palace and boasted the most bucolic scenes in the realm. A perfect wedding picnic—one his wife proudly commended him on after she changed out of her wedding gown.

He deemed the realm could continue with the celebrations. In all his recollections, he had never known a wedded couple to last more than a few hours without secretly leaving.

Kneeling on one knee, Rory placed his palm on the ground. The Goddess greeted him on the whisper of a gentle breeze, and the warmth of her love infused him. "Thank ye. I shall and always will be your warrior. Ye were correct, as always. Love is our foundation and the greatest power of all."

Rory stood and went to his wife, who was now basking in the sun on a quartz bench. Her eyes were closed, and he could make out every curve under the gossamer rose-colored gown. Desire swelled instantly as he bent to place a kiss on her lips.

"Hmm…ye taste like cloves and wine," she murmured and opened her eyes.

"How did Thane find us?"

Erina shifted on the bench and he joined her. "When ye left to go fetch some wine and food, he came charging through the trees. I am beginning to think this is *his* favorite spot. The air is warm and the grasses lush. He always did like the water and a comfortable spot under a tree."

"Would ye like me to send for your sheep? He can resume his duties here."

She shielded her eyes from the sunlight, watching the animal continue with his antics. "Nae. Let him roam free." Erina turned her attention to Rory. "Although, why not take him to your mother's home? He enjoys watching over Angelica. Since your mother has graciously agreed to care for our daughter while we have some private time together, we can send him there. I dinnae ken why I had not thought of this alternative plan."

Rory cupped her chin. "Because your focus was elsewhere."

Erina scooted closer to him and wrapped her arms around his neck. "Do tell," she encouraged.

He could make out the swell of her ivory breasts, and his hand brushed across her pert nipples. "Did I tell ye I love ye, wife?"

Erina narrowed her eyes in thought. "Nae. Not for several hours."

In a flash, Rory brought her onto his lap, nudging his swollen cock against her. "For shame. Should ye punish me?"

Giving him a saucy grin, she replied, "With pleasure."

"Before I let ye have your way with me, there is one gift that was given to both of us by Aelish."

Erina drew back. "My grandmother has given us a gift? Why did she not mention it at the banquet table?"

"Because part of her message regarding the gift was for me. Several months ago, I asked permission to see the Master Apothecary to bind my scar. Do ye ken what I was told?" He sighed and looked away. "Return when your heart has healed."

"Your heart is now healed, my husband," she acknowledged.

"But not the scar on my side."

Erina traced a finger over the puckered skin on his side. "Nor are mine."

Rory held out his hand and a golden pouch appeared within his palm. "This is her gift to us, *mo ghrá*. To heal the remainder of our wounds."

Erina regarded the pouch in confusion. "I dinnae understand."

"Your grandmother, Aelish, has visited the healing caves of Graecove. She has procured the ancient stones and made a powder. Only the Master Apothecary has the power to use these magical gems that were brought from our homeland."

Confusion furrowed her brow. "Does this mean…can she take away the pain? The ugly scars?"

Smiling, he removed her from his lap and stood. "Trust me. Show me your legs."

She bit her lip, but complied and placed her legs on the bench. Bringing her gown above her knees, Rory emptied a portion of the dust into his palm and sprinkled it over her damaged skin.

"What a pretty color—" She winced and brought a fist to her mouth.

"Aye, she told me there would be itching and pain. Ye must wait for a bit." Rory dropped the pouch onto the ground and brought her into his arms.

She clenched her eyes shut. "How long is a *bit* in your world?"

Chuckling softly, he kissed her brow and strode toward the stream. "Remember, time moves more slowly in this realm."

She made a garbled sound as he entered the water.

Opening her eyes, she glanced around. "And why are we in the water?"

"*I* am in the water," Rory corrected.

"Oh for the love of the Goddess," she complained, though a smile tugged at the corners of her mouth.

Gently, Rory lowered her into the river. The water came only to her knees as she clung to his shoulder. Soon her features relaxed.

A choked sob escaped from her lips. "I dinnae feel

any more pain." Erina bent over and inspected the skin. "Sweet, beautiful Goddess! The scars are gone!" She covered her face with her hands and burst into tears.

Rory lifted her back into his arms, cradling her against his chest. His heart constricted with joy and love for her.

Time passed and her tears lessened. She hiccupped and wiped at her nose. "'Tis wondrous, but I must confess, I have ye to thank for healing me. Though the fire left me in pain most of the time, ye made me feel beautiful."

"Your beauty steals the breath from me." He sought out her lips and kissed her passionately.

She nipped on his lower lip. "Your turn for healing."

Making his way from the river, Rory countered, "After I make love to ye."

"Nae," she protested, wiggling to free herself from his arms.

Rory placed her onto the ground. Picking up the pouch, he handed it to her. "If ye would do the honors?"

"Aye, most assuredly." Erina removed a small amount and smoothed it over Rory's scar.

Instantly, he let out a hiss and waited for the allotment of time to pass. In the meantime, his lovely wife had walked to the table and returned with a pitcher of water.

"Ready?" she asked.

"Aye."

He watched as she poured the water in a steady stream down his side. Within seconds, the scar had vanished, and the skin lay smooth beneath his markings. Rory's fingers trembled as he wiped them over his skin. "Now we are both healed."

Erina dropped the pitcher onto the ground and wrapped her arms around his waist. "I love ye."

Rory skimmed his hands down her back. Cupping her bottom, he grazed his teeth along her neck. "As I love ye. Let me pleasure ye out on the land."

After breaking free, Erina slipped out of her gown in a seductive dance. "First, I must choose the perfect spot."

He arched a brow, and his cock tightened in pain. "A new game?"

"Aye, and this time ye cannot use magic."

She sauntered away, giving Rory a luscious view of her bottom. "Ye are torturing me, *mo ghrá*!"

Casting a glance over her shoulder, Erina's eyes glittered like the sea on a calm day. "Nae, my husband, only pleasure."

"I shall give ye one minute to reach your destination. And then prepare yourself, wife!"

Her laughter filled the air when she took off running toward the field of opulent wildflowers, and Rory stood transfixed by the beauty that had captured his heart and soul forever.

Glossary of the Fae Realm

CATHEDRAL OF TREES: A place of worship and where royal ceremonies are held.

COURTS OF THE FAE: Special chambers where the Fae Order discuss and advise on the laws of the land.

FAE APOTHECARY: A special healer and a place where one can purchase or create medicinal herbal remedies.

FAE COUNCIL: A group of nine Fae members who proceed and advise over the laws, especially those governed by the Fenian Warriors.

HALL OF REMEMBRANCE: A place where the Fae can visit to reflect on their life's journey through mirrored images.

KEEPER OF KNOWLEDGE: Archibald McKibben, Bard of the Fae. He is responsible for keeping a historical record of all events pertaining to the Fae within both words—human and Fae.

LIBRARY OF THE ANCIENTS: All the knowledge the Fae brought with them to Ireland.

PLEASURE GARDENS: A vast, luscious, sensual garden where the Fae may find others for sexual pleasures.

REALM OF SORROWS: When a Fae becomes trapped in his own misery and sorrow. Ultimately, they become a shadow of their former self and go mad.

ROOM OF REFLECTION: The Fae prison.

Note from the Author

In doing research for *Oath of a Warrior*, I came across hundreds of cases pertaining to witches and the witch trials in Scotland. The records of Scotland's witch trials spanned over a period of 200 years during the 16th and 17th centuries. However, I did find evidence of several women being burned, or executed in the late 15th century. This was a dark period in Scottish history, exposing a culture of fear and panic that cast a cloud over much of Scotland.

Some of the charges brought against these individuals ranged from belonging to a coven, receiving herbs from the Queen of the Faeries, and using charms against another person. It did not matter if you were a servant or upper class, either. If you wanted to rid yourself of someone, all you had to do was accuse them of being a witch.

Erina was a wonderful character to write and one I knew who would appeal to Rory. She loved her garden and animals, tended to those who required healing, made love charms, and believed in the old ways. A perfect combination for any to accuse her of dealing in the black arts. Yet, she never saw herself as a witch. Only someone who was different. Sadly, even in this century, we tend to look at others who don't walk the same path as the majority as odd.

I hope you've enjoyed Rory and Erina's story. It was a tale of healing, renewal, and a second chance at love. Next in the *Legends of the Fenian Warriors* is Liam MacGregor's story—*Trial of a Warrior*. If you recall, Liam is awaiting trial for breaking a high Fae law by taking Aidan Kerrigan back in time to help rescue Aidan's daughter, Aileen in *Dragon Knight's Medallion*. I'm calling Liam's story adventurous!

A word about the author...

Award-winning Scottish paranormal romance author, Mary Morgan resides in Northern California, with her own knight in shining armor. However, during her travels to Scotland, England, and Ireland, she left a part of her soul in one of these countries and vows to return.

Mary's passion for books started at an early age along with an overactive imagination. She spent far too much time daydreaming and was told quite often to remove her head from the clouds. It wasn't until the closure of Borders Books, where Mary worked, that she found her true calling—writing romance. Now, the worlds she created in her mind are coming to life within her stories.

If you enjoy history, tortured heroes, and a wee bit of magic, then time-travel within the pages of her books.

Visit Mary's website where you'll find links to all of her books, blog, and pictures of her travels.

http://www.marymorganauthor.com

www.ingramcontent.com/pod-product-compliance
Lightning Source LLC
Chambersburg PA
CBHW050024030726
47506CB00001B/108